The
Other Version

eve blakely

QUEEN B INK

First published in Australia by Queen B Ink, Sydney.

ISBN-13: 978-0-646-86679-6

www.eveblakely.com

To my boys,

*I love every version of you that
ever was and will be…*

Chapter 1

OLIVIA

The uber comes to an abrupt halt on the corner of Maine and Geraldton in Milton's central business district, exactly two blocks from the Salt Factory. God, why is it that there are absolutely zero uber drivers that can (a) actually drive and (b) get you to the exact location you ask? Like their jobs are that hard.

"Where did you tell your dad we were going?" Katerina asks as she scoots sideways out of the car.

"Library," I reply as I follow her lead.

"And he believed you? Dressed like that?" she asks incredulously, gesturing to the low-cut romper that adorns my petite frame.

It's a piece that had been given to my mother by some up-and-coming designer during fashion week. People are always giving her things. It's ironic really, how many free things rich people are given.

"Please," I scoff. "He barely glanced in my direction when I told him I was going out. I could have told him we were going to work the street corner and he wouldn't have bat an eyelid."

Maybe I'm exaggerating, but most of the time my father's head is buried in his laptop and his phone glued to either ear. He always puts his job ahead of me, of my mum. Ahead of everything really.

"Is it me or did you down a cup of instant bitch before we left?" Katerina smirks. "I'm getting some seriously negative vibes from you right now. I mean, you know, more than usual."

"Shut up." I roll my eyes and give her a playful shove. She laughs, rocking backwards on her Manolos before regaining her balance. "I guess I'm still pissed about Sean."

Sean is my boyfriend, though lately it seems like we barely ever speak. Actually, it doesn't just seem that way. It's exactly that way. When I'd told him I wished we could spend more time together he'd brushed it off, explaining to me instead how important it is for him to be studying right now so he can get in to medicine next year at Milton University. I get it. It's our last year of high school. Investing time into our futures is important.

Maybe I'm envious of the fact that he knows what he actually wants to do with his life. Maybe I just want to have fun before I have to grow up and adult. Either way, I didn't pressure him. There's no way I'm going to be portrayed as one of those nagging girlfriends that no guy wants hanging off their arm.

"Forget Sean." Katerina throws her bony arm around my neck as we near the Salt Factory. She raises an eyebrow suggestively with a wicked grin. "Guys suck. Let's get wasted."

Katerina is many things. To her friends, she's kind, caring, protective and nurturing, but if you get on her wrong side she will bring the wrath of hell down upon you. She is earth, wind, fire, and ice. And she's my best friend in the world.

The Salt Factory is an exclusive club, frequented by only a handful of kids from Hampton Ridge College, the local private school in our town. The select few of us have three things in common. Fake ID, social status and, of course, money. It's amazing what you can get away with when you're loaded.

I shadow Katerina toward the door of the club. Her long, auburn waves stretch behind her like flames, her sequinned cami glistening under the neon sign as we bypass the hopeful wannabes waiting in the queue and attempt to slink behind the velvet rope.

An arm shoots out in front of us, forcing us backward, then a strong hand wraps its way around my upper arm.

"ID," the bouncer insists sternly as he folds his arms over his chest, his dark eyes piercing into ours.

He's tall, built from lean muscle, but he can't be more than a few years older than we are. He seems completely unfazed by Katerina's resting bitch face, nor does he react to the bitter scowl I aim back at him.

"You must be new here," I state, my voice icy. "First of all, you touch me again and you'll be dealing with my lawyer. Secondly, we're regulars here. We keep you in business. Therefore, we keep your pathetic little pay checks coming."

He raises both eyebrows and takes a step back, then condescendingly says, "Well, sorry princess, but it's my job to check ID."

Katerina's eyes roll dramatically but she pulls out her counterfeit ID regardless, handing it over with a perfectly

3

manicured hand. The bouncer takes it and folds it over several times in his palm.

He gives a half laugh. "I think you girls should head home. It's past your bed time, isn't it?

"Excuse me?" I say, disbelievingly. "Where's the other guy? The one that's normally here? We'd like to see him."

"Why?" he responds. "You think he can't tell a fake ID when he sees one, princess?"

Ugh. I shudder at his overuse of that word.

"You have no idea who I am, do you?" I smile mockingly at him, my hands resting confidently on my hips.

"Should I?" he asks, combing a hand through his dark, unkempt hair.

"There he is!" Katerina screeches, as she spots the usual door man lingering just inside the club. Then, turning to me, she asks, "What was his name again? Seth? Stan?"

The new bouncer follows our gaze. "That's Mitch," he says, looking at us as with distaste. So, we didn't remember the guy's name. Big deal. "His name is Mitch."

"Yeah. We get it." I hiss, not even attempting to hide my annoyance.

Katerina calls to Mitch, thrashing her arms about in a desperate attempt to get his attention. This no-hoper has severely underestimated who he's dealing with here. There is absolutely no way in hell that we won't get our way tonight.

We always get our way.

Mitch, finally seeing us, meanders over. "Is there a problem here?" he asks.

"Actually, yeah," the other bouncer says, handing him Katerina's fake ID. He folds his arms across his chest again, a stupid grin plastered across his face.

Mitch takes the ID, and without even so much as a glimpse at it, hands it back to Katerina. "It's all good."

Lifting the rope, he allows us inside and as we pass them I hear him say, "That's Victor Petersen's daughter."

I'm not sure if I heard the new guy correctly over the loud music, but it sounded as though he said, "Who?" I guess he isn't just new to the club. He must be new around here. Period.

We sashay through the crowd, absorbing the stares of pretty much everyone around us. Young hotshot business men trying to mark their place in the world and old, gross corporate washouts, well passed their expiry date. I ignore them, but Katerina enjoys it as usual.

I spot the bar manager, a tray of cocktails floating gracefully on his outstretched arm. "Enzo! Babe!" I call out over the reverberating bass beat.

Enzo immediately dumps the tray of drinks on the bar and ambles in our direction. "Olivia Petersen and Katerina Van Sant! To what do I owe the pleasure?" he greets us in his usual flamboyant manner, embracing us both with air kisses. "What can I get you?"

"Well, a private booth would be nice." I flash him my most persuasive smile, clasping my hands together as though in prayer. "Pretty please!"

"Oh, I'm all booked out tonight, babes." Enzo replies, waving his hand theatrically.

"Oh, no!" I pout. "I just really wish we had somewhere we could sit without these perverts staring at us all night."

"Maybe we should find somewhere else to go instead," Katerina adds.

We definitely have no intentions of doing so, but Katerina knew the thought of us leaving the club would make Enzo sweat.

"Look, we're totally booked, but I'll see what I can do." Enzo pulls an iPhone from his shirt pocket and saunters away, probably to somewhere quieter. Within minutes, he's back and leading us to a booth of our own.

We spend the next hour sipping back cosmopolitans from the white suede lounge in our private booth, gossiping about this week's scandalous events.

Katerina tells me that Jessica Lawrence and Matt Holden had the most epically embarrassing break-up in first period on Thursday and were back together by Friday lunch. I tell her about how Sheree Ackers had finally announced she was into chicks, much to the dismay of Brent Waterhouse who has been crushing on her since the third grade. And rumour has it that Brian Attfield's dad showed up in the school office demanding that his son's grades be changed or else he would stop his rather large donations coming. There was never a dull moment at Hampton Ridge College.

"Brian Attfield is so hot though," Katerina says as she plucks an olive from the complimentary canape platter and pops it between her teeth. "Cheater or not. Whatever that guy got up to this past summer has earned him some serious biceps!"

I laugh. It's obvious by her hooded eyelids that she's getting very tipsy, but then again, so am I. "You think so? I hadn't really noticed."

"Of course, you didn't! You've got total tunnel vision for Sean."

"Ugh! No. No talking about Sean. I was almost in a good mood," I reply.

"What do you mean? You love Sean, don't you?" she asks. A waiter places a jug of water and two glasses between us. A not-so-subtle hint if I've ever seen one.

"Yeah. I do." I answer.

I do, don't I? Sean and I have been together for over a year and I love spending time with him. It's just that lately he only wants to spend time with me when it's good for him.

"You guys are cute together. But I still think you should have made out with Jesse Bradman when you had the chance." Katerina is referring to the hot pool guy her mum employed over the summer, one half of the Bradman twins, who was apparently totally into me. His brother Taylor had been all over Katerina.

"Oh my god, girl! You must be totally trashed right now! You know I would never cheat on Sean."

I've done a ton of crappy things in my life, I'll admit it. I ridiculed Jeannie Purcell in the eighth grade when she finally got her period. I fat-shamed James Vardan when he tried out for the football team in tenth grade because he could barely run a quarter of the field without stopping. I can lie my way into any place and there are no lengths I won't go to when I want something. The truth is I've done a bunch of shit things and I'll probably continue to. I mean, who doesn't? But if there's one thing I definitely am not, it's a cheater.

"I'll be back in a sec. I have to go to the bathroom." I stand, smoothing out my romper as I make my way to the ladies' room, leaving Katerina chewing on her straw and bobbing her head along to the beat in an out of time fashion.

I enter the immaculately decked out restroom and perch on the edge of a crimson suede ottoman situated in the spacious sitting area off to the side. I reach down to adjust the strap of my shoe that's been cutting my circulation for most of the night. If I'm being honest, these shoes have had my feet in a world of pain since the moment I put them on, but I'm a sucker for fashion and they're Jimmy Choo's. Enough said.

The walls of the restroom drown out the club's music, giving way to the audible moans that echo from the cubicle behind me. There's a breathy sigh followed by a low, deep grunt, combined with the repetitive rattling of the cubicle door. Someone is getting lucky in here tonight.

Katerina will be mad she missed this. I can imagine her crouching at the door of the cubicle waiting to snap a pic of the culprits with her phone, or pulling some kind of cruel but hilarious prank. With the click of the lock, a man emerges momentarily, only to be dragged back in by his partner in crime for one last embrace. A woman laughs softly as he pulls away from the door. I recognise him. He's the bartender that served us our cosmos earlier.

I smile to myself. Good for her, whoever she is. The bartender is hot.

The woman says something undecipherable, to which he replies in a whisper. "Okay. I gotta get back to work. I'll see you soon."

Ignoring me, he beelines for the exit.

I rise unsteadily to my feet. The cocktails have definitely blurred the edges and I form a silent prayer that the drive home in the uber will sober me up. I let the wall take my weight until the head spin subsides.

The woman appears from the cubicle. Her cheeks are flushed, her eye makeup slightly smudged as she stumbles on a pair of too-high red heels.

I observe her, unnoticed, from the corner of the room, as though in a dream. Her air of confidence captivates me, demands my attention. I'm under her spell, both struck by the familiarity of her reflection in the mirror and baffled by my own sense of naivety.

I watch as she reapplies her lipstick, swipes at her uncouth mascara and tousles her messy blonde curls.

Curls that are identical to mine.

My lungs are empty of air. My feet are stuck, frozen in their place on the marble tiles below. I blink, desperate to dissolve this vision before me, but she remains, unable to be unseen. My heart battles with my sceptic mind, for although this woman seems completely foreign to me, she is no stranger.

A crack rips through my chest.

A shrill sound echoes off the granite walls. My iPhone. A text from Katerina.

Did you get lost in there? LOL! I'm ordering another round.

As I inhale sharply, I realise I've been holding my breath. The woman looks up, her wide hazel eyes meeting mine in the reflection.

"Olivia," she gasps, her voice barely a whisper.

"Mum."

Chapter 2

LIV

I walk the esplanade aimlessly, as I've done every other day this week. Cliff Haven is quiet today, even more so than usual. I slouch down lethargically onto the bench seat at the end of the pier, welcoming the warmth of the late afternoon sun on my face. A gentle breeze sweeps orange leaves from the ground, whisking them in lazy circles, entwining a small piece of crumpled paper in their midst.

Curiously, I lean forward and retrieve the wrinkled note. Smoothing out the creases from the middle to the edges, I hold it closer to read the fine print. It's a job advertisement for a local café, The Haven. I recognise the name and know exactly where it is too, just a few blocks from where I now sit, back up on the esplanade.

The community noticeboard stands a few feet away, so I stroll over to it, pull a tack out of the cork, and stab it precisely through the centre of the top of the small page.

There. I was saving the environment, and now some lucky person would get a job. My good deed for the day. I wonder how many honourable deeds it would take to erase all the bad I've done.

I stare at the words on the advertisement. "Seeking wait staff for busy seaside café. Must have a positive attitude and a friendly demeanour. No experience necessary."

I don't have experience. Positive and friendly? I'd have to work on that, but of all the words on that flyer, one of them stands out.

Busy.

It would be nice to be busy. If there's one thing I need most right now, it's a distraction. Without another thought, I rip the paper from the notice board, tearing the top of it in the process and march back up the esplanade to the Haven Café.

A petite woman with a blonde pixie cut stands behind the kiosk, counting money from the till. Her head snaps up when she hears the little bell ding above the door as I enter. "Sorry, we're about to close."

For a second, I hesitate, unable to form words. I seem to have lost my vigour on the way up the hill. "I know. Are...are you the manager?" I look back down at the flyer, searching for the contact name. "Carla?"

"Yeah," she answers, matter-of-factly.

"I'd like to apply for the waitressing position." My voice is smaller than I intend it to be.

"Oh, I see." She closes the till, leaving her position behind the counter and gestures for me to sit down at a table with her. "Do you have a resume I can see?"

I feel more comfortable standing, but out of respect, I take the seat across from her. The metal legs scrape unpleasantly along the terracotta tiled floor.

"Uh, no. I actually only just saw the ad. I can bring you one though." I mentally scramble for things I could write on a resume that doesn't exist yet.

"That's okay," she replies with a smile. She has a sing-song voice and certainly embodies the friendly demeanour stated on the ad. "What's your name?"

"Liv," I reply automatically, folding my hands nervously in my lap.

"Liv," she repeats. "That's pretty. Is it short for…?"

"No," I cut her off, a little too abruptly. "No, it's just Liv. Liv Peters."

She seems stunned by my rudeness and I immediately feel guilty for snapping. I didn't mean to.

"Sorry," I mumble, tucking a stray, espresso brown tendril behind my ear.

"Well, Liv. Why don't you tell me a little bit about yourself?" She folds her toned tanned arms across her chest, which only heightens my anxiety.

Fantastic. If she's waiting to hear about my greatest achievements, she's about to be sorely disappointed. I pick at my fingernails nervously under the table, wondering where I should begin. What do I tell her? That I killed my social status so now I have no friends? That I flunked high school and can't get into university?

Or I could lead with my favourite one. That I, single-handedly, destroyed my own mother.

"Well," I begin. "I finished high school last year."

"Okay. So, you went to Cliff Haven High?"

"Uh, yeah." Great. Add 'liar' to that list of qualities.

"And do you go to university now? Are you looking to work part time?"

"No. I'm not a student. I can be available to work whenever you need me."

Busy. That's what I want to be.

She studies my face as I speak. I sense some austerity under all of that friendly, though I guess that's probably appropriate criterion for a café manager. I'm afraid she can see right through me, see all the damage.

"Okay. Well, we work on a rostered system here, so it's generally just part time, but there are extra hours every now and then. We've been getting a little busier lately, which is why I've decided to hire an extra person."

"Okay," I reply, not sure what else to say.

She eyes the Chanel handbag resting in my lap. God, what was I even thinking coming down here? I wonder briefly how many other twenty-year-olds have walked into her café asking for a job sporting a bag that costs more than a waitress's monthly salary. I stand, ready to get the hell out of here, but just as I think she's about to dismiss me, she does the complete opposite. "The café opens at 8am tomorrow, so I'll see you at half past seven to set up."

"Really? You're hiring me?"

"If you still want the job, yes."

It will never cease to amaze me how quickly life can change. One action, whether it's your own doing, or left up to fate, can set you on a whole new path.

"Thank you," I stammer. "I won't let you down." And strangely enough, I half believe myself.

The drive back home to Hampton Ridge takes about forty-five minutes, thanks to the frequent windy bends and low speed limits on the way up the cliff, but I quite enjoy it. For me, driving alone is an opportunity to increase the volume of my rock music of choice and zone out for a while. It's my

13

favourite way to escape reality. I try to tell myself that I don't mind spending so much time alone.

In my experience, people are overrated anyway.

Once I reach the top of the ridge, the sun has almost set and the bright city lights of Milton are becoming visible below. Milton lies to the right. Cliff Haven, although I can't see it in the dimming light, way further down on the left. Milton Hospital is lit like a beacon and I think of my dad, who would be down there somewhere, performing surgery or holding meetings, or whatever else he does that keeps him away from home for hours on end.

I drive down the main boulevard. The deciduous trees that line the streets sway in the wind, their ochre leaves contrasting with the purple, orange glow of the sunset.

There's no denying that Hampton Ridge is aesthetically a gorgeous place to live. It's a sanctuary between the city and the sea, full of beautifully landscaped gardens and spacious parks.

Too bad the people here suck.

Mayfield Boulevard runs through the centre of Hampton Ridge, a street lined with picturesque mansions. They're the kind of houses you find in dream home magazines, complete with manicured lawns and enormous swimming pools.

At the end of the boulevard, my family home rests on the back of the highest cliff. I use the term 'family home' loosely. In actual fact, my family home is a seven-bedroom, five-bathroom Victorian style mansion, with a grand upstairs balcony held up by stone columns, and a tennis court that I'm pretty sure has never been used. 'Family' is now just me and my father.

Pulling into the long cobblestone driveway, the sheer grandeur of this place stirs a loneliness within me. The external lighting, designed to create a soft hospitable glow, somehow makes me feel anything but welcome.

Fumbling with my keychain, I locate the button on my garage remote and raise the wide panelled door of the six-car garage, which is way too big considering we only own two cars. My dad had always planned to buy a project car, but he would have no idea what to do with one and no time to learn.

I round the end of the hall, entering the kitchen, lit only by the crystal pendant lights above the stone benchtop. A figure sits perched upon a bar stool.

"Tessa! Oh my god, you scared me!" I shout as I clutch at my chest.

Tessa usually leaves at six and it's now almost six thirty. I wasn't expecting her, although I'm grateful for her presence. There's something really depressing about coming home to an exceptionally large, empty house.

"Tessa, what are you still doing here? It's late." I place my handbag and keys down on the bench.

"*I* scared *you*!" she exclaims. "Liv, I've been so worried! You scared the hell out of me. Where have you been?"

As I near closer, the concern on her face becomes apparent. Guilt wraps me with its iron fist at the thought that I've made her worry. It was never my intention. Tessa is the kindest person I've ever known, and God knows, she's had her fair share in putting up with my shit over the years. In the past, our relationship could have been described as tumultuous at best, but now I consider her the one true constant in my life.

"Why? Did something happen?" A sense of panic rises in my chest, my eyes fixating on the soft frown creases that appear on her forehead when it's wrinkled with worry.

A lump forms in my throat as I remember the last time she'd worn that expression. It had been the night she told me my mother was gone.

"No. Nothing has happened." She shakes her head and with it the concern evaporates. "You didn't answer your phone when I called! I tried four times already! I didn't know where you were!"

I let out a long breath of relief. It was easy for me to forget that I had someone looking out for me, someone who worried about my whereabouts, when my parents previously had so often never been present to care. I pull my phone from my handbag. Sure enough, there's a notification illuminating the screen. Four missed calls. Disappointment floods me at the realisation.

"Oh. I was driving. It looks like I must have turned the Bluetooth off by accident." Truthfully, I never really bother to check my phone that much these days because no one ever calls me. "Oh, Tessa. I'm sorry."

"You're starting to worry me, Liv. I don't want to sound like your father, but you can't keep wandering through life. You've been through so much and I understand that, but you …"

"Tessa! Calm down. I'm okay." I hold her steady by her petite shoulders and look her straight in her chocolate brown eyes. "I'm actually glad you're still here. I have some news."

"Well, it better be good," she teases.

"I got a job!" I say, the hint of excitement in my voice surprising even myself.

"A job? Where?" she asks.

"At this café in Cliff Haven. It's really cosy. It has this little nook off to the side where you can read books. You would

16

love it." I pluck an apple from the fruit bowl on the counter and take a bite. "I start tomorrow."

"Cliff Haven? What were you doing down there? I thought you hated that place."

"I don't mind it. It has a certain charm about it," I tell her.

I don't bother explaining that I've been going down to Cliff Haven almost every day for the past couple of weeks. It was Katerina that hated going to Cliff Haven. She'd said it was a dump full of townies that would never make anything of themselves. It's the one place in the world that she will never go, which makes it the perfect place for me.

"Well, that's great! Congratulations!" There's nothing but kindness and pride in Tessa's eyes as she holds out her tanned, olive arms, pulling me in a huge, comforting hug. "See, I told you, Liv. You are destined for wonderful things!"

"Settle down, Tessa!" I laugh. "It's just a waitress job." I roll my eyes and wrap my arms around her.

"No, my dear. This is the start of things to come. You'll see. I have a good feeling about this!"

To say Tessa was an optimist would be an understatement. Her sweet nature and ability to be genuinely happy for other people make her a rare find in this town. These are some of the many reasons why I love her. To be honest, she is, without a doubt, the reason I'm not a self-indulged brat. I've come a long way with her love and guidance, but I have no idea if I can live up to this vision she's created of me inside of her mind.

"What's wrong, Liv?" she asks me, sensing the dismay that must be written all over my face.

"What do you think my dad will say?" I ask her.

She gives me a look that says, "Come on, we both know what your father will say." She's probably right. Even though

17

it's just a waitressing job, it could be a step in the right direction for me because at least I will no longer be standing still, but convincing my father of that won't be easy. He expects more of me. He's been dreaming of me following his footsteps into medicine since I got my first doctor's playset at five years old and I've shattered those dreams into oblivion.

"Let's not worry about it right now. What you need to worry about is that you are doing what's right for you. Are you doing what's right for you?"

"I think so," I reply. "For now. I just need some time. You know, to figure things out."

"Good," she says, snatching the half-eaten apple from my hand and waving it dramatically in the air. "Now, this is not dinner! Come on. I'll fix you something to eat."

Chapter 3

OLIVIA

The blindfold is uncomfortable and scratchy, flattening my eyelash extensions and smudging my makeup.

"Seriously! Do I have to wear this thing?" I complain, aware of the whiny high-pitched tone in my voice.

"Not for much longer," my father booms as he directs me down the driveway with firm hands on my shoulders. Then, as he unties the blindfold and lets it slide off my face, he shouts excitedly, "Happy birthday!"

His arms are splayed out in the direction of my birthday present. Parked in front of me is a brand-new, A-Class Mercedes convertible, my reflection staring back at me from its glossy sheen.

I jump up and down a few times and scream, "Oh my God! Is it for me?"

Of course, I know it is. I've been expecting it.

"Absolutely. I can't believe my little girl is finally turning eighteen." My father squeezes me in a tight hug and plants a kiss on my forehead.

"Ugh! Dad, you're going to ruin my makeup." I pull away from him, checking myself in the side mirror and tucking the blonde tendril of hair that has come loose from my braided updo during the unblindfolding.

"Men, huh?" My mother reaches out, attempting to touch the back of my hair. "They have no idea how many hours we sit in the salon chair."

I know she's only half kidding but considering how true it is, having spent the entire day perfecting my platinum blonde colour at Luxe Hair and Co, her joke irritates me.

"Just don't touch it, Mum!" I slap her hand away, then swiftly pull it back in to catch a glimpse of her watch, purely to see what time it is, not to admire her taste in jewellery. It's the watch she bought on one of our many shopping trips together. I'd told her the Chanel one was classier, but for some reason she'd opted for a plainer, less expensive option. "When are you guys leaving?"

Half of Hampton Ridge College will be here any minute and the last thing I want is my parents lurking around at my eighteenth birthday party.

My mum conceals her disappointment at my eagerness for her departure under a hostile demeanour. "Now, actually," she snaps. "Our driver is almost here. Call us if you need anything."

I can't help being particularly aggressive toward my mother. Who could blame me after that night at the Salt Factory? She'd told me that she wouldn't cheat on my father ever again. She'd tried to justify it by saying that Dad hadn't been showing her how important she was to him and that there were other 'things I didn't know about.'

She'd basically bribed me. I would keep her secret if she kept quiet on the fact that Katerina and I had been partying at the Salt Factory. I doubt there was anything my father could do to punish me if he found out, but I couldn't let Katerina take the fall. It wasn't fair, but I couldn't do that to my best friend.

I continue playing with the strands of loose hair, torn between whether to leave them down or pin them back up.

"Olivia, did you hear your mother?" There is irritation in my father's voice, though I don't know what his problem is. I'm the one trying to pull off the greatest party of my life. My parents need to get out of here already.

"Yes! I heard you! I'll be fine," I retaliate, challenging his impatience.

"Okay, we're staying at the Shangri-La. Call us if you need anything."

"I will. Has the housekeeper organised the caterers?"

The housekeeper hears my question and shuffles over. "Yes, Olivia. They will be here at seven."

"Great. But you won't be. Right?" I know I'm being rude, but I don't really care. No one ever seems to react to the way I behave. As it turns out, Olivia Petersen can say and do pretty much whatever she likes.

I catch the housekeeper rolling her eyes as she turns away from me. "I'm leaving now," she mutters, then glancing back at me she adds, "Oh. And, Olivia?"

"Yes," I respond, without looking up.

"I do have a name you know," I hear her say.

I ignore her and shift my attention back to my parents, flashing my best fake smile. "Okay, bye, Mum. Bye, Dad! Love you!"

"Goodbye, sweetie," they both say, each giving me another hug, although not as tightly this time.

"Oh, I almost forgot!" exclaims my mother, reaching into her Birkin bag and pulling out a flat package wrapped with designer paper and an impeccable silver bow. "Happy birthday, my darling girl. I hope you'll use this."

"Thanks, Mum." I smile half-heartedly as I take the package, with no intention of opening it immediately. Whatever it is will have to wait because Sean's BMW is coming up the driveway. "I'll open it later."

"Oh, okay." It's not hard to detect the disappointment in my mother's voice, but she turns nonetheless and with my father by her side, heads for the black, stretch limousine that awaits them on the curb.

Sean strolls toward me, then wrapping himself around me, he lifts me up and kisses me roughly on the cheek. He whispers in my ear. "Happy birthday, sexy."

"Put me down, Sean," I say, unable and unwilling to hide my annoyance.

"Nice ride!" he says, skimming the roof of my new car with his fingertips.

"Yeah, it's nice, but he didn't get the right colour." I'd asked my father for a custom red, but I guess he thought he knew better.

"Gunmetal is sleek. I like it," he replies, as he follows me into the house like a lost puppy. "That's unfortunate that I missed your dad. I wanted to talk to him about the benefit next week. He said he was going to put in a good word with the professor for me."

"Yeah. How unfortunate." I say, sarcastically, as I reach for my mother's vodka bottle on the top shelf of the glass cabinet.

"Don't be like that, Olivia." There's that tone again. It's the same tone I hear constantly in my mother's voice, in my father's voice. Disappointment.

"Like what?" I shrug.

"Every time I mention Milton you get all defensive and moody," he answers.

"Because it's all you ever talk about. Seriously, who are you dating? Me or my dad? It's like you only ever come over here to talk to him."

It may sound harsh, but it's true. I've only invited Sean here a handful of times and every single one of those times he's wound up talking to my dad about his dreams of a career in medicine.

My father is the best cardiac surgeon in the state and a director on the board at Milton Hospital. A recommendation from him would provide Sean with a better chance of being accepted into the medical program there, and he knows it.

I understand that he's looking out for his future, and maybe I'm being petty, but I can't help feeling upset that all his attention is focused on his career prospects, instead of on me.

"Come on, you know it's not like that," he says, snaking an arm around my waist.

"He's already writing you a reference. What more do you want?" I don't want to start an argument before everyone arrives, but he's making it impossible.

"Nothing. Just you," he leans into me, attempting to plant a kiss on my lips, but I push him aside.

"Everyone will be here soon. I have to go check on the caterers." I already know that the caterers won't be here till seven. The housekeeper told me so, but it gave me an out.

23

It annoys me that Sean can't see the real reason I'm upset. I know he can't read my mind, but I wish he would make more of an effort to understand me.

The truth is that I'm torn between my mother and father's aspirations for me, while having no idea what my own are. My dad has always wanted me to follow his footsteps into medicine, but my grades will never be enough to get me there and that fact left me feeling like one huge failure. My mum believes I could get early acceptance into the Milton Conservatorium of Music, but lately, she pisses me off so much I want to take a sledge hammer to my piano as a big 'fuck you' to her. Besides, we're young. Are we really meant to have it all figured out already?

"What's that?" Sean asks, pointing to the ornately wrapped giftbox I'm still carrying.

"Oh, just a present from my mum." I toss the box onto the kitchen counter. "I'll open it later."

"That reminds me," he says, pulling a small box from his jacket pocket. "Happy birthday, babe."

Sean holds out a Tiffany blue box, his chestnut brown eyes boring into mine. I instantly feel guilty. Maybe he does care about me after all.

"You went to Tiffany's for me?" I lift the lid on the small giftbox, revealing its contents. A Tiffany bow bracelet, a dainty platinum chain with a diamond encrusted bow in the centre.

"Well, you did tell me how much you liked it about three hundred times." Sean cups my face and kisses me on the cheek, then his mouth moves over mine. This time I let him.

"Thank you," I say, as I squeeze him tightly. "Help me put it on. I wanna wear it right now. Katerina is going to be so jealous!"

Chapter 4

LIV

My phone resonates maddeningly from my bedside table.
I set my alarm to a tone called 'charming bell', but at five thirty
in the morning it is anything but charming.

Waking up at this hour feels completely foreign to me. I
slam my hand down on the touch screen. A number of
different apps open up as my fingers fumble to shut off the
sound. With my eyes only half open, I finally find the snooze
button and the incessant bleeping ceases.

Resting my head back onto the silk pillowcase, I'm
overcome with a strong urge to stay in bed and ignore the
alarm. Then I remember that this is my life now. I'm a
responsible, employed adult and I'm determined to function
as one. Tessa's voice replays in my head as I remember our
conversation from the previous night.

You are destined for wonderful things.

Maybe she's right. Maybe she's insanely delusional, but
nonetheless I reluctantly stumble into the shower.

Although I don't need to be at the café until 7:30am, I plan
to arrive a little earlier to prove my commitment to my new

boss. And to myself. And if I could impress my dad, that would certainly be a bonus. I want to show him that I can actually function as a person again. That I can survive on my own.

Dad arrived home from work at a reasonable hour last night and I was able to have a very brief chat with him before he strode off to the shower and then bed.

It wasn't uncommon for us to go a few days without seeing each other. We're often like two ships passing in the night. When we talk, it's rarely about anything that actually matters. Never about how we really feel.

And never about Mum.

But at least last night I was able to tell him about my new job. As I'd suspected, he hadn't been too thrilled but for different reasons than I'd thought. Although I'm sure he wasn't over the moon that his only daughter was now a lowly waitress, he'd genuinely seemed concerned about my wellbeing. All this time I've been anxious about disappointing him by doing nothing with my life, but last night he seemed more concerned that I was launching myself out into the world before I was ready. It's nice that he cares, but it kind of makes me feel like a needy child.

I never thought to ask Carla about what she considers appropriate attire for work. I'd taken note that yesterday she'd been wearing jeans and a t-shirt so I figure as long as I look neat and presentable, casual wear will be okay. I slip into a short, black denim skirt, throw on a white tank top, and layer it with a light grey, cable-knit cardi, which I guess I won't need for long. Cliff Haven is usually warm and sunny during the day, but up here on the ridge, it's always windy.

I pull my deep brown hair into a half up style. The edgy shoulder length bob I've adopted doesn't quite allow for a full ponytail. I'm not big on wearing a lot of makeup these days, so I apply a tinted moisturiser to my lightly freckled complexion, accentuate my hazel eyes with a slick of black mascara and wipe a light sheen of clear gloss over my lips.

I pause for a second, remembering how my mother would never even go as far as the mailbox without a full face of makeup. Tessa had told me that she hadn't always been like that. In her younger days, when I was just a kid, my mum had rarely worn makeup. She didn't need it. She was a natural beauty, but over time the housewives of Hampton Ridge had worn down her self-esteem.

I stare at the girl in the reflection. She stares back. She still holds sadness within her expression, but there's something dancing in her eyes that wasn't there yesterday.

Hope.

She hasn't given up yet. There is still fight left in her. For the first time in a long time I hold onto the belief that just maybe, she's going to be okay.

I lean down to put my lip gloss back into the dresser drawer when my eyes drift over the music books my mother gave me on my eighteenth birthday. I hadn't known it then, but it would be the last birthday I'd ever get to spend with her. Not that I'd devoted much of my time to her. I was too preoccupied with impressing the people I'd called friends.

Now those people are gone, and so is she, and all I'm left with is a handful of papers bound in soft, black leather.

What I wouldn't do to relive that day, how different I would spend it. If only I had another chance to tell her that I loved her and I accepted her.

I lift the book from the drawer, running my hands over its smooth cover and tracing the embossed letters with my forefinger. I open it and read the inscription inside, written in my mother's elegant handwriting.

My dearest Livvie,

Always follow your dreams. They know the way.

Love Mum

Sorry to disappoint you mum, but it's not always that simple.

I slam the book shut. I know now that my mother had her own battles to fight, but these words were still useless coming from her. Even so, it's the only piece of her that I have left and I feel compelled to have it close to me. I stuff the book inside my handbag and tiptoe down the staircase quietly, in case my dad is still sleeping.

I arrive at the Haven at ten past seven. The town is practically empty at this hour. Apart from a couple of early morning joggers sprinting toward the pier, I can't see anyone else. The only sound comes from the cawing of birds near the foreshore. A sense of tranquillity permeates the atmosphere, with the sun having not long ago risen from the water's edge in the distance.

My plan to arrive early seems to have backfired. Carla hasn't arrived yet, and without keys to get inside, I have no choice but to wait for her out the front. I peer through the window, mentally preparing myself for what tasks may lay ahead for me.

As I step back, a movement in the reflection catches my eye. I spin around, scanning the opposite side of the street. A guy leans against a run-down shopfront on the corner across the road. I've never really paid much attention to it before on my day visits to Cliff Haven, but looking at it now, I can see it's a pub. The sign above the door reads 'Steve's Tavern.'

I wonder what has brought this guy to be standing outside a pub at this time of the morning. I contemplate the fact that maybe he's trying to break in, but then the sound of metal ringing travels across the street and I realise he's holding a set of keys.

It's hard to tell from a distance, and with the morning sun penetrating my line of sight, but he looks like he couldn't be more than a couple of years older than I am. He wears a black leather jacket and his brown hair is almost shoulder length. He glances over in my direction and I turn away, not wanting him to think I'm watching him. Even though I am.

Whatever.

Carla's voice startles me from behind. "Hello, Liv. You're here bright and early!"

I gasp, clutching my chest in shock as I twist around. "Good morning," I say, politely, and slightly out of breath from being scared half to death. I was so focused on the guy across the street I hadn't heard her coming.

"Sorry, I shouldn't have snuck up on you like that," she says, apologetically.

I laugh nervously. "That's okay." I will my heart rate to return to normal. "It's just so quiet around here."

"Yeah," she agrees. "But the customers will be pouring in soon." She plucks a set of keys from her small, blue messenger bag and begins unlocking the door, delegating my tasks as she does so. "Okay, let's get to work. I need you to take all the chairs down from the tables while I set up the registers. Kristen should be here any minute to help you out."

"Okay, great!" I say, probably a little too enthusiastically. I am both nervous and excited to get to work.

To be busy.

"Dammit," Carla says, as she fumbles with the lock. "The lock is stuck. I keep telling Charlie to replace it. He's our chef, but he also comes in handy when things need fixing. That is, when he actually remembers to fix them." There's a loud click as the lock releases and Carla pushes the door open. "Ah, there we go! Just close that door behind you. We'll open up at eight."

As I gently press the door closed, I notice the guy across the street is still there. His gaze lingers on me for a few seconds until he realises I'm watching him too. He averts his eyes to the ground, and with his hands in his pockets, he walks off in the direction of the beach. I try not to read too much into it as Carla helps me find a place for my belongings. Then I begin pulling the chairs from upon the tables.

"Sorry, I'm late! I must have somehow accidentally turned my alarm off and only woke up, like, fifteen minutes ago. Can you believe it?" A young woman barges through the café door, sending the bell above it into a frenzy.

And no, I can't believe it, because the first thing I notice about her is her beauty. No one should look this gorgeous fifteen minutes after waking up. She's stunning, even without makeup, with long dark chestnut hair cascading down her back.

The second thing I'm aware of is her confidence. It exudes from her in a way that demands the room's attention. Not in an arrogant way, but in a way that suggests she's unapologetically herself. I know who she is, although we haven't met. This is Kristen. And I instantly like her.

She smiles as she approaches me, her hand extended in a welcoming handshake. "Hi, allow me to introduce myself. I'm Kristen. You must be Liv. Carla told me she found our newest team member!"

"Hi," I reply, awkwardly. "Yes. That would be me."

"Awesome. Now, let me help you with that." Kristen catches the barstool I'm attempting to lift from the counter as it slips through my grip.

"Oh, God! I'm so sorry!" I cry out, half expecting her to be impatient with my clumsiness, but she only laughs which makes me laugh too.

After taking all of the chairs down from the tables, we help Carla prepare fruit salads, yoghurt, and muesli. I'm introduced briefly to Charlie, the chef, as he fusses around in the kitchen, organising things for the day ahead. When Carla reverses the 'Closed' sign on the café window to 'Open,' the first customers begin filing in like bees swarming to pollen.

Things become so hectic at the cafe that Carla, Kristen, and I (mostly I), struggle to keep an efficient pace and I have to wonder if this is considered exceptionally busy, or if this is what I'll be subjected to on a daily basis.

Kristen does her best to train me on the basics while holding down the fort, but the breakfast rush seems to run directly into the lunchtime rush and I find myself getting flustered. When my own stomach starts to rumble, I regret my decision to skip breakfast this morning. The blueberry muffin I'd scoffed during my short morning tea break hadn't been enough to curb my hunger for long.

When the lunch time customers have finally dispersed, I hurry over to clear a large table, where previously, a group of eight people had been sitting.

Lifting the stack of food crusted plates between my wrist and the crook of my elbow requires strength and balance, as well as some serious concentration, but it only takes one single person to waltz in through those open stacker doors to throw my entire world off its axis.

The world slows. My mind races in overtime to put this picture together. It doesn't make sense.

He doesn't belong here, with his black suit pants and silver-grey tie, the expensive dress shirt with its sleeves rolled up to the elbows a blinding shade of white. His dark eyes meet mine as he rips a pair of Prada sunglasses from his chiselled face.

Everything is all wrong.

The unpleasant crashing sound of the plates shattering as they hit the terracotta floor snaps everything into focus, assuring me that he is not, in fact, a figment of my imagination. This is actually happening.

Suddenly mortified, I crouch to the ground and begin sifting through the large pieces of broken china. Then I feel him beside me, see his large hands reach for a fragment of porcelain. The air thickens with the scent of expensive cologne. I hold my stare on the floor in front of me, not daring to look up at him.

There's no mistaking the person those hands belong to. They're the hands that once held me, once comforted me.

They're the hands that betrayed me.

"Are you okay?"

It's been so long since I've heard his voice. Hearing it now stirs up a range of emotions within me. Mostly anger. I level my eyes with his.

"What are you doing here, Sean?" My face feels as though it's on fire. With rage, shame, or guilt, I'm not sure. Probably all of the above.

"I was in the neighbourhood."

"Yeah, right," I sneer.

"Sorry. That was a lie. I saw your dad this morning at the hospital."

Damn it. I'd forgotten about how often he was in contact with my father. Milton hospital was a teaching hospital, which meant Sean spent more time with him than I did.

"And?" I can't believe this happening. And on my first day of work, of all days.

"I wanted to see you. Can we talk?" He leans in close to me, his breath warm on my neck.

"There's nothing to talk about."

It was so typical of him. He'd always been selfish. He wanted to talk so he came down here, with no consideration for my feelings, or the fact that I might not want to talk to him, or that it's my first goddamned day of work and now I'm embarrassed and I'll probably get fired.

"Please?" he pleads.

"I have nothing to say to you."

"Look, I know you hate me, but I came all the way down here for you." He says it like he's done me some sort of favour.

"I never asked you to." My words come out through gritted teeth. He's come all this way just for me? Wow. Lucky me. My hero. I hate that there's a part of me that's curious about him, and even more for what I say next. "My lunch break is in fifteen minutes. Meet me at the bookstore next door."

He nods and leaves me with a colossal mess to clean up, a situation with which I am familiar. By now, Kristen and Carla are coming at me with a mop and bucket.

"What happened?" Carla demands. I shudder to think she's probably realised what a terrible decision she's made in hiring me.

"I'm.. I'm so sorry, guys. I'm an … idiot." I stutter, feeling the heat rise in my cheeks. "I guess I tried to carry more than

I could manage." I frantically pick up the pieces, throwing them hastily into the bucket.

Kristen is more sympathetic. "It's okay. These things happen. Man, if I had a dollar for every plate or glass I've broken," she laughs casually. "It's happened to all of us." I can tell she's only trying to make me feel better, but I'm grateful.

Carla doesn't appear at all pleased but seems to sense how flustered I'm becoming. "Slow and steady next time, okay? Go on and take your lunch break, Liv. We can take this from here."

Feeling helpless, I utter a small "okay" in agreeance and gather my bag from the storeroom. I would have been relieved to be removed from this situation if it weren't for the one that awaited me. Out of the frying pan and into the fire, Tessa would have said.

When I get to the bookstore, I find Sean perusing the medical encyclopaedias. What a surprise. I guess some things never change. I sit down on a small blue sofa in the corner.

"Well, let's get this over with. What is it that's so important you had to come all the way down here?"

He turns when he hears my voice, his forearm muscles straining as he places the heavy book back on its shelf. "I've missed you bossing me around," he smirks, looking down at me. "I've missed *you*."

"That's weird. You didn't seem to miss me when you were hooking up with my best friend." I fold my arms across my chest defiantly.

He inhales sharply. "That's fair. I know I made a huge mistake."

I sigh as Sean drops down next to me on the sofa, his elbows resting on his knees. "I like your hair," he says. "It suits you."

I ignore his compliment. "A huge mistake? Is that what you're calling it? What you did was unforgiveable. Don't you get that?"

"I know. Katerina said all this stuff about you. She got in my head. She manipulated me."

"Wow," I say, my eyes widening in disbelief. "Poor baby. You're a big boy, Sean. Grow up." I stand, ready to walk away when he reaches up and grabs my elbow, his hand lingering for longer than it needs to.

"Please. Just hear me out," he says.

I give him an impatient look, throwing one hand up in the air for dramatic effect.

"I know I screwed up, Olivia."

I shudder, hearing my full name. I'd left Olivia Petersen up on the ridge this morning, as I've done every morning for the past few weeks. Up there, I am her. Former socialite and daughter of the state's best cardiac surgeon, but down here, I can be whoever I want to be.

Down here, I am just Liv. And I will do everything in my power to prevent anyone making the connection between the two. To keep them from figuring out that I'm an extremely complicated girl trying to live a simply normal life.

"I'll never forgive myself for what I did to you. I can't get you out of my head. I've met other girls. I've tried to move on, but each time I have the same problem." He stands up in front of me, too close, gently reaching for my hand, his brown eyes seemingly sincere. "They're not you."

"Yeah? Well, look around. In case you haven't noticed, I'm not me anymore either." I snatch my hand away from his.

"Don't say that. You just need some time. Maybe it's this place. Working here in that café. Maybe it's not the right fit for you."

I glare at him suspiciously. "Did my father send you here?"

"No! I swear he didn't. I saw him this morning. He only told me where you were. But I'd be lying if I said we both aren't worried about you."

"After everything you've done, you have the nerve to come down here and tell me how to live my life. I mean, you honestly sound like you just expect me to forgive you right here and ride off into the sunset with you."

A lone tear escapes, forming a track down my cheek. Shit. This is not how I envisioned my day going. It wasn't so much that Sean was getting to me, but rather the possibility that my father could have sent him here.

"Olivia," Sean says softly as he attempts to reach for me again. "We both made mistakes."

I slap his hand away. "We're done here."

I storm out of the bookstore and head toward the ocean, praying that Sean doesn't follow. I collapse onto the park bench by the pier and breathe deeply, allowing the warm ocean air to fill my lungs. I will the rhythmic lapping of the waves to soothe me. The sea is like magic to me. It never fails to calm me down.

Sean's words echo in my head. We both made mistakes. I'm well aware that for every one of Sean's faults, I have my own. I was never the perfect girlfriend for him and we were never in love. I can see that now. I am one hundred percent sure that my relationship with Sean is dead, never to be revived, but it isn't Sean that has me rattled. It isn't what he did that sent a tear rolling down my cheek. It was what he had said.

36

What if he's right?

What if this place is a bad fit for me?

What if I can never escape from who I really am?

"Are you okay?" A husky voice pulls me from the depths of my chaotic mind, startling me more than it should.

I jump in my seat, panicked. God, I have got to stop being so jittery all the time. A guy, probably a little older than me, with dishevelled brown hair and a silver eyebrow ring sits next to me on the old, wooden, paint-chipped park bench. He nurses an apple-red acoustic guitar on his lap. He smiles at me, flashing a set of perfect, straight, white teeth as he chuckles quietly at my reaction.

Maybe it's because I'm still wired from the altercation with Sean, or that I'm suddenly pissed off at the entire male species, but it makes me angry. I mean, honestly, who does this guy think he is? He literally scared the shit out of me and then laughed. I defensively shift further away from him on the bench.

"Sorry. I didn't mean to freak you out or anything." His voice is calm, fluid like the ocean. If I wasn't so annoyed, I might have even said it sounded sexy, but I am annoyed, so I push that thought to the back of my mind.

"Well, what did you expect, you creep?" I shout, without even looking at him. My eyes are still trained on the surf ahead. "You can't just linger around people and expect for them to be comfortable about it! I mean... really?!"

I didn't mean to be such a bitch, but seeing Sean has provoked something within me and now this poor guy is on the receiving end of my wrath.

My hand comes up to my forehead and I sigh. The guy goes silent and I begin to think that maybe I really have upset him. I shift my body toward him, reluctantly preparing an apology in my mind.

I raise my gaze to his. He's still smiling, which should have only exacerbated my petulance, but it doesn't. Because after years of seeing only fake smiles, it surprises me to see one so real.

He beams back at me, his entire face emanating light. Sparks dance in his grey-green eyes that seem to mirror the ocean before us, and I dissolve. It's cliched, I know, but they're the kind of eyes that have the ability to make you lose your train of thought, the kind that render you speechless. I've forgotten why I'm angry.

"I'm sorry," he says, still grinning, then his smile fades into concern. "But are you?"

"Am I what?" I question.

"Are you okay?" he asks, cautiously. I probably freaked him out with my outburst. For all I know, he might actually think I'm insane.

"Yes," I reply, although my head shakes as if to say I'm not. "No. I don't know. It doesn't matter."

"Wow, you're wound really tight." He places his guitar pick between his teeth and combs a hand through his messy hair, pushing back the strands that have fallen onto his face. I realise now that he's the same guy that watched me from across the street this morning.

"Yeah, sorry, just …I … I'm having a bad day." I manage to choke out. I suddenly feel drained and regret tugs at me for being so rude. "I have to go."

He ignores what I've said, extending his hand out to me.

"I'm EJ," he says, "Cliff Haven's resident creep. Apparently."

As embarrassed as I am for insulting him, he seems completely undeterred. His eyes flicker under the hot sun and the corners of his mouth lift again, forming a crooked smirk. His mood is contagious and I find myself smiling back at him. I thank my lucky stars that he has a good sense of humour, or else this conversation could have taken a completely different turn.

"Liv," I reply, accepting his hand shake, and then attempting to poke fun at myself I add, "Crazy girl from out of town that freaks out about everything. Apparently." His hand is warm and surprisingly soft.

"Oh, yeah? Where are you from?" he asks.

"Hampton Ridge." I answer without even thinking, then mentally reprimand myself for letting my secret slip.

So far, Carla is the only one that knows where I live, and that's only because I had to fill out my address on my employment contract. If she's figured out that I lied about going to Cliff Haven high school she hasn't mentioned it yet.

"Oh," he says, raising his eyebrows and pointing to the cliffs to the right of us. "You live up there?"

It's hard to tell by his tone whether he is impressed or disgusted.

"Uh, yeah. Why? What is that supposed to mean?" I ask warily, though I already know.

I'm used to being judged by my postcode. He probably thinks I'm some sort of conceited, stuck-up rich snob, but the reality is, I'm a lot worse than anything he could dream up in his head.

"Nothing, I ..." He pauses with a slight shake of his head and the light leaves his eyes. There's a stark contrast between his current demeanour and that of five minutes ago. "I met someone from Hampton Ridge once."

I get the impression that he didn't like this 'someone', and knowing what I know about the residents of Hampton Ridge, I can't blame him.

"Well, now you've met two. Anyway, I really do have to go." I glance down at my watch.

Carla is going to kill me for being gone so long. I'll be lucky if I have a job left to go back to.

"Okay," he says. The darkness in him shifts a little. "Maybe I'll see you round, crazy girl."

I half laugh at this new found nickname as I roll my eyes. "Maybe you will."

Somehow, the prospect of that doesn't bother me one bit.

As I pace back up the hill to the Haven café, the melodious hum of guitar chords follows me. Despite the awful day I'm having, the sound fills me with a sense of hope.

Maybe it isn't too late to turn this day around after all.

Chapter 5

OLIVIA

"Good morning, Olivia." I squint as my father's voice hollers from the kitchen table. It's hard enough to pretend I'm a normal non-hungover school girl ready for a double period of maths as it is, without adding my dad's thunderous voice to the equation.

"Hey." I force out a reply. I throw my bag down onto the countertop and press some random buttons on the coffee machine, hoping it spits out something edible and highly caffeinated. "Where's mum?"

Dad slams his laptop shut and slides it into his briefcase. "Upstairs. She isn't feeling well this morning."

In other words, she's hungover.

I don't know why I bother asking. I suppose I'm hoping for a different answer. Something like, "She's in the garden planting flowers," or "Right behind you. Can't you smell the fresh pancakes?" But those are things a normal mother would do. Not my mother.

"The benefit must have run pretty late last night?" I say, referring to the charity gala my parents had attended.

For what this time, I have no idea. Hell, the people who attend them rarely have a clue what they're throwing their money at. I'm really just making conversation to be polite. Truthfully, we have nothing to talk about anymore. These days the only thing we have in common is our address.

"Actually, the benefit is tonight," my father responds.

"Are you sure?" I ask, confused. "I'm sure Mum said it was last night."

"No. Definitely tonight. I was working last night. There was a major emergency at the hospital." He picks up his briefcase, then kisses me quickly on the forehead. "I'll be working late tonight. Make sure you do your homework."

When I hear the door close behind him, I rifle through my bag, searching for my phone. I scroll until I find Mum's message.

Definitely sent yesterday.

Mum: *Meeting Dad in Milton for the benefit. We'll be home late.* X

If Dad was working, then where the hell was she?

Chapter 6

LIV

My second shift at the café turns out to be more successful than my first. I managed to get through the day without breaking anything, Sean never showed up to ruin my life and I met Sammi, another waitress. I'm finally starting to get the hang of the cash register and coffee machine after spending the morning training with Carla.

Following my lunch break, Sammi approaches me. "Hey Liv. Some of us are going over to Steve's after closing. You wanna come?"

"Steve's?" I ask, wondering if Steve is another employee I haven't yet met.

"It's the pub across the road. We go there pretty much every Friday for drinks after work," she answers, tucking a honey blonde ringlet behind her ear.

"Oh, Steve's Tavern!" I respond, remembering the guy standing below the sign yesterday. His smooth husky voice and crooked grin enter my mind.

"Yeah. That's the one."

"I don't know. I don't want to impose on you guys. Maybe I'll just head home."

I wrestle with the decision. I'm here to reinvent myself, but with opening up to new people comes a greater risk of exposed secrets. I know it's in my best interests not to get involved, and yet I can't seem to fight this gravitational pull toward human interaction. I enjoy being in their company.

"You wouldn't be imposing at all." Sammi's expression is genuine. "You're one of us now!"

Her words tug at my heart. Whether I like it or not, I'm a part of something now that I hadn't been last week. I'm forming relationships with these people.

"Yeah, sure. It sounds fun." Maybe I could just make an appearance.

Sammi claps her hands in excitement. "Yay! Kristen will be so happy you're coming."

When the final customers leave the café, we busy ourselves with our closing duties. There's a different vibe this afternoon, anticipation hanging in the air. Sammi hurriedly wipes tables down, I place chairs and stools upon countertops and Kristen gracefully slides the mop along the floor in between us.

Carla and Charlie won't be joining us at Steve's. Carla has plans with friends and Charlie's daughter is having her 10th birthday party at a local bowling alley, so when five thirty finally rolls around, Sammi, Kristen and I head across the street.

I can't help feeling a little underdressed. Sammi wears a cute top and blue jeans, while Kristen looks ultra-chic in her knee-high boots and pleated mini skirt. I make a mental note to wear something a little nicer next Friday than the cut-off denim shorts and black off-shoulder tee I'm donning tonight.

From the outside, Steve's Tavern doesn't look like much. Its rustic exterior could definitely benefit from a fresh coat of paint. Like most of Cliff Haven's buildings, it was probably constructed last century, but Steve's lacks the regular maintenance that the other shopfronts seem to have had.

As I step inside, it becomes obvious that the interior is just as antiquated, the "open" sign above the door, now illuminated in neon blue, being the pub's only modern addition. Yet, despite the lack of contemporary décor, I feel welcome from the second I enter it.

There's something comforting about it's scratched, wooden floor boards creaking beneath my feet, something humbling about finding myself in a place that isn't brand new and shiny. Unlike the upscale restaurants and bars in Hampton Ridge that are overly congested with the judgmental eyes of upper-class snobs, Steve's Tavern is old-school. And I like it.

"Sammi, go grab us that table!" Kristen points to a table in the corner, situated next to a platform that appears to be a small stage. "We'll get the drinks. You want your usual?"

Sammi gives a thumbs up as she beelines for the table, and I follow Kristen. The bar is packed and I can tell we're in for a long wait.

When we've almost reached the back of the line, an evidently drunk guy stumbles into me. He grabs my arm to steady himself as he falls forward, his beer breath warm on my face. I estimate him to be about sixty years old.

"Oh hey, darlin'," he slurs. "If ya wanna come home with me, all ya hafta do is ask!"

I attempt to wrestle my arm free, but his grip is tight.

"Leave her alone, Tommy. It's time you went home, don't you think?"

I freeze at the sound of the voice coming from behind me.

A husky voice.

A sexy, husky voice.

I cringe inwardly, not sure if I'll ever muster the courage to turn around.

"I'mma not ready to gooo yet," the old man responds, releasing me, and straightening himself.

"Suit yourself. But I'm still not serving you," the smooth voice answers.

The drunk guy ambles off and I slowly turn to greet my rescuer. Before I can say anything, Kristen throws her arms around his neck and cries, "EJ! How are you?"

"I'm good, Kristen. How are you?" he replies, returning her hug.

"Yeah, pretty good! Well, uni sucks at the moment but, you know…" Kristen trails off, then remembering I'm standing there, she enthusiastically slings an arm over my shoulder, pulling me forward. "Hey! This is Liv! She's our new girl."

"Hey, crazy girl." EJ says, leaving my cheeks burning with humiliation and Kristen totally confused.

"Do you guys know each other?" Kristen asks.

"We've met," EJ grins. His grey-green eyes hold mine. "Hi."

"Hi," I reply.

I'm nervous. Why am I nervous? The bar is loud, but his eyes seem to block out all sound. And if that isn't enough, the guy's biceps are distracting as hell, on full display thanks to the graphic muscle tee he wears. I never noticed how tanned and radiant his skin was yesterday.

"Can I get you guys something?" he asks, heading around the opposite side of the bar.

"Yes. That would be amazing." Kristen replies. Sammi's over in the corner and she wants her usual. I'll have a vodka and lemonade. Liv, you want one?"

"Hold the vodka. Lemonade's fine."

"No worries." EJ says as he begins preparing our drinks.

When he's done, I pull a fifty from my wallet and hold it out over the bar.

"Don't worry. First one's on the house." He waves my hand away.

"No, it's cool. You don't have to do that. I can pay."

"Keep it," he says. He grins at me again and I think I'm going to melt.

"Okay, thanks," I say, shyly.

What is wrong with me? Why is it taking every ounce of my self-control not to get lost in his eyes?

I carry my lemonade while Kristen juggles the other two drinks and we return to the table.

"That was some speedy service," Sammi states, as she takes a sip of her bourbon and coke.

"Perks of knowing the staff," Kristen replies with a wink.

"Does he always give out free drinks?" I ask.

"Sometimes," she answers. "His dad owns the bar and he manages it, so he can do what he likes."

"His dad is Steve?"

She nods, slurping some vodka lemonade through her straw, "Steve's great. And EJ is really sweet."

It occurs to me now that maybe she's dating him. It would explain the hugging and their apparent closeness.

"Oh, is he your boyfriend?" I ask.

Kristen laughs. "No!" She waves her hands in front of her, as though I've just asked her the weirdest question in the world. I don't know why I'm relieved to hear that. "He's like a little brother to me," she continues. "Our families are really close. We pretty much grew up together."

"Oh cool," I say, casually. "So, this is the place to be on a Friday night in Cliff Haven, huh?"

"Yeah. Either this place or there's usually some pretty cool parties happening." Sammi answers.

"Where are you from, Liv?" Kristen asks me.

I've unintentionally made it completely obvious that I'm not a local. I'm supposed to be reinventing myself, but as it turns out, I'm really bad at it.

"Uh, well, I kind of just live up on the cliff. I never used to come down this way much I guess." I speak quickly and then swiftly change the subject. "So, what are you guys studying? You both go to university?"

"Yeah. I want to be a teacher," Sammi answers. "Primary school."

Why does that not surprise me? I've only known Sammi for a day, but the teaching profession suits her down to a tee.

"That's awesome," I reply. "I can totally see that for you. What about you Kristen?"

"Psychology." Kristen pokes at the ice in her otherwise empty glass with her straw.

"Wow. That's impressive," I say. I mean it, although it somehow makes me feel vulnerable to know that about her. Did Kristen have the ability to analyse my personality? Could she see through to my fragility?

"Yeah," she replies. "Most days I'm sure I've chosen the right path, but other days I honestly wonder what the hell I'm doing. It can be pretty full on, but definitely interesting and worthwhile."

"What about you, Liv?" Sammi asks.

"Me?" I twirl a strand of hair nervously. "I'm kind of a work in progress."

"Okay, so…" Kristen begins to speak, but is abruptly cut off by Sammi. I'm thankful for the diversion.

"Hey, Kristen! Henley's over there! Is he still having a party tomorrow night? We should all go!"

"Who's Henley?" I ask.

"Alex Henley. Kristen's boyfriend," Sammi states matter-of-factly.

Kristen rolls her eyes. "Was. He *was* my boyfriend. As in, he's not currently my boyfriend. And the party isn't for another week."

"You guys are off again?" Sammi asks.

"It's complicated." Kristen doesn't seem eager to offer any more information than that.

"Henley is the drummer in the band that plays here." Sammi fills me in. "He's Kristen's on-again off-again boyfriend. Currently they are off."

"Hello? I'm sitting right here!" Kristen says, sarcastically. "Speaking of the band." Her eyes wander to the small stage in the corner and she shifts uncomfortably in her chair.

I follow her gaze. A tattooed guy paces the stage, tapping a set of drumsticks. He's tall, rugged, and muscular with longish blonde hair. He's attractive, and although I don't know either of them well, I can easily imagine them as a couple. There's an obvious tension in the air between them.

A moment later, EJ leaps onto the stage, grabs a guitar from the corner and hangs it upon his neck. It's a different guitar to the one he cradled at the pier yesterday. This one is electric, its body a polished turquoise that gleams under the dim pub lights.

He tunes the strings, gently plucking them individually and pausing to listen to each one. The concentration on his face is actually adorable. He strums a few chords, stealing a glance in our direction. I watch his jaw tick as he swallows, adjusting, and readjusting his guitar strap.

"EJ's giving off a weird vibe," Kristen says. "He looks nervous or something."

Weird. I'd had the same thought, but dismissed it due to the fact that I really don't know him at all. EJ leans into the microphone. "Hey everyone. Hope you're all having a great night tonight. We're Eight Oceans Away and we're gonna play a few songs for you."

"Wooooooo!" Kristen shouts, then turning to us to clarify her response, she adds, "That was for EJ, not Henley."

"Uh huh. Sure." Sammi nods, an eyebrow cocked sarcastically, then gives a loud wolf whistle.

By now, two other band members have taken the stage. The lead singer, a pretty blue-eyed guy with messy dirty blonde hair, stands front and centre. A tall, lean guy struts to the right of the stage, nursing a bass guitar, his dark hair falling over his face.

They dive straight into their first song, an energetic bass-driven alternative rock ballad. I like their style instantly. It isn't what I would have listened to in the past. Sean's addiction to hip hop music and Katerina's love of dance tracks hadn't left a whole lot of room for me to explore my own genres. I now have a deep appreciation for rock and indie music.

I try not to stare, but it's hard to keep my eyes off EJ. If he'd been nervous before, as Kristen had suspected, there's no trace of it now. He nails the guitar solo, his bottom lip curling as he focuses on the strings, his biceps flexing with the weight of the guitar in his arms. He seems to fade into the song, like he's forgotten the audience before him. He's not here with us right now. He's somewhere else entirely. It's a sensation I'd once been familiar with, but those days now seem like a lifetime ago.

We order another round of drinks and watch the band play the rest of their set. They play eight songs in total. When Henley descends from the stage, Kristen seems eager to get the hell out of here. I gather from the snippets of information Sammi has revealed throughout the night that her relationship with Henley has always been complicated.

"Sorry guys. I think I'm gonna head home. I have a huge assignment to work on tomorrow. Besides, this is awkward." She gestures uneasily in Henley's direction.

"That's okay," Sammi replies, glancing down at her phone. "My roommate just texted to see if I need a ride home, so I might take her up on that offer."

"Will you be okay to get home, Kristen?" I ask. "Yeah, of course! My apartment's just around the corner. What about you? We should walk you to your car." Kristen tosses her bag over her shoulder and readies herself to leave.

"Oh, its fine," I reply. "I parked close by."

Three of the band members have gathered around a table near the bar throwing back beers, but EJ is nowhere to be seen.

"Hey Cayden," Kristen calls. "See you guys later. Say bye to EJ for me, okay?"

The bass player tips his beer in our direction and nods his goodbye. "Sure thing."

The air has grown cold when we step onto the pavement outside the tavern. Cliff Haven sure looks beautiful all lit up at night. Fairy lights twinkle from within the hedges that line the streets. I'm awestruck by the serenity in the atmosphere, and after the girls have gone their own separate ways, and despite being a little cold, I feel inspired to take a quick walk down to the beach. I'm not ready to go home yet.

I've almost reached the end of the esplanade, where the glow of the streetlights give way to the stars. In the darkness, I hear the sound of footsteps on the pavement far behind me, increasing in their pace.

Cliff Haven has felt like a safe place to me up until this point, but I suddenly tense at the thought of being the only one out here. Between the loud music from the pub and the laughter on the street, would anyone even hear me if I screamed?

"Hey!" A voice calls from behind me, muffled by the sound of the crashing waves ahead. The tone is deeper, male. My fear intensifies as the footsteps draw closer, and just as I'm trying to decide between which direction to run, he calls out once again.

"Hey!" He isn't far behind me now.

I spin around quickly, my eyes meeting a tall, dark figure. I inhale the scent of leather and vanilla, mixed with a subtle tinge of beer. My hands instinctively grasp at the stranger's chest in fear and I try to push him away. I search for his face, but with the glow of the town lights behind him, I can only make out his silhouette.

"Liv," the voice calmly says. "It's me. It's EJ."

I take a step back, allowing my eyes to adjust to the night. I can see him now. I see his perfect skin, silver under the light of the moon, the sparkle in his eyes. How is it fair that such long, luscious eyelashes could belong to a guy? I exhale a shaky breath. My walls come up, and in turn, my panic converts to anger. I can't help it. It's how I'm wired.

"Jesus Christ!" I yell. "You couldn't have led with that?"

"I'm sorry," he says, simply.

"You're really trying to live up to this whole creep mentality, aren't you?" I ask, rudely, I admit.

EJ has come to stand beside me now, although he doesn't respond to my question. I glance sideways to find him grinning at me in the darkness.

"Are you laughing at me?" I ask, incredulously.

"I'm sorry," he chuckles, then does his best to maintain a serious composure. "I'm sorry. Really. I am."

"Well, I'm glad you find me so amusing." I state.

"Ok, look," EJ says, turning to face me. "Please don't be mad at me. I really am sorry. It won't happen again. I promise."

I turn towards him. "Really? And how can you be sure?"

"I'll … start wearing a bell." EJ deadpans.

I've never seen anyone say something so ridiculous with such a straight face. "A bell?" I fight to contain my laughter. I don't want to give him the satisfaction.

"If that's what it takes," EJ quips.

We stand like that, staring at each other for what seems like ages, but is probably only a few seconds. What is it about this guy that both captivates me and infuriates me?

"I'm sorry," he says again, and I can tell he means it. "Look, let's start this whole thing from the beginning. I'll go first." He clears his throat, then says, " Hi, Liv. Nice night, isn't it?"

I gape at him in bewilderment.

"This is where you say, "Why, yes EJ! It's such a lovely night. And now it's even better because you're here!"

"Wow," I say, battling the urge to smile and failing.

"Yes! Mission complete," EJ remarks.

"Huh?" My brow furrows in confusion.

"I made you smile." He winks at me.

"Oh. Right."

"It's a great smile. You should do it more often," he says, rubbing the back of his neck with his palm.

"I'll try, I guess." If only he knew, I've been trying for so long.

"You like the beach, huh?" he asks.

"Yeah, I guess so." I begin to walk towards the water, EJ falling in step behind me. The waves fall and tumble onto the sand, black in the night, with the exception of the silvery foam that shimmers under the gleam of the moon. "I like the ocean. It makes me feel free."

"You are free," EJ responds from over my shoulder.

In so many ways, he's right. I nod. "Yeah. I guess. I just mean, it makes me feel alive."

"Yeah. I get that."

I turn to face him, realising only now that he's carrying something in his right hand. I instantly recognise it.

"Is that..?" I point at the flat, rectangular object.

"Oh, right. Yeah." EJ holds it out toward me. "That's why I followed you. You left this back at the bar. It was under the table."

I take the music book from his grip. "Thank you. It must have fallen out of my bag somehow."

"No problem. And I'm sorry again, for scaring you."

"Thanks. This means a lot."

I'm more grateful than he will ever realise and guilt gnaws at me that I've been so mean to him. All he's done is show me kindness. I couldn't live with myself if I lost that book. I shiver as an icy blast of wind rolls in from the sea.

"Are you cold?" EJ asks, as he starts shedding his jacket.

He drapes it over my shoulders before I even have a chance to respond, and I find myself enveloped in warm, vanilla scented leather.

"Thanks," I reply. "But my car isn't that far. I should get going."

"I'll walk you," he says, nodding toward the street.

"Thanks," I say softly, clutching the music book to my chest.

When we reach the esplanade, I direct EJ down the dark alley that leads to the parking lot where my Mercedes awaits.

"Just over there," I say, pointing to the furthest car space in the lot.

"That's your car?" EJ questions, as he strides toward it.

"Yep," I reply.

I'm guessing he's now just realising that I'm from the 'rich' part of Hampton Ridge if he hadn't already.

"Wow. It's amazing," he says, eyeing the exterior. I wonder what he would think of my dad's Tesla.

The irony isn't lost on me. This constructed heap of painted metal, with its black, leather interior and shiny, chrome wheels would make me the envy of most of the teenagers in Cliff Haven, maybe even some of the adults. But it makes me feel like a hypocrite. Every. Damn. Day.

"Well, I guess I should be going." I say, awkwardly. "Thank you. For walking me here, and for the book." I hold up the music book and give a small smile.

"No problem." He shoves his hands in his pockets, his body tense in the cold night.

"Oh, your jacket!" I begin taking the jacket off, but he reaches out and stops me.

"No. It's cool. Keep it for tonight." His fingers gently brush the back of my neck as he readjusts the collar, sending

55

tiny sparks of electricity down my spine. After a beat, he shrugs and adds, "I'll be seeing you around."

He opens the car door for me and I settle into the driver's seat, placing my bag and the music book beside me on the passenger seat. "I guess you will."

This time when he grins at me, I can't help but smile back. I'd be lying if I said I wasn't intrigued by EJ. That it doesn't feel like some sort of magnetic force is at work when he's near, drawing us together. For all the effort I've been putting into distancing myself from people, he makes me want to know him in ways that I've never known anybody else.

And as I drive away from Cliff Haven, the scent of leather and vanilla fills my car. I've never more ardently anticipated the possibilities of the future.

Chapter 7

OLIVIA

"I want to go shopping," I announce as I hover over my mother lying lazily on the cabana beside the pool.

"Fine. Take my card," she replies flatly, not bothering to even move or look in my direction. "My purse is in the kitchen."

"I want you to come with me, Mum. Come on, please!" I plead.

"Oh, not today Olivia." She groans as she leans forward, taking a sip from her crystal scotch glass. Her large designer sunglasses slip down her nose, subtly revealing bloodshot eyes.

"Please. We haven't spent any time together lately. We could go to that Chocolateria you love so much. It'll be fun!" I know my words are wasted on her even before I say them.

My mother has been preoccupied lately and I'm becoming increasingly desperate to find out what or who she's been turning her attention to, and although I'd never admit it, it pisses me off that she seems to have better things to do than spend time with me.

"Olivia, I'm tired. I'd just like to rest before I have to go to this benefit with your father tonight. It's going to be hard enough to keep my eyes open through all that boring drivel as it is. Besides, the last thing I need is extra calories. You should know that."

It's unlike my mother to refer to charity events in such a negative manner. It may be the norm for the other desperate housewives of Hampton Ridge, but my mother's generosity and consideration for others has always separated her from them in that sense. Something is definitely up with her, but I'll disregard that for now because she's given me an opportunity to ask her where she'd really been last night without sounding accusatory. This is my chance to catch her in a lie she obviously forgot she'd ever told.

"I thought the benefit was last night," I muse.

"What?" Her expression remains hidden behind the oversized glasses, but the shock is evident in her voice.

"You told me you were meeting Dad in the city last night for the benefit."

"Uh," she stammers. "No. That was for something different. I was with the girl's last night."

"The girls? Which girls?" I ask. I still don't believe her. Her text had said she was meeting my father. She's hiding something. The alcohol is tripping her up. She's losing track of her own lies.

"Olivia, what's with the interrogation? You can see I'm absolutely exhausted." She waves her scotch glass dramatically. "With your father's business at the hospital growing, it seems there's an event every night these days. I'm honestly so busy I can't keep up."

I fold my arms across my chest. I would pity her if I weren't so furious. Finally, she removes her sunglasses and straightens up, deciding I'm worth a mere morsel of her attention. She reaches for my hand, taking it in hers. "I'll make it up to you next week, okay? But in the meantime, my credit card is in the kitchen. Buy yourself whatever you like."

With that, she drops her sunglasses back down on her nose, takes a long swig from her scotch glass and settles back into the cabana. I turn on my heel, ignoring the tears that sting my eyes, and head straight to the kitchen for her credit card.

Look on the bright side, Olivia.

At least you were able to catch her before the slurred speech kicked in.

Chapter 8

LIV

An entire week has passed and I haven't seen EJ. Not down at the pier during my lunch break and not on the street near the tavern. I'm only rostered on for a few days this week but Carla called me in today because Sammi is sick. Truthfully, I would be happy to work way more hours than she is giving me so I happily agreed. Not for the money, but for the distraction.

My mind has become overwhelmed with thoughts lately, although EJ has created a nice diversion from all the background noise in my head, as much as I hated to admit that. I'd try to convince myself that the only reason he occupied my mind at all was because I had to return his stupid jacket.

His dumb, stupid jacket that smells like him.

I'd started to think that maybe he didn't care if he got it back at all, but that wouldn't have been consistent with what Kristen had told me after she'd seen it draped over my forearm as I'd walked into the café on Tuesday morning.

"Umm. What's that?" she had said, cautiously pointing at the jacket as though it was a bomb that might explode on impact.

"It's EJ's jacket. Do you know if he'll be around today?"

"EJ? As in... my EJ?" She had looked at me like I was an alien from another planet and I had wondered whether she had lain some kind of claim over him. I remembered her saying he was like a little brother to her and I got the feeling she was super protective of him.

"Uh huh," I answered, hesitantly.

"Are you sure that's EJ's jacket?" She turned the leather over in my arms, exposing the zip on the left pocket, the letters E and J sewn underneath. "Oh, wow! That's really EJ's jacket!"

"Yeah. It's no big deal," I'd assured her, and then given her a brief run-down of the events that had occurred after leaving Steve's Tavern.

"No freaking way!" She had shaken her head in amazement. "He must seriously trust you."

"With his jacket?" I had scoffed. "It was cold. He's a nice guy."

"You don't understand. EJ loves that jacket. I've never seen him not wearing it. His sister bought it for him for Christmas, like, three years ago and he hardly ever takes it off. Trust me, he must like you."

I had brushed her theory aside. We'd only just met and whether EJ is interested in me or not, nothing serious could ever happen between us. I'm too damaged for that.

Today is Friday, and I'm hopeful that the band will be playing at Steve's, which means I can go there after closing, return the jacket to EJ and get the hell out of there, before his sea-green eyes can mesmerise me into oblivion. Or maybe I could just give it to Kristen and she could return it.

"Hey Kristen," I say casually when the lunch rush dies down. "Will you be heading to Steve's after closing?"

"No. Sorry." She sounds disappointed. "I have to go to Henley's parent's place tonight. It's his dad's birthday so the family are putting on a dinner for him. By the way, Henley's having a party tomorrow and you have to come. He just got a new place so it's kind of a housewarming thing but it'll be wild."

"Oh," I say, surprised, "So, I take it you and Henley are back on then?"

Yeah, you could say that." Kristen smiles. "He's a great guy. He just knows how to push my buttons. I mean, boys, right?"

"Well, that's great. I'm glad you guys sorted ... whatever it was ... out," I say, realising I had no idea why they had broken up in the first place. It would have been rude to ask anyway. Still, I'm happy for them.

I continue restocking the napkin holders on the counter when she speaks again, "He'll be there."

"What?" I ask, raising my gaze to hers.

"EJ." Her lips lift at the corners in a devious grin. "He's working tonight."

I roll my eyes at her, fighting the urge to smile.

"Liv!" Carla shouts to me from across the now empty café, "Can I see you for a minute?"

"Sure," I leave the napkin holders and meet her behind the register.

"Liv, I'm so sorry to ask this of you. I know you probably have plans this weekend, but is there any way I could get you to help out tomorrow afternoon? Sam just called. She has tonsillitis so she's out for the rest of the weekend." She's becoming more flustered with every word.

I'm already rostered on for the morning so I'll be coming in anyway. A few more hours wouldn't hurt. I almost laugh at her assumption that I might have made plans. I never have plans. "Of course, Carla."

"Are you sure? I promise to give you Sunday off."

"It's fine. No problem at all," I smile. I'm genuinely happy to help. Any excuse to get me into Cliff Haven and away from Hampton Ridge.

"You're a lifesaver!" she exclaims, gratefully.

When the registers have been counted and we're officially closed up for the day, Kristen dashes out in a hurry, excited to see Henley.

I cross the street, clutching EJ's jacket, the leather cool and smooth against my skin. I'm anxious. I've somehow managed to unintentionally work myself up over this whole thing. Damn Kristen for putting ideas in my head. I take a deep breath and put them to the back of my mind as I push open the heavy, wooden door to the tavern.

Get a grip, Liv.

The bar is fast becoming inundated with eager customers wanting to purchase cheap cocktails before the close of happy hour. Even through the swarm of people, I spot him straight away, cradling an acoustic guitar in the corner of the stage. This time, it's the same apple red guitar he had with him when we first met at the pier. He places it on the ground in front of him and begins testing the microphone. I wonder if the band will be playing without Henley. Maybe they have a back-up drummer.

"Testing," EJ's cool voice echoes through the bar. When he's satisfied that it's up to his standard, he picks up his guitar, hangs it around his neck, and tweaks the tuning pegs.

I can tell instantly that things are not going to go as I'd planned out in my head. I can't just throw the jacket at him while he's playing, especially if it's as important to him as Kristen had made out. I'll have to wait until he finishes his set, or at least takes a break. He tips the microphone and strums a few chords, which I soon realise serves as the introduction to his first song. EJ is going solo tonight.

The song is a mellow, acoustic ballad, and drastic in contrast to the songs he played with the band the previous week. Captivated by the cool edge in his voice, I'm stuck in my place near the door.

It's not only his voice that moves me. It's the lyrics too, sad and poignant. The song weaves a heartbreaking tale of love and loss, and even though he doesn't know I'm here, it's as though his words were written only for me. He performs it so intensely, it's impossible to believe that it isn't personal. I'm indescribably affected by him. Goosebumps form on my skin as his lyrics wind their way into my veins, an invisible tether connecting his heart to mine. When a tear tracks its way down my cheek, it comes as no surprise.

EJ's energy tonight is vastly different from the few encounters we've had before tonight. Although I don't know him at all, being around him at the pier and at the beach I'd felt a certain light emanating from him. He emits such positivity and happiness, but during this performance, it's as though that flame has been snuffed. It has me wondering what has happened in his life. What's his story?

The song ends and the crowd cheers as he hops off the stage momentarily to take a swig from the water bottle on the closest table. He ascends the stage with more momentum than before, strumming an upbeat acoustic number and, just like that, it's as though the light has switched back on, that sparkle in his eyes returning.

He plays the second song with enthusiasm. There's no denying his talent. Both his voice and his guitar skills are beyond amazing, leaving no doubt that his band is lucky to have him.

He pauses before his third song, leaning into the mic. "Thanks guys. I appreciate it," he says to his audience. "I'm gonna sing another one but this one's kinda new. So go easy on me, okay?"

The crowd whoops and his chuckle echoes through the room.

This new song is more chill than the last. It gives me Jack Johnson vibes, with a bit of Ed Sheeran thrown in. I find myself getting lost in the melody, but then the lyrics grab my attention and my heart catches in my throat.

"She's the new girl in town,
She has a thing for the sea,
She said it makes her feel free
And alive."

"Well, I got nothing figured out
But I can say with certainty
That she makes me feel free
And alive."

What. The. Actual. Fuck. I can't breathe. Surely, it isn't possible that he is singing about me. I tell myself this is pure coincidence, that he's singing an original, new song that vaguely details our last meeting.

"She's a little bit of crazy
In this mixed-up world,
But I see something in her
That I've never seen before."

Okay. This is all sounding too specific and weirdly intimate. My nerves transform into panic and I'm overcome with a desperate need to remove myself from this situation. I'm not proud of it, but I'm about to do the most childish and cowardly thing a person can do.

Run.

I could easily slip out unnoticed, but that doesn't resolve the issue of returning the jacket, which suddenly feels like lead in my arms. Knowing what Kristen told me about its importance and the song lyrics that are now embedded in my brain, it's blatantly obvious to me that I'm not meant to be the one protecting it. This is all wrong.

I recognise the guy sitting at the bar from last week. He's the bass player from the band, whose name I can't, for the life of me, remember. He skulls a beer while a couple of scantily clad girls hang off his every word.

"Hey," I tap him on the shoulder to get his attention.

He whirls around on the bar stool, giving me an annoyed look, which quickly morphs into a sleazy grimace. He eyes me like a lion would a piece of meat. Gross. He's a pig, but he will serve my purpose.

"You know EJ, right? You're in the band?" I question him.

"Yeah, I am," he boasts, shifting his body toward me. I ignore his perverted stare.

"Great. Look, I have to be somewhere but I need to get this to him," I say, handing him the jacket. "Would you mind?"

"Uh, sure," he says, visibly disappointed with my disinterest in him.

I practically throw the jacket at him, then burst through the door and out onto the street. I lean against the tavern's external wall, allowing it to take my weight.

I can still hear EJ's beautiful voice as the end of the song draws near. There's no point trying to hold back the tears that force their way down my face.

I cry because his song scares the hell out of me, but also because it's beautiful, amazing, and wonderful. And I cry because this should be a happy moment, but I can't allow myself to feel happiness without chasing it down with a shot of gut-wrenching guilt.

I curse myself.

I curse my life.

Because if I was someone else with someone else's life, this story would have a different ending.

But I am who I am.

And EJ deserves better.

I raise my gaze to the dark sky above. There are no stars tonight. No tiny bursts of light to break up the blackness. Something sinks inside of me as I realise how poetically the empty sky sums up my existence.

I'm a black hole.

And I can't suck EJ into it.

Chapter 9

OLIVIA

"Are you okay?" Sean asks me.

"Yeah, I'm fine," I answer, although I'm positive the irritation is evident in my voice.

I lean against the bricks near the front door of Sean's friend's mansion. What was his name again? Daniel, Dylan… Something like that.

I don't want to be here. I'd rather be at the Salt Factory with Katerina but Sean had practically insisted that I meet this guy he'd known since he was in primary school, because he'll be going to Milton University too. Like I care.

After a moment, the large, cedar door swings open revealing a short, plump woman with dark hair and pale skin.

"Hi," Sean says to her. "We're here to see Dane."

Dane. That's his name. Why am I so hopeless with names? Oh, that's right.

Because I don't care.

The woman waves us inside and leads us through to the alfresco area where a group of guys and girls lounge on large wicker sofas, their faces illuminated by the cobalt blue light glowing from the in-ground pool below.

"Sean, you made it." A guy I assume to be Dane saunters toward us. He's tall and tanned and wears a suit, much like Sean's. "And you must be Olivia," he says, taking my hand in his and squeezing it gently.

"Yeah. Nice to meet you," I return the gesture, feigning interest. "Nice place."

"Thanks," he answers. "It'll all be mine someday."

Jesus Christ. What a douchebag.

I never thought it was possible to be sick of money, but I'm starting to feel as though it turns people into egotistical monsters. But if that's true, what does it make me?

Dane gestures for us to take a seat. "Make yourselves comfortable. What can I get you to drink?"

"Vodka and soda," I reply, out of habit.

Sean throws me a disapproving look, then shifts his attention back to Dane. "Just beer for me. Whatever you have is fine."

"Sure thing," Dane says, then calls over his shoulder to the housekeeper. "Bianca, did you get that?"

The housekeeper nods, then waddles off in the direction of the outdoor bar. This Dane guy can't even be bothered to get drinks for his own guests? Still, he knows his housekeeper's name, so I guess he has one up on me.

"Olivia, Sean tells me you're going to Milton too." Dane balances a scotch glass in one hand, the other deep in his pocket.

What is this guy? Fifty?

"Maybe," is all I can be bothered to say.

I know Sean has high hopes of me hitting it off with his old friends, but I can already sense that they're not, nor are

69

they ever going to be, my people. Dane annoys me, simply by the way he's standing, if not for the cockiness in his demeanour.

The trio of girls huddled together on the outdoor sofa are eyeing me curiously, and it only takes a quick glance at them for me to understand why. All four of them are wearing monochromatic suit jackets, their hair twisted elegantly into sophisticated chignons. Their outward appearances pale in comparison to mine, outshone by my red strapless Valentino mini dress and ice blonde waves.

Despite their wary stares, they must decide I'm worthy of their company. A tall brunette with severe crimson lips calls to me, gesturing for me to join them on the sofa.

"You must be Olivia," she says. She has her hand extended in welcome, although I feel anything but. "I'm Veronica and this is Elizabeth and Calista."

Whatever. I don't bother to commit their names to memory.

"Nice to meet you all." I smile robotically.

Get me out of here.

"So," Lizzie begins, or maybe it's Calista, "We hear your father is the legendary Victor Petersen. What's it like having such an influential man as a dad?"

Influential man? Kill me now.

It becomes apparent that my father is going to be the main topic of conversation here. I live in the shadow of an 'influential man.' No one will ever want to hear the stories of my own life. Is that why I'm applying to Milton? Because the only way to make something of myself and be someone other than Victor Petersen's daughter is to gain a title and add to my already increasing bank balance?

"It's a hard act to follow." I immediately chug down my vodka and soda when the housekeeper places it in my hand. To my relief, the girls laugh.

"Seriously, though," Veronica says. "What your father has done for Milton hospital has been revolutionary. He is an inspiration."

"Yes, the man is a legend," I respond, hoping my sarcasm isn't too obvious.

Up until now, I haven't really thought about what my father actually does, let alone what he has done for the hospital. All I know is that he's gone a lot, but I guess with the title he holds comes a huge amount of responsibility, which he obviously manages like a true professional, whether I care to admit it or not. But I didn't come here to talk about my father.

Why did I come here?

Oh, I remember.

To make Sean happy.

Laughter erupts from the other side of the courtyard. Sean appears to be enjoying himself. I'm not sure why he even needs me here. I'm getting so sick and tired of being his precious arm candy.

The housekeeper places a tray of glasses filled with what looks like lemonade or sparkling water down on the table in front of us.

"Betty, would you be able to bring me another vodka and soda?" I ask her.

"It's Bianca," she replies sternly, her eyes on my empty glass. "And why don't I just bring you the bottle?"

"Thanks. That would be great." My eyes level with hers, but I don't smile.

She doesn't look amused but wanders off toward the bar. The three other girls watch, their mouths wide open in disbelief, as though they can't tell if I'm joking or not.

Then Elizabeth begins to laugh, her shrill cackle echoing throughout the courtyard. "Oh, you're bad!"

"Yes," I say, with a straight face. The other girls join in the laughter. It seems they have decided I was joking.

For the record, I wasn't.

Chapter 10

LIV

On Saturday morning the staff at the Haven are buzzing with the anticipation of Henley's upcoming party.

In an effort to distance myself from EJ, I declined Kristen's offer to tag along with her, making up an excuse about not feeling well.

I don't want this to be my life. I don't want to feel like I should be avoiding EJ, but there is obviously something between us, a fondness, that I can't reciprocate.

"I hope you're not coming down with something too," she had said, as she'd reached up and gently inspected my forehead for a fever. Her sincere concern made me feel guilty for the lie.

When my shift ended, I walked directly to my car. I didn't want to meet anyone along the way that might try to talk me into going to Henley's. The old me would have jumped at the chance to party. It's funny how things change.

I drive home as fast as humanly possible without breaking the speed limit, and manage to arrive at Hampton Ridge just after six. Cherry blossom petals float whimsically from the trees, some landing on my windscreen as I manoeuvre down the boulevard. There's an air of calm and yet, from the top of the cliff, I can make out a storm cloud rolling in the distance.

Footsteps fall on the stairs as I enter the house and I think of Tessa. I miss her and I suddenly long for the opportunity to vent to her about all the things that have happened this week. She's become my person over these last few years. My hopes of seeing her are dashed as it dawns on me that it's Saturday and she would be at her own home with her family.

Instead, I round the bottom of the staircase to meet my father. Us being home at the same time is such a rare occasion. I pause to watch him struggle with his tie in the full-length mirror. Even after all these years, he can never get it perfect. It had been Mum's specialty, but with her gone, I'd adopted the task after streaming a YouTube video on repeat.

"Need some help?" I smile at him; my reflection visible behind him now in the mirror.

He shrugs and gives me a hopeless smirk, signifying what I already know – that he has absolutely no idea what he's doing. I reach up to his neck, smoothing the tie between my hands and form the perfect knot.

"Is there another charity benefit tonight?"

"Yes," he replies. "For the McHale Foundation. What are you up to? Would you like to come with me? It might be good for you. Get you out on a Saturday night."

My dad's pity is more than I can stand. It almost makes me wish I'd gone to Henley's party so I didn't feel like such an anti-social loser. Almost. I contemplate his invitation for the mere fact that it would impress him to see me attend.

The McHale foundation is a great cause to support and Dad has done a lot of remarkable things in collaboration with them, but I have too many bad memories of being at those events.

The McHale foundation was founded in 1996 by my father's good friend, Dr Albert Flynn. It aims to raise money for updated medical equipment in paediatric units in hospitals all around the country. They're also trying to get a grant to open up another hospital in the district. While I can't argue that they've been hugely successful in everything they've achieved, I only wish that the people that attended these kinds of functions cared about the cause.

Most of them were preoccupied with their appearance, always seeking gratitude and power for their donations. A genuinely caring and giving person doesn't need praise. It wouldn't surprise me if half of them didn't actually know where their money was even going.

Not to mention the incessant questions they would bombard me with about where I saw myself in the future, and the boastful comments that would follow about what their sons/daughters were doing, and which top ranked institution to which they'd been accepted.

"I'm actually not feeling all that well tonight. I just want to get some rest, if that's okay," I tell him, spinning the same lie I'd told Kristen.

"Sure," he answers, placing a warm hand on my shoulder. "Take care of yourself. Get some rest."

His voice drips with disappointment as he turns for the stairs. I hate letting him down but I don't have his strength. Somehow, Dad has always been able to stand above the lies and gossip that this town has spread about us. I don't know how he manages to never let it get to him. Either he hides his emotions well, or he has way more courage than I could ever hope to have.

"Hey, how was work?" Dad glances back at me over his shoulder.

"Good," I respond, surprised. It's the first time he's asked about my job, although I can't really blame him for not having asked earlier when we've barely seen each other. "I've made some new friends."

"That's good." His tone is positive but there's sorrow in his expression.

"I know it isn't what you want for me." I nervously tuck a loose strand of hair behind my ear. It's one of the most vulnerable things I've ever said to him.

"I only want for you to be happy," Dad replies earnestly, his hand resting on the staircase banister.

I nod. "I promise I will come to the next benefit." Despite it being the last thing I want, it's important for Dad to know that he has my support.

"Okay. It's next month. I'm hosting it."

"Even better," I say, ascending the stairs to my room.

I fling myself dramatically onto my king size bed, allowing the cushy pillows to take the weight of my head. A head that is heavy with stress and anxiety, probably due to this double life I'm attempting to lead.

My dad's shouted goodbye travels up the stairs, followed by the soft click of the front door as it closes behind him.

I briefly ponder what Kristen would be up to at the party as my fingers curl around the TV remote. I flick through the channels and stop when I see That 70's Show is on. I've always loved that show. No matter how bad my day has been or what kind of mood I'm in, it never fails to distract me.

Except for right now. My thoughts drift to EJ, and the song that I haven't been able to get out of my head since last night.

I'm frustrated. I'd thought that this new life I was creating would be a way to start anew, and yet here I am, running from the intimacy that comes with friendships, afraid that someone might actually learn the truth.

I frown in confusion at the humming sound coming from my handbag at the end of the bed. Is my phone actually ringing?

I rummage through my bag and pull it out. An unknown number illuminates the screen. I hesitate. The last time I'd answered an unknown number was after returning to school for final exams. That was when the abusive texts and prank calls had begun. But that was well over two years ago and I have a new number now, so the chances of that happening again are slim. I nervously swipe the answer key and lift the phone to my ear.

"Hello?" I say, softly.

At first, there's no reply. Then muffled music comes through the speaker, mixed with a few faint voices, then followed by distant laughter. "Hello," I say again, this time a little louder.

I wait, but there is no reply. I lower the phone from my ear, ready to end the call.

"Hi. Is this Liv?" I hear a voice, deep and husky.

"Yeah. Who is this?" I ask cautiously, though I already know.

"It's EJ." He answers confidently.

I freeze. My breath hitches in my throat. By the sounds of the background noise, I assume he must be at Henley's party. Where else would he be on the night his friend was throwing his first big party in his new place. Why is he calling me? How did he even get my number?

"Hello? You still there?" he asks.

Speak, Liv. Say something.

"Uh, yeah," I stammer, still in shock. "How did you get this number?"

"Kristen gave it to me. Don't hate her for it. I gave her a really hard time," he says, laughing. "She told me you were feeling sick. I wanted to make sure you were okay."

Of course, it had been Kristen. Most of the Haven staff have my number now.

"Yeah, I'll be okay. Just a headache." I answer, although now my nerves are getting the better of me, contributing to the sudden churning in my gut. The background music fades out, and I assume he must have walked away from the party.

"You sure?" he questions. "Because if you need me to come up there and check on you, I'd be happy to."

My heart races, beating against the walls of my chest at the thought of EJ visiting me in my house. "What?"

"I mean, if you need some company."

"You want to come over here?" I ask him in disbelief.

His confidence amazes me, in a good way or a bad way, I can't decide.

"Oh, well if you insist," he says, spinning my question to suit himself. I swear I can hear his crooked smirk through the phone. "Okay, sure. I'm on my way."

"Are you serious?" I ask sceptically.

He can't be serious.

I'm once again both infuriated by his arrogance and swayed by his charming persona. I contemplate screaming at him through the phone the way I had at the pier and at the beach, but I stop myself. Something tells me that no matter what I say, he's going to do what he wants. And some small part of me finds that impressive.

"Meet me at Highview Park," I sigh, resigning to the fact that this is actually happening.

"See you in half hour," he says, and then I hear the sound of the ignition starting before the line goes dead. He's already in his car.

I look down at myself. I'm still wearing the outfit I'd worn to work today, and probably smell like kitchen grease. Not that I'm trying to impress anyone, but I decide to have a quick shower and freshen up. I throw on my ripped, black skinny jeans and a tank top. I don't want to be flattered that this guy is leaving his friend's party to drive up a mountain for me, but my heart races all the same. I slick on some clear lip gloss, pull on my ankle boots, and snatch my house keys from my bag.

When I leave the house, the sky is purple blue ahead, painted with streaks of orange and crimson, but the dark, grey storm cloud I'd seen earlier has started closing in behind me, coming in off the ocean.

As the park comes into view I see an old, red, beat-up ute parked on the curb. EJ leans against it, his silhouette defined by the brilliance of the sunset behind him. He's wearing his jacket again, and a pair of mirrored aviators shield his eyes.

I curse my heart for racing so fast as the heat rises in my cheeks. I lecture myself inwardly for having such a reaction, because the truth is that EJ doesn't know me. Not at all. And if he did, there's no way he'd be wasting another minute of his time with me.

"Hey," he says.

"Hey." I'm not sure what else to say and my reply is followed by an awkward moment of silence.

"So... you come here often?" he jokes, attempting to break the ice.

"You could say that." I laugh. "You?"

"Oh, always!" he exclaims.

"Really?" I ask. It's hard to tell if he's serious or not.

"No. Never." He deadpans.

I feel a smile tug at my lips and I nudge him playfully in the shoulder. My reflection stares back at me from the mirrored lenses of his aviators and a wave of uneasiness washes over me at not being able to see his eyes. He follows me to the picnic table in the middle of the park.

"So, shouldn't you be at your friend's party?" I question.

"Yeah. I was there. But, you know, I thought it was gonna be better than what it was."

"Better?" I ask. "Better how?"

He grins at me, flashing his gorgeous, white teeth. "I thought you were gonna be there."

"Wow. That's a line if I've ever heard one." I smile shyly, self-conscious all of a sudden.

"Yeah, I guess." He smiles back at me, then removes his sunglasses. I'd thought his aviators were intimidating, but they have nothing on the clear, sea-green eyes that now penetrate mine. "Doesn't make it any less true though."

I suddenly can't look at him. I hang my head toward the ground and nervously dig at the damp dirt with the toe of my boot.

"I didn't feel great, so I came home," I tell him, which is not as much of a lie as I'd intended it to be.

The butterflies are flying harder and faster, twisting my stomach in knots. Never before have I had such a physical reaction to another human being. It hits me that he's really interested in me. And I have nothing to offer him.

He sits on the picnic table with his feet resting on the bench seat below. He motions for me to join him, so I do. Not wanting to lead him on, I position myself further down the table. "That's too bad. Thanks for returning my jacket by the way."

I wince. It hadn't occurred to me until now that me giving his jacket to the bass player made it obvious that I'd been in the tavern last night. That I'd heard him play.

"I'm sorry I didn't stick around. I had to get home."

His smile fades. "Did you? Or did you hear my song and completely freak out?"

I've hurt his feelings. Lies have never gotten me anywhere in the past so I decide to go with honesty this time.

"Okay. Yeah. I did."

"It wasn't meant to freak you out," he says, running a hand through his hair. "Sometimes lyrics come easily. I write about what motivates me."

"And I motivate you?"

"You inspired me." His eyes burn holes right through mine again, his eyebrow ring gleaming as it catches what little light is left in the sky.

"You don't know anything about me."

"But I'd like to." His expression is sincere.

No, you wouldn't. If you knew what I'd done, you wouldn't want anything to do with me. You'd be running in the opposite direction.

"Look," I begin, pausing to gather the right words. I don't want to hurt him. "I can't be in any kind of relationship. I need to focus on my future. That's all I have time for right now." It comes out harsher than intended, but it's necessary.

"Ouch," he murmurs, looking down at the damp grass between his feet.

I've offended him again and it makes my stomach churn. I'm about to apologise when he looks back up at me wearing his signature crooked grin. "Do you think you can make time for a new friend then?"

"You want to be my friend?" I ask.

"I'll take what I can get." He holds out his hand for me to shake on it. "Friends? Come on. Say yes, and I can drop this whole stalker creep thing I've got going on."

I bite my bottom lip as I contemplate his offer, then slowly link my palm with his. His hand is warm and smooth, and much bigger than mine. I push the butterflies down. If we're going to be friends, they're going to have to behave themselves.

He holds my hand longer than necessary, and then says, "I have to warn you though. If we're gonna do this whole friends thing, you're gonna have to stop biting your bottom lip like that."

"And you're going to have to stop saying things like that." I flash him a warning look.

"Fair enough," he says, withdrawing his hand from mine.

Thunder rumbles overhead and we both instinctively look to the sky. The heavy, grey clouds have finally made their way above us. Rain starts to fall in thick, heavy droplets. The only shelter in the park is on the other side of the barbeques about thirty metres away. I let out a shriek as I jump down from the table. Laughing, we both make a run for cover.

"Man, it's really coming down!" EJ calls out, as we race across the park together.

The soft ground squishes beneath our feet, having already been dampened by a previous storm. When we've almost reached the shelter, I lose my footing. My left heel sinks into a small hole in the muddy soil. Crying out, I grasp EJ's jacket, taking him by surprise and sending him flailing forward into a huge puddle. Miraculously, I manage to stay upright.

"Oh my god!" I cry. "I am so sorry!"

Humiliation warms my cheeks. I brace myself for EJ's response. His favourite jacket is trashed. He will surely be furious with me.

But he isn't. I watch as he rolls over onto his back in the middle of the giant mud puddle, the rain still pouring down on him from above. His whole left side is covered in sludge.

And he's laughing.

It's the kind of laugh you laugh when you're uninhibited, when nothing in the world can touch you. Only seeing him in this moment, do I remember what that feels like. I haven't laughed like that since I was a child, but watching him lie there cackling at himself makes me laugh too.

I've always thought that there was something unique about people who can laugh at themselves. It's a quality my friends in Hampton Ridge never had. They'd always taken themselves too seriously.

"Are you okay?" I ask, still standing in the now torrential rain. I reach down to grab his wet muddy hands and help him up out of the mud.

EJ stumbles to his feet. "Do you throw all your friends in the mud? Or am I special?"

This makes me laugh even harder and I feel a weight lift from my chest. In fact, I can't remember the last time I laughed so liberally. My hair is a wet mess, plastered to my head in knotty strings. Our clothes are drenched. I'm sure I look hideous, and for the first time in my life, I don't care.

"Hey, wait." EJ places his hands on my shoulders, looking intently at my face. "You've got something right there."

With his index finger, he draws a muddy line down the length of my nose.

"Hey!" I shout, but I can't help smiling.

"Sorry. Couldn't resist." He gently swipes a wet strand of hair from my face.

His fingers only just graze my skin, but it's enough to spark every nerve ending in my body. His eyes are intense as they search mine, and I have to wonder how much of me he sees.

Do those eyes see how much I want to kiss him in this moment?

Do they see how much his smile affects me?

Does he know that if they search deep down to the depths of my soul, I might just completely unravel?

It's all too much. He is too much. I pull my gaze unwillingly from his.

"I guess we better get you cleaned up then," I mumble.

Taking EJ back to my house is risky. The last thing I want is for him to be in my space, but I can hardly send him home drenched in rain and mud, especially when this was all my fault.

I formulate a plan in my head. I'll let him use the bathroom, and then I'll tell him he has to leave. My house is only four houses down from the park and we're already completely saturated, so it makes sense to leave EJ's car on the curb at the park entrance and walk. When we reach the front gate, EJ stops dead, gaping up at the house.

"This is where you live?" he asks. It's just a question, but it comes out more like an accusation.

"Yeah," I sigh. "Come on."

I enter the code on the keypad and the gates swing open. He's probably wondering what my life must be like having grown up in a place like this. Whatever he's thinking, it's probably not even close to the reality. I wait for him to say something else, but he stays silent.

He follows me to the front door, where we kick off our shoes. I dump them in the mud room sink before leading EJ up the stairs.

Our house has five and a half bathrooms. It wouldn't be appropriate to take him to my ensuite, so I lead him to a different one that adjoins a guest bedroom, located across the hall. Boundaries are necessary if our new found friendship is ever going to work.

I can't remember the last time this guest room had been used, but I know there are spare clothes in the wardrobe. My dad ordered Tessa to stock them after having to accommodate one of his closest business partners from interstate when he'd made an urgent visit. I slide open the heavy wardrobe doors and rummage through the drawers. I pull out a pair of navy tracksuit pants and a white t-shirt. They look like they're roughly his size.

"I'm so sorry. I still can't believe I pushed you into the mud," I say, spinning around to face him.

"It's all good. Don't worry about it." EJ replies, running his index finger along the spines of the books on the shelf across the room. He points to a rare, old copy of The Great Gatsby. "Wow, someone likes to read. Is this a first edition?"

I move toward the bookshelf, my wet jeans creaking as they stick to my legs.

"Ugh. Yes." I answer, "I hate that book."

He's right. It's a first edition. It probably holds some monetary value, but to me, it's worthless. It had belonged to my grandparents on my mother's side of the family.

"That's harsh. It's a classic," he argues, his tone amused.

"It's shallow and tasteless. It's the epitome of everything that's wrong with this world," I mutter. "It's a lesson on how not to live your life."

85

"Whew," he whistles, taken aback by my fiery response.

I'm a little stunned myself about how abrasive I've come off.

"And how should we not be living our lives exactly?" He speaks slowly. His hair is sticking up in a cute way, half caked in mud, almost distracting me from his question.

"By wasting it seeking money and possessions, and the approval of those that don't deserve it," I answer. "Anyway, it's just a stupid book."

"A stupid book that you're pretty fired up about," he says, turning to face me.

The truth is, I had to read Gatsby for tenth grade English. It had struck a chord with me. I likened my dad to Gatsby, always working to live in a house he was barely in, trying to buy a woman that he couldn't keep. The superficiality of it hit home, but I'll be damned if I'm going to let EJ in on any of that.

"Yeah. Well, like I said before, you don't know me." I shrug, reaching for the book in his hand, and shoving it carelessly back on the shelf.

"Right," he agrees. I look away from him, but I feel his eyes on me. "But like I said before, I'd like to."

His hand reaches for mine and I raise my gaze to his. He smells like rain and earth. As much as I will it not to, my heart seems to skip a beat as the intensity between us heightens. We're already on the verge of breaking our friendship pact.

I swallow, looking down at the floor nervously, and whisper another apology. "I'm really sorry about your jacket."

His fingers entwine with mine, which somehow gives warmth to my cold rain-soaked body. "Relax. It's just mud. It's fine."

"Yeah, I know. But I know it means a lot to you." I cringe inwardly as the words leave my mouth. I've made it obvious that Kristen and I talked about him behind his back.

He takes a small step away from me, his hands falling to his sides. "And how do you know that?" His brow knits in confusion and I sense a hint of annoyance in his voice. I'm startled by his sudden change in mood.

"Oh, no reason." I play down my response. "Kristen just told me your sister gave it to you or something."

"Oh. Is that all she said?" he asks, cautiously.

"Yeah." I get the impression there's something he isn't telling me, but I don't push it. If I'm entitled to keep my secrets, then I guess he should be too. "I'll get you some fresh towels."

I swing open the vast linen closet across the hall and pull out some towels to take back to EJ. When I return to the guest bedroom, I find him in the ensuite. He stands, shirtless, taking in the view of the cliff edge and the ocean far below.

"This bathroom is amazing. I'm in heaven right now," he says. I watch as he admires the marble stone bench tops, the large frameless shower, and the double spa bath in the far corner, while doing everything in my power to act like I haven't noticed his tanned, naked abdomen. "Can people see in from out there?"

He's referring to the floor to ceiling windows that make up the complete length of the room.

"No. It's tinted. We can see out, but no one can see in," I say to him, still trying not to stare at his toned upper body. "I know. It takes some getting used to."

"Wow," he breathes.

"Yeah," I shrug.

I wonder what he would think if he knew this was not the biggest bathroom in the house. Although this bathroom is large, it's only about half the size of the one in my bedroom. I set the towels down on the sink.

"I'll leave you to it then."

"Thanks," he grins.

I close the door behind me, pausing a minute to lean up against it, allowing myself to blow out a shaky breath.

God, Liv. What are you doing? Don't get involved here.

I hurry to my room and change into a pair of black gym pants and a loose purple tank. I'm yanking the top over my head when a loud bang echoes throughout the house as the front door slams shut. I dart into the guest bedroom quickly, before hearing the soft thudding of footsteps on the stairs. I freeze.

Dad's home.

I glance at the clock on the shelf. It's only seven thirty. He's barely been gone for an hour and a half. This is extremely unusual for him. Panic rises in my chest. My dad is home, and there's a guy in the bathroom taking a shower.

Sure, I could tell the truth, but I'm not sure he would believe me. Would he think that this was why I never went to his charity benefits? That all the nights he worked late, I've been shacking up with a guy in his house?

I know one thing for certain. When he climbs to the top of those stairs, he'll hear the shower running, if he hasn't already, and he'll wonder why. I have my own private bathroom and therefore, no use for the guest bedroom ensuite.

I could lie. I could say that it was a girlfriend in the shower. But who? He knows I no longer speak to anyone from Hampton Ridge. He knows I spend all my free time alone. Even if I lie and tell him it's Kristen, he might linger around wanting to meet her. His footsteps draw nearer. I'm becoming desperate. I'm not proud of what I do next, but it's the only thing I can think of.

I quietly turn the handle and slip into the bathroom, resting my forehead on the back of the door. I slowly press it closed; the lock barely audible as it clicks shut.

I pray that EJ will stay silent long enough for me to get his attention. I turn at the sound of the shower door opening and see EJ's head emerge through the gap, an amused but confused smirk spreading across his face. He doesn't seem at all concerned that the fogged-up glass has left little to the imagination. I hold a forefinger to my lips, motioning for him to be quiet, and close my eyes tightly. The shower faucet shuts off.

"Olivia." My dad's voice booms through the door.

"Uh. Yeah, Dad?" I reply with my eyes still closed, my chest rising and falling with every breath as I fight to keep my voice steady.

I turn back to face the door, away from EJ. It's extremely difficult to hold a conversation with my father, knowing EJ is naked in such close proximity.

"Is everything alright? Why aren't you using your own bathroom?" Dad asks.

"Um…I tried to but the… um…shower head is broken." I battle to contain the shakiness in my voice, while hoping to God that he doesn't immediately go to my room to check.

"Oh, right. I see. I'll have Tessa call a plumber on Monday morning."

"Ok," I answer. "You're home early."

As soon as I say it, I hope it doesn't sound suspicious. How the hell will I get EJ out of here with my dad down the hall?

"Yeah, I forgot some documents that Dr. Flynn wanted to take a look at."

"Oh. Okay." The sound of rustling towels comes from behind me.

"You sure you're okay in there?" Dad inquires again.

"Yep!" I force a chipper tone, trying to sound as natural as possible.

"Alright, well I have to head back out. They're waiting for me."

Thank God he isn't staying.

"Okay. See you in the morning."

I listen for the padding of feet on the carpet as he walks away. After a moment, I crack the door ajar slightly, awaiting the sound of my father's footsteps on the stairs, followed by the heavy thud of the front door closing. Only then, do I breathe a sigh of relief and shift my attention back to EJ.

He's standing closer than before, a towel draped around his waist, droplets of water still clinging to his muscular shoulders. His eyes appear greener under the downlights as they pierce right through me. I beckon my heartrate to slow down.

"That was close," I breathe.

He takes another step towards me, saying nothing at first, heat radiating from his bare skin. Then after what seems like forever, he smirks with one eyebrow cocked, and whispers.

"Are you gonna turn around so I can get dressed? Or is this something you do with all of your friends?"

A laugh escapes me, followed by a nervous eyeroll, then I turn to face the door. I'm hyperaware that I could just leave the room, but I don't.

"What does your dad do?" EJ asks.

"He's a doctor," I downplay, not bothering to elaborate.

He doesn't need to know everything. Besides, we've breached enough boundaries tonight.

"Oh, cool," he says. "And who's Tessa?"

"She's my aunt. She stays here sometimes."

Lies seem to come too easily to me these days. I don't know why I don't tell him the truth. It's already obvious to him that we are well off financially. What difference would it make for him to know we had a housekeeper. Lots of families have housekeepers, but lots of other families don't. Not that I would ever wish Tessa away, but I guess for a second, I want to belong to one of those other families.

The normal families.

"Your dad wants your aunt to call a plumber? No offence, but why can't he call one himself?"

"He would, but he's really busy," I mumble, nervously placing a stray strand of hair behind my ear.

I feel warm, strong hands on my shoulders as EJ whirls me around to face him. I catch sight of myself in the reflection of the glass, my shoulder-length dark hair still damp and unkempt from the rain, my body petite in comparison to his. I find myself wondering how anyone could make a pair of sweat pants and plain tee look so sexy. If I'd thought his touch was warm before, it's like he's on fire now. Between his body heat and the steam that continues to fog up the room, I've become unsteady. I lean into the sink for support.

"You alright?" EJ asks.

"Yeah, it's just hot in here," I exhale.

I'm not all right. I'm far from all right. My heart is fighting with my mind. My knees are weak, and every instinct I have is telling me to dive headfirst into something my brain knows would be a very bad idea.

He grins cheekily. "Well, yeah it is."

Once again, his confidence both annoys and impresses me, making me want to laugh and scream at the same time. I attempt to shove him playfully, but he catches my arm, holding it down at my side. His eyes dance with mischief as his free hand slowly moves to my face. He runs his thumb down my nose and cheek, gently wiping away the mud he smeared there earlier. I swallow hard and contemplate whether he can hear my heart pounding. He closes the gap between us, our foreheads now only inches apart. He pauses to gauge my reaction. It would be so easy to give in right now, to reach up and lay my lips on his.

Instead, I turn my head. "Time to get you out of here." My voice is hoarse, barely audible.

He pouts mischievously in response, but steps backward toward the stone counter. With space once again between us, I can finally breath again.

I throw his rain-soaked clothes at him, then he reluctantly follows me down the staircase and into the mudroom, where he collects his muddy converse sneakers. I lead him through the lobby and out through the front door.

The air is cooler now that the sky has darkened. It's no longer raining and the clouds have dispersed to reveal a starry night.

"Well, Liv. It's been a pleasure." EJ says, jokingly. I wonder if he wishes he'd stayed at Henley's party.

"I'm sorry. For all of it." I apologise. "Tonight has been so…"

"Fun?" EJ beams as he finishes my sentence.

I realise he's right, though I don't want to admit it out loud. Despite everything, I've had more fun tonight than I've had in a long time.

'I'm not sorry. For any of it," he says, his voice soft and low, as he combs a strand of my hair behind my ear.

I stiffen at his touch and then defensively take a step back.

Heart.

Mind.

Heart.

Mind.

They are at war with each other, but my mind always has to win out. It has to.

EJ seems to take the hint and shifts away from me.

"Well, I better get back up there. I've gotta go break my shower head," I joke. "I guess I'll see you next week."

"You can count on it," he smiles back at me as he strolls out into the night.

Somehow, I know I can.

Chapter 11

OLIVIA

"Wow," I groan, cradling my pounding head in my hands. I run my fingers through my tousled curls and rub my throbbing temples, squinting to avoid the harsh light of the sun. "Thank God that's over. Mr. Morgan put me through pure torture in English this afternoon. I thought it would never end. What did we do last night?"

My memories of the previous night's events are hazy. I vaguely remember dancing on tables and obviously, there was tequila.

"Oh, you know. The usual. Dancing, tequila shots, and of course, we didn't have to pay for a single one." Katerina grins devilishly at me before returning her concentration to her fingernails, which she is meticulously filing. "That guy was so hot."

"Oh, that's right! You mean, the guy with the tatts?" I roll my eyes, flashing her a playful grin. "The one you ignored me for all night long."

Images of Katerina flash through my mind, of her mini skirt riding up a little too high as she downed a shot of red liquid, (I have no idea what) and threw herself all over some guy. If my memory serves me correctly, and let's face it, the chances of that were slim, the guy was, in fact, hot. Not that I was looking. I have a boyfriend, but Kat is a flirt. I couldn't count the number of times we'd gone to a club or bar together and left separately because she'd found some 'hot guy.' She drove me crazy sometimes, but she was my best friend.

"Guilty. Hey, have you got plans tonight?"

We sit on the concrete stairs that lead to the front office of Hampton Ridge College. School has been out for at least half an hour, but my mother is yet to pick me up and Katerina is hanging around for her younger brother to finish detention, something she has to do quite regularly. Normally, I'd have my own car here, but today Sean had offered to drive me.

"Oh! We could go to that club with the hot bouncer!" she suggests excitedly, her eyes lighting up at the prospects of seeing another 'hot guy.'

Usually, I'd jump at the chance to party all night with her but today I'm physically incapable.

"Well, I was supposed to go over to Sean's but he cancelled on me," I reply, still rubbing my aching temples. "He said he has to go through university applications with his dad."

She fishes a pastel, mint coloured nail polish from her Gucci tote bag and begins unscrewing the lid.

"On a Friday night?" she questions sceptically, flicking her long auburn waves over her shoulder, her perfectly sculpted brows knitting together. "Yeah, right. It's only the beginning of the semester. We have ages to do that."

It doesn't make sense to me either. Literally, nobody else is worrying about that right now, except for maybe the science freaks and geeks that sit behind the lab, not that I would know.

I retrieve my phone from my black Chanel handbag, the smell of new leather permeating my senses and sending another wave of nausea over me. There are no texts or missed calls from Sean. As odd as his excuse seems, I don't feel up to arguing with him tonight. I'm hungover and lacking in energy. Besides, if he doesn't want to spend time with me, it's his loss.

I open up Facebook and scroll downward. I have four hundred and sixty-two Facebook 'friends' and yet, there's never anything exciting in my news feed. A selfie of some girl I barely know, a video someone has posted of a cat, another selfie, a shared chain letter post - the kind that threatens you with death or seven years bad luck if you don't immediately share it with fourteen of your closest friends, another selfie.

Boring.

But then I see something that captures my attention. Lori Hutchison, a tenth grader, has taken her own selfie, blowing a kiss from her plump, rose-pink pout. She's wearing some trashy, white, lace two-piece outfit that makes her look way more mature than her sixteen years. She looked like a baby this morning when I'd seen her walking the hall of the English block, but here she looks at least twenty. What bothers me most about the picture is the caption underneath it. "Getting ready to partaay! - with **Sean Lundgren, Logan Hepworth** and **Jenn Simmons**."

"Oh my god," I mutter under my breath, too exhausted to give it the dramatic reaction it deserves.

"What's up?" Katerina replaces the lid of her nail polish and fans her wet glossy fingernails as she glances over my shoulder.

She squints as she reads the caption, then slowly, her eyes widen in disbelief. "Ugh! Why has Skankerella tagged your boyfriend and his best friend in her post?"

"Who knows?"

I'm too hungover to give a shit. If Sean is really planning on partying with tenth graders tonight when he'd told me he was working on his uni applications, he'd better be prepared for my wrath tomorrow.

I stare at Lori's thin frame and her crystal blue eyes, lined precisely with winged eyeliner. Why would Sean choose to spend time with Lori over me? What does she have that I don't have, besides a serious Instagram following and a new skincare line her daddy bought her for her sweet sixteenth? I shove the phone back into my bag, a little too aggressively, and then go back to cradling my head. Could today get any worse?

In my peripheral vision I sense Katerina's eyes on me. After a long moment, she finally speaks, carefully and cautiously. "Are you worried that he's, you know, cheating on you?"

Way to go stating the obvious, Katerina.

I know that in her own way she's only trying to be supportive, and yes, there is every chance that Sean is cheating on me. In fact, it seems pretty apparent right now. Maybe Lori is just looking for attention, but she wouldn't have tagged Sean in the post if there were zero truth to it. Sean lied to me. He'd given me a lame ass excuse and ditched me for someone else. Somebody who was two years younger. So, yeah, it's not looking good for him.

"I can't think about it right now," I say, hoping it will shut her down. It doesn't.

"Speaking of cheating…" she says, guardedly. *No. She isn't going to go there. She couldn't possibly do this to me right now.* "How's it going with your mother?"

I grit my teeth. Katerina is my best friend. She's always there when I'm down, usually with tequila or vodka in her outstretched arms. She's the only person whose advice I'll take concerning hair, makeup, and fashion. When it comes to scamming money from her parents or flirting her way into a bar, she is a wealth of knowledge, but she has never known how to choose her moments and subtlety has never been her forte.

"Fine, I guess." I answer through clenched teeth, hoping she'll take my short, blunt answer as a hint to end the conversation.

It's no secret that my mother had cheated on my father in the past. The whole school knew about the time she'd been busted in the elevator of the Fullerton Hotel with her massage therapist. Of all people to have discovered their hot and steamy encounter, it had to have been none other than Sean's mother and town gossip, Carol Lundgren. The news hit the entire community of Hampton Ridge within a day.

I never understood why it was so newsworthy. This was Hampton Ridge for god's sake. Another desperate housewife cheating on her rich, pre-occupied husband was hardly remarkable.

I was only glad that I'd been the one to find her in the Salt Factory restrooms this time. Three years had passed since her last known previous infidelity, meaning the dust had finally settled. The last thing our family needed was to open old wounds.

Maybe Katerina has taken a clue after all because she changes the subject and her tone. "You wanna come over mine and hang out?" she offers.

I cringe as I inhale a waft of her nail polish, the toxic fumes burning through my nostrils to my aching head.

"No, I actually still have a headache. I just want to get home. Thanks though."

I'm not lying. My head is killing me, but maybe Lori Hutchison's selfie bothers me more than I'm letting on.

"You're mad at me. I'm sorry for asking about your mum." Her expression is one of remorse.

"I'm not mad. It's okay," I reply, although it's a lie. Katerina is the person I'm closest to in this world and yet I always fear confrontation with her. When it comes down to serious issues, I can never just come out and say what I truly feel. "I mean, it's not something that I like to talk about, but I'm not mad. I really do have a crazy bad headache."

"Okay, well I might hit up my mum's liquor stash tonight if your headache miraculously disappears and you change your mind. There'll be tequila?" She taunts me playfully in a sing-song voice.

She's trying to tempt me with my favourite poison, but her efforts are wasted. The image of Lori Hutchison's slutty two piece is now burned into my memory, threatening to transform my headache into a migraine. Still, I appreciate what she's trying to do.

"You are the devil," I say flippantly, slapping her on the knee. I stand, smoothing out my plaid school skirt and hang my bag over my shoulder.

"I thought you said your mum was picking you up today," Katerina says.

"I guess not," I reply.

She gives a sympathetic frown. Mum was supposed to pick me up. She was supposed to do a lot of things. I've been slowly getting used to not relying on her for anything for a while now.

"I'll see you later."

"Not if I see you first," she jokes, making devil horns on her head with both of her index fingers. Despite the fact that my head burns like it's on fire, and I'm still annoyed by Katerina's questions, I manage a weak laugh at her attempt to cheer me up.

I turn and begin the arduous journey up the incline to the highest house on the cliff, leaving Katerina there on the steps blowing the mint green polish on her fingertips.

Chapter 12

LIV

I stare at the crisp white ceiling from the comfort of my bed. I figure it has to be past seven, by the way the sun glows from behind the shutters, its golden light creeping into my room through the slats.

I'd barely slept last night, and yet I'm energised in a way that I've never been before, thanks to the image of EJ wrapped in nothing but a fluffy, white towel that's now etched in my memory. I'm suddenly hit with a pang of guilt for wishing I'll never forget it.

Normally, after a sleepless night, I would be moody, irritable, and reluctant to get out of bed. Today is different. All I can think about is getting out into the sunshine and soaking up its warmth.

I'm suddenly aware of all the things I've been missing while isolating myself from the world. The sun, the air. The people. I somehow feel more alive, or at least like I'm ready to feel alive again.

Of course, there are still many aspects of my life that I want to keep private, but it's as though I'm seeing the glass as half full instead of half empty, that with everything life has thrown at me, there is still so much that I should be thankful for.

My phone chimes from my bedside table. I grab it, disconnecting the charging cable and will my blurry eyes to focus on the screen. It's a text from Kristen.

Hey girl! You feeling better today?

For a second I have no idea what she's talking about, then I remember the illness I faked yesterday afternoon to get out of going to the party. I type a reply and hit send. I keep it brief, deciding not to mention anything about the events of last night. If and when I tell her, it's a conversation that we need to have in person.

Yeah, thanks. I'm all good now. ☺

I place the phone down on the bedside table and then sink back into my cushy pillowtop mattress. I really do want to get out into the sunshine, but a few more minutes in my cosy bed won't hurt.

My phone sounds again to my right. Letting out a sigh, I roll over and reach for it. Kristen probably wants to tell me all the juicy details about the party. When I see the notification, it's another text, but it's not from Kristen. It's from an unknown number, but I intuitively know whose.

Good morning, friend.

Obviously, it's EJ. To my own surprise, a wide grin spreads across my face and I realise my reaction to him is completely out of my control. I'm in trouble.

I type back a quick reply, not really knowing what to say. I settle on a simple, *Good morning* ☺.

A few seconds later another message comes through.

EJ: *You get that shower head sorted?*

I smile, thinking again of our narrow escape last night.

102

Me: *It has somehow miraculously repaired itself.*

There's a knock on my bedroom door. "Come in," I call out.

The door cracks open and Dad sticks his head in. A jolt of panic creeps in. I hope he hasn't come to check out my not-so-broken shower head.

"Morning," he says.

"Morning," I reply.

My phone dings again.

EJ: *Guess you won't be needing that plumber.* 😊 *It was good seeing you last night.*

I feel the heat rise in my cheeks. God, I'm blushing. As much as I try to deny any connection between us, there's definitely something there.

"It's nice to see you smiling." My dad's voice brings me back from my thoughts. "Is that from one of your new friends?"

"Yeah," I answer.

Something like that.

No. Definitely like that.

Just friends.

"That's great. I just came by to let you know I have to go into the city this morning to pick up a new suit. I should be home around lunchtime though."

"Okay," I reply. I'm hearing what he's saying, but my mind is elsewhere.

Dad backs away from the door, closing it behind him as he leaves. Another text lights up my screen. This time it's Kristen.

Kristen: *What you up to today? I'm gonna go hang out at Little Bay Beach… could use some company if you're up for it?*

My first instinct is to decline Kristen's invitation. It's what I do. I've become accustomed to being an outsider, a loner.

But for once in my life, since things had drastically changed more than two years ago, I find myself wanting more. Since getting the job at the Haven, I've developed a sense of what it might be like to have real friendships, and I want in on that. Despite the fact that getting close to anyone terrifies me, I long for the chance to feel a part of a bigger connection.

I type back a quick reply and launch myself out of bed.

Me: *Sounds great. I can be there in an hour.*

I dance over to the French doors that open out onto the balcony, pushing them open in one swift movement, feeling the warmth as the sun's rays infiltrate the space. I step outside, inhaling the balmy air. The ocean seems bluer today. I glance down to the left, where the ridge opens up below and the tiny town of Cliff Haven lie, nestled among the coast line. I can make out several small coves, one of which is Little Bay Beach. I'm struck with a sense of contentment gazing at that tiny town in the distance and the prospect of opportunity it fills me with.

I shower, slip one of my favourite sundresses over a plain black bikini, and grab my sunglasses and a towel.

When I arrive at Little Bay Beach, Kristen is already on the sand, sitting upright on her towel, smearing sunscreen over her fair skin. Her chestnut locks are piled in a messy bun on top of her head.

"Hey!" she calls out when she sees me and pats the sand next to her, motioning for me to join her.

I lay out my towel beside her and she offers me some sunscreen, which I accept. I'd completely forgotten about that in my haste to get down to the beach.

I haven't been to Little Bay before. I've never even really been a 'beach' person despite growing up on the coastline, but it is actually a beautiful hidden gem. I guess up until now, I've always considered myself a city person, with the exception of yacht trips and luxury cruises. Little Bay Beach is a tiny cove in comparison to the others, with white sands and calm, crystal clear waters.

"How was last night?" Kristen asks.

"Last night?" Stunned, my face falls in complete shock. Does she know something about what happened last night? "What do you mean?"

"You said you felt sick," she replies slowly. A small smile tugs at the corners of her mouth, but disappears just as quickly. "Did you manage to get some rest?"

"Oh!" I answer. "Yeah. It was just a migraine. Painkillers took care of it. How was the party?"

"Oh god. It was crazy! So many people showed up." She flicks her sunglasses on top of her head. "I guess it was a good thing you skipped it because it was so loud. I'm surprised nobody called the cops. It was fun though. Except for when this guy we knew showed up being a total dick and ended up getting pushed in the river."

"Wow. Really? Sounds wild." I respond, thankful for the definite subject change.

"Yeah. Karma's a bitch," she laughs and then adds, "Henley's place is so amazing though. He basically has the river in his backyard and there's this little jetty. Not that he has a boat or anything, but his cousin said he could borrow his dinghy while he's working up north." Her expression then shifts from cheerful to revulsion and her eyes roll to the back of her head. "Oh my god. Pack of douchebags at two o'clock."

105

I follow Kristen's line of sight out past the shoreline. A bunch of muscular guys hang off the back of a yacht, laughing and carrying on.

I squint, focusing to get a better look. I know this boat well, having been a passenger on it in the past. It belongs to Sean's father. I panic for a second, then realise there's no way he'll be able to recognise me here on the sand if he's onboard. I can only just make out the boat, but it's definitely Bryce Lundgren's. The bright red slide that adorns the side of it is a dead giveaway. And I'd bet all my money that Sean is one of those douchebags.

"Sorry," Kristen apologises with a slight shake of her head. "I just know their type. Rich, preppy assholes with nothing better to do than spend daddy's money. I know, I shouldn't judge, but I've kinda been there."

"Really? You were a rich, preppy asshole?" I joke.

Conversation with Kristen always comes easy to me, but still I tense at her comment. Clearly, if we'd met a couple of years ago we would not have been friends.

"Well, not exactly," she laughs. "I used to go to this posh private school. Not around here. It was like four hours' drive away. My parents were well off. Until they weren't."

"Oh. What happened?" I get the impression that Kristen's idea of "well off" is vastly different to mine.

"My dad left my mum for his receptionist and refused to pay child support. The kids at school were relentless when they found out. We couldn't afford the tuition fees so Mum packed us both up and moved us out here."

"Shit. I'm sorry," I say.

I'm interested to hear about Kristen's past. Maybe we have a few more things in common than I'd originally thought.

"Don't be. It all worked out okay in the end. I love it here. And my dad got what was coming to him," she says, with a wicked grin and a cocked eyebrow. "He went bankrupt."

"Seriously?" I ask. "Wow. Karma really is a bitch."

"Yep," she agrees, with a chuckle. "Anyway, enough about him. Next Friday is gonna be so fun. We're thinking drinks at Steve's first to watch the band and then another party at Henley's after. Not as big as last night, but still awesome. You have to come."

"Uh, okay. I guess." I say, hesitantly.

I can't help that the first thought that enters my mind is that EJ will probably be there.

"Oh, and you're totally welcome to come stay at mine after so you can have a few drinks if you want to ..." she begins.

"That's okay," I stop her. "I actually don't drink. But thanks for the offer."

"Ever?" she asks.

"Never," I answer bluntly.

"Can I ask why? Do you have, like, a medical condition or something?"

"Nah, nothing like that," I mumble. "Just trying not to repeat my mother's mistakes." This is the best way I can think to answer her without giving too much away.

"She can't handle her booze, I'm guessing," Kristen says, sympathetically. "You could say that." I shake off the memories that threaten to surface, my eyes trained on the ocean in front.

"Are they still together? Your parents?"

"No," I say. This is a total understatement.

"Divorce is tough. I know first-hand and now I'm watching Henley go through it with his own parents. They're trying to work on it but it's hard." She squints in the sunlight, then flips her sunglasses back down to rest on her nose.

Kristen has a talkative nature and an endearing way of going off on a tangent. It makes it easier for me to keep things to myself when she's busy making her own assumptions. I choose to ignore her commentary on divorce because I don't want to divulge the real reason my family has become divided. I will tell her. Just not today.

"I'm sorry to hear that. Is that why he moved out?"

"No, not really. He's been wanting his own place for a while now. He just turned twenty-four so it was the right time for him. Anyway, you're still welcome to stay over so you don't have to drive home late," she offers. "Where exactly do you live anyway?"

I pause. I don't want to lie to Kristen. I can see that she is a genuinely good person. Besides, if I don't tell her she'll find out from EJ or Carla eventually, but after what she'd just told me about her family, I dread her reaction. I take a deep breath and let the words tumble out of me.

"I live in Hampton Ridge."

"Okay. Wow." A look of regret passes across her face, then she brings her hands to her mouth dramatically. "Oh god, Liv. I'm so sorry about what I said before. I basically bagged out all of high society and your family is probably loaded to be living there and that explains the car you drive and that expensive bag you carry around…"

"Kristen, it's okay." I place an arm around her shoulder. "You didn't say anything that wasn't true. And the bag was a gift."

She sighs with her head in her hands. "I'm not usually this judgmental, I promise."

"It's really okay. Also," I pause, and then at the risk of sounding like a spoilt brat, I add, "I hate that car."

"What?" she shouts, incredulously, but with laughter in her voice. "What do you mean you hate it?"

"It's the bane of my existence," I joke. "No, but seriously, I don't hate it. I just hate all that it stands for, you know. Maybe I'll sell it one day."

"So, you can buy a small island with your profits?" Kristen snorts.

"Oh! Come on!" I swat at her thigh with my hand and give her a playful shove. "You know it's not worth that much. Maybe I could just get one of those yachts." I gesture to Sean's father's boat, which has now moved further out to sea.

My comment sends Kristen into a fit of laughter and I find myself giggling along with her. I've never had someone I could make fun of my wealth with before, and I'm grateful to have someone not take me so seriously for a change. It's nice not taking myself so seriously either. After a moment, Kristen settles down and readjusts herself on her towel.

"No offence," she says cautiously, "but why do you work at a café in Cliff Haven?"

"I guess, I just want something different. You're right about high society. It's fucked up. I don't want to be like the rest of them." I've managed to answer her question truthfully, but without oversharing.

"I really respect that." She looks at me wistfully. After a moment she jumps to her feet, then nods toward the ocean. "Come on. Let's make some waves out there."

Kristen reaches downward for my hand and pulls me up. Her kindness and thoughtful words have sealed our friendship and as we walk into the sea, any trace of awkwardness has evaporated. We immerse ourselves in the salt water, waist-height, letting the lazy waves flow and ebb over us.

A few moments pass before Kristen's attention is drawn back to the shore.

"I think that's EJ and Henley," she says, shielding her face from the sun with her forearm. She must notice the mild panic that sweeps over me because she grins and then asks, "He called you last night, didn't he?"

"Uh, yeah," I reply, timidly. "You gave him my number!"

"I hope you're not mad at me for that. It's just, he seemed interested in you and, I don't know, I thought you seemed like you could do with having a person like him in your life," she says with a shrug. "Now that I know you a little better, I'd say I'm right."

I want to ask her what she means by that. A person like him? Why? What is it about me that makes her think I'm the kind of person who needs anyone in my life?

But I'm so stunned by her comment, I say nothing.

Kristen waves and calls out to Henley and EJ. When she has their attention, they reciprocate with a wave.

"Just promise me something," she says, turning back to me.

"Sure. What is it?" I ask.

Her eyes wander back to the shoreline. To EJ.

"Don't hurt him. God knows he's had enough heartache already."

She gives me a small smile and I wait for her to elaborate, but she doesn't. And it doesn't feel right to ask.

It had been obvious to me from the moment I'd seen Kristen and EJ together that they have a close relationship and that she's very defensive of him. It doesn't feel right to

110

intrude on that, so I stay silent and watch as EJ and Henley make their way toward the water. Toward us.

Chapter 18

OLIVIA

"Olivia, come sit with me." Mum beckons me from the grand piano, patting the space beside her on the cushioned bench.

I've just spent an hour with Katerina, discussing celebration plans for her birthday at the end of the month. She's tossing up between a lavish party at home with ice sculptures and topless waiters with one of her favourite bands playing live, or chartering a luxury yacht to a private beach. Knowing Katerina, she'll probably end up doing both.

The last thing I expected was for my mother to be home when I returned, let alone to find her fully sober. It appears she's having one of her rare, good days. As far as I can see, her scotch glass is nowhere in sight. I contemplate punishing her, rejecting her offer out of spite, but she's still my mother. Despite our differences and the many ways she's disappointed me, I haven't given up on her yet.

"What's up, Mum?" I drop my bag to the floor and take the place next to her on the bench.

"Play with me." Her fingers dance gently over the ivory keys.

Chopin. Nocturnes. It has always been her favourite piece.

"I'm not really in the mood today," I state. Truthfully, I'm never really in the mood to play at all these days.

"Please tell me you haven't given up on applying to MCM," she pleads.

MCM. Milton Conservatorium of Music. Mum has dreamt of my acceptance there since birth, I'm sure.

"I don't know. I don't know what I'm doing." These are probably the most honest words I've ever uttered.

"I get it." Mum stops playing and turns to me. I can't quite read her expression, but there's an inner turmoil captured within it. Sadness, maybe? Regret? "I know I haven't made things easy for you lately either. But I'm trying, Olivia. I'm really trying."

I let out a sigh. I'm tired of all of it. Of her behaviour, her lies, her broken promises. And I'm tired of myself. Of feeling as though I'm being pulled in every direction. Of feeling like I have to be multiple different people to please everyone in my life.

"I just don't want to see you give up on your dreams. I want to see you succeed," she continues, her fingers once again trailing the keys.

"You mean like how you gave up on yours?" I retaliate.

It's a low blow. I know it as soon as the words leave my mouth. Her fingers stop dead, her hands falling into her lap.

"Olivia, that's not fair." Her glassy eyes threaten to spill tears.

She's right. It isn't fair. My mother had abandoned any chance of having a career to raise me. She'd been in her second year of medical school when she'd met my father and become pregnant. Sure, a lot of other women in her position may have been able to continue pursuing their dreams, but she hadn't had the support network. She hadn't come from money like my father and throughout her life she'd constantly had to defend herself to my father's parents, who labelled her a gold digger right from the very beginning. Secretly, I always wondered if she resented me for how her life had turned out.

"I know. I didn't mean that." It isn't much of an apology but it's all I can offer right now.

"There's so much you don't understand," she whispers as a tear escapes down her cheek.

I'd beg her to tell me everything, to make me understand, but my patience is wearing thin and I'm losing my will to listen. Maybe I've given up on her after all.

"I wanted to tell you that I'll be going away for a little while." Mum wipes the tears from her face and rises from the bench.

"What do you mean?" I ask, stunned. "For how long?"

She clears her throat. "A few days. Maybe a week."

She smoothes out her dress with her palms, collects herself and strides out of the room before I can ask any more questions.

Where the hell could she possibly be going for a week? Was she planning another bender? A vacation with one of her boy toys?

Whatever. Maybe it's better if I don't know.

Chapter 14

LIV

EJ visited the café three times this week. Each time I'd fought hard against his attempts to flirt with me, although I have to admit it's getting ridiculously difficult.

The impression instilled in my mind of him enveloped in that fluffy white towel has now been replaced with a new mental image of his chiselled pecs at the beach last weekend. That chance meeting had been awkward enough, without me gaping at him stupidly as he stood there shirtless, the waves lapping at our ankles, his boardies riding just low enough to take my mind back to the night before, when said towel had clung low on his tanned, toned abdomen.

Neither of us had dared to mention the shower debacle, though it was obvious from Kristen's body language that she sensed something between us.

It's now Friday. The Haven café will be closing in the next few minutes and Kristen and I will be heading to Steve's Tavern. Sammi had declined to join us last minute. She still isn't feeling her best self after recovering from tonsilitis.

As Kristen had summarised last weekend on the beach, the plan was for the band to play their set, then we would all head over to Henley's to hang out.

Things have proven to be pretty hectic this week. I've worked every day except Tuesday, though as promised, Carla has given me this weekend off.

Being a working-class citizen is completely foreign to me. I go home each night feeling exhausted, but the reward of feeling like an actual person again is well worth it. I've had the chance to befriend some regulars, including an elderly woman named Mabel, who has a penchant for peppermint tea and macarons.

There's no doubt that changes are occurring within me. I've substituted cynicism for anticipation, bitterness for contentment. There are still large parts of me that I'll forever keep closed off, but I welcome this happier version of me regardless. It's good to long for something again, whether it be friendships or gatherings or visits to the beach.

I finish wiping up the remnants of lettuce and ketchup from the table by the window, then re-enter the kitchen where Kristen is disposing of today's uneaten salads.

"You all done?" she asks me.

"Yeah, just finished." I reply, throwing the cloths into the sink.

"Okay, cool. I'll just finish washing up these salad containers and we can get out of here."

She seems tired tonight. I grab a dish towel from the shelf above.

"I'll dry," I smile. "It'll be quicker."

"Thanks," she sighs and then confirming my assumptions, she adds, " I can't wait to get out of here."

"Rough week?" I ask.

"That's for sure. I had this really important exam yesterday. I studied all week for it, but I think I may have only just scraped by. Seriously, all I wanna do right now is get a little drunk."

"I'm sure you did better than you think. It must be hard to balance work with study."

It's just an observation and obviously not something I have any experience with unless you include balancing studying with partying. Even then, considering I'd barely made it through high school, I'd hardly have called that balance.

"It can be. But I don't have much choice. I need the money. And I don't normally get super drunk on the weekends or anything, but sometimes I just need to let off some steam, you know?" She closes her eyes and grits her teeth after the words leave her mouth. "Oh my god. Of course, you don't! You don't drink. I'm so sorry, Liv. I didn't mean anything by it."

"It's okay!" I laugh. "I get it."

If only she knew she was preaching to the choir. I'd once been the queen of drinking to avoid my problems. I had it down to an art, but that's information I'm definitely not disclosing right now.

I place the clean salad containers in the cupboard below the counter while Kristen wipes down the sink, then we lock the door behind us and cross the road to the tavern.

There are more customers at Steve's than I've seen previously. Most of the tables are occupied, and the line to get a drink is miles long.

"Wow," I say, scanning the overcrowded bar. "It's crazy in here."

"Yeah," Kristen replies, raising her voice above the noise. "Most of these people have probably been invited to Henley's. He knows a lot of people."

"Wow," I say again. "I thought you said the party wouldn't be as big as last week."

"Yeah," she answers casually. "It won't be."

Is she kidding? How many people must have shown up to Henley's place last week for this to be considered smaller? I haven't been to a party that crowded, or a bar for that matter, in a long time. My social anxiety heightens. I've spent so long confined in my own bubble that the idea of being around so many people gives me claustrophobia.

I don't have time to dwell on it for long. EJ is standing on a chair in the corner near the stage, his arms outstretched above his head, waving us over. He's obviously been here for a while and been able to hold a table for us all. That, or he just reserves tables whenever he likes because his dad owns the bar. Probably the latter.

For him to be able to see us through this crowd, he must have been awaiting our arrival. That realisation also makes me nervous. I inhale deeply and will my rising heartrate to slow.

Be cool, Liv.

"Hi," he says, giving Kristen a quick hug before embracing me in his open arms.

The scent of his leather jacket sends me dizzy, in a good way though. He must have had it cleaned because it looks brand new. Is it me, or does he hold onto me for a little longer than necessary?

Kristen takes a seat next to Henley and wraps her arms around his neck, kissing him in a full-on public display of affection. There are no other vacant seats, so I hover awkwardly.

"You can take my seat. We're going up now." EJ gestures to the stage, then leans into me, his lips gently skimming my ear, his breath warm in my hair. He speaks just loud enough for me to hear. "Don't worry. I won't sing any songs about you tonight."

With a cheeky wink, he heads up onto the stage with the others. After he slings his guitar around his neck, he turns to look at me, his crooked grin lifting the right side of his mouth.

"I'm going to go find the biggest cocktail they make in this place," Kristen states. "I'll be back. Do you want anything?"

I laugh, glancing at the massive line up at the bar. "Good luck with that. Maybe just water for now."

"No worries." She struts off in the direction of the bar and I turn my attention back to the stage.

I can deny it to EJ, but I can no longer deny it to myself. I'm attracted to him. I'm hooked on the way his lip curls in concentration as he adjusts the tuning pegs of his guitar, the way his eyes twinkle when he glances over at me and catches my stare. I suddenly find myself wondering how long his list of ex-girlfriends might be, then feel jealous of them, even though at this point, they're just in my mind.

Get a grip, Liv. We're just friends.

And that's all I have time for.

It's all I can risk at this point.

Kristen returns promptly with a gigantic fishbowl cocktail glass filled with blue liquid adorned with fruit pieces, its rim dusted with a coating of sugar and coconut. "Mission accomplished," she says happily, cupping her hands around the drink as though it's her prized possession.

"How the hell did you manage to get that so fast?" I ask. "And what the hell is it?"

119

"Well, to answer you first question, I'm pretty. And it's a blue colada Hawaiian thingy… or something. I don't care. It looks good."

"Well, firstly, good for you," I respond. "And secondly, fair enough."

We both laugh and then our attention shifts back to the stage as the band begins to play. Between listening to their set, Kristen manages to down another cocktail, although the second one she retrieves from the bar is not quite as large. EJ is true to his word and doesn't perform any songs about me. By the time they've reached their last song of the night, Kristen's body is swaying lethargically to the music in an out of time fashion. It's refreshing to see her so happy and carefree. I'm not used to alcohol having that kind of influence on people.

At the end of the band's set, Kristen and I go outside to wait for the guys to pack up their equipment. We stroll across the road, Kristen slightly wobbly on her feet, to where the Haven is situated. I stop at the window of the building next door and peer through the glass. It's dark, but it looks empty, apart from a few paint cans on the floor at the back, and some timber leaning up against the side wall.

"What do you think they have planned for this building?" I ask Kristen.

"Which building?" She's struggling to focus her eyes on where I'm pointing. "Oh, in there! I don't know. That place has been vacant for ages. Oh, look at that cute dress! Liv, that would look so cute on you. We're so going shopping there next week…" Kristen trails off, her eyes fixated on a dress on a mannequin in the window of a boutique store up ahead.

"If you say so," I say, laughing.

Kristen misjudges her next step, tumbling over the gutter.

"Whoa!" she cries, as my outstretched arms strain to save her from the pavement. They manage to stop the full blow, but still they fail, and we're both sent crashing to the ground, luckily not too forcefully.

I cry out in surprise as my hands hit the concrete, preventing me from obtaining any actual injuries.

"Those cocktails may have been stronger than I thought," Kristen slurs, declaring the obvious.

"You think?" I say sarcastically.

"Shut up!" Kristen swats at my shoulder playfully and misses, swaying in the process.

She giggles, and then I laugh loudly when a random thought enters my head. What would Sean and Katerina think if they saw me now? Rolling around, laughing in the gutter with my new friend. Oh, the horror! And the best part of all of it? I'm not even inebriated.

But I'm having fun. And my new friend is awesome. She's not a violent drunk. She doesn't want me to be something I'm not. She isn't like them. She's simply a real person that has decided to harmlessly let off some steam.

For a second, I wish that I was drinking too, so I could feel what Kristen is feeling. But I know that drunk Liv would be less like drunk Kristen and more like my drunken mother.

Whatever. I don't need alcohol. I'm content. At least, I'm learning to be. Even if I do feel more like a fraud with every passing day.

"Hey party animals!" EJ calls to us from across the street. "You guys coming or what?"

We amble to our feet and hurry over to Henley and EJ. Henley's house is only a ten-minute walk from the tavern. The guys walk a little further ahead of us with the other band members, and I spend most of the walk supporting Kristen as she struggles not to stumble in the most outrageously high platform boots that she normally moves in with ease. I'm thankful that I opted to wear my converse high tops.

When we arrive at the house, the walk has sobered Kristen up a little. We enter through a gate in the low picket fence that leads straight out into the backyard. Kristen's description had been accurate. Henley's place has a certain charm to it, with a long stretch of grass leading down to the tree-lined banks of the river and a private jetty, visible from a distance, thanks to multiple strings of fairy lights.

There are people scattered out on the lawn in groups. If I had to guess, I'd say there were probably about eighty people already here. Henley guides us up a set of rickety old steps to the back porch where a few others have gathered.

"There's beer in this fridge. Feel free to help yourself." Henley points to a small retro fridge just inside the back door. "EJ, come help me with the rest of the drinks. They're out in the garage."

"Yeah. Sure." EJ steals a glance back at me, before following Henley through the house.

"I need to go to the bathroom," Kristen says. "I'll be back in a minute."

Before I can beg her not to leave me alone, she's gone. I hang around at the top of the stairs, too hesitant to lean on the old railing in case it can't hold my weight. I move over to the far wall of the balcony and wait for Kristen to return.

Music begins to blare from a speaker in the back room of the house. More people arrive and the balcony becomes too overcrowded for my liking. I glimpse down at my watch. Ten minutes have passed and Kristen and Henley still haven't returned. I'm becoming anxious. I don't know how I thought this night would go, but this isn't it.

I bravely enter the house through the back screen door and find myself trapped between bodies in the packed living room. In that moment, EJ appears in front of me like my own personal saviour.

"Hey. Where's Kristen?" he asks.

The clarity in his eyes stuns me. In a good way. Always in a good way.

"She went to the bathroom. Over ten minutes ago." I'm aware my impatience is evident and increasing by the second, but I'm relieved to see him.

"Uh huh. I'm betting she found Henley and got distracted." He holds up his fingers to form quotation marks as he says the word 'distracted.' "You want a drink? I can go grab you a lemonade?"

"Thanks," I say, gratefully. "That would be nice."

He shuffles his way through the congested living space, leaving me alone again in a sea full of strange faces. I curse under my breath. I should have declined his offer so he didn't leave me.

Overwhelmed, I take a few steps back until I reach the balcony again. The last party I'd attended had been Katerina's, but this is vastly different to the kind of parties I'm accustomed too. For starters, it isn't filled with rich, fake people concerned with everybody else's business.

If it were, I'd be the girl at the centre of attention, lapping up compliments from everyone at the party and congratulating myself on choosing the right shade of lip gloss. But that version of me was a far cry from the one that stands here now, and I'm glad for that.

"Hey." I'm startled when a raspy voice echoes in my ear. "I'm Cayden."

I spin around, meeting the eyes of the bass player from EJ's band. He's stumbling all over the place, a can of Jack Daniels lodged in his left hand. His eyes are all over me in the same way they were the night I gave him EJ's jacket in the bar. He's obviously too drunk to remember that we've spoken before. There's something about him that makes my insides heavy like lead.

"Hi," I say nervously, wishing he would go away. I turn my back to him hoping he'll get the hint. He doesn't.

"You wanna take a walk with me?" he asks, moving around until he's in front of me again.

"No, thanks." *I just want you to go away.*

"Aww. Why not?" He slaps a hand against his chest in mock heartache.

My intuition screams at me to get away from him, as far as humanly possible. I take the stairs down to the back lawn two at a time, but he stumbles close behind.

"Come on," he persists, reaching for my elbow to spin me back around.

His mouth twists in a sleazy smirk. He brushes away the long dark strands of hair that fall across his face, revealing something I hadn't noticed until now. A deep scar forms a jagged line from the top of his left eye down to the base of his jaw. I've never seen him before in my life, but there's something familiar about his voice.

"No," I say firmly, crossing my arms in a defensive stance.

"Hey," he says again, softer this time. A look of recognition passes over his features. "Do I know you from somewhere?"

"I doubt it," I reply.

"You look familiar. I've seen you before." He stares at me, his hand reaching out to sweep the loose strands of hair out of my face.

I shudder at his touch, at the scent of alcohol and cigarettes on his breath. He's obviously so intoxicated that he's mistaken me for someone else.

"I was at Steve's last week. I gave you EJ's jacket." That would be where he remembers me from.

Through the crowd of people gathering in front of us, I catch sight of EJ making his way toward me, a can of lemonade in his left hand. He smiles at me and then, just as quickly, his face fills with concern. I can only imagine the story my expression tells. He forces his way through the throng of people until he reaches me, then swiftly grasps Cayden by the shoulders and throws him backwards.

"Get your hands off her!" EJ yells, his eyes flickering like blue green flames.

"Dude! I know her!" Cayden shouts.

EJ looks from me to Cayden, confusion flooding his features. "Is that true? Do you know him?"

I shake my head, too bewildered to speak. I want him to know how grateful I am for him being here, but the words don't come.

"You're drunk, dude. Go sleep it off," EJ mutters to Cayden, picking up the can that fell from his hand in his haste to protect me.

Cayden backs off, holding his arms up in surrender, defeat in his eyes. "Whatever man. She ain't worth it, anyway."

"What did you just say?" EJ lunges toward him, their faces now only inches apart.

The crowd has given us their attention now, forming a circle around the three of us. Countless pairs of curious eyes are trained on me, the new girl at the party, who's apparently followed by drama everywhere she goes, no matter how hard she tries to escape it. Social anxiety curls its way around my lungs.

This isn't me. I'm not this girl any more. I can't be her. And I can't breathe. I need air. I turn and push past them all, running until I reach the river. I follow the string of fairy lights along the timber beams and slump down at the end of the jetty, allowing my legs to hang off the edge.

From down here, the party's music is a muffled hum, giving way to the sounds of frogs and crickets chirping and the gentle lapping of the river below. If it weren't for the fact that I'd just caused a huge fight among two friends, I might have found it peaceful. I sense a presence behind me. I don't know how, but I know it's him.

"You alright?" EJ's voice is like music in the stillness of the night.

I inhale and run my fingers through my hair. "Yeah, I'm fine. I just needed some air."

He sits down beside me, so close that my right knee brushes his left, sending goosebumps over my skin.

"I'm sorry about Cayden. He can be a real dick when he's drunk."

"It's okay. I mean, he is a dick, but I'm fine," I say, not even trying to hide my dislike for him.

"No, it's not okay." EJ's jaw ticks in frustration. "He's a real asshole sometimes, but he's harmless. He would never have hurt you."

"Sorry, I know he's your friend and all." I don't know how deep his relationship with Cayden goes, and despite Cayden being a jerk tonight, the last thing I want to do is offend EJ.

He sighs as he lays back on the dock, folding his arms behind his head. "He's my friend, but he's a dick."

"Yes. We've established that he is a dick," I grin.

"Yeah." EJ smiles back, his white teeth glowing in the faint light. "Plus," he adds. "He knows I like you."

I turn to look over my shoulder and gaze down at him in curiosity. His honesty shouldn't surprise me anymore, yet it still does. The air is electric as his eyes meet mine. "Come on. It's not like I've tried to hide it."

He's right. He's made it obvious that he's interested in me since the very beginning, but I've spent too many hours convincing myself that there's nothing between us to cave in now. There's too much at stake for me to go jumping into a relationship, if that's what he even wants. For all I know, he has other plans in mind and entertaining this connection could make for nothing more than a passing fling.

"I don't understand why," I say.

"You're not like everyone else," he says, as though he's read my mind.

"How do you know that?" I'm not convinced that this isn't just a line he feeds every other girl before making his way into their pants.

"Because of the way you make me feel. Because you were right to be freaked out about me writing that song about you. Because no one else has ever inspired me that way before." His eyes are focused on the starry sky above, his expression pensive and then suddenly, his lips form a devilish smirk. "And because of the way you blushed so hard when you saw me in your bathroom."

Heat rises in my cheeks at the mention of that night and I'm relieved that the only light comes from the stars and the fairy lights surrounding us. "You noticed that, huh?"

127

"It was cute." He laughs and then his smile fades. "I'm not going to pretend that I know you, because I don't. I only know what I feel."

"That's fair." He doesn't know me and if I have my way, he never will. My past is complicated and my present is a complex work in progress.

"How come you're not on social media?" he questions me.

"How do you know I'm not?"

"Because I tried to stalk you," he admits casually, looking upwards to the sky.

"Creep," I mutter teasingly. "I can't believe you looked me up."

It's true. I don't have Facebook or Instagram, or any other social networking platform. Not anymore. Not since cutting ties with everyone I knew in Hampton Ridge. There was a time when I'd needed my whole life on display for the world, relished in the number of likes and shares, but now I simply want privacy.

"Sorry," he laughs. "I was curious. I mean, you live in Hampton Ridge. You drive an insanely impressive car and yet, you're completely grounded."

He has me wrong. I mean, yes, he got two out of three right. I live in Hampton Ridge and I have a nice car, but I'm clearly not who he thinks I am. I'm not worthy. I'm someone who has made too many mistakes. Unforgiveable mistakes. I've hurt people, mentally and physically.

I let my own mother die.

My eyes begin to well. A tear escapes, rolling down my cheek. I squeeze my eyes shut in an attempt to keep the rest of them inside.

"Hey," EJ says gently, as he sits upright beside me. "It's okay."

With his palm cupping my cheek, he wipes the stray tear gently with his thumb. His touch is warm, his hand strong and there's this pulling in my chest, a sense of longing. It's what I imagine home must feel like. But I don't deserve his comfort.

"I'm not her. This idea you've created in your mind of who I am, it's all wrong."

"Liv, it's okay," he whispers. As if sensing my need for space, he folds his hands in his lap.

"It's not. You don't understand." I sob. "I'm not a good person."

"I think you're wrong. That's not what people see when they look at you. It's not what I see." His eyes bore into mine and for a second I almost believe that he really can see me.

I break away from his stare and lay back, my head resting gently on the jetty. "Do you ever wish there was another version of you out there somewhere?"

"Another version?" he asks. "Like, a future version?"

"Yeah, maybe," I answer. "Or just an alternate version, walking the Earth somewhere. I sometimes think that maybe she's out there. This other version of me. She's me, but she's brave, and she's good. And she's doing everything she's supposed to be doing."

EJ lies back next to me. Moments pass and we don't say anything. Neither of us seem to feel that there's a need for words. We let the crickets and the frogs and the river and the faint hum of music in the distance fill the silence, and the brightness of the stars above fill the sky.

"So, this other version of you." EJ finally breaks the calm.

"Yeah?" I reply, turning my face to watch him. His eyes are still on the sky above.

"I bet she has a musician boyfriend that works in a bar." He pauses. "I mean, if she really is doing everything she's supposed to be doing."

I laugh. How does he always know the perfect thing to say?

"You're beautiful when you laugh," he says, glancing sideways at me. "I'm gonna make you see, Liv."

I swallow the lump that forms in my throat. "See what?" I dare to ask.

"You. And that there's something between us."

"There's not," I lie.

He shrugs, and then says matter-of-factly, "It's only a matter of time before you give into my irresistible charms."

"You're infuriating. You know that?" I'm only half kidding when I say this, as I spring upward into a sitting position. "How are you so sure of yourself all the time?"

"Is that how I seem?" he asks. Hurt fills his expression.

"I guess. Yeah."

He sits up beside me, staring straight ahead at the river, silver under the light of the moon. He takes a deep breath, as if preparing himself for what he's about to say next.

"I just think we should all say what we really mean. Life's too short no to. We're always wasting our words. We waste our moments. I don't want to waste mine."

When EJ's eyes meet mine this time, there's something missing. The light has left him, the same way it did when he'd played that sad song in the bar. I'm reminded that there's another side to EJ than this charming, fun, spontaneous one that I've been privileged enough to encounter. He is more than confidence and charming one-liners. Underneath his nonchalance, something brews below the surface.

Kristen's warning echoes in my head.

God knows he's had enough heartache in his life already.

How self-absorbed was I to assume that I'm the only one of us with problems? Could it be possible that EJ is just as lost as I am?

"Is there something you want to talk about?" I ask him.

He shakes his head, still observing the river. "Not tonight. I just wanna be here. With you."

I cover his hand with mine and we sit on the jetty for another hour, not saying anything else at all.

Chapter 15

OLIVIA

I return home from school and climb the staircase to my room. I feel like shit. Katerina and I went to the Salt Factory last night. Mum has been gone longer than anticipated and I'd decided to make the most of her absence. My head throbs now and the last thing I need is the incessant whirring of the vacuum cleaner the maid pushes around in the upstairs loungeroom.

"Argh! Shut that off!" I yell, clutching my head in my hands, probably a little too dramatically.

To my surprise, she actually listens and the noise ceases almost immediately. "Your mother called the house looking for you today," she says urgently.

"So what?" I spit.

I figured she would have. I've been ignoring her calls all day. My mother had said she'd be gone a few days. Then a week turned into two. Why would I want to speak with this woman that has abandoned me? She made a choice to leave. It's my choice to reject her calls.

"Olivia, I think that's a little harsh," the housekeeper says.

"What's it to you?" I hit back at her comment. "You're the maid. It's not your job to get involved in our business! You have no right to an opinion here."

She sighs. "Your dad didn't tell you where she is, did he?"

I roll my eyes. I'm still annoyed with her for sticking her nose in where it isn't wanted, yet I'm curious to know what she knows. It wouldn't surprise me if my father didn't even know where she really was. My mother had spun so many tall tales about her whereabouts in the past, she was probably lying somewhere tangled up in her own giant web of lies.

"Why don't you enlighten me?" I dare her.

"You need to ask him," she says. "It's not my place."

"Oh, now you've decided it's not your place?" I ask, my tone dripping with sarcasm.

She sighs again, but pays no mind to my attitude. The kindness and concern in her expression only fuels my frustration with her. Why does she have to be so annoyingly nice to me when I never reciprocate the same sentiments to her?

"I think you better sit down." She guides me over to the couch and gestures for me to sit opposite her.

"I'm fine right where I am." I fold my arms across my chest defiantly. I won't allow her to tell me what she thinks I should do.

Her eyes roll in response to my stubbornness, but then her face fills with something I'm not used to seeing. Sympathy. "Your mother is at Ryker's."

"Ryker's?" I ask, stunned. "You mean ... as in, Ryker's Institution?"

She nods. My brain works overtime, attempting to comprehend what she's telling me. Ryker's Institution is a rehabilitation clinic for mental illness and addiction. I know

133

that because it was where Jenn Simmons' older brother had spent several months after being diagnosed with depression after leaving high school.

"Yes," she answers simply.

"She's being treated for alcoholism then." It's more of a statement than a question.

"There may be more to it than that." She purses her lips into a thin line, clasping her hands together in her lap. "You really should be talking to your father about this."

"What do you mean? What more is there? She's an alcoholic," I say.

My mum drinks. She drinks way too much. If she just stopped, all of our problems would go away. The maid smiles sadly at me. I don't like it. I'm disgusted by her pity for me.

"They suspect your mum may have bipolar disorder. But I shouldn't be discussing this with you. You really need to talk to your dad."

"How do you even know this?" I ask, disbelievingly.

"I spoke with your mother today. She told me everything. She hasn't been able to call until now. Once admitted, they took her phone, and they don't allow contact with anyone outside."

I don't want to believe her. I want it to be a lie. But I'm not that far gone in my denial to realise that what she's saying makes total sense. My mother has always been friendly with the maid. She has no reason not to be honest with her about this. But what does all this mean? Questions and doubts infiltrate my mind, swarming like bees. I have the sudden urge to sit down after all. I collapse onto the couch, feeling instantly drained.

My mother had been admitted. For bipolar disorder. She'd been right when she'd said there was so much I didn't understand, but should this diagnosis of a mental illness excuse her from all of the shit she's done? Does it justify all of her wrong doings? All the times she's never been there for me as a mother? All the times she has lied?

"What happens now?" I ask the maid, unable to make eye contact.

"I'm not sure." She relocates to the position on the couch next to me. "I assume they will explore treatment options."

I nod, now incapable of hiding the fear that is no doubt displayed across my face. "Okay."

"Everything is going to be alright." She rests a hand on my shoulder, rubbing it gently. She's trying to comfort me, even after I've been such a bitch to her. "Now that your mother has been given a diagnosis, they can start the appropriate treatments. It's likely she has suffered with this for a long time."

Although I hold grave concerns for my mother after hearing the news of her condition, there is something else that plagues me. Something that I know in my heart will continue to haunt me, that I will question for the rest of my days. I turn to the woman beside me. Unintentionally, my voice comes out as a mere whisper.

"Tessa." I pause. "What if I'm just like her?"

Chapter 16

LIV

"What are you doing on Friday?"

EJ has crazy eyes when I meet him at the pier during my lunch break. He is all pent-up energy and enthusiasm. If I hadn't come to know him a little, I might have suspected he was high on something. But I'm slowly learning that there are many sides to EJ.

"Why?" I ask cautiously, as I perch on the park bench. "What's going on?"

He paces back and forth in front of me, running his fingers through his hair. "I have an announcement." He lets out a long breath.

I study his face for some kind of clue as to what he's about to say. "Sounds serious."

"I'm gonna do something crazy," he states.

That much I had guessed. "Like?"

"Guess."

"Shave your head?"

"Jesus Christ, no! What do you think I am? Certifiable?"

I laugh. "Okay, good. That would be a waste of great hair. Just tell me then."

"I'm going skydiving!" he declares, holding his arms out for effect.

"What? Well, I didn't see that coming." My eyebrows rise in awe and then the realisation of what he's telling me sinks in. "You are certifiable! That's insane!"

He throws his head back as he chuckles. "I know. I'm going on Friday. You have to come and watch me!"

"Oh, damn. I can't. I'm working Friday." To my own surprise, I'm genuinely disappointed that I can't be there for him. Carla has me rostered on for Friday and with it still being so early on in my employment, I'm not sure how she'll react if I ask her for time off. "Who else is going with you?"

"No one. You're the first person I've told."

"Will your parents go watch you?"

"No way! They aren't gonna know about it. My mum would kill me."

My thoughts drift back to the party and I remember how miserable EJ had been at the end of the night, when his light had dimmed. I don't know enough about EJ to determine his moods but my instincts practically scream at me that he should not be jumping out of a plane alone.

"Can you do it Saturday instead?" I offer.

"No. It has to be Friday," he answers, shaking his head defiantly.

"Really? They won't let you change days?" I ask again.

"They might. But I'm not going to. It has to be Friday." He's adamant. For some reason, Friday's date is important to him.

"Aren't you scared?" I ask him.

The idea of free falling out of a plane at fifteen thousand feet didn't appeal to me in the least. In fact, I could think of nothing worse.

"Yes!" he answers, as though the adrenaline is already coursing through his bloodstream. "I'm freaking terrified!"

"So why are you doing it? You're crazy!"

"I might very well be certifiable," he laughs. "But they say it's the things we fear most that are worth doing, right?"

"They do?" He's probably right about that, but I wouldn't know. I've been a coward my whole life. If only I was as brave as he was, I might have the guts to find out one day. "I have to get back to the café," I say, glancing at my watch and downing the last of my Sprite.

"Yeah, I have to pick up the afternoon shift at the bar. One of the guys called in sick. Come on, I'll walk with you."

"Okay." I smile, grateful for his company.

"Maybe you can elaborate on what you were saying before."

"Huh? What was I saying?" I ask, confused.

"About how I have great hair," he grins.

I give him a playful nudge with my elbow as we stroll back up the hill. When we reach the café, EJ crosses the road to the bar and I look up to find Kristen waving from the Haven's front window.

"What's going on with him today?" she asks, as I walk through the door. Even Kristen has sensed EJ's adrenaline.

"He's gone completely nuts. He told me he's booked in to go skydiving next Friday. Can you believe that?" There is a sceptical tone to my voice.

To my apprehension, she doesn't share the same opinion.

"Wow! Good on him!" she says in amazement, tossing me my apron from the wall hook.

The lunch rush is now dispersing and there's a lot to clean up. Kristen and I have settled into a routine and we work well as a team.

"He's crazy though, right? I mean, he sounded so insistent on doing this." I stack some dirty plates from the table by the window and load them into Kristen's arms.

"Wait," Kristen dumps the plates on the counter and spins around. "What day did you say he's going?"

"Friday. He said it had to be Friday. To be honest, he was a little irrational about it."

Her attention shifts to the wall calendar behind the counter.

"April 22nd," she says solemnly. "That's not so crazy for EJ. It actually makes perfect sense."

"What do you mean?" I ask. "Does that date hold some kind of significance?"

"April 22nd is his sister's birthday. She and EJ always used to talk about skydiving for her 21st."

"Oh," I say, confused. "So why isn't he doing it with her? He told me he was going alone."

Kristen sighs and her face is overcome with sadness. "He hasn't told you."

"Told me what?"

Kristen pauses for a moment. She squeezes the bridge of her nose with her thumb and forefinger, her eyes glassy.

"Liv, I probably shouldn't be the one to tell you this." Her voice is quiet, cracking as she forces the words out. "She died."

"What?" I gasp.

My heart aches for EJ, but now I understand. Everything suddenly makes sense. The conversation about his jacket in my guest bathroom. The reason the jacket is so important to him in the first place. The lyrics to the sad song he sang in the bar. And the unrelenting darkness that seems intent on swallowing his light.

"He obviously finds it so hard to talk about. I don't blame him." Kristen swipes at a lone tear as it slides down her cheek. "It's hard for me too."

"You guys were friends." It's more of a statement than a question. I remembered Kristen saying that hers and EJ's families were close.

"The very best," she confirms. "In a way, she was kind of like a sister to me too. I'm okay. I think about her a lot, but it's been a couple of years now. EJ hides it well, but he hasn't been the same since the accident. I don't think he ever will be."

"Accident?" I ask.

At that moment, a group of uni students barge through the café doors, occupying the table by the window. "I'll go get them some menus," Kristen says, then turns her focus back to the tasks at hand.

I want to know more, but between the onslaught of customers and the dishes that continue to pile up, the opportunity to talk about it doesn't arise. I also sense that Kristen doesn't want to be pressed for more information today.

I get why EJ hasn't told me. Somethings are hard to put into words, like the pain and anguish of losing the people closest to you. I can sympathise with the inability to talk about heartache when it feels as though all your pieces lie broken.

My mind stays with him for the rest of my shift. I can't seem to break away from the melancholy after what I've learnt. I contemplate the possibility that this is why EJ and I have such a strong connection, that EJ had been right when he said there was something between us. We are two damaged souls tethered by an invisible bond, bound together by loss.

"Hello? Earth to Liv." Sammi's voice pulls me from my thoughts.

"Sorry. What were you saying?" I ask.

"Carla put you on mop duty."

"Oh. Sure." I rush around the back to the storeroom to collect the mop.

I'm still so deep in thought, I don't hear Kristen's footsteps behind me. "Are you okay?" she asks.

"Yeah," I answer. "But, what you said about EJ before. I feel bad for him."

"I know," she says, with both kindness and grief in her eyes.

"I need to ask you a favour. Do you think you could do something for me? I wouldn't ask if I wasn't desperate."

"Depends," she shrugs, combing away a glossy brunette strand. "Do I get chocolate?"

"Definitely. So much chocolate," I promise.

"Okay," she said. "What is it?"

"Do you think you could cover my shift on Friday? Pretty please," I beg, clasping my hands together in mock prayer. "There's something really important I need to do."

"Friday, huh? It must be extra important," she says knowingly.

I nod. My grasp tightens around the neck of the mop as an overwhelming sense of anticipation comes over me. Suddenly, all I can think about is getting the hell over to the bar and telling EJ that my plans have changed.

As if sensing my impatience, Kristen smirks and takes the mop from my hand. She nods towards the back door. "Go."

"But Carla will freak if I just leave."

"There's only twenty minutes left of your shift," she smiles. "Go out the back way. I'll tell her you were struck with a migraine."

"You're the best," I beam. "Thank you. I mean it. Thank you."

I'm grateful to have a friend like Kristen in my corner. I take a silent oath to repay her for her generosity, and with more than just chocolate. I hastily untie my apron and toss it in the hamper, hurrying toward the door.

"Hey, Liv," she calls.

"Yeah?" I say, as I turn back in the doorway.

"He's lucky to have you."

I smile and nod in her direction, then rush across the street and burst through the doors of the tavern, scanning the room for EJ.

I see him gathering bottles of alcohol together behind the bar, but there are no waiting customers. I speed towards him. It's my turn to look irrational and adrenaline fuelled.

"I'm coming on Friday," I stammer, out of breath as I lean on the bar for support.

He turns at the sound of my voice, beaming at me. "Are you sure? Was it okay with Carla?"

"It will be."

"Yes! That's great! I'm so glad you'll be able to watch!"

He's buzzing with excitement again. I watch as happiness radiates from him. The glow that he emanates makes it impossible to believe that he could ever be in pain. I wouldn't mention his sister, wouldn't pry for information about what happened to her. I sense that in due time, when he's ready, he will tell me himself. Besides, I am the queen of keeping secrets. Asking him to share his private thoughts would be the ultimate hypocrisy.

"I don't want to watch," I say, still breathless.

A look of confusion and perhaps, a little hurt, passes over his features. "Why?"

"I'm jumping with you."

I watch as his signature grin spreads across his entire face, and I swear to God I've never seen anything more perfect.

Chapter 17

OLIVIA

"Daniella! Anne-Marie!" Katerina holds out two wax-sealed, rose gold envelopes with a tight-lipped smile. "Be there, bitches!"

She's chosen the school lunch hour to distribute invitations to those she deems worthy of attending her birthday celebrations. She meanders away, not bothering to hear either of their responses. They will be there. No one would dare pass up an invitation by Katerina Van Sant. I tag along beside her, feigning interest whenever she starts going into detail about the event. With everything going on at home, I'm just not in the mood for Katerina's extravagance today.

"Jessica." She pauses further down the hall, towering over Jessica Morgan intimidatingly. "I would have loved for you to come to my party, but I really think it's best you rest up at home. For the baby's sake."

Both Jessica and the friend that stands beside her gasp in horror, all eyes tuning in to see what the commotion is.

"I'm not pregnant," Jessica announces, timidly.

"Oh!" Katerina says in mock astonishment. "You might want to tell your bloated stomach that. Maybe lay off the cheeseburgers."

Jessica marches off, visibly upset and on the verge of tears, her friend following in tow. Katerina snickers, then looks to me for a reaction. I don't have one today. This is the part where I'd normally add some commentary and congratulate her for a job well done. She'd made a loser cry. Bravo.

"Well, you're off your game today," she says. "What's going on?"

"Nothing." I don't tell Katerina that my mum is at Rykers. I'm still foggy on all the details myself. And as much as I hate to admit it, I'm anxious about what she'll say to me and how she might treat me. I shudder to think that it could, one day, be me on the receiving end of Katerina's snarky remarks. "Maybe that was a little harsh though."

"Really? This coming from the girl that single-handedly took down James Vardan when she fat-shamed him and made him quit the football team? I'm pretty sure he developed an eating disorder after that."

She's right. I was awful to James Vardan, and it hits me now in this moment like a blow to the gut. At the time, it seemed like no big deal, but hearing her bring it up again now, I feel a strong pang of guilt for my efforts. Is it possible I'm growing a conscience? I surprise myself with what I say next.

"Maybe I shouldn't have done that either."

"Are you kidding?" Katerina scoffs. "The Jessica Morgans and James Vardens of the world belong on the bottom of the food chain. It's just how the world works. They're trash and we're elite."

I nod but I no longer believe her words. "Yeah. You're right," I say anyway.

"So, I've almost got all the details finalised for the party. My Dad knows the owner of Twisted Ivy and he's agreed to shut the whole place down for my party. For a high price, obviously." She rolled her eyes.

"That's incredible!" This time I actually am impressed.

The Twisted Ivy is an ultra-chic bar and restaurant in Milton that's often frequented by celebrity royalty. Chris Hemsworth has been known to eat there when he's in town, and someone once said they'd seen Justin and Hailey Bieber dining there a couple of times.

"I know. It's great, right? And there's gonna be a red carpet at the entrance and this huge banner with my face on it! My party planner has everything covered, except for live music. Apparently, there's some big charity music festival on the same night and my top choices will be performing there instead," she says, sounding annoyed.

"Oh, damn." I go over the names of some of the bands I know in my head. "Oh! There's this great underground band I've been listening to on Spotify. They aren't really that well known yet but…"

"Um, I'm gonna stop you right there." Katerina cuts me off mid suggestion with a manicured hand raised in dismissal. "There's no way I'm going to have some trashy garage band play at my party."

I raise my eyebrows at her disrespectful tone. She must notice because she begins to apologise. "Sorry, Olivia. I don't mean to be a total bitch, but this is my eighteenth birthday party. I want everything to be perfect."

"I get it," I reply. "But don't you think the giant banner of your face might be overkill?"

"No way! I'm about to turn eighteen and inherit a fortune."

Right. Of course, you are.

"Oh my god! What is Kaylee Anderson doing with one of my invites? There's no way that whore is coming to my party."

Katerina sashays away in Kaylee's direction with a flick of her long, mahogany locks. She doesn't seem to notice that I'm no longer trailing her.

Chapter 18

LIV

It's Thursday. This time tomorrow, EJ and I will be free-falling through the air, anticipating the release of our parachutes. My chest constricts at the thought. God, what have I signed up for? Skydiving has never been on my list of things to accomplish in life. I've never been a 'bucket list' kind of person, but EJ's excitement had gotten the better of me.

Of course, it isn't just his enthusiasm that motivates me, but also his vulnerability. I feel as though I'm carrying a weight now that I know of EJ's loss. It's on my mind constantly, particularly today. Hence the reason I'd stuffed up an elderly couples' meals this morning and given poor diabetic Mr. Hudson a sticky date pudding in place of his usual spinach and ricotta omelette.

When I park in the driveway at home later that day, there's a couple of text messages on my phone. One is from Kristen checking what time she has to be in to cover for me tomorrow. I quickly shoot her a reply and thank her once again.

The other text is from EJ, letting me know that he will pick me up on the way to the sky-diving range. It makes sense, considering the range is located to the west of Hampton Ridge, right on the cliff's edge.

There's a fluttering in my gut as I respond. I hope I have it in me to follow through with this. I almost bump into Tessa as I enter the foyer.

"Who is he?" she questions; her eyes narrow.

"He?" I answer, confused. "He who?"

"Oh, don't you play coy with me, Liv. I know there's a boy!" Her voice is a loud whisper, a grin breaking out across her features.

My eyes widen as I try to hide my smile. Tessa has always been able to read me. "I don't know what you're talking about," I lie.

"Uh huh. Sure," she says sarcastically. "You've been acting different for weeks. Don't think I haven't noticed."

My smile falters. She had noticed a change in me weeks ago?

"A good change!" she says quickly, seeing the despair that must fill my eyes. "I meant that in a good way. You seem happy, Liv."

"Thanks. I've still got a long way to go, but I'm working on it." In all honesty, I'm still overcome with crippling guilt during my moments of happiness. In so many ways, I don't deserve them.

She places a hand on my shoulder. "None of us have it together, Liv. Don't let anyone fool you." Tessa glances down at her watch. "Oh shoot. I really have to go. Mila's dance recital starts in twenty minutes. Your father is in the kitchen."

"He is?" I can't conceal my surprise. Dad hasn't made it home in time for dinner in weeks.

"He sure is," Tessa replies, and then cringing, she adds, "And he's cooking."

We both know that my dad doesn't have the finest culinary skills. I laugh softly, wincing back at her. "Wish me luck."

"Good luck." She speaks with sass while she palms the air. "I'm out of here. But next time I wanna hear about this new boy that's got your head all up in the clouds."

"Sure thing." I chuckle as she shuffles off down the hall.

Dad is in the kitchen burning chicken. Smoke wafts up toward the ceiling, sending the smoke alarms into a frenzy. He frantically waves an oven mit underneath it until the ear-piercing bleeping ceases. I run to his aid, turning off the stove and thrusting the pan, which is now enveloped in orange flames, into the sink and flip on the tap.

"Maybe we need to hire a chef." Dad looks at me helplessly.

"You're not here often enough to warrant a chef." I dismiss his suggestion. A look of hurt appears on his face and I worry that I've offended him with my nonchalant remark. "I just mean you eat out so often, it wouldn't be worth it."

"I know," he agrees. "But I want to be here more."

"You do?" This revelation shocks me. My dad has always been in love with his work. Always found fulfilment in saving the lives of people and all of his extra-curricular activities. He practically invented the glorification of being busy. "Are you talking about retirement?"

"Semi-retirement. Let's not get ahead of ourselves."

"Of course," I laugh. "Is that what you want?"

"I think so. I realise I'm not getting any younger. I think I'm ready to pass on some of my responsibilities. Make more time for things I've always wanted to do." He tosses the oven mit onto the counter and rubs the back of his neck. "Be here for you more often."

The irony isn't lost on me. When I'd needed my dad's comfort and love, he'd thrown himself into his work, and now that I'm learning to stand on my own two feet, he's ready to give up some of his responsibilities for me. But I can't be mad at him, can't blame him. He'd only been doing what he thought he had to do to survive his own pain. Pain that was so big, it overwhelmed his being and left no room for me. So instead of being angry for what the past has taken from us, I smile at him, hopeful for what the future may bring.

"I think that could be great."

"Maybe I might even take a cooking course," he jokes. "But for tonight, pizza or Thai?"

"Pizza," I suggest, and then hope to God I won't throw it back up tomorrow.

We eat pizza in front of the tv, which is new for us. It seems we really are turning over a new leaf. When Dad asks me if I have plans for tomorrow, I lie and tell him I don't. I'm not sure why I do that. Maybe knowing EJ's parents don't know about it either influences my decision. Kristen is the only one that knows of our plans and it's as though there's something sacred about that. After dinner, I excuse myself to get an early night.

Sleep doesn't come easy. My anxiety is high thinking about tomorrow. In a positive way or a negative way, I can't quite tell. The skydiving range is so close to where I live that I often see parachuters sailing to the ground in the distance from my window. If it's quiet enough, their screams and cries of exhilaration can even be heard, like whispers on the wind. I've never, in my wildest dreams, considered that one day someone might hear mine.

A million thoughts race through my head. I think of my mother and what she would think of it all. I think about my dad wanting to make more time for me. My mind wanders for hours, reflections and ideas whirling in my head until they come full circle back to one person.

EJ. The guy that takes risks to go after the things he wants, even though there's no guarantee he will get them. The guy who wears his guitar around his neck and his heart on his sleeve. The guy with eyes so intense that they rival the depths of the ocean. A man so full of life, and yet tormented by death. We're connected in ways that words can't explain. How long can I deny my feelings for someone I'm willing to leap from the sky with?

My eyelids flutter open to the sound of drums and a familiar guitar riff. I'm not sure what time sleep had eventually come for me but the clock on my night stand tells me it's now 7am. I'm disoriented momentarily, trying to figure out where the song is coming from. It takes a second for me to realise that it's blaring from my phone.

I'm looking to the sky to save me. Looking for a sign of life. Looking for something to help me burn out bright.

I slam my palm down on it in an effort to silence Dave Grohl's gravelly voice as it serenades me from my bedside.

Make my way back home when I learn to fly high.

I finally recall the song title. Learn to Fly.

I blink until my eyes come into focus. It isn't my alarm. EJ is calling me. After another moment of confusion, I come to the realisation that he's somehow changed my ringtone. Still sleepy, I swipe the answer button and fall back onto the pillows.

"Foo Fighters," I answer, rubbing my eyes. "Clever."

EJ's chuckle echoes through the speaker. "I knew you'd appreciate it. I had some help from Kristen."

"Of course you did. Typical." Sarcasm drips from my voice.

"How's it going? Are you awake?" he asks.

"Um. Yeah." I respond.

"Right. You're talking to me. Sorry, that was dumb." He's rambling.

I can sense his nervous energy through the phone and I have to remind myself that this day is of great significance to him. It's his sister's birthday. And she isn't here.

"No, it's all good," I reassure him. "I'm awake. At least, I am now."

"Please don't tell me you've come to your senses and changed your mind."

"No. I'm still just as mental as ever," I joke, letting out a nervous laugh.

"Awesome. I'll be there in an hour."

"Okay. See you then." I speak calmly, but inside I'm beginning to freak out. We are now counting down a matter of hours until we'll be plunging from an aircraft into oblivion.

When EJ ends the call, I spring out of bed with anxious enthusiasm, which is definitely a new way for me to behave at 7am. I decide against eating for fear that breakfast will not remain where food should remain and open up my closet to get dressed.

What does one wear to a skydiving adventure? I find myself wondering. I know I'll be changing for the jump but I still want to look cute in the meantime. It's colder today than usual, with the seasons beginning to change, so I settle on a pair of jeans and a white t-shirt, then layer it with a suede aviator jacket. How fitting.

By the time EJ arrives, Dad has long since left for work, and Tessa isn't due to arrive for her shift for another hour. Relief washes over me knowing I won't have to explain to Tessa where I'm going. I hate lying to Tessa, not that it's a new concept for me. Shame makes an unwelcome pinch in my chest as I recall all the lies I'd used in the past to sneak away with either Katerina or Sean. But I tell myself this time is different. I'll tell them both eventually, but for right now, I'm savouring this secret.

EJ pulls up in his beat-up red ute five minutes early. He steps out of the truck and walks over to me as I'm locking the front door, his hands thrust deep into the pockets of his ripped blue jeans. His muscular chest fills out a grey t-shirt with the logo of a band I don't recognise on it.

"You ready?" he asks. His light green eyes twinkle with mischief and something else. Anxiety maybe?

"No," I state, frankly. I toss my keys into my bag. "Let's go."

He chuckles, shaking his head in amusement at my bluntness and turns toward the car. As I follow behind, I tried not to focus on the way his back muscles flex underneath his t-shirt, or the light splattering of freckles at the base of his neck. I blow out a long breath. How is it that even when my mind is occupied with a million different emotions, I can still find ways to appreciate how attractive EJ is?

When the ute pulls out onto the main road, I'm struck with panic. My heart pounds so hard against the walls of my ribcage that a wave of nausea threatens to empty what little is left in my stomach.

Am I really about to do something this crazy? I'm not the daring type. This isn't me. I lean forward in the passenger seat, fighting to get air back into my deflated lungs. I lurch sideways as EJ veers onto the side of the road.

"Are you alright?" He turns to me, worry in his features.

"Yeah. I'll be fine." I manage to say, still focusing on getting my breathing back to normal and my heartrate down.

"Really?" He doesn't seem convinced. "You look kind of pale."

"Yeah, I'm okay. You didn't have to stop. I'm good." I look at him then, as if making eye contact with him will prove to him that I am okay. I want to be okay. I want to be able to do this for him.

"Are you sure? I'm not really buying it." He reaches up to my shoulder.

His touch sends heat through my entire body, and it's then I realise that I might be more afraid of my feelings for him than I am of the thrill-seeking adventure that awaits us. One glance at him and I'm lost in his eyes again. I force my gaze away from his, the chemistry between us like an electric charge. On top of my anxiety and everything else, it's too much.

"I'll be okay," I repeat. I don't know which one of us I'm trying to convince. It occurs to me now that I haven't asked him how he's doing. I don't want him to know that I know about the magnitude of what we're about to do. I still believe he'll tell me, if and when he's ready. "How about you? Are you doing okay?"

"Don't worry about me. I'm great." He tries to sound cheerful, but his expression tells a different story. I see his fear. I hear it in the tremor of his voice, but more than fear, there's a hollowness within him. I wonder if he knows I can see through him, or whether he thinks he's doing a substantial

155

job of fooling me. "You know, you don't have to do this right? You could just watch from the ground."

Even with the worry and loneliness he must be experiencing right now, he's attempting to comfort me. He's giving me an out, but I won't let him. I know I'll never come close to being a substitute for his sister, but I can't let him do this alone. I won't. He was never meant to do this alone.

I decide to lighten the mood. "Oh, right. I see what's happening here," I joke. "You're just afraid I'm gonna be so much better at this than you."

"Ha!" EJ laughs, baring a set of perfect white teeth, and it's like watching grey clouds lift from a blue sky.

I did that. I made him happy, even if only for a moment.

"What can I say? You just get me," he says sarcastically, holding a hand over his heart. "Actually, I'm really scared of throwing up in front of you."

"Oh! Gross!" I exclaim and we both laugh.

"Seriously though, Liv. I had no idea you were such a badass." He glances at me sideways. His tone is neutral and I'm not sure whether he means this as a compliment.

"What do you mean? How?" I ask warily.

"I mean, you just seem like… I don't know." He trails off.

"Like what?" I ask, curiously.

"Don't worry. I'm not gonna say it because no matter how I say it, it's just going to sound bad." He looks away from me.

"Just tell me." I roll my eyes at him. "You can't say shit like that and then not tell me."

He sighs. "Okay. All I meant was, you're like this total mystery. You live up on the ridge and you drive a Merc. Not to mention that designer handbag you carry around. I mean, jumping out of a plane? It just doesn't seem like something you would do." He lowers his gaze to the floor of the car in front of me where my Chanel handbag lay.

"You think I'm a shallow, spoilt princess." It's a statement, not a question. I know how I must look to those around me, but having heard him mention my car and hometown previously at Henley's party, his words instil anger in me.

"No!" he cries, pain crossing his features. "No. I know you aren't shallow. That's not what I meant."

"You of all people should know that nothing is as it seems, EJ." I blurt it out without thinking.

He's hurt my feelings and I'm lashing out in revenge, but as soon as the words are in the air, I want to take them right back.

He turns to me, pain and confusion encompassing his beautiful, tanned face. "What is that supposed to mean?"

"Nothing," I say, turning to look out the passenger window. In an attempt to change the subject, I defensively ask, "How the hell do you know what a designer handbag looks like anyway? I didn't realise you were so up to date with the latest in fashion accessories."

"Well, now who's being judgmental?" he scoffs, but he's smiling. "I only know because it's the exact same one my sister begged my parents for a couple of years ago for Christmas. I don't think she ever expected them to actually buy it for her though."

The car falls silent. Guilt grasps at my heartstrings at the mention of his sister. She's the reason we're doing this to begin with. This isn't the time or place for us to be arguing over trivial bullshit. There are bigger issues at hand.

"Look, I didn't mean to be a bitch. I'm sorry." I say, softly.

I see him glimpse at me sideways in my peripheral vision, but I refuse to make eye contact. I didn't peg EJ as the type to judge by appearances, but I can't blame him for it. It's true. I am, in the eyes of everyone else, a spoilt brat from Hampton Ridge that does, indeed, drive a Mercedes and own a wardrobe full of designer fashion, but what these people don't know about me is that I would give it all away in a heartbeat for some normality, to have my mother back here with me.

"Neither did I. I'm sorry too. I didn't mean to offend you. I just meant that you surprise me is all. It's one of the things I like about you." EJ replies, sincerely. "And I'm trying to put on a brave face, but I'm kinda shitting myself here."

I feel awful. His 'badass' comment had been a compliment after all and my stupid walls had gone up in defence and ruined everything. The sign for the skydiving range comes into view up ahead.

"Last chance. We could bail right now and go do something else. Something on land." My attempt to persuade him is only half-hearted. I know this is important to him, but a big part of me wishes he and his sister had planned something much tamer to do on her birthday instead.

EJ smiles as he turns left down the long driveway. "Too late now."

We pass under a canopy of overgrown trees, their leaves all shades of purple, orange and yellow, which give way to a clearing, where a few small aircraft come into view. EJ parks out the front of an oversized, grey shed and then comes around to meet me as I climb out of the truck. He sets a hand on the small of my back. "You okay?"

"Yeah. I'm a badass, remember? Let's do this." My words don't hold their intended amount of enthusiasm.

My hands shake visibly as my fingers grip the straps of my handbag, but determined to get through this I stride ahead toward the shed. I've only taken a few steps when I feel EJ's hand in mine. Part of me wants to shake it away, but his touch is comforting and it fills me with warmth. And somehow I know we both need each other in this moment.

Inside, a man sits behind a large wooden administration desk. Despite being middle aged, he is extremely physically fit. The interior walls are lined with photos of aircraft and people performing jumps.

The man stands up to greet us, but I'm not paying attention to him. Instead, my eyes scan the walls in a blur before becoming fixated on one particular random photograph. It depicts a young woman, probably not much older than I am now. Her face is fully encompassed by fear. The wind blows her cheeks out in a distorted fashion, while her tandem instructor gives a huge smile and the thumbs up gesture. If I was scared before, I'm terrified now.

I involuntarily squeeze EJ's hand tighter, then realising what I've just done I look to him. I expect him to be grinning smugly at me again, ready to taunt me with some joke or 'badass' comment, but his expression only holds apprehension.

"You really don't have to do this. Just watch from the ground," he tells me.

I shake my head at him, my stare locked on his. His eyes reflect the rebellion and determination in my own. I don't know what it is about this guy that makes me care so much, why despite my obvious fear, I'm still willing to hurl myself out of a moving plane.

A voice snaps us both back to reality. "Hello?" We both turn to the man behind the desk at the same time. "Do you have a booking?"

"Hi. Yes, we do," EJ stutters. "I'm Emmett. And this is Liv."

EJ's name is Emmett? Oh God. I'm only just now learning the actual name of the guy I'm about to risk my life with. What is wrong with me?

The man shakes EJ's hand, and then mine. "Welcome guys. I'm Scott, and that guy over there is Max," he says, pointing to a guy who appears to be Chris Pratt's doppelganger talking to a couple of women on the other side of the room. "We'll be taking you guys up today, but first I need you to sign some paperwork, and then we'll get started with the training video."

He leads us to the large desk and hands us a pile of forms each, which are basically full of information on all the risks involved and a waver we have to sign to say it's okay if we don't make it. After we literally sign our lives away, we are taken to a room where an introductory video is played for us. The video is followed by a demonstration by Scott.

The ladies that Max had been talking to have been laughing and making jokes throughout the process. They seem pretty relaxed about the whole thing, which is a whole lot more than can be said about me and EJ. We've barely spoken two words to each other since signing the papers and it's clear we're both freaking out on the inside.

Scott disappears into the office and EJ asks me a few more times if I'm okay after the demonstration. I tell him I am, but I'm fairly sure he can see through the lie. The truth is that I've become so comfortable on the couch in this tiny waiting area, the idea of leaving it to fling myself from an aircraft is nothing short of miserable.

"You guys ready?" Scott calls, his head poking around the door frame.

I'm not ready. In fact, after watching the DVD I'm ready to get the hell out of this place. But I haven't forgotten why we're here and what is at stake, so I launch to my feet and politely tell Scott that I'm raring to go.

"Is he okay?" Max mouths, gesturing at EJ.

EJ is staring off into space, too wrapped up in his own thoughts to hear Scott's voice or to even notice that I'm no longer sitting next to him on the couch. He's staring out the window, deep in concentration. I could take a wild guess about what exactly is on his mind. Or who rather. She was supposed to be here with him.

I gently nudge his shoulder, so as not to startle him. "EJ," I say, softly, "It's time."

EJ jerks under my touch, then his sadness is suddenly replaced by fortitude. I'm certain that this experience means more to EJ than anyone else here today.

"Let's do this," is all he says as he gets up, clapping his hands together once.

We are given nylon jumpsuits to wear over our clothing before being fitted with our parachutes and taken to the aircraft. As the plane engine roars to life, the surrealism hits me. This is really happening. When the plane has scooted along the runway and we've begun to ascend into the air, EJ jolts forward, his arm muscles swelling as he seizes the underside of his seat.

"What's wrong?" I ask him.

"Nothing. I've just never been on a plane before."

My eyes widen and I almost choke on my laughter. "You what?"

He's never been on a plane before. Like, ever. And we're about to jump out of one. This guy doesn't do anything in halves.

Being a small plane, it's nothing like the planes I've travelled in first class to exotic places on vacations with my parents. It's bumpy and rough and a little scary. Even scarier is the sight of the ground from above, as all of the people spectating below shrink to the size of ants before our eyes. My unease only proves to increase as we reach new heights.

"How high are we right now?" I call over the engine to Max, who is busy securing a parachute and harness around himself and EJ across from me.

"About seven thousand feet," he replies.

"Right," I answer, pondering that thought. "And how high do we have to go?"

"We're going to fourteen thousand," he yells back over the engine.

Oh my god. We're only half way up. It definitely already feels like we're high enough. I glance at EJ. He's laughing at me, probably because of the shock that's no doubt written on my face. I would scold him for it, but I'm pleased to see that wide grin of his. I like seeing him happy.

A few minutes later we've reached our goal of fourteen thousand feet and Scott begins edging us both toward the door of the plane. I feel some tugging and pulling as he re-checks the straps that connect me to him. Then the door of the plane opens and we're blasted with air.

Any information that I may have retained from the introductory video vanishes in an instant, leaving only the picture of the girl in the shed flashing in my mind.

"Okay who's going first?!" yells Max.

EJ and I exchange a look. The cheeky smile that he'd worn only minutes ago has evaporated. His usually tanned face is now void of colour. Hesitation lingers in his expression as he swallows hard. I couldn't deny that if he suggested leaving right now, I'd one hundred percent be tempted. What he'd said in the car earlier was true. Olivia Petersen doesn't jump out of aeroplanes. She isn't programmed to participate in spontaneous, risky activities. She isn't this person at all.

EJ is shaking his head now, and part of me wants to reach out to him and tell him that it's okay. We don't have to do this. But the other part of me knows that he does have to do this. I know that if he chickens out, he'll regret it. We're here to do this for his sister, and somehow I know that if I go first, he will follow.

Olivia Petersen doesn't jump out of aeroplanes. She isn't this person at all. But maybe Liv Peters is.

"I'll go first," I call above the engine noise.

EJ's eyebrows lift in surprise at my response, and it's as though my words snap him out of it. A hint of optimism crosses his expression, and if I'm not mistaken, admiration. Scott edges me further toward the door until my trembling hands are gripping each side of the cold metal door frame.

"Wow. That's high," I murmur under my breath to no one in particular.

Despite my fear, the view is amazing. I can see the skyscrapers of Milton in the distance, the place where Cliff Haven lies on the edge of the sea, and in between, the vast range that divides it all. Opening up below us like a giant split in the earth is the gorge known as Hampton Ridge.

"Hey, Liv!" EJ calls out to me over the engine. I turn back one last time to see his face, all seriousness, before his usual cheeky grin returns. "You must really like me!"

I can't reply even if I want to, because I'm free-falling out of the plane, tumbling at what feels like a thousand miles an hour. It's absolutely terrifying. I can't breathe. The air sticks in my throat, and I feel like I might have a full-blown panic attack mid-air.

"Just enjoy it!" Scott's words sound distorted in my ear. "Breathe!"

Enjoy it? How the hell am I supposed to enjoy hurtling to my death at the speed of light? I seem to surpass the sensation of fear and move into anger.

I'm angry at Scott for jumping before I was ready.

I'm angry at myself for agreeing to go along with this.

I'm angry about the fact that EJ had lost his sister in the first place.

And that my mum isn't here anymore.

We continue to free-fall, the air pummelling me like a plastic bag caught up in a cyclone. I picture the girl in the photo from the shed, such fright on her face. I don't want to be like her. I want to be like the others that I'd seen float so gracefully from my bedroom window and Highview Park. I wanted to be in control. Of this situation, and of my own life.

"Breathe." Scott's voice rings out through my head again, but this time I listen.

I inhale. Then when my lungs are refilled with air, I realise it isn't so bad. Or maybe I've just become used to it. I'm still free-falling, but instead of letting the air beat the crap out of me, I let it lift me. I'm flying.

EJ and Max pass us, then an extreme jerk signifies the release of the parachute. We bounce upwards ferociously, then slow down to a graceful glide, still fast but considerably calmer. It hits me that maybe this is what life is like too. Not knowing where you're going, until all of a sudden, you do.

As we float lower to the ground, Highview Park comes into focus. I picture myself laying there beneath the fiery leaves of the sugar maple trees, looking upwards to the mysterious floaters in the sky.

Then I see myself. Or a different version of me, at least. She's the girl that lets life pass her by, who misses opportunities because she fears failure, who watches other people soar with man-made wings.

I'm still that girl, yet somehow I'm different. I left something behind in the plane, a heavy piece of me that has only weighed me down.

I'm still lost, but maybe being found is overrated. Maybe the lesson is in the journey, in the uncertainty. The only thing that makes sense to me right now is EJ. He makes me a better version of myself, and he'd kept true to his promise. That he would make me see me.

When we finally land, it's a little rough, but I'm so euphoric that nothing could bother me. I'm re-entering the earth knowing something that I didn't know before. That everything is going to be okay. One way or another.

"Woohooooooooo!" EJ cries from across the field. He scrambles up off the ground and unclips himself from the parachute. I want to run to him, but my legs don't seem to know how. He starts toward me, staggering at first, until he rediscovers his balance. When he reaches me, he embraces me in a massive bear hug, lifting me of the ground in his arms.

"Can you believe it? We did it!"

"Yeah. We did it." I repeat his words, seemingly unable to find my own.

He puts me down and we walk through the green, grassy field back to the shed, where we strip off our jumpsuits and give thanks to Scott and Max for looking after us.

When we get in the car to leave the skydiving range, it's still only late morning. It's weird to be confined into such a small space. The adrenaline is still pumping through our veins and we can both barely sit still, like our emotions have been multiplied tenfold and there isn't enough room to fit them in the car with us.

"Hey, let's go to Highview Park," I suggest. "I feel like I might explode if I go home and sit indoors."

"Yeah, cool," he simply replies.

EJ goes quiet after that. I'm on such a high that I could speak a thousand words to a complete stranger, but he suddenly appears too overwhelmed to really say anything.

We arrive at the park and walk over to the same picnic table we'd sat at the night we got caught in the rain. EJ jumps up onto the bench and sits on the table, resting his feet on the seat below. I follow his lead, taking the space beside him. Above us, the sky has turned overcast, with only a few rays of sunshine slipping through the clouds.

"Look," I say, pointing up to the sky.

Several parachuters come into view overhead. It's otherworldly to think that we'd just been where they are. We watch as they drift downward, until EJ finally speaks.

"I can't believe we did it," he says in awe.

"I know! It was amazing, wasn't it? I can't even begin to explain that feeling, to be above the rest of the world, it was so…"

"Liberating." He finishes my sentence.

"Yeah. That's exactly how it felt. It was like…" my voice trails off when I realise EJ's head is down between his knees.

It takes me a moment to figure out that he's crying. I'm an idiot. In all my excitement I'd missed the sadness in his voice. With the adrenaline rushing through me I'd forgotten all about his sister and the reason we were here in the first place. I rest my palm on his back.

"EJ?"

His shoulders shake beneath my hand and then he straightens up, covering his face with his palms.

"She was meant to be here." His words come out muffled through his fingertips. "She should be here."

He drags his hands down in front of him and I watch as a tear moves down his right cheek. I shift closer to him on the bench. His pain is affecting me in ways I can't explain. All I know is that I want to take it from him. I need to fix him.

"Your sister," I whisper.

I understand that admitting what I know about his sister's birthday and their skydiving plans is risky. I know that it leaves a chance for him to be furious at me for deceiving him, but when he looks at me through glassy, bloodshot eyes, there are no traces of anger or hate. Instead, they reveal the fragility that he's tried so hard to keep buried.

"She died." He swallows hard before continuing. "There was an accident and she drowned. It was a while ago now, but I don't know…" He rubs his face again with his palms. "She had this crazy plan that we would go skydiving together on her twenty first birthday. I made a bet with her that she'd never go through with it. That she would chicken out. But she never got the chance." His voice cracks slightly. "It was a bet I would have been happy to lose."

"I bet she'd be happy to know you kept up your end of the deal." I struggle to hold my own tears back as I place a hand on his knee, my fingers grazing over the ripped denim of his jeans.

EJ conjures such raw emotion when speaking of his sister that my own psychological scars begin to rise to the surface and I force them way back down. This is about EJ. Not me.

"I'm sorry I didn't say anything before. It just hurts so much to talk about her." He pinches the bridge of his nose and squeezes his eyes shut.

"Don't be sorry. I get it." I understand the anguish of losing someone so close to you, but he has no idea I'm speaking from personal experience. "I'm sorry she isn't here."

I lay my head on his shoulder and weave my fingers through his.

"You already knew," EJ says. "That's why you jumped with me, isn't it?"

"Yeah," I sigh, my head still on his shoulder.

"You really are badass."

"Yeah," I say again, lifting my head to look at him.

"I can't believe you did that." His tone is awe filled, his eyes searching for something within mine.

I try to look away, but with his arm outstretched toward me, EJ cups my cheek in his palm, lifting my face upward to his. He's so close now our foreheads are almost touching. Every fibre of my being fires with electricity as I melt into him. I can't fight this anymore. I don't want to fight it anymore.

My hand slowly reaches out for him and I grab a fistful of t-shirt near his waist. His body tenses as my fingers graze his abdomen through the material, and I pull him into me. His breath is warm on my cheek and then his lips are on mine, moving slowly and softly. His fingers stroke my jawline, then move to the back of my neck and into my hair.

I lose myself in him, in his beautiful, yet troubled soul. For years I've closed myself off from new opportunities, from new people. I formed a wall of ice around me, an impenetrable shield to protect me from getting hurt, but in turn, I prevented myself from experiencing incredible connections like this one I have with EJ. Somehow, he's managed to break through that wall and instead of being mad about it, I can't be more grateful.

EJ's phone begins to vibrate from his pocket. He pauses, his lips still on mine, as though considering whether to take the call. He chooses to ignore it, kissing me some more. I pull away from him, not because I want to, but in case the phone call is important.

"You should call them back."

"Okay," he sighs, reluctantly reaching for his phone. "It was my dad."

He hits the call button. I appreciate that he doesn't move, doesn't try to walk away or be secretive about the conversation he's about to have. I love that he's an open book, but it plagues me with guilt that I can't offer him the same sentiment.

"Hey, Dad... Yeah... Whoa, really?... Lunch? Hang on a sec," he says into the phone, then turning to me he asks, "Do you like seafood?"

"Yeah," I answer curiously.

He speaks into the phone again. "Okay, I'll be there in an hour. I'm bringing a guest."

He pauses, grinning at the shocked look on my face, then says goodbye to his dad before ending the call and shoving his phone back into his pocket.

"What was that about?" I ask hesitantly.

"You're coming back to my place for lunch with my parents."

"Your parents?" I say, stunned.

Things are moving way too fast today. How have I gone from being so determined that there's nothing between us to meeting his parents? And on his dead sister's birthday of all days.

"You're freaking out," he states.

"No," I lie.

"You're such a bad liar," he laughs.

"Okay. Yeah. I'm freaked out. Parents tend not to like me all that much," I admit.

"That's crazy! They're gonna like you," he replies.

"How can you possibly know that?" I ask.

It's true that in the past I didn't have a great track record with my friends' parents. I'm fairly certain Sean's parents wouldn't be opposed to having me burned at the stake.

"Because *I* like you," he says simply.

I roll my eyes. There's no point in arguing with him. I know him well enough by now to know he's stubborn as hell and won't take no for an answer. "Fine. But why did you tell him we'd be there in an hour. It only takes forty minutes to get there from here."

He cocks an eyebrow. In his low husky voice he says, "Because I was hoping to kiss you again before we leave."

He leans into me, but I quickly interject. "Wait! I need to know something about you first."

"What's that?"

"Tell me, Emmett," I say, leaning in close. "What does the J stand for?" If we're going to take things to the next level, I at least have to know his full name.

"James," he whispers breathily in my ear, then kisses me until I'm once again immersed in his world.

I'm gone. If this is what it feels like to be lost, then I never want to be found.

Chapter 19

OLIVIA

It mocks me from its platform in the foyer, like a dark menacing monster. I'd spent so many hours weaving intricate melodies on its keys, forming harmonies with my very fingertips. It had been my first love, the thing responsible for unshackling me from this persona I've been forced to fill. When the notes permeated my core, I wasn't acting a role. I was me.

But as I look upon it now, I feel nothing but anxious frustration and confusion. Because I'm not entirely sure why I've become so disengaged from the thing I once loved to do most.

Is it because my mother and I are becoming increasingly disconnected with every passing day? I hover above the piano and press gently on middle C. The sound hums through my being, but instead of feeling joy and peace, I only feel pain and distaste. I slam its glossy lid shut and storm in the direction of the stairs.

"Oh, hello Olivia!" My mother's voice startles me.

She doesn't sound like herself. The drugs have left her a mere shell of the woman she once was. They tone down her personality, the good parts as well as the bad. She's been home for two weeks now, and we've failed to form any kind of connection. I don't know how to be around her. And as much as it kills me to admit it, I still worry that I'm destined to follow in her footsteps.

"Hi, Mum," I say, softly. "How was your day?" It comes out awkwardly but this is me trying.

"Okay," is all she offers. Her voice has an almost musical tone to it.

She's probably been sitting and staring at the wall for most of the day, like she has done every other day this week. Dad barely communicates with me about her condition, so I'm mostly left to wonder. Wonder when my mum will return to herself. If she will ever return to herself. And it isn't like I want her to go back to her lying, cheating ways, but I long for the familiar all the same.

The doorbell chimes, and sadly, I'm thankful for the distraction. I turn into the foyer and open up the big cedar front doors. Sean greets me with his hands. They wrap around me, travelling from my waist up under my shirt, while his lips press forcefully against my mouth. I pull away, pushing his hands from me.

"Sean, stop."

"What's wrong?" he asks, reaching out to embrace me again.

"Nothing. Maybe I just don't want to be mauled before you've even said hello to me. I'm not really in the mood." I don't even try to hide my irritation.

"Okay," he says, sullenly. "Can I come in at least?"

I sigh, then shove the door the rest of the way open, allowing him to follow me inside.

"Oh! Sean!" My mother leans on the staircase banister, seemingly dazed. "Is that you, Sean?"

"Uh, hi." Sean appears only slightly stunned by my mother's unusual demeanour. "Yes, it's me."

My face heats and my nostrils flare. With shame or fury, I'm not sure. Maybe a little of both. My father appears at that moment, coming to my mother's aid. He's been working from home frequently, when he can, since mum returned. I catch quiet moments between them sometimes, see flickers of tenderness. Of love. It's still there, even after everything. He begins ushering her back to the sitting room.

"Come on, Elle," he speaks gently to her. "You need to rest."

I climb the staircase, Sean trailing closely behind. When we reach my bedroom, he closes the door. He grabs me from behind, his lips brushing my neck, his fingers tangled in my hair.

"I've been thinking about you all day," he whispers gruffly into my ear.

I shove him away for the second time in a matter of five minutes. "What the fuck is wrong with you? Did you not notice the absolute shit show you just walked in on downstairs? Are you that out of touch with reality? Or are you just a heartless, insensitive jerk?"

Sean looks back at me, astonished by my reaction. "I'm sorry. You've never really given a shit about your mum being wasted before."

What he's saying isn't untrue. In fact, in the past, when my mother had done embarrassing things under the influence of alcohol, I had used Sean as a distraction. Only now I knew, it

173

wasn't merely the effects of alcohol that had her acting that way. Mental illness had played a role in it too.

I collapse onto the edge of the mattress. "She's not drunk, Sean."

"What do you mean?" he asks matter-of-factly.

"My mum wasn't spending time at a health retreat. She was at Rykers."

I'd thought the health retreat story had been a great cover. A way to glamorise my mother's absence. How impressive she was, flitting from shopping sprees and fancy clubs to high end health and wellbeing spas.

"Oh. She was in rehab." It isn't a question. He says it nonchalantly, in the same manner you might say "she was at the mall" or "she was at a restaurant," which only serves to remind me how messed up the world is today. And how messed up Hampton Ridge can be.

"Yeah. But that wasn't the only reason she was there. She was diagnosed with a mental illness. She has bipolar disorder." I try to hide the fear in my voice.

"Shit." He curses, rubbing his palms on the back of his neck. "What exactly does that mean?"

"I'm still figuring that out. My dad isn't saying much so I only know what I've read online. The way that Tessa explained it to me is that she will have manic and depressive episodes. When she's manic, she does things she wouldn't normally do. She gets impulsive. And then when she gets depressed, she barely leaves her bedroom."

"That sucks, babe. I'm sorry." He drops down onto the mattress beside me. "Wait. Who's Tessa?"

"She's our housekeeper." I answer condescendingly, despite not calling Tessa by name up until a few weeks ago myself.

"Right. Of course," Sean replies, as though he knew this all along.

I sigh. "I don't know what to do. It was almost easier when she wasn't here. I don't know how to treat her and what to say to her. Then again, she probably doesn't remember the things I do say to her, she's so out of it all the time. It's like even though she is here, the meds make it seem like she's just a ghost. Like she's here, but she isn't really here." I know I'm ranting, but I can't help it.

"What happens now?" he asks.

"I'm not sure. They'll adjust her meds, if necessary. Dad says it could be a while before she's herself again. Whatever that means."

"It'll be okay, babe." Sean rubs my back in a circular motion, then his hand finds its way to my neck. His forefinger traces a line along my jaw.

"You're the only person I've told about this. I don't want anyone else to know. Not even Katerina."

He nods, his brown eyes seemingly sincere. He doesn't seem at all surprised by my willingness to hide my mother's illness from Katerina. I wonder if it's because he knows how lethal the information could be in her hands. Or does he merely think I'm withholding because I don't want it to dampen her party plans, which are well and truly underway.

"How about I make you forget all about it all for a little while."

Sean cups my cheek with one hand, while using the other to investigate beneath my shirt. His fingers creep under the hem of my blouse and then his mouth is on mine, hot and suffocating. It turns out both of my previous assumptions are incorrect. He hasn't really been listening to me at all. He's only here to fulfil his sexual needs. I shove him in the chest as hard as I can.

"God! You can be such an asshole!" I cry. "You need to leave."

"Are you serious? What's your problem?" Sean stumbles backwards toward the bedroom door, shaking his head at me.

"If you don't know what my problem is, there's something very wrong here."

"You know what? Fine. I'm gone."

I look away, not bothering to see him out, and cross the room to the balcony doors. The ocean is grey today, just like my mood. An ocean liner comes into view, far out on the horizon. Out there, it's nothing more than a tiny black spot against the contrasting red sunset, alone in a big, deep sea. Just as I am all alone here, in a sea of insignificance.

Sure, people are envious of me. I have what others only dream of.

Hundreds of thousands of Instagram followers. Check.

The hottest wardrobe. Check.

The sexiest boyfriend. Check.

Yet, it all feels suddenly irrelevant. We waste our time on these material things, these meaningless relationships. We measure self-worth by how hot our wardrobes are, how expensive our cars are, and how many strangers like our posts on social media. It's all bullshit, isn't it?

As removed as I am from everything in this moment, I know in my soul that there's one relationship I'll regret not saving. I inch my way silently down the stairs, the plush carpet squishing between my bare toes. Mum is sitting at the piano with her hands by her sides on the bench. She stares ahead, dazed, her thoughts faraway. I shuffle onto the bench beside her.

"Play with me, Mum?" I encourage her softly.

She turns carefully until she's facing me, blinking in slow motion. I've never seen her like this before. So fragile.

"No. I want to listen." Once again, her voice doesn't sound like her own.

I nod sadly. Then my fingers rediscover the keys, my heart finds its home and the music transports our minds to somewhere else.

Somewhere better.

Chapter 20

LIV

EJ lives on the water, but to say I'm amazed when I see his parent's house would be an understatement. Like many of the other beachfront properties in Cliff Haven, it has its own jetty. It's only about a tenth of the size of the mansion I live in, but to me, that's its greatest appeal.

I love its quaint cottage vibe and the stony path that leads down the side from the front yard to the back, embellished with gardens that have obviously been meticulously created.

Although I haven't even set foot inside the residence, I can sense that it's more than just a house. It's a home.

A melody of wind chimes choruses from the back deck as a woman, that I assume must be EJ's mother, throws open the old paint-chipped back door, her arms adorned with platters of food.

"Hello!" she welcomes us, happily.

EJ runs to her, taking the platters and moving them to a wooden picnic table that has been set up on the lawn. She lunges forward, arms outstretched, and to my astonishment, embraces me in what has to be the warmest hug I've ever received from a stranger. "You must be Liv!"

"Uh, hi, Mrs…" I begin, reciprocating the gesture.

"Oh please! Call me Maggie," she shakes off my attempt at a formal greeting, her warm arms still wrapped firmly around me.

This is a genuine hug. Not one of those 'because you have to' hugs, but a real hug. She smells of lavender and almonds. Her blonde hair, in a half up style, falls just below her shoulders and she wears a casual maxi dress with a floral print on it. It reminds me of a dress my mother wore in an old photo, where she'd held me as a baby.

"I've heard so much about you already!" she says with excitement.

"Mum!" EJ interrupts, and then mutters under his breath. "Be cool."

I feel myself blushing at the fact that EJ has mentioned me to his mother.

"Dad!" EJ calls to a man standing on the jetty, wearing boardies and a long-sleeved Rip Curl t-shirt, who appears to be struggling with a heavy bucket. 'Hang on. I'll help you."

"It's great to have you joining us for lunch, Liv." Maggie's tone is friendly and inviting, though her voice softens when she says, "I'm sure EJ has told you about what today is."

"Oh. Oh my God. I'm so sorry," I start to say, awkwardly. "If I'm overstepping by being here, I can go."

"No. Not at all!" Maggie waves a hand at me. "I was only going to say thank you."

"Why?" My brow furrows in confusion.

Today, she was meant to be celebrating her daughter's twenty-first birthday. A daughter who, sadly, never lived to see this day. Why could she possibly want to thank me?

179

"We're going into our third year without having Mads here. Every year on her birthday, EJ disappears. He never tells us where he goes. None of his friends can tell us either, so we know he goes alone," she answers, placing a hand on my arm. "He seems in much better spirits this year, and I somehow think we owe that to you."

"Oh," is all I can gather in response to her admission.

"EJ has sacrificed so much. He got early acceptance into Bruxfield, but when Mads passed away, he couldn't bear to leave us."

I'm shocked by her words. Not because Bruxfield is the most prestigious music conservatorium in the country; I have no doubt EJ is talented enough to be accepted, but that EJ was on a similar path as me before both of our futures were derailed, and that somewhere along the way, his mother has been given the completely wrong impression of me. That I will somehow be the person that saves EJ from darkness. If anything, he's the one bringing me into the light. Her words leave immense pressure on me. What if I can't be the saving grace for EJ that she's hoping for?

"I hope you like snapper, Liv." EJ's dad wanders toward us, with EJ following closely behind carrying a bucket that appears to be full of fish.

"Liv, this is my dad," EJ says.

Like EJ, his father is quite tall with a muscular build. He has the kind of glowing tan you would expect on someone who lives this close to the sea. Although I'd been to the tavern a few times, I'd never actually met Steve, or even seen him.

"Hi, I'm Steve," he says, as he extends his hand.

"I'm Liv," I say nervously, as I lean forward to accept his handshake.

I grip his hand gently, surprised to find it cold, hard, and smooth. It doesn't feel at all like skin. I gasp when it becomes detached from the rest of his arm, sliding out of the sleeve of his shirt and onto the grass below. "Oh my god!"

It takes me a second to realise his arm is prosthetic, at which point I become aware that my reaction is terrible. My hands fly to my gaping mouth. I'm mortified. "I'm so sorry! I can't believe I did that. I didn't mean..."

I stand there in utter astonishment, not knowing what to say next. A long sigh coming from EJ's direction catches my attention. EJ palms his forehead. My eyes dart back and forth between EJ and his dad.

"Dad. Come on. Seriously?" EJ moans. His cheeks have turned a shade of rose pink as he looks away in embarrassment.

Steve lets out a huge belly laugh. "Sorry, couldn't resist."

"Please excuse my husband for his inappropriate behaviour," Maggie says, arranging the salad servers on the table. "He does this all the time when he meets new people. Thinks he's hilarious."

"I got you pretty good, though," Steve chuckles. I can see where EJ gets his mischievous grin.

It dawns on me that I've become the victim of a bizarre practical joke. Once the initial shock has worn off, I find myself laughing along with Steve. "You definitely did. EJ never mentioned you...um...not having both arms."

"Ah, it's no big deal," he says, waving his good hand nonchalantly. "It makes for a lot of laughs when I meet new people. It was cut just below the elbow so I still get a lot of use out of it."

Not a big deal? I'm surprised at his ability to see any positivity in losing an arm, but then again, I've come to realise that EJ has an optimistic attitude too. It's something he, no doubt, has inherited from his father.

"How did it… I mean…never mind," I stutter. I'm curious about Steve's arm, but I don't want to appear rude.

"How did it happen, you mean?" Steve asks.

"Well, yeah," I answer.

"Just went out for a surf one day and a bronze whaler bit my arm clean off," he says, weirdly casually.

"Oh, wow! I'm sorry." I don't really know what to say to him. I've never met anybody that has any amputated limbs.

"Don't be. You should have seen the other guy," he jokes, light-heartedly. "I got a few punches in with my good arm."

I laugh, turning to EJ. He's still shaking his head as he mouths the words "I'm sorry" to which I can only grin at. He's cute when he's embarrassed.

Steve reattaches his prosthetic limb quickly and expertly, and begins reaching for the bucket of fish EJ carried up the hill from the jetty. EJ snatches the bucket away from him.

"It's fine, old man," he quips. "I'll help you barbeque them. Geez, how many of these did you catch today?"

"Heaps," Steve says sheepishly.

"Ahem," Maggie clears her throat loudly, from beside me.

"Okay. One. Your mother caught the rest," Steve admits, slapping his good hand on EJ's shoulder as they both begin walking to the back deck of the house, where I assume the barbeque must be.

"Wow, you caught all those fish?" I ask Maggie, impressed. I've never been fishing before and it sure as hell wasn't something my own parents did.

"Yes," she answers, ushering us both over to the table. "Come sit. Would you like a drink? EJ tells me you like lemonade."

It made me smile to know EJ had told his mother such a small detail about me. Almost as though he knew somehow that I'd be coming to his house one day all along. "Yes. I do. Thank you."

"Tell me, Liv," Maggie says, pouring the cloudy liquid from a jug into a plastic cup. "What is it that you do?"

"I work at the café across from the bar," I answer simply, taking a sip. "Is this homemade?"

"Yes! I just made it this morning," she replies.

"It's really good." I'm not exaggerating. This is the best lemonade I've ever tasted. EJ's mum is shaping up to be a real Martha Stewart type.

"Thank you. You're too kind. I know you work in the café, but I mean, what is it that you do? Like, what do you enjoy?"

"Oh. Right," her question perplexes me. She's talking about hobbies and past times, and I don't know how to answer her. The things that had once given me joy now bring me nothing but frustration and unhappy memories. "I guess I'm still figuring that out."

"Well, don't wait too long. Life is short." She knows the true meaning of those words in the same way that I do.

"Yeah. You're right. I'm so sorry for your loss, by the way." I take in a shaky breath, anxiously tucking my hair behind my ears. "I didn't get a chance to say that before."

"Thank you," she says, with kind eyes.

Sitting here at the table with Maggie, I absorb the view of the sea. A tiny boat bobs gently, anchored to the jetty. There are ripples at the water's edge where the reeds meet the soft, white sand. There are so many small details, so many features that can't be seen from an isolated mansion on a cliff. It makes me wonder how EJ could be so impressed with the view from my bathroom window when he has all this to look at.

Feelings of sorrow stir within me as I realise how different his upbringing has been from my own. I'd been raised in a palace with every material thing I could ever dream of and yet, I consider him the lucky one. His house is filled with so much love and that's something that no amount of money can ever buy.

After a few moments, EJ joins us. His knee nudges mine under the table. "The fish is almost ready."

"Good." Maggie reaches for the lemonade and pours a cup for EJ. "What did you two get up to today?"

"Actually…" I begin.

"We went and saw a movie," EJ says loudly, cutting me off.

Maggie is so easy to talk to, I'd forgotten that our skydiving experience was a secret. Maybe EJ wants it to stay that way. Maybe knowing what we did today would be too much for his parents when their daughter is no longer here.

Or maybe, the thought that their only son had participated in such a dangerous activity would terrify them.

"A Movie? On this gorgeous day! Stuck inside a movie theatre is no way to spend a day like this!" Maggie exclaims, walking over to help Steve with the platter of cooked fish as he makes his way to the table.

EJ playfully pulls faces behind his mum's back. I have a feeling that if only she really knew what we'd been up to, she might not be as shocked by it as he thought she might be.

"Everybody, dig in!" Steve gestures to the array of platters as he joins us at the small table.

It's heartening to sit down to a family meal, all be it with a family that isn't my own. My dad has been making more attempts to eat dinner with me when he can and we occasionally see each other in the morning, him downing cups of coffee and me eating something quick before running out the door. But family dinners have never been on our list of priorities, not even when Mum had been around.

"I still can't believe you caught these fish yourself," I say to Maggie.

The fish is cooked to absolute perfection. I don't know if Steve cooks at the tavern, but it's obvious he's had a lot of practice.

"Oh yes, I love fishing! It relaxes me. There's a great spot for it right down past the jetty there," she says, pointing to the shore. "EJ can show you sometime."

EJ glances at me sideways, a small smile on his lips. He appears uncomfortable at his mum's remark, probably because we haven't defined our relationship yet and he's scared he might freak me out even more.

To my own surprise, I find myself thinking that it will take a lot more than that to scare me away.

"I don't know," I say hesitantly, scooping some salad onto my plate. "I've never been fishing before."

"Never?" Maggie's looking at me as though I've just told her that I never learnt to tie my shoes, or that I've never seen the sun.

"No, it's not something my parents have ever been into, so I guess it's never crossed my mind." The thought of my dad with a fishing rod in his hands makes me want to laugh, although it's probably something he would really enjoy, if he ever stopped working for half a second.

"Well then, you'll have to come fishing with us!" Maggie says, excitedly.

I look at EJ. He's beaming back at me but mouths the words "I'm sorry" again.

I smirk in his direction and then turn to Maggie. "Why not? That sounds great."

"Maggie catches the most fish out of all of us. If anyone can teach you anything, it'll be her," Steve says, as he stabs a cherry tomato with his fork.

"That's actually true," EJ agrees.

"Damn it!" Steve curses, pulling his phone out of his pocket.

"The fridge again?" I hear EJ ask.

"Yeah," he replies. "I'm gonna have to go check it out."

"That's okay," EJ says. "I'll go have a look at it. I have to take Liv home anyway."

"You sure?" Steve asks, then he turns to me. "This damn fridge at the bar is on its way out. It keeps alarming when the temperature gets too high. Anyways, if you can look at it, EJ, I'll arrange a repairman to be there first thing tomorrow."

"No worries, Dad."

I finish off the last of my fish and thank EJ's parents for their hospitality.

"Thank you so much for lunch," I say to Maggie and Steve, gratefully. "It really was incredible. And it was so nice to meet you."

My words are sincere. It truly has been a pleasure to be welcomed into their home. There's something uplifting about being around grounded people. I've encountered few people in my life with such depth and strength of character, and I feel that absence like an ache in my bones.

"You're welcome, Liv. Don't be a stranger." Maggie hugs me goodbye.

"Yes. You're welcome any time," Steve says, his eyes kind.

EJ and I get back in the ute and begin the drive to Steve's tavern.

"Your parents are cool," I say, once we've pulled out onto the street.

"Yeah, they aren't bad." I wonder if he knows how lucky he is. I'm pretty sure he does. EJ doesn't seem like the kind of person to take anything for granted. That's the greatest thing about him. "What are your parents like?"

I hesitate. I'm torn between wanting to tell him and not wanting to ruin what has already been an emotionally charged day for him. I decide the truth can wait for another day.

"They're okay, I guess."

"Just okay?" he asks.

I remembered the day I'd spent at the beach with Kristen, when she'd assumed my parents were divorced.

"Yeah. My dad's always working and my Mum doesn't live with us anymore. Divorce." I lie. I need to change the subject. "Isn't the tavern open today?"

"No. This is the one day of the year that we don't open. Mum and Dad like to stay home and do something in honour of my sister."

"Of course," I nod, then reach out and give his shoulder a squeeze. He smiles at me, then leans forward to turn up the radio.

We drive back towards town, along Seacliff Drive, with the windows rolled down and the music loud. The calming ocean air soothes my soul, and I promise myself I'll never get tired of it. For the first time in a long time, I'm happy.

We pull up on the curb outside the bar and EJ lets us inside. The bar is different without the people and the lights and music. The only sounds that disturb the silence come from the fridge alarming somewhere in the back and the clomping sound of my boots on the wooden floor as I follow EJ to the bar.

He catches me by surprise when he whirls around in front of me, clutching my hips and swinging me around so that my back is against the bar. He presses into me, his mouth on mine, gentle at first, then increasing in hunger. My hands find their way to his neck, then my fingers entwine in his hair. He feels like coming home and going on vacation all at the same time.

"I've been waiting this whole time just to do that again," he breathes, his eyes gleaming with lust.

"Was it worth the wait?" I tease.

"Always," he answers, as his kisses travel down my neck.

My knees are weak under his touch and I'm grateful for the support of the bar behind me. I've never been kissed this way before. EJ kisses me with intention, with purpose. Behind us, the fridge continues to beep, and I reluctantly pull away from his arms.

"You better go take a look at that fridge," I say, nodding toward the sound.

He lets out a low growl of frustration. "I'll just be a second. Don't you go anywhere." With a quick peck on my cheek, he sighs and then disappears behind the bar, into the storeroom out the back.

Today I've been pushed out of my comfort zone in more ways than one. I'd watched a movie once, where the main character had asked, 'how many truly great days can you say you've ever had in your life?' I don't remember the movie, or even what it was about, but that question had resonated with me. Because at the time, I couldn't really think of one. There was not one day that I'd put above all the rest. Until now.

My attention shifts to the small stage. I inch over to it and step up onto the platform. In the corner at the back stands an old, upright piano that faces the side wall of the bar. I'm not sure why I didn't notice it before.

This piano is at least fifty years old, made from cast iron and mahogany. They don't even make them like this anymore. It appears neglected, covered completely in a layer of dust, but I'm enchanted by it. I gravitate in its direction and pull out the vintage stool from underneath it. I sit down on the worn velvet, cushioned seat. The once varnished lid now has a matt sheen in places where the polish has worn off. I lift it to reveal the yellowed ivory keys, all of which are still intact, although they've seen better days.

I don't even know if they all work or if the piano is in tune, but my fingers find their home on them, drawn to them like magnets.

Maggie's words resonate in my head.

What is it you do? Life is too short.

I exhale, my hands trembling over the keys. I press them delicately and discover that the piano is reasonably in tune. Maybe someone has been maintaining it after all. My fingers move slowly at first, then pick up tempo as I find my rhythm within the song. Muscle memory takes over and my hands weave a slow and haunting piece my mother had written. It had been the last one she had composed herself, before the illness really took hold.

I haven't touched my own piano in over two years. I don't know how I summon the courage to start playing this one. Maybe I'm still high on adrenaline. Maybe EJ's effect on me is greater than I imagined. For some reason I'm letting these walls I've built around myself fall. My hands continue to wander until it feels as though I've left my body. I no longer have control of the keys. It's as though I'm not playing them, rather they're playing me, the piano becoming an extension of who I am. I breathe out as I hit the final note, and it's then that I realise I've been holding my breath.

"Liv?" EJ's voice pulls me from my trance. "Whoa."

His words come out cautiously, like he knows I'm somewhere else, and doesn't want to startle me. Kind of like how you aren't supposed to wake a sleepwalker. He looks at me now the same way Carla had looked at me the day of my first shift at the café. Like a puzzle with a missing piece. I thrust my head into my hands, not sure what to say or do next.

Laugh? Cry? Run?

EJ, oblivious to my current state, skips up on to the stage and takes a seat next to me on the old piano bench. I'm afraid it won't hold the weight of both of us, but somehow it does.

"That was amazing! Why didn't you tell me you could play?"

"I can't. I don't," I falter, hot tears pricking at the back of my eyes. I'm closing up, rebuilding those walls.

"What do you mean? That was great! You are seriously talented." He's so energetic, waving his hands around the way he does when he's gets passionate about something and then combing his fingers through his hair.

"I shouldn't have done that. It was stupid." I'm getting defensive. I wish I had a magic wand that I could use to wave this all away and go back to the moment before my hands touched the keys.

"No, it wasn't. I can't believe you never told me you're a musician," EJ continues, his hand resting gently on my lower back. I can't tell if he's staring at me in disbelief, or if maybe he seems a little hurt that he's just discovered I've been keeping a secret from him, which I basically was. Little does he know, it's not my biggest one.

"Why would I?" I question. It comes out harsher than I mean it to and EJ recoils, removing his hand from my back.

"I'm in a band. I'm into music. You obviously are too. We have that in common. I mean, Liv…" He isn't going to let this go.

"I'm not into it!" I yell, shutting him down. "I used to be, but I'm not now. It's just not my thing anymore."

His eyes flicker with anger and hurt. His jaw clenches.

"I don't believe you," he challenges, his voice low and determined. "Because what I just saw? You were definitely into it. You were so far into it that you were lost in it."

I bite my lip uneasily, sense my nostrils flare. I want to be open with him. I want to tell him that although it was cathartic to play again, the pain of losing the one person that had taught me about music is too excruciating to bare. That every note and every chord is like a dagger to the heart, reminding me that she isn't here anymore, and that it's all my fault. How can I tell him that? How can I stand to have him look at me the way everyone else does?

"Look, EJ. Can we just drop it?" I say, my voice almost a whisper.

"For now," he answers. "If you do one thing for me."

"What is it?" I raise my face to meet his.

Sadness floods his eyes, but the light is still there. I don't ever want to be the reason that light goes out.

"Find whatever it is that's holding you back from playing. And use it. It will only hurt for a little while, and then it will heal you. I promise."

I don't have to know his life story to understand that he's speaking from experience. I know enough. I've heard his songs. It annoys me that I know he's right, and even more that he can see me, see my grief.

Music is and always has been the way I express myself, but getting past the pain to the healing part? That's terrifying. I want to scream at him that life isn't that easy. But who am I to challenge him when he's overcome so much loss? When he's already found the best possible version of himself.

I swallow the lump that forms in my throat and nod. "I'll try."

EJ strokes my hair, then lowers his head to mine and gently plants a kiss on my forehead. It's only a small gesture, but it means so much.

"Did you fix the fridge?" I ask.

"Temporarily," he says softly. "Come on. I'll drive you home."

He rises from the bench, then holds out a hand to me. His palm is warm, comforting. He pulls me into his chest and keeps me there, his strong arms encasing me, his breath in my hair. I don't deserve his understanding.

"I'm sorry I went into bitch mode again," I murmur into his chest.

"I think I can forgive you for that," he says. "You're too cute to be mad at."

I laugh quietly. "It's been a long time since I've played and…" I begin to try to tell him something, anything, but the words get caught in my throat.

"Hey, it's okay. You don't have to say anything. I get it." He holds my face in his hands and kisses my lips, slow and passionate. His hands slide down to my hips, sending heat down my spine. "You know what you were saying that night about how you hoped there was a version of you out there that's doing what she's supposed to be doing?"

"Yeah," I nod. In light of today's events, I expect him to joke about me having a musician boyfriend again, but what he actually says catches me completely off guard.

"For the record," he whispers, nodding subtly at the piano. "I like that version."

Chapter 21

OLIVIA

I gaze up at Katerina's oversized head, struggling with the notion that Katerina herself can't see how undeniably cheesy and ridiculously conceited it is to lord a giant banner of yourself over one of the city's finest establishments. Then again, I suppose I would have thought it was awesome a few months ago, maybe even have been envious.

Twisted Ivy is humming with energy as we enter, Sean's hand held firmly on my lower back. It's a gesture of ownership, a reminder that I am one of his possessions.

"Oh my God! You're here! Finally!" Katerina's squeal gets louder as she draws closer, shoving whoever is in her way until she reaches us.

"Happy birthday, gorgeous!" I throw my arms around her neck and give her a quick squeeze.

My enthusiasm is forced, but I hope I'm doing a sufficient job of acting like I want to be here. I should want to be here. Katerina is my best friend in the world. I can't understand why it feels as though we're drifting apart. It isn't her fault that my life has become a mess.

THE OTHER VERSION

"Thanks babe!" she shrieks in reply. "Come and check out the ice sculpture. It's insane!"

We dissolve into the crowd in the direction of the alleged ice sculpture, leaving Sean to fend for himself. Katerina stops abruptly in the midst of a mass of people when she spots a server carrying a silver platter loaded with an assortment of sandwiches.

"Um, excuse me. What the hell is this?" Katerina pinches at one of the sandwiches with her thumb and index finger, inspecting the filling with a look of distaste. "Ham and cheese? Are you kidding me? My parents have paid for premium gourmet cuisine, not this subpar picnic food."

"I'm sorry Miss Van Sant. I'm just serving the food as I've been directed to." The catering assistant, a woman that looks to be in her early twenties, appears calm and collected despite Katerina's condescending tone.

"Oh, I'm sure you *are* sorry," Katerina says, sarcastically. "A sorry excuse for a waitress! If you still wish to be directed to do anything ever again, you better fix this. I can have you out of a job faster than you can raise those nasty man brows of yours. Do you understand?"

"Loud and clear, Miss Van Sant." The woman, reluctant to take Katerina's orders, seems resigned to the fact that her threats are most likely true. It's easier to obey than pick a fight with the devil herself.

Katerina turns to me after the server heads back through the kitchen doors. "Can you believe this shit? I thought this place was supposed to be high end."

"You know what you need?" I ask her.

"To not be surrounded by idiots?" she scoffs with an eyeroll.

"Well, there is that." I consider, then gesture to a large bottle of champagne behind the bar. "Or maybe one of those."

Katerina flashes a diabolical grin. "That could easily make all the idiots disappear."

I saunter toward the bar, flash a smile at the bartender and point to the champagne bottle resting in the ice bucket behind him. "We'll take that one there."

"Yeah? Two glasses then?" The bartender finishes drying the champagne flute in his hand and tosses the small towel over his shoulder, his clear blue eyes penetrating mine.

"We'll take the bottle," I reply.

"That one? That's a 2012 Louis Roederer. It costs over four hundred bucks."

"Oh really?" I say in mock horror, then I wink at him. "Better give us one each then."

The bartender smirks at me, a glint of something in his eye. Is that lust?

"She's kidding," Katerina jumps in. "Just one bottle to share will be fine."

I lean into Katerina. Pouting, I whisper into her ear. "Party pooper."

"I can't help it. My parents have been willing to give me practically anything for this party but they're keeping a close eye on alcohol consumption."

The bartender finishes pouring the Louis 'whatever-its-name-is' into two champagne flutes and we each take a sip.

"Hmm. I expected more for over four hundred bucks," I think out loud.

The bartender gives a half-hearted laugh and smiles wickedly at me, his eyes glinting mischievously under the bar's fluorescent lights. If it wasn't for his arrogance, I would have found him attractive.

A loud crash from behind us pulls my attention away from him. The woman server that Katerina had terrorized earlier lies sprawled in the middle of the floor, shards of broken porcelain surrounding her, along with a couple of dozen oyster shells and their fillings.

"Fucksake!" shrieks Katerina from beside me. "That's it. Her job won't survive past tonight. She's done."

With that, she pushes away from the bar, intent on exacting revenge on this pitiful woman. I know I should be supportive of my friend, but I don't have it in me to watch her berate the server further. There's enough drama in my life without adding to it with this superficial bullshit. I need an escape.

I snatch the champagne bottle from the bar and move in the opposite direction. I sneak out the side doors and into a courtyard lined with twinkle lights and vines draping from all directions. Twisted Ivy no doubt lives up to its name.

The courtyard is empty, apart from two older men that sit off to the side, and another guy that looks like a staff member smoking a cigarette in the corner. I lean against the wall on the far side of the courtyard that backs onto the restaurant, where I can virtually be hidden from view. I swig the champagne straight from the bottle, letting it soften me from the inside out.

I know I have to face the party soon. Mingle with all my so-called friends. Be Sean's doting girlfriend. Pretend that my life is as perfect as everyone else thinks it is.

But for now, I'll take this moment. I'll close my eyes and let the burn of the alcohol consume me. Let it paint this grand illusion of my life and how it's supposed to look.

"Busted." A male voice bursts through the shadows.

For a second, I think Sean has found me. Where is he anyway?

"Who are you hiding from?" The bartender asks, leaning up against the wall beside me with one arm.

"Everyone," I answer. "Not that it's any of your business."

"Fair call," he responds, with a single nod.

"Shouldn't you be behind the bar, serving the city's elite," I ask, sarcastically, bringing the bottle to my lips.

A deep chuckle breaks his serious expression. "Wow. Is that what you call yourself?"

"I used to." I say, bitterly, swigging another mouthful of champagne. Bubbles of froth stick in my throat.

"Really? So, who are you now?" He moves in closer to me until I can feel the heat of his body, smell his cologne.

"No one," I answer, wishing it were true.

How nice it would be to just be no one. But that can never be. Not so long as I am the daughter of Victor Petersen and his mentally ill wife.

The bartender watches as I haul the champagne bottle to my lips once again. I'm tipsy now. As I pull it from my mouth, he wraps a hand around mine and drags the bottle upward, taking my hand with it. He draws a long sip. His eyes glint with danger and desire. I can't decide whether it frightens or entices me. His body is closer now, his head bent toward mine.

"You were right," he says, his voice low and breathy. "It's not that great for four hundred bucks."

There's a dull clang as he throws the empty bottle into a trash can in the corner. Then his hands move to my hips, holding me against the wall, his lips come down roughly on mine. He tastes like champagne and cigarettes. Do I want this? Part of me does. Part of me wants to let go, to give into the danger and the unknown, but the other part of me knows it's wrong. I'm Sean's girlfriend and I'm not a cheater. I'm not like my mother.

I push at his chest with my forearms, turning my head away from his. "Stop. I can't."

"Come on," he beckons, attempting to kiss me once more.

"No. Don't. I have to find my boyfriend."

"She said stop." A voice comes from the other side of the courtyard.

It's the staff member that had been smoking in the corner. He steps out from the shadow now, stubbing out his cigarette on the ground and flipping his long hair out of his face. He looks familiar, but I can't quite think of where I've seen him before.

"Yeah. I heard her." The bartender holds his hands up in surrender.

I don't stick around to see what happens next. I burst through the doors of the Twisted Ivy. My eyes struggle to keep up with my head as I look for Katerina. I search the sea of faces until it seems they have all blended together.

I'm not sure how many minutes have passed when a hand grips my wrist and hauls me to the edge of the room. When we are clear of the crowd, my eyes find Katerina's. She looks extremely stressed.

"Where have you been?" she asks, her anxiety building as she speaks. She seems flustered with me. Angry even. Does she know what just happened in the courtyard?

"Nowhere. Just getting some air."

She glances over my shoulder. Worry fills her features. "Maybe we should go outside. I think I need some air too."

My eyes follow hers to the dancefloor to see what has caught her attention. Lori Hutcherson is grinding away on some guy. Her arms are around his neck, her eyes closed. His hands rest on her lower back dangerously close to her ass, his mouth only inches from her neck. I squint under the blinding disco lights, and then the realisation hits me like a freight train.

Sean.

I move forward, aware that Katerina is pulling on my arm from behind, attempting to draw me back in the opposite direction. Why is she trying to hide this from me? I reach Sean and Lori, gaping at them for several seconds before they realise I'm standing there. They're clearly immersed with each other so deeply they've forgotten there are eyes on them.

"Well, isn't this cosy?" I state, my voice straining above the club's music.

Both of their heads snap in my direction, the same expression plastered on both of their faces; guilt, quickly followed by narcissistic composure. Sean opens his mouth to speak.

"Don't." I hold up a hand in protest.

I begin to move toward the side exit. Sure, I'd literally just been kissed by a stranger, but I'd had the decency to tell him to stop. I wanted to be faithful to Sean. I'd done the right thing, only to come in here and find him getting way too handsy with this wannabe influencer.

"Olivia!" I hear Sean's pleas from behind me. "I can explain."

"Actually, I really don't think you can."

"Please, Olivia!" Sean grabs my shoulders, spinning me around to face him. "We were only dancing!"

"Dancing? Your hands were practically on her ass. You were basically dry humping each other there in full view of everyone!"

Lori hasn't come to Sean's aid. I figure she's probably climbing back under whatever rock she crawled out from. Katerina stumbles clumsily up behind us in her too-high heels.

"Stop, Olivia!" she says, as discretely as she can considering the situation. "You're starting to cause a scene."

I gawk at her incredulously. "A scene? That's your concern right now? That I might make a spectacle at your precious party?"

"You know what?" Katerina glares at me through winged eyeliner and dramatic lashes. "You're being a shitty friend. Not just tonight either. You've been bitchy for the past few weeks. What's going on? Are you like…jealous of me or something?"

A fury rages from within, my anger now focused entirely on Katerina. It was one thing for my boyfriend to betray me, but my best friend of over ten years? A crowd forms around us. Katerina isn't smart to start something with me here. I'm a ticking timebomb ready to detonate.

"Jealous!" I cry in frustration, vaguely aware of the way my voice is beginning to slur. "Of what? Your fucking ham and cheese sandwiches? Of your giant fucking banner?"

"Oh, fuck off, Olivia!" Katerina's words sting.

Never in the history of our friendship has she spoken to me with such disdain. I guess I haven't ever been this harsh to her either, but I'm not the one trying to downplay my best friend's boyfriend's betrayal for the sake of my party.

"No. You fuck off!" I scream. "I'm not jealous of you! If you weren't so stuck up and self-absorbed you might realise there are bigger things to worry about than this fucking party!"

I know it's not entirely fair to blame Katerina for not supporting me lately. I haven't opened up to her about my life, but if she hadn't been so obsessed with herself she surely would have noticed that there has been a change in me.

Sean's hands clutch my shoulders, attempting to draw me away from the crowd. "Olivia, we should go. Come on."

"I'm not going anywhere with you, asshole. I'll see myself out." With that, I free myself from his grasp and charge away, fully intending on leaving the party, but not before I do one last thing.

The bartender, resuming his duties behind the bar, watches as I storm in his direction. "You wanna get out of here?" My face is hot and flustered.

The bartender doesn't say anything, but the twisted smirk on his face gives me his answer. He turns briefly, removing another champagne bottle from the ice bucket behind him. Then he swings himself athletically over the bar and follows me out into the courtyard, through the exit and onto the street, seemingly not giving a damn about whether his job is at stake.

"What happened back there?" he asks.

"Nothing." I throw myself down onto a park bench. "Just the rest of my life imploding. Aren't you gonna get fired for walking out on your job?"

The champagne makes my legs feel heavy, my head dipping like one of those bobble-headed figurines tacky people put on their car dashboards.

"Nah. I clocked off twenty minutes ago." He takes a mouthful of champagne.

"Huh? Why were you still there behind the bar?" I reach for the champagne bottle in his hands. I know it's a bad idea to keep drinking, but I'm only up for making poor decisions tonight, so I down a few big gulps then hand it back to him.

"I was watching you. You intrigued me." He leans closer, wrapping an arm around my shoulders, pulling me into him.

My chest aches at the realisation that this guy has given me more attention in the past ten minutes than my boyfriend has given me all year.

Fuck it. Maybe he can help me get the image of Sean and Lori Hutchison out of my head. I thrust forward, grabbing clumsily at the collar of his shirt. Our mouths connect, mashing together messily. I wonder if it's the alcohol that makes him seem like such a good kisser. Still, he's hot and dangerous. A bad boy. And there's a thrill in that.

An unknown amount of time passes before we're interrupted by a figure looming over the park bench. "Dude, really? She's wasted. What are you doing?"

The bartender pulls away from me, a sigh escaping him. "Come on, man. We're just having a bit of fun."

"Yeah," I pout. My words are slurring together even more than before as they mimic his. "We're just having some fun."

I blink furiously, my eyes battling to focus on the person standing before me. It's the other employee from Twisted Ivy. Once again, I'm struck with a sense of familiarity when I see his face.

"Hey! I've seen you somewhere before!" I say, my eyelids heavy. "Why do I know you?"

The guy shoves his hands in his pockets, sighing as though my drunkenness is such an inconvenience to him. "I work at the Salt Factory."

"Ah! The Salt Factory. Of course," I slap my head comically, too inebriated to care whether I look like a fool.

I've lost my best friend and my boyfriend tonight. Why not my dignity too?

"I'm gonna call you a cab," he says, pulling a phone out of his pocket.

"No! I'm hanging out here with…" It only occurs to me just now that I don't know the bartender's name.

"Actually, he's just leaving," the new guy says, his eyes piercing the bartenders.

The bartender challenges his stare with his own. "Whatever, man."

He stands, glancing down at me one last time and then ambles off down the dark street. The other guy replaces him on the bench beside me, scrolling through the contacts on his phone.

"What are you doing?" I ask him. My eyelids suddenly feel heavy.

"I'm calling you a cab." He doesn't look up from his phone.

"Please don't call me a cab. I hate public transport. It's gross." Even drunk out of my mind, I still have it in me to be a diva. The champagne is frothing around inside me like waves on a turbulent sea.

"Do you have a better idea? Is there someone you can call?"

I think hard for a moment. As hard as one can think when their brain is only semi-functioning. I can't call my dad. Aside from the fact that he's probably working, I can't let him see me like this after what he's been dealing with at home with Mum. A sudden pang of guilt hits me as I realise how disappointed he'll be in me. I must be growing a conscience.

There's only one person I can lean on right now. She's the only person I can trust.

Tessa.

I locate her number in my phone, listed under 'Maid.' I make a mental note to change that when I'm more coherent. She picks up on the fourth ring.

"Olivia?" Her voice crackles through the speaker, filled with worry. I barely ever call her, and never this late.

"Tessssa," I slur.

"Olivia, where are you? What's wrong?" She's frantic now.

"Can you come get me?" I sob. Hearing the compassion in her voice fills me with emotion.

"Where are you?"

"Um.. I'm…" I scan the street for a street sign, anything that might indicate my location, but my vision is a blurred mess.

The guy holds out his hand to me, gesturing for me to pass him the phone. I listen as he rattles off directions and landmarks to Tessa so she'll be able to find me. He ends the call and hands the phone back to me.

"Thanks," I sniffle. "You don't have to hang around."

"Yes, I do," he says, simply.

"Why are you being so nice to me? Do you want something from me?" I shiver in the cold night air.

"I'm just trying to help you." The guy takes off his jacket and wraps it around my shoulders. I welcome the warmth of his body heat. "I don't want to be reading about some girl being mugged in the park tomorrow when I'm drinking my morning coffee."

"Oh."

"That's kind of sad though."

"What is?" I question.

"That that's where your mind goes when someone offers to help you."

"Yeah," I nod.

Chapter 22

LIV

All Kristen wants to talk about the next day at the Haven is the jump. "What was it like? Was it crazy? How was EJ? Were you scared out of your mind? Was it exhilarating?"

These are just some of the many questions she bombards me with as she bursts through the doors in her usual whirlwind manner. The café isn't due to open for twenty minutes, but we've almost finished setting up.

"Yeah, it was totally crazy," I tell her.

For me, 'the jump' had taken a backseat to the rest of yesterday's events. Strangely, the plunge I'd taken with EJ had proved to be more significant to me than the one I'd taken from the plane.

When sleep had come for my exhausted mind and body last night, it had been restless and brief. Everything played out in my head on repeat, every molecule in my body coming alive with adrenaline. Skydiving, the kiss, meeting EJ's parents, the piano. I'd opened a door, allowing EJ into my life, and I'm still coming to terms with the inertia of it all.

"Liv! Hello? Where are you right now?" Kristen's voice echoes distantly, growing louder as it pulls me away from my thoughts.

"Sorry. What?" I ask, in a daze.

"Wow. It must have been some kind of day, huh?" Kristen says smiling, eyebrows raised with her arms crossed over her chest. She examines my face as if she'll find the answers she's looking for printed on my forehead.

"It was insane. There's just no way to describe the feeling, it's like your heart is in your stomach. Like, it was so terrifying but it was also just… so fun! And so freeing." I smile, realising I've not only just described what it felt like to jump out of a plane, but what it felt like to kiss EJ.

"Wait," Kristen says, curiously. "Did something else happen?"

"No," I lie. Heat rises in my cheeks as I turn away from her and start refilling the napkin dispenser.

"Liar!" she accuses. "Something happened. What are you not telling me?"

"Nothing," I say, self-consciously. "It just… it ended up being a really good day."

"A really good day?" she questions, her eyes squinting in suspicion. "You're keeping something from me."

Kristen gives me side eye as she helps me with the napkins, but she doesn't press me for more details.

A knock on the window startles us both. We look up to see EJ waving energetically, a grin spreading across his face. He seems different somehow, or maybe I'm seeing him in a new light. He beckons me to him. Kristen's gaze burns into my back as I thrust open the sliding door and slip outside.

Before I can even say anything, EJ scoops me around the waist and with one hand supporting my lower back and the other gently moving from my cheek into my hair, he leans down and his full bottom lip brushes mine. When the kiss deepens, everything goes white, as though I'm in a dream. I can think of nothing but how affectionate and beautiful this human is as he envelopes me in his solid arms. He's too good and it leaves me reeling for more.

"Good morning, friend," he says, in his sexy, husky voice.

I would have laughed at his 'friend' remark, if I weren't busy trying to get my breath back. I cringe inwardly, knowing without a doubt that Kristen has seen us from inside.

I glance over my shoulder. Sure enough, there she is, watching us in amazement, her mouth wide open in wonder. She starts to clap her hands comically, while dancing laps around the table she's setting up.

"Someone's had their coffee this morning," EJ says, nodding toward Kristen, still holding me close.

I laugh. "She hasn't, but I don't think I want her to. She has enough energy for the both of us. Did you come by for your usual?"

"No. Just wanted to see you." EJ twirls a piece of hair that's fallen on my face, then tucks it behind my ear. "I haven't been able to stop thinking about you."

I smile at his admission. "I know that feeling."

"It's pure torture," he grins, then he kisses me again so deeply, I'm out of breath again when he pulls away.

"Mmhmm," I agree. "I wish we could do this all day, but I have to get back in there. Carla's probably already annoyed that I'm out here. Plus, I have to go clarify this little scenario to Kristen. She looks like she might explode if she doesn't get some form of an explanation."

He pouts playfully as I unwillingly drag myself away from his warm embrace. "Come see me at the tavern when your shift ends?"

"Sure. I'd like that." I step back into the Haven and close the door behind me.

He winks at me through the glass, then turns to cross the street.

I couldn't have kept the juicy details from Kristen if my life depended on it. It's written all over my face. Between waiting tables and washing dishes, I tell her everything. Well, mostly everything. I leave out the part about the piano at the tavern.

"You even met his parents? Well, that was a productive day!" Her eyes are wide with excitement, then her expression changes to one of interest. "Wait. Did Steve pull the whole fake arm prank on you?"

"Yes!" I laugh. "He got me good."

Kristen throws her head back in laughter, accidentally sloshing soapy water all over the floor. It seems so natural to be talking to her about all of this and so far removed from my past life in Hampton Ridge. Still, the reminders of who I used to be are always there.

"Kristen, do you think that maybe this is all happening too fast. I mean, I don't even know what *this* is."

"I don't know," she answers. "Only you guys can know that for sure. But EJ's been through so much. I don't think he's dated anyone in forever. Maybe you shouldn't try so hard to define it and just go with it. You both deserve a little happiness."

"Yeah," I reply. What Kristen says makes sense. There's no reason to ruin what we have by overthinking this or trying to put a label on it, but one phrase in particular keeps repeating in my head.

EJ's been through so much.

She's right. EJ's heart is not to be toyed with. If he and I are going to do this, we have to do it right. I need to be the kind of person he deserves. He'd shared details about the most painful loss he's ever experienced, allowing me to gain a sense of who he is inside, to see into his heart. There would be no room for secrets with EJ. He's an open book and I owe him the same level of transparency. If I can't give him that, the kindest thing I could do for both of us would be to walk away right now.

My phone vibrates in my apron pocket and I pull it out discretely. A text from EJ brings the screen to life.

EJ: *I think yesterday was the greatest day of my life. I seriously can't stop thinking about it.*

I shoot him back a quick reply.

Me: *Me too. I can't believe we actually jumped from a plane.*

He replies immediately.

EJ: *I wasn't talking about that part. ;)*

I know now, that walking away will never be an option. We're in too far to turn around now. We've waded far out of the shallows and into the deep blue, with nothing but the unknown surrounding us.

I will tell him about my past. And about my mother. Soon. But I need to buy some time while I figure out how.

"I'm glad you've found happiness with the local bartender, but can we please keep the texting to a minimum in the workplace." Carla's stern voice snaps me to attention.

"Sorry, Carla," I wince.

"It's okay," her voice softens. "I remember being young. I really am happy for you both."

211

"Uh, thanks," I respond, not sure how to take her well wishes.

"You know, the day I met you, I knew there was something about you. I saw that Chanel handbag you carry everywhere with you and I thought, who is this girl and why is she here in my cafe? She looks like she bears the weight of the world on her shoulders. You don't seem to be carrying so much of that today."

I blink back at Carla, not sure what to say. I often wondered what had led to her hiring me on the spot that day.

"Everything is gonna be okay, Liv," she says, placing a gentle hand on my shoulder. "One way or another."

"Thanks, Carla," I reply. I believe her.

"Back to work," she says, her eyes crinkling at the corners as she smiles.

"Yes, boss," I say, then busy myself with clearing the table in front.

The rest of the day drags, although imagining what EJ is up to lessens the gloom of the monotonous tasks ahead, until finally the close of day comes. I finish placing the last of the chairs upon the tables and then mop the floor, a job I hate with a passion.

I often watched Tessa mop our marble floors at home. Leave it to her to make mopping look so graceful while she swished from side to side, humming old Whitney Houston songs. She once told me that it was like therapy to her. I don't share the same opinion, but it was so like Tessa to see the good in everything, even the mundane. Suddenly, I miss her. I hope she'll still be there when I arrive home tonight.

"See you tomorrow, Carla," Kristen calls as she exits the kitchen, pulling off her apron and hanging it neatly on the hook. She turns her attention to me. "Oh, hey! Before I forget, next Friday we're having a send-off at Steve's for Sammi. She got a teacher's aide position, so she's leaving the café."

"Oh, wow! That's great for her! I had no idea."

"Yeah, she told us yesterday," she says. "But you know, some of us were off having the time of our lives with cute guitarists."

I roll my eyes at her comment and she laughs.

"So, you'll be there? Friday?"

"Yeah, no worries," I say, but then I realise that Sammi's farewell would fall on the same day as my dad's benefit. "Oh no, wait. Friday? I can't do Friday. I have family stuff."

"Bummer. You can't blow it off?" she asks.

"I wish I could."

I mean it, too. Not only will I be missing Sammi's farewell, I'll also be missing the opportunity to watch EJ on stage with the band again. But I've fobbed so many of my dad's invitations already, it wouldn't be right to ditch him again, especially when he's hosting this one.

"Damn," she pouts. "Maybe us girls will have to have our own catch up later."

"Sounds like a plan," I agree.

Not long after Kristen leaves, it's my turn to hang up my apron and make an exit. I say goodbye to Carla and head over to the tavern to see EJ as promised.

It's still early, so business is yet to pick up at the bar. Sure enough, in an hour or two the place will be packed out. My heart skips a beat when EJ's eyes lock with mine. He finishes serving an older man, then leaps around the bar in my direction, the cutest smile plastered over his face.

"Finally," he murmurs into my ear as he snakes an arm around my waste. "I've been waiting forever for you."

213

"I know the feeling," I say in response. I've missed his presence more than I realised. I reach up and lace my arms around his neck. His lips graze my jawline, driving me insane.

"Please tell me you have a day off tomorrow."

"I don't, actually," I reply.

"Damn." Disappointment floods his features.

"But I get off at midday," I say, hopeful. I'd say anything to bring that smile back to his face.

"Yes! Really? Please tell me you don't have plans after," he pleads, playfully.

"I don't have plans after."

"Okay. That's awesome! I really want to show you something." EJ seems genuinely excited about whatever plans he's concocted in his mind.

"Show me something like…" I press him to elaborate.

"It's a surprise. All I'll say is that it's my favourite place in the entire world."

"Sounds intriguing." I smile at the way his eyes light up when he speaks. It's clear that this place he wants to show me means something to him and I feel privileged to be invited.

"Will you come with me?"

"Absolutely." I watch as his grin widens. We've already jumped out of an aircraft together. At this point, I'll go anywhere with him.

He cups my face in his palm and kisses me slowly, sending me weak in the knees. A few seconds later, we're interrupted by a loud commotion. Loud squeals and cheers resonate through the bar, catching EJ's attention.

"Oh great," he sighs. "Well, this is my cue."

I steal a glance over my shoulder when he releases me from his embrace. The shrieking and laughter come from a group of young women, all of them wearing bridesmaid sashes except for the pretty blonde they surround. They whoop and holler as they adorn her with a flashing tiara and costume veil.

"Looks like you're in for a wild night," I joke teasingly.

"You have no idea," he rolls his eyes with a shake of his head. "I gotta go serve them but be ready at midday. I'll come get you. Wear something comfortable."

"Comfortable?"

"Yeah. And pack a change of clothes." He winks at me, his teeth skimming over his bottom lip as I stand there, confused by his request. He pecks me on the lips and then scurries back behind the bar.

"What can I get you ladies?" I hear him ask, though his eyes are still on me. I push the heavy door open and he waves at me before turning to make whatever drink the woman has requested.

I stroll out of Steve's and back to my car, pondering all the possible places EJ might be taking me tomorrow where I'd need a change of clothes and something comfortable.

But mostly, I wonder how in the world I'd gotten so lucky, and what the hell I'm going to do in this life to make sure I deserve it.

Chapter 23

OLIVIA

Monday morning isn't kind. I skulk into school alone, with a heavy head and heart. A weight in my skull because somehow my hangover has still not fully dissipated, and an anchor in my heart knowing that my boyfriend no longer wants me and my best friend will probably never forgive me for ruining her party.

There's no doubt that Saturday night had been a low point for me. My lowest of lows. I can't even begin to fathom the shame that's eating me over the things I did with that bartender. I'd never randomly hooked up with a stranger before. Of all the crappy things I've done in my life, losing my dignity and self-respect is probably the worst. Afterall, if I don't have that what do I have?

I'd never been more grateful for Tessa than I was on Saturday night. When she pulled up on the curb of that deserted park in Milton, she may as well have been a knight in shining armour on a white stallion. I won't forget the way she took me into her arms and lead me to her little hatchback.

Never before have I seen so much love and compassion radiate from one person. I'd spilled my heart out to her about what had gone down at the party. I told her about Sean flirting with Lori, and that Katerina had been less than supportive when I'd gotten upset. I did, however, leave out the part about the bartender, telling her only of how I'd taken a bottle of champagne and got myself completely wasted.

Tessa had agreed, all be it reluctantly, that informing my father of my drunken state would only upset and stress him out further when he already had so much on his plate. It was decided that she would keep my secret if I promised never to do it again.

"Do better," she had said to me.

And so I vowed to be better. To put that horrid version of me into the past and become someone I could be proud of. The first step would be to make things right with Katerina. We may have said some aggressive things to each other at the party, but we've been friends for too long to just give up on what we have.

As I move down the corridor of the main building, I become aware of several pairs of eyes on me. With my head down, I shove my text books into my locker and slam it shut.

"Can we talk?" a low voice whispers in my ear.

It's not who I'm expecting, although I shouldn't be surprised.

"What do you want, Sean?"

"I want to apologise. I came round to your place to see you on Sunday morning. Your dad said you stayed at Katerina's house. I knew that wasn't true. I was worried."

"You could have just called Lori to keep you warm."

A defeated sigh escapes his lips. "Look, I'm sorry, Olivia. She came over to dance with me. I had no idea where you and

Katerina had gone. The next thing I knew she was all over me, but you have to believe it meant nothing."

His words actually sound genuine, though we never actually discussed the night that he'd been tagged in Lori's Instagram post.

I look up to meet his gaze, his eyes pleading. He's either a great actor or this is true remorse. I'm hit with guilt when I remember what I'd done in retaliation. Sean may not have betrayed me, but I'd deceived him, a fact he isn't aware of to my knowledge. The shame sends a sick feeling into the pit of my stomach.

I reach out for his hand, my fingers skimming his. "You promise nothing happened? You don't have feelings for her?"

"Only you, babe." He wraps his arms around me, smothering me in his chest. I'm relieved to have this second chance, but the shadow of guilt remains, poisoning me from the inside out.

I release myself from his grasp. "Come over after school?"

"Of course," he says, then nods to something behind me. Someone. "I think someone else might want to talk to you."

I dare a glimpse over my shoulder. Katerina clutches her laptop to her chest, looking as anxious as I feel. The tension in the air is palpable. I move slowly toward her; all eyes in the corridor now trained on us.

"Hey," I say.

"Hey," she says in reply, and then to the prying crowd of people that can't keep their stares from us, she shouts, "Nothing to see here, morons! Go back to your pitiful existences!"

The comical way the crowd disperses earns a slight giggle from both of us. "Idiots," I jeer.

"Are you okay?" Katerina asks, sympathetically.

"Are you? I ruined your party. I feel so bad about how I dealt with things. I was just so upset when I saw Sean with Lori…" My eyes well, tears threatening to spill down my cheeks.

"I know. It's okay. I probably would have done the same thing. But were you okay? I mean… when you left? Where did you go?"

"Nowhere," I lie. It isn't lost on me that although she's asking if I was okay after the party, she hadn't been concerned enough to follow me on the night.

"What do you mean? You're not gonna tell me where you went?" Her tone is accusatory and I fumble for the right words to keep her from getting mad at me again.

"No. I…" I avert my gaze, my eyes firmly stuck on the floor, afraid that if Katerina looks into them she'll see through my façade. "I just called Tessa to come and pick me up. I didn't want to bother my dad."

"Your maid? Why?" she asks.

"My dad has had a lot going on lately." I nervously tuck a tendril of hair behind my ear.

"Okay," Katerina says. I can tell she doesn't believe me.

"With work. He's just been really busy." I want to tell her about everything that's been going on with my mother, but now isn't the right time.

"Right," she responds. "So, everything was fine after you left. You just went straight home?"

"Uh huh. Yeah," I lie again.

Katerina nods slowly, a questioning look in her eyes. I get the sense that she knows something more than she lets on.

"I'm really sorry about what I said. I didn't mean any of it, Katerina. You're my best friend and I can't imagine my life without you in it." This time the tears do fall.

219

"Shh… I know. It's okay. I didn't mean what I said either." Katerina wraps her free arm around me, the other still clasping her laptop. "We're okay. It's all okay."

"Sean's gonna come over today. He apologised for everything."

"That's great. Just promise me one thing." Katerina releases me from the hug.

"What's that?" I ask, attempting to wipe the tears away without smudging my mascara.

"That you'll come to me when there's something bothering you. You can tell me anything." Her words are sincere, but there's something about the way she delivers them. Something almost threatening. Maybe I'm being paranoid. My own guilt and shame are getting to me.

"I know. I will." I nod.

"No secrets," she says sternly, but with a smile.

"Of course."

And just like that, all my intentions are thrown out the window, my vow to be a better human sitting in the trash. In a matter of minutes, I've managed to deceive my boyfriend and my best friend. At least things will go back to normal. I'm not sure I can handle change at this point.

When the morning bell rings, we disperse in different directions, like a pair of non-polar molecules repelling from each other.

Chapter 24

LIV

As planned, I attend the café for my morning shift, but midday can't come fast enough. I'm desperate to see where this mysterious favourite place of EJ's is. He told me had a few errands to run for his dad, but that he would come by the café to pick me up after, and promised me an afternoon to remember. I spend the morning hoping the tank top and shorts I've worn will suffice and watching the clock in anticipation.

"That clock isn't gonna tick any faster just because you're staring at it you know," Kristen says, as she eyes me from the counter. "Got somewhere to be?"

"Is it that obvious?" I frown back at her, gathering the remnants of a toasted cheese sandwich from the far table near the window.

"Yep." That's Carla. "Let me guess. You're seeing the guy from the bar today?"

"No!" I say defiantly, determined to prove her wrong.
They both laugh.

"So where is he taking you?" Carla asks.

"I don't know. He wouldn't say. Just that it's his favourite place." I turn to Kristen. She's known him for years. "Do you know where that is?"

"Me? No idea," she answers, unhelpfully.

I guess I'll just have to wait and see. I continue clearing the table when a figure enters my peripheral vision on the opposite side of the glass.

Cayden's hunched over form looms on the footpath outside, his death stare directed straight at me. The scar on his cheek appears silvery and pink in the light of day, his hands shoved deep into his pockets. An uneasy feeling churns in my gut. His presence makes the hair stand up on the back of my neck. For a second we both just stand there, him glaring, me with my eyebrows knit together in confusion. Then he simply turns and walks away.

"Wow, someone really has it in for you. What did you do to piss Cayden off?" Kristen gives an awkward half laugh, somewhat breaking the tension in the atmosphere.

"I have no idea," I answer, trying to shake off the evil stare that's now embossed in my memory. "But you saw that right? I'm not imagining it."

Maybe he's still angry about what had gone down at Henley's party. He'd been so drunk, I highly doubt he'd even remember all the details of that night. Is there some weird jealousy thing going on between him and EJ?

"I wouldn't worry about him. He's harmless," she says with a wave of her hand. "He's got some issues, but he'll be okay once he gets his life back on track."

I hear Kristen's words but I'm not sure whether I believe her. There doesn't appear to be anything harmless about the way he scowls at me. I consider asking her what she means by him having issues, but it isn't my business and I refuse to make it so.

Then EJ drifts through the door of the Haven, providing the perfect distraction.

To my relief, he's dressed casually, in boardshorts and a blue tie-dye muscle tank. It makes me glad that I'd opted to wear my swimsuit underneath my outfit.

"Good afternoon, ladies," he calls out as he tips his baseball cap off and then rearranges it backwards on his head.

"Oh, thank God!" Kristen groans. "Take Liv away from us, EJ. She's putting us all on edge here."

"Hey!" I say defensively, giving her a warning look so she doesn't embarrass me further. Then to EJ, I ask, "So, where are you taking me?"

"I told you. To my favourite place. I hope you don't need to be anywhere later cause I'm planning on cooking you dinner."

"Hmm, I'm impressed." I untie my apron and throw it into the linen bag in the corner. "And I'm all yours."

"Hey Carla, do you have any raw seafood scraps out the back there?" EJ calls to Carla who's busy in the kitchen, just out of view.

I make a sour face behind EJ's back and mouth to Kristen, "Seafood scraps?"

She stifles a laugh and then mouths back, her face a picture of sarcasm. "Romantic!"

I cringe as Carla calls in reply, her voice echoing through the kitchen. "Sure, I'll see what I can scrounge up."

"Thanks." EJ turns to me, lifts me up in a hug and pecks me on the cheek. I try not to laugh as Kristen pulls faces behind his back.

It dawns on me how natural this all feels, to have a real friend and this amazing guy that likes me enough to want to show me his favourite place on earth. Nothing about this feels forced or fake and I consider for a second that maybe I'm actually succeeding in reinventing myself in this town.

But that seed of doubt is still there, implanted in my mind. I try not to feed it, but the truth is, I'm scared to death. Each and every passing day is a step closer to the moment that everyone will discover that my whole persona is a lie. I need to find a way to tell EJ the truth.

But not today.

Seafood scraps or no seafood scraps, I'm not going to let anything ruin this day.

Carla emerges from the kitchen carrying a plastic garbage bag. It's obvious from the smell of it that it contains the raw seafood that EJ has requested and I assume that, as it's inedible for human consumption, he must be taking me fishing. Not a far leap, considering we'd talked about it the day I met his parents.

I say goodbye to Carla and Kristen and follow EJ to his ute. He takes my bag for me and secures it in the back, then he holds the passenger door open for me. I pause to kiss him on the cheek before ducking inside the vehicle. He smiles at my gesture as he closes the door. I inwardly gush at how adorable he is.

We drive all the way back through Cliff Haven until we reach Bentley, the next suburb across. After a few more minutes, we enter a dirt track, marked with large tyre marks that wind further into the trees. EJ dodges large puddles where he can, but there are some he can't avoid. We drive through them, the car dipping and rocking, as muddy brown water splashes up onto our windows.

"Do you have any idea where we are?" he asks me.

"No," I say. "None. But I hope you do. You're not planning to bury my dead body out here, are you?"

His face takes on a serious expression for a moment, then he cocks an eyebrow. I stare blankly at him, which only makes him break out into a grin, sending us both into fits of laughter.

"Creep," I mutter jokingly.

We come to a stop in a clearing. EJ exits the car and begins emptying the tray of his ute. I jump out of the truck, surveying the area with total confusion. He's brought me to a tiny bare section in the midst of all of these trees. There's nothing around us but mud and shrubs.

"Uh, what are we doing?"

"Here." He hands me a back pack. "We can't go any further in the car. There's no road. We walk the rest of the way."

My eyebrows escalate involuntary. "We walk?" I repeat. "Through all of this?" I gesture to the trees and shrubs in front, but even as I do I can see a faint trail through the foliage.

"Yeah," he says casually, adjusting the other backpack on his shoulders.

"How far do we walk?" I fumble to get the backpack on.

I realise I'm at risk of sounding like a spoilt child.

"Not far. About five kilometres." EJ positions the fishing rods and a small tackle box so he can carry them all in his right hand. "That okay with you?"

"Just five kilometres? Oh, yeah," I say, defiantly but with a hint of sarcasm. Now isn't the time to admit that I've never hiked through the woods in all my life. "That's totally fine. Let's go."

As we trek through the trees, the sun shines mercilessly overhead. It's turning out to be a sweltering day. The skinny dirt trail is slightly damp from recent rain and there are patches of mud all around. We walk in silence, me persistently following EJ, wondering where the hell we could possibly be going, and how on Earth this has anything to do with EJ's favourite place.

We come to a wider part of the track that's been flooded by recent rain and a giant puddle of about five feet round takes up the entire path. It has to be at least a foot deep. A large log from a fallen tree provides a makeshift bridge across it. I watch as EJ delicately springs up onto the log and acrobatically makes his way across. It's obvious that he has done this before.

When he reaches the other side he turns to me. "Do you want me to hold the backpack for you?"

I consider letting him help me, but stubbornly, I want to show him I can manage all on my own. Tenacity is a trait of mine that only seems to come out in the presence of EJ. If he had been any other guy, I'd be making him carry me over that puddle like a queen.

"It's fine," I say. "I'm totally fine." I'm acutely aware of my overuse of the word 'fine.'

EJ nods with a sheepish grin, sensing my determination. I place my right foot up on the log, which is a step higher than I thought it would be. When my left foot reaches the log, I sway a little, but with my arms out to balance myself, I slowly make my way across the log bridge.

He holds out his hand to me as I get closer, which I instinctively take. Our eyes lock, his filled with mischief to match the crooked grin he wears, before his palm, smooth and slightly sweaty underneath mine, jerks sideways, sending me flailing into the mud.

"EJ! What the hell?" I shriek. "Are you crazy? Why did you do that?"

I angrily curse at him as I drag myself out of the sludge, but he isn't listening. The fishing rods drop to the ground beside him. He's laughing uncontrollably, with his back arched and his face to the sky. I look down at my once-white tank top, now a gross shade of brown. Mud is splattered from my converse sneakers all the way up to my thigh.

My anger dissipates as I watch him, the way he laughs like he has no care in the world. I'm transported back to the night in Highview Park when I'd first seen him like this. There's something so free about it that it makes me glad he'd thrown me in the mud, because it's worth it to see him this happy. I also love the fact that he doesn't treat me like a fragile porcelain doll. For the first time in a long time, I've found someone that makes me feel like an actual person.

"I'm sorry," EJ manages to say through laughter. "I had to. It was payback."

"Payback?" Before I even finish the word I know he's referring to the night in the park, when I'd accidently pushed him into the mud. "Oh! I see!" I say, nodding. I bend down and pick up a large wad of sludge. "Then you better run."

He stops laughing when he realises what I'm about to do.

"No. Come on, babe. Please. You don't want to do that."

He holds his hands up, but instead of backing away from me, he draws nearer. He reaches out, attempting to pin my hands, but it's too late. I smear fistfuls of mud onto his cheeks and finish by wiping my hands down his blue shirt, feeling the hard muscle tense beneath it.

"You got me." He wraps his arms around my waist and I throw mine around his neck, standing on my toes to kiss him. Then he reaches down to the ground and flicks more mud up in my direction. I scream playfully as I respond by throwing another wad.

When every bare inch of skin is covered in mud and our hair matted in chunks, we pick up our things and keep walking. EJ assures me we're nearly there but I'm no longer bothered. I'm grateful to be out here enjoying his company with the sun shining on our mud crusted faces. About five minutes later, the sound of running water becomes apparent. We are close to a stream.

"Okay, we're almost there. It's just through the trees here. Close your eyes." EJ holds my hand.

"Why? Are you gonna throw me into the rapids or something?" I joke.

"There's that attitude I know and love," he jokes, and then, rolling his eyes, he adds, "Just do it."

I cover my eyes with my hands and he guides me through the last section of trees. Twigs snap beneath my feet. I nearly stumble but EJ keeps me upright.

"Okay. Open them."

I remove my hands. My jaw slackens in awe. My voice comes out in a whisper. "Wow."

The sight before me is absolutely breathtaking. A river, water as clear as crystal, streams at my feet. On the other side, a giant wall of rock stands tall with water cascading down. I'm overcome by the sheer beauty that nature has to offer, and at the same time, sad for the ignorance I had before realising places like this existed.

So many people in Hampton Ridge have never experienced anything like this, too oblivious to journey past what they think beauty is. Luxurious yachts and day spas and extravagant hotels. I'd travelled the world over with my parents, yet I can completely understand why this place right here is EJ's favourite. It's mine now too.

"What do you think?" he asks.

"I love it." I take his hand in mine, still staring ahead at the stream. "Thank you."

"For what?"

"For everything. For bringing me here."

For showing me how to live again.

His eyes connect with mine, and the affection I find in them jolts me. EJ and I operate on the same wavelength, and I don't know if I'll ever get used to how perfect that is.

He smiles down at me, squeezing my hand gently in his. "Come on, let's clean up."

We drop our gear on the sandy bank and I follow EJ into the cool water. With lazy strokes, we swim to the waterfall on the other side, allowing the heavy drops to shower down on us, ridding our hair and skin of dried mud. I find a place on a large flat rock, warm from the sun. I ring the excess moisture from my shoulder length hair and secure it into a messy bun. I glance at EJ, notice him watching me silently from the water below.

"What?" I ask.

He paddles to the edge of the rock and hoists himself up next to me. "Do you even realise how amazing you are?"

"Yeah, right," I scoff. "You are." He places a loose tendril of damp hair behind my ear, his fingers grazing my jawline. "You're gorgeous."

I reach up to his neck and pull him close. His skin is cool from the water, but his lips are warm as they mesh with mine. When we'd first met, I'd tried so desperately to deny the chemistry between us. I'd wanted to stay away from him so badly, because the thought of getting close to anyone scared the hell out of me. With his hands stroking my face and my fingers in his hair, I realise I've never failed at anything so badly in all my life. And I'm glad.

A sigh escapes me as he breaks away. I try to reign him back in. "Let's go back to the other side," he says.

"Do we have to?" I'm unwilling to move from both my place on the rock and my position in his arms.

"Yes. I'd love nothing more than to keep kissing you forever, but we have dinner to catch."

"Right." I say reluctantly, moving back into the water. I'd forgotten we came here to fish.

I climb onto EJ's back and he carries me through the river to the other side. He takes off his shirt, laying it out on a large flat rock to dry. Seeing him shirtless takes my mind back to the night in my guest bathroom when heat had radiated off his bare torso. It had taken all my will power to keep my hands to myself that night, and now I don't have to. I follow his lead and strip off my white tank top, revealing the pale blue string bikini I'm wearing underneath.

"Holy shit." EJ groans, reacting to my near naked top half. "Jesus, Liv. That's not going to be distracting at all."

"Sorry. You want me to put it back on?" I say, gesturing to my tank top with a cheeky smirk.

"Nope," he replies bluntly, then gets to work setting up the fishing lines. "So, I'm not really that great at this. My mum is the real expert, but she showed me a few tricks."

I cringe as he threads a slimy piece of prawn onto the hook, its barely attached head flapping in the process. It looks to me like he knows what he's doing just fine.

"I'm not sure I want to touch that." There's no point trying to hide my disgust.

"What? This?" He waves another piece of unidentifiable seafood near my face.

"Eww!" I dodge his hands. "Gross, EJ."

"Don't worry," he laughs. "You won't have to. Come on, I'll help you cast it out."

"Okay," I stand, grudgingly.

I don't want to hurt his feelings, but it's obvious I'm not as into this as he'd like me to be. In all honesty, all I want his lips on mine and his hands all over me.

I half get my wish as he hovers behind me, his arms outstretched in front. He places the rod in my hands, holding them as he does so. My back is on fire where his bare skin meets mine.

"So, all you have to do is swing it and release the line as you let go." With his hands over mine, we sway as he swings the rod back and then forward.

The prawn covered hook sails through the air and lands a short distance from us in the middle of the stream. EJ let's go and then goes about setting up his own rod.

"What now?" I ask, already a little bored, and missing EJ's close contact.

"Now, we wait." He casts his line out a few metres from mine.

"Do you really think we are actually going to catch some…" I gasp, unable to finish my question, as a strong tug warps the end of my rod.

"You've got something!" EJ says excitedly. "Wind it in."

"Ah, okay," I mutter as I struggle with the line. It feels heavier than I could ever have imagined. "I don't think I can."

"Yeah, you can!" EJ encourages me. "Just try and hold it still and keep winding."

I follow his instructions and about half a minute later a silvery fish becomes visible, flapping and splashing in the shallow water. I haul it up onto the beach and suddenly my fear and lack of enthusiasm is overcome by excitement.

"Oh my god! I actually did it! I caught a fish!"

"You did!" EJ moves toward me to help, but I'm so caught up in my excitement I'm already kneeling down trying to pick it up and remove the hook. When I've freed the fish from the line, I look up to catch EJ smiling at me.

"And you're not even worried about touching it."

I laugh. "I guess it's not so bad."

The fish turns out to be a decent size according to EJ and his fish sizing chart, so we keep it. After that, I reel in two more, but EJ isn't as lucky. It doesn't seem to bother his ego. He's happy for me to be the provider of tonight's dinner.

We lay on the sand in the late afternoon, and as the sun descends behind the cliff face, EJ lights a bonfire and erects a small pop-up tent. The back pack I carried in is actually a picnic satchel that holds a cooler bag inside of it. EJ rummages through it now, pulling out a packet of chips, and throws me a can of lemonade.

When he asks if I want to help him clean the fish, I politely decline. Touching it had been my limit. I don't think I could handle seeing it gutted too. I lay out the picnic blanket from the bag and sit down next to the fire, taking a sip of my drink, while I watch EJ in the distance.

The sky is streaked with shades of violet and orange as the daylight dims, giving way to the night. I can't think of a time when I've ever felt this content. Even the times I'd been happiest during my childhood, I'd never felt as free as I do now. Almost every happy day in my past had been marred by my mother's moods. I realise now that it hadn't been entirely her fault. It was the disease.

There's only one thing holding me back now, one thing I need to do to relieve this constant feeling of guilt in my gut. I have to tell EJ about my past.

"You okay?" EJ's voice pulls me away from my thoughts.

"Yeah. I was just thinking."

"The fish is ready to cook," he says, pulling out a small fry pan from the picnic satchel. It's beginning to resemble Mary Poppin's bag. I wonder what else he could possibly have fit into it.

"You really came prepared," I admire.

"I'm used to it. My dad and I always used to go camping." He prods at the kindling with a long stick.

"Can't say I've been camping all that much," I say, then I add, without thinking, "Except there was this one time in France." Realising what I've said, I stiffen, slowly turning to gage EJ's reaction.

His eyebrows are raised in surprise, and something else. Annoyance, maybe? "France?"

"Uh, yeah," I stammer. "It wasn't really proper camping though. More like glamping. You know? The big tents that have air conditioning and bathrooms and all that?"

"Right," he says, looking away. "Sorry, I don't have one of those."

I've upset him.

"It was awful," I say in an attempt to make him feel better. "Trust me. This is way better."

"Yeah? How's that?"

I haven't convinced him yet, but I'm telling the truth. I travelled to France with my parents on vacation and we took a last-minute camping trip, or glamping trip as they'd called it. I was only ten years old at the time and had found the trip immensely lonely.

"Because you're here," I answer, shifting closer to him, and resting my head on his shoulder. "I meant what I said. I love this place."

"France, though? What else don't I know about you?"

So many things.

Judging by his reaction to knowing I've travelled to France, now doesn't seem the right time to also mention that my father is Victor Petersen. Once he knows who my father is, he'll also know who my mother was and there will be nothing left to hide. He'd then associate me with the reckless, teenage socialite I once was, in what feels like a lifetime ago.

I shrug off his question. That is a story for another time. Relief floods me when EJ leans in and plants a gentle kiss on my forehead. It appears he's willing to let this go for now.

We eat the fish with a delicious salad that EJ's mum had made, and when we're fully stuffed, we lay back onto the picnic blanket, using the pack as a pillow. I settle my head into the curve between EJ's arm and his chest and he wraps his arm around my shoulder.

"What were you planning to do if we didn't actually catch anything?" I ask him.

"I brought a ton of extra potato chips in that bag," he answers. I laugh and shove his chest playfully.

The stars come into focus above, framed by the trees surrounding us, their twisted branches like arms reaching out toward each other. Between the melodic sound of the flowing stream, the crackling of the fire and the warmth of EJ's body, I feel as though I could fall into the most peaceful sleep I've ever had.

"This place is pure magic," I sigh. "How did you find it?"

"I found it with my sister. One day I'd come home from a really shit day at school. I failed some test and this girl I liked told me she wasn't interested."

"Stupid girl," I joke.

"Yeah, I thought so," EJ chuckles softly. "My sister saw that I was down and she told me to get my head out of my ass and go on an adventure with her. So, we came out here with no idea where we were going, and by some miracle we found this stream."

"Your sister sounds like the kind of person everyone needs in their life."

"Yeah. I was definitely blessed to have her." EJ strokes my hair gently. "Now every time I need to get my head out of my ass, I come up here."

"Is this where you usually come on her birthday?" I ask. "Your mum mentioned you go somewhere. She said no one knows where."

"Yeah. I guess, now you know."

"I can keep a secret," I whisper, tucking my head deeper into EJ's neck.

"Do you ever wish you had a sibling?"

"Sometimes," I answer. "I always used to want a little sister when I was a kid."

"I can't believe it's just you and your dad in that big house. That's insane. That house is amazing."

"It's not all it's cracked up to be," I say.

"In what way?" EJ shifts onto his elbow, watching me curiously. I hope I'm not coming off as a poor little rich girl again.

"Well, it's like…" I search for the right way to describe it without revealing too much. "It's not just the house. It's the lifestyle that goes with it. I'm expected to act a certain way, to dress a certain way."

It would have been easier to tell him who my father is, but I'm not ready to make that kind of confession. Victor Petersen is practically famous in the district for his work, but he's also famous for something else. He's the widower of Elle Huxton.

"There are too many expectations?" He sounds like he understands, but I don't see how that's possible.

"Yeah, exactly," I say.

"Why do you care?" he asks.

"What do you mean?" My eyes narrow, his question catching me off guard.

"I mean, why do you care what people think?"

It's such a straightforward question, but the answer is complicated. Why do I care? Maybe it has something to do with being raised by two perfectionists, or that I used to hang out with the most superficial people imaginable. I only know that it hurts to hear someone say something nasty about me or my family. I can't explain those reasons to him because I don't want him to see me as weak. To know that I'm not strong enough to rise above it.

"I don't know."

"Well," he says. "Maybe you're your own worst critic. Maybe you shouldn't care so much."

I laugh. "It sounds good in theory, but you don't know my dad."

"Is he strict?" I'm flattered by EJ's interest in me. I've never had someone listen to me so intently before. Ironically, there's so much I can't say.

"Not so much. He just wants me to be someone that I'm not."

236

"Like, who?" he asks.

"I don't know. Like him, I guess. He would love for me to be a lawyer or a doctor or something, but it's… it's not for me."

"Do you ever see your Mum?"

"No." A tear forms in the corner of my eye at the mention of my mother.

I have an opening to tell EJ right now about everything, but I know I won't. I'm too afraid.

EJ glances down at me. "You miss her." It isn't a question.

"Yeah, I do, but we had a difficult relationship. She was an alcoholic and she was depressed. I'm scared all the time, that I might end up like her."

"You won't."

"You can't know that." There are so many things I should tell him but the words are caught in my throat.

"You seemed determined not to. I know you're a good person, Liv." His faith in me is humbling, but he doesn't know anything about me. Not really.

"I used to be different. I used to drink. A lot. I was wasted most of the time."

"Is that why you don't drink anymore?" he asks, weaving his fingers through mine.

"Yes." I blink away new tears as they well in my eyes. "I'm really not who you think I am."

"You're exactly who I think you are. I told you, Liv. I see you."

"I'm not. My life was a mess. I was a mess."

"So what?" His blatant question throws me. "So what if you were a mess? You're not now."

"That's debatable," I mumble.

"Come on. Be serious. You didn't want to be an alcoholic so you stopped drinking. That was you, Liv. You did that."

He's right. I have the power to take things into my own hands. I get to decide who I want to be. And once again, he's right about what he'd said at Henley's party. That one way or another he was going to make me see myself. Words fail me. I don't know how to respond. All I know is that when I look into his eyes, my whole heart is full.

"Stop obsessing over this past version of you, okay?" his eyes plead with mine. "I don't know everything about you, or what you were like before, but I don't have to. Because I know who you are now. And everything you ever did in your past led you here. It led you to me. That's all I care about. Okay?"

I nod as EJ wipes the tears from my cheeks, his olive skin glowing in the light of the fire. He lowers his head down until his lips are on mine and delivers what is, no doubt, the greatest kiss of my life. His hand traverses from my face to my neck as the kiss deepens, continuing downward until his fingers climb under the edges of my swim top. Heat fills my body as his hand discovers my breast, tracing my cleavage.

I still have so much I want to tell him. Need to tell him. But words don't seem important right now. I'm overcome with so much affection for him, this person who has made an effort to look right into my core, to sift through all of its ugly parts and find pieces of beauty.

My hand moves down his chest and abdomen, and when my fingers curl under the waistband of his shorts, he groans into my mouth. He moves over the top of me until his body is pressing down on mine. My hips roll upward involuntarily when I feel how much he wants me.

His kisses become softer as they move from my lips down to my breasts. When his mouth finds mine again, I wrap my legs around him and thrust my fingers into his hair.

Being with EJ isn't like being with Sean. EJ is considerate. His touch is tender, his attention greater. With EJ, I know I'm adored. He makes me feel things, both mentally and physically, that no one else has ever been capable of doing.

We both fall asleep on the picnic rug underneath a lightweight blanket by the fire, and I swear it's the best sleep I've ever had. I wake with EJ's arms still around me, one underneath my head and the other draped across my waist.

The sky is lighter, though the sun hasn't fully risen yet, painted with hues of blue, purple, and yellow. I watch EJ as he sleeps peacefully, his breathing slow, strands of chestnut brown hair falling across his forehead. I could watch him forever. His eyelids flutter open momentarily, filling my vision with green and grey, before closing softly again as he pulls me close to him.

"How long have you been awake?" he murmurs, his voice gravelly.

"Not long," I whisper back, not wanting to disturb this moment.

I reach up and brush his hair back from his forehead, my fingertips tracing their way downwards along his jawline. He purrs under my touch, leaning forward to kiss me once gently on the forehead. "This is too good. I don't want to leave."

"Same. Do you think anyone will miss us?"

He chuckles. "I think they'll miss you. As much as I'd love to be greedy and keep you all to myself, we can't stay."

When he opens his eyes a moment later, I let myself get lost in them again. Those grey-green ocean eyes had drawn me in from the very first day we'd met. I know it wasn't that long ago, but what I feel in my heart for him runs deep. I can't fight this notion that the universe has brought him to me somehow. To pull me from the darkness. To save me. And despite him not knowing everything about me, he's the only one that's ever really taken the time to see me. He's my person.

"Promise me you'll bring me back here one day," I whisper.

He smiles. "I promise."

Reluctantly, we leave the comfort of the picnic blanket and pack up our stuff. We eat a quick breakfast and then hike the five kilometres out to the ute. My car is still parked in the alley behind the Haven, so EJ will take me there.

"You got plans for today?" EJ asks once we get onto the road.

"Other than going home to take a shower? No."

"Hmm," EJ says cheekily. "You need help with that?"

I laugh. "I think I can manage."

"It wouldn't be the first time we've been alone in your bathroom together. Just saying," he adds.

My cheeks flush at the memory of EJ's naked form in the spare room ensuite.

"It does sound enticing, but the thought of my father walking in scares the shit out of me."

"Yeah, me too." EJ agrees.

"What about you? You have any plans?" I ask.

"I think I'm meeting up with the band later. Cayden wanted to run over some of our new material."

"Oh, cool." I try to sound upbeat, but my words come out flat.

"Are you okay?"

"Yeah. Fine. It's just…" I struggle to find the words. As much as Cayden freaks me out, I don't want to come between their friendship.

"Cayden." EJ finishes my sentence for me. "Did he bother you again? What did he say?"

"No. He didn't say anything at all. He just stood there and stared at me through the café window. It's fine. I just wish I knew what his deal was."

EJ's frowns. "Don't worry. I'll talk to him."

"No, EJ." I counter. I don't want to say anything harsh about his friend, but I'm beginning to get worried. If EJ upsets him, who knows what he might do? "I don't want you to talk to him. I know he's in your band and everything, but there's something really off about him."

"He never used to be like this." EJ sighs. "He's had a tough couple of years, too. But he'll be okay." EJ's words mirror Kristen's from yesterday.

"You said that before, but we've all been through a lot, and we don't all act the way he does."

"It's different with him." EJ's jaw clenches.

"Why?" I wonder aloud.

What happened to Cayden to make him so miserable?

"He and my sister were together."

"Together? As in dating?"

"As in engaged."

"Oh my god."

"Yeah. He was completely devoted to her. We all thought they were too young to be making the decision to get married, but whenever they were together no one could deny that they were made for each other."

"Wow. From what you've told me about your sister, I can't imagine her being with someone like him."

"Like I said, he was a completely different person before all of this."

"Wow," I say, again.

"Yeah. It gets worse." EJ continues. "He was with her the night she died. When she was drowning, he jumped into the river to save her. He dove straight down onto some metal and got cut up pretty badly. He was lucky he survived himself."

"The scar on his face," I muse.

He nods. All of a sudden, I realise why Cayden is the way that he is. His whole life had been ripped away from him in an instant. The plans he'd made with EJ's sister. The life he thought they would have together.

Gone.

No wonder he hates me so much. It can't be easy to see EJ moving on with me, or to see anyone experiencing any kind of romantic happiness at all. After spending these past couple of years without her, he's no different to the rest of us that have lost the people we love. We all clutch desperately to any kind of joy, no matter how brief it may be.

With this knowledge, I stop seeing Cayden as a threat.

He's a victim.

One that needs help.

Chapter 25

OLIVIA

There's no doubt left. Our relationship is toxic. I know it now. I think I've known it all along, but denial is a bittersweet enemy. I've always felt like Sean only spent time with me because he had ulterior motives, but sitting in the living room last night, hearing him butter up my dad in the next room, exactly two days after the worse fight we'd ever had, I'm positive of it.

I forgave him for the dancefloor fiasco with Lori Hutchison. But did I do it because I actually wanted to restore our relationship? Or because of the guilt that persisted over what I'd done with the bartender at the Twisted Ivy?

And would Sean be happier with someone like Lori if he hadn't chosen to be with me because he wanted my father to write him a reference for medical school?

My head is stuffed with a million thoughts. Not just of Sean, but of Katerina too. We'd made up after our fight at her party, but I couldn't help thinking there was something threatening behind every word she spoke to me. Last night, after Sean left, she'd texted me once again, questioning whether there was anything I needed to tell her. Anything that I wanted to confide in her about. A dreaded weight took shape in my gut at the thought that maybe she knew more than she was letting on. But surely I was being paranoid.

Right?

My mother beeps the horn at the car in front. "Come on! What are you waiting for?" she shouts out the window.

"Mum! You're embarrassing me." I reprimand her. The last thing I need is for her to draw attention to herself right out the front of my high school. I silently curse my dad for needing to borrow my car today because his is in the mechanics.

"Sorry, but some of these kids need to learn how to drive properly."

She isn't wrong, but she's acting differently today. Come to think of it, she's been acting differently for the past few days as well.

"Are you okay, Mum?"

"Of course!" she says, cheerfully. Too cheerfully. "I'm just impatient, that's all."

I nod, not quite sure whether I believe her. The doctors had said she would eventually adjust to her medication. Maybe she finally has.

"Okay."

The car in front finally moves on and she continues to drive forward to let me out on the curb. "Have a great day at school, sweetie."

Sweetie? Well, this is new. "Okay, Mum. I'll see you this afternoon."

I exit the car, adjusting my bag on my shoulder. When I look up, I'm met with the stares of several students. Even James Vardan is giving me the evil eye. What is their problem?

I guess some of them aren't aware that the drama from the party is old news. Whatever, they'll get over it soon.

I do my best to ignore the unwanted attention, but when I reach the main building I'm finding it difficult to tolerate their judgmental gawking. I slip into the first-floor bathroom, seeking refuge in a stall. I'm inhaling some deep breaths in an attempt to redeem my composure, when a bunch of tenth graders burst through the door.

"Did you guys hear about Olivia Petersen?" I hear one of them say.

"Oh my god. Yes. She's so tragic." I recognise this voice. Lori Hutchison.

I peer through the crack in the door. I see Lori pouting in the mirror, applying her lip gloss, while a couple of her minions watch with hairbrushes in their hands. I don't know their names, but I remember their faces.

"What happened?" says the third girl.

"So, the other night, she went totally psycho when she saw me dancing with her boyfriend. Then, apparently, she got completely wasted and hooked up with this random waiter from the restaurant."

"Whoa, that's insane." The girl on Lori's right drops her jaw in surprise. "But why were you dancing with her boyfriend?"

Lori shrugs her shoulders, lip gloss still in her hand. "He's hot."

"Fair enough."

These girls used to follow me around every party I went to like I was royalty. Hearing them talk shit about me now is surreal, like I'm stuck in another dimension. The irony isn't lost on me, that they look a lot like younger versions of myself and Katerina.

"But I heard that's not even the worst part," the other girl interrupts.

"Huh? What do you mean?" asks Lori.

"I heard her Mum is a psycho too. She just got out of Rykers because she has some major mental problems."

My hand flies to my mouth in shock and I fight to contain a sob. Bitter tears sting my eyes, threatening to spill down my cheeks.

"You're kidding!" Lori says in surprise.

"Nope. Apparently her mother's a slut too. Cheats on her dad all the time. Probably where Olivia gets it from. She's crazy just like her."

I want to throw open the door of the stall and confront these bitches. I want them to know I'm hearing every word, make them pay for being so callous. But instead, I stand frozen, watching them attack me from the small crack between the hinges, tears tracking their way down my cheeks and most likely making a hideous mess of my mascara. What purpose would it serve? They're only speaking the truth.

"How do you know all of this?" one of the other girls asks. I'm too upset to care which one.

"Katerina Van Sant."

"What?"

"Yep. She told a couple of people that she saw Olivia leave with the waiter from the party. And that Sean had told her about Olivia's mother being mental."

"Wow. How pathetic."

"Katerina tried to get her to admit it, but Olivia wouldn't tell her. She lied to her face and acted like nothing happened. Apparently she gets wasted all the time too."

I watch as both girls scoop up their bags and head for the bathroom door, their heels clapping irritatingly on the tiles.

The bathroom falls quiet until my tears, silent up until now, turn into gut-wrenching sobs. I'm in shock at how quickly my life has spiralled into something else entirely, but also of how cruel the human race can be. I shudder at a distant memory, of being at Sean's party a few years ago when I, myself, had been so rude to those girls.

I'd betrayed Sean and Katerina at the party. And now they had both betrayed me. Were they doing this to exact revenge on me? Katerina would have been pissed at me for lying to her about the champagne and the bartender. She probably told Sean, who then would have spilled about my mother being in Rykers in retaliation. I'd deceived them both and they'd sought a way to punish me for it.

Sure, there's some truth to what has been said. I did get wasted from time to time, but apart from the other night, I was usually the least drunk between me and Katerina. I'd kept the truth from Katerina and Sean, but I had my reasons for that. And now suddenly I've been branded a psycho.

Life as I know it has come to an end. I'm no longer the girl everyone admires. I'm the girl everyone loves to hate.

I'm a liar.

I'm an alcoholic.

I'm crazy.

And there's only so many times you can hear the same lies before you start believing them yourself.

Chapter 26

LIV

My phone vibrates from the ottoman in front of me. I feel Tessa's eyes on me as I reach for it. A text from EJ illuminates the screen. It simply says, "*missing you*." I couldn't contain the smile that spreads across my face if my life depended on it.

"Ahem." Tessa clears her throat loudly from beside me.

"Sorry," I laugh. "It's from EJ."

I look at the clock. It's almost seven, meaning he would be about to begin his shift. It's nice to know he's thinking of me, even when he's busy.

"Well," Tessa says. "It seems this guy really has you smitten."

"Yeah, I guess he does." I feel my smile falter.

"Uh-oh," she says. "What's wrong?"

"Nothing." I shake my head as though it will rid me of the negativity that's entered my mind.

Tessa's eyebrows knit together in concern. "It doesn't look like nothing."

"He doesn't know who I really am," I admit. "He said he doesn't care about my past. That now is all that matters. But somehow I don't think that sentiment applies with me."

"I see," Tessa empathises. "Look, there's no denying you've had a difficult past but you can't let that interfere with what's to come. It sounds like this guy understands that even better than you do. Tell him. You might be surprised."

"Maybe." I want to be as optimistic as Tessa, but the fear of losing EJ holds me back.

"So, tell me more about him. What's he like?"

I get Tessa up to speed on all the facts about EJ over a delicious pasta meal that she's cooked. I tell her about his sweet nature and his exceptional musical talents. I skim over the details of the amazing night we shared by the stream.

In typical Tessa fashion, she's thrilled for me. She expressed her excitement over me finding new, amazing friends at the café and a guy that had, in her words, 'brought the sunshine back.' Overall, we could both agree that even if it turned out to be temporary, taking the job at the Haven had been a positive move.

We put the leftovers in the fridge for Dad, for when he returns home from work. His assistant had left a message earlier saying that one of his routine surgeries had complications and would run longer than expected.

I help Tessa clean the kitchen and then after she leaves, I go up to my room and shower. I sprawl out over the king bed, suddenly feeling emotionally drained. I flick on the TV, trying to tune out the thoughts that crowd my brain.

I've become invested in an episode of Friends when my phone starts ringing. It's EJ. The same smile that filled my face earlier when I'd received his text doesn't come this time. Instead, my excitement is replaced with anxiety. Because I know the time is drawing closer when I'll have to be honest with him. Our relationship can't sustain any secrets.

I swipe the answer key. "Hello."

"Hey, beautiful!" EJ's voice is cheerful, though the background noise I expect to hear is non-existent. Maybe he's out in the store room.

"Hey. How are you?" I ask him.

"I'm better now that I'm talking to you."

"Oh, really?" I smile at that. "Hey, did you end up talking to Cayden yesterday?"

"No," he replies. "He never showed up and he didn't answer his phone."

I don't know why I'm relieved to hear this, but a part of me has seriously begun to think that Cayden could be dangerous. "Okay. Weird. Anyway, how's work?"

"It was boring."

"Was?" I ask. EJ usually works till at least eleven. "What do you mean? Where are you?"

"I'm standing outside your house."

"What?" I blurt out as I leap off the bed, pulling the curtains away from the window.

There he is, standing at the back of the house, peering up at my balcony.

"You're crazy! If my dad sees you lurking outside he'll kill you!"

"Is he even home?"

"Well, no but... How did you even get past the gate?"

He holds up his arms and cheekily flexes his biceps. Of course, he's athletic enough to climb an eight-foot-high fence.

"Aren't you going to let me in?"

"Give me a second." I sigh as I skip down the stairs two at a time. When I open the front door, he's all eyes and smiles.

There's no way I can be mad at him for this impromptu visit. I throw my arms around his neck and kiss him.

"Good to see you too," he says, as he kisses me back.

"Come on." I take his hand and lead him up the stairs to my bedroom.

"Wow." EJ stops in the doorway, surveying my room. I watch him, confused. "Sorry. I forgot how big your house actually is."

"Yeah. Well, it's a mansion. Bright and shiny and big," I say, sarcastically. It seems my cynicism is making a comeback.

EJ detects the change in my tone. "Are you okay?"

"Yeah, sorry." I sit down at the foot of my bed.

Friends still plays out on the TV. It's the infamous episode where Rachel discovers Ross has cheated while they were on a break.

"Holy shit! How big is your TV?"

"I don't know. One hundred inch or something." I'm not sure where the annoyance in my voice is coming from. In the past, I'd had people befriend me without the best intentions because I had money, but EJ has never struck me as one of those people. "Aren't you supposed to be working?"

"Yeah, but like I said in my last text, I was missing you."

He flops down beside me on the bed and butterflies stir in my gut. The only guy to ever enter my bedroom before was Sean and I had nowhere near the same feelings for him as I do for EJ. My mind skips back to the other night, when I'd gasped under his touch, unable to get enough of him.

'Wow. I'm a bad influence on you. Your dad is gonna hate me." I give a half-hearted laugh.

"Impossible," he says, leaning in so close I can feel his breath on my neck, as his lips scrape the skin under my jawline.

I want to kiss him back, to wrap my arms around him, because he is all of a sudden everything to me. The person who brings colour into my grayscale life. But my head is battling with my heart. How can I let this go further without being open with him about my past?

"You can't just leave work because it's boring, though," I argue.

"Well, look at you sounding all mature and shit!" he jokes, raising one eyebrow playfully. "I can actually. My dad's the boss. What's going on with you? Is everything okay?"

I sigh. "Sorry. It's not that I'm not happy to see you. It's just that I don't want you to get in trouble."

"Relax. Henley's covering for me. I told him I owe him one."

"Oh, okay. That's good." I'm relieved that he won't be getting in trouble, but this unexpected visit has put me on edge for some reason.

"Do you wanna hang out Friday night after our gig at the tavern?" His hand lightly strokes my face and he draws me in to kiss him.

"Okay," I murmur, then realising I can't, I pull away from him. "Oh, wait. I can't. I have this…family thing."

"Oh." He seems momentarily disappointed, then suddenly optimistic. "You know, parents love me. I could tag along. Make things less boring for you?"

He's full of hope, but I'm about to crush him. I say nothing and he withdraws from me, sensing my coldness. Tell him, Liv. Just tell him who your father is.

"I'm sorry. It's just this thing with my dad."

"And what? I'm some kind of secret you keep from your dad?"

"It's not like that." Another pang of guilt rips through me.

It's exactly like that.

"Okay. Sorry, but for someone who says they're happy to see me, you sure are acting like you want me to leave."

"I don't. It's just going to be this boring thing for my dad's work. Honestly, it's just a bunch of stuck-up rich snobs in a room vying for each other's approval."

"Oh, so I won't fit in. Is that it?" He's frustrated. He rubs the back of his neck and wanders over to the window.

"What? No!" I follow him as he steps out onto the balcony. Truthfully, he won't fit in, but that's exactly the reason I like him so much. "I mean, yes. You won't fit in, but that's a good thing. Trust me."

"Liv, I know we come from two different worlds. I just didn't know that it was ever going to be a problem." Despite his obvious discontent, EJ never raises his voice to me.

I'm stunned. My head fills with all the things I should say to him in this moment, but they're things once said, I can never take back. We do come from two different worlds, but I don't think he realises how different. I stay silent. Because that's what I do. I self-sabotage.

"You don't know me, EJ." I finally say, softly, unable to keep the sadness out of my voice.

"Yeah, and whose fault is that?" he questions. "No, screw that. I do know you. I know that you're beautiful. I know that you're smart and funny. I know how whenever you get nervous, you tuck your hair behind your ear. That when you care about someone, you'll do anything for them. Including jumping out of a plane. I know that you're so talented. God, when you played the piano that day… I've never seen anything like it."

My eyes sting with the threat of tears. EJ isn't finished.

253

"I know that you could do anything that you put your mind to, but I know that you're scared. And I know what you're doing right now. You're pushing me away because it's easier for you to shut people out than to let them in."

I stiffen at his words because they're true. If I let EJ be mad at me, then I'll never have to tell him the truth. It is easier to push him away. But there's nothing easy about watching the pain in his eyes and knowing that I'm the reason for it.

"Guess what, Liv? I'm not going anywhere. And you have a chance to be great. A chance that some people never get. Stop hiding from it."

A chance that some people never get.

He's referring to his sister. A soul taken too soon. Her dreams, whatever they may have been, never realised. I turn away, unable to look at him anymore, wiping tears from my flushed cheeks. I feel his hand on my shoulder and then he's in front of me.

"Liv, I'm sorry. I didn't mean that…" he trails off, his eyes shining like sea glass.

I don't want to hear his apology. I don't want him to take back the words I deserve to hear. But more than that, I'm angry. Angry at myself mostly, but angry at him for calling me out so blatantly. I'd always admired EJ for his honesty, but right now it seems cruel.

"What about you?!" I cry in frustration.

His brow furrows in confusion. "What about me?"

"Bruxfield?" I question him. If he's going to dish it, he has to learn to take it. "You have a chance too, and instead, you're hiding out here in some small-town bar." His jaw clenches as he swallows hard. He hangs his head, running a hand through his unkempt hair. "Yeah. I know about that." I say. I know it's not fair of me to throw this in his face.

"Okay. You got me. I got into Bruxfield. Over two years ago." He throws a hand up in the air in defeat and leans back to rest on the balcony. "It's three hundred kilometres away, Liv!"

"Are you ever going to go?"

"I used to think about it. About just packing up and leaving town. Getting as far away as I could from everything and everyone."

"Why haven't you?"

"My parents need me. And now, there's you."

"Don't do that. Don't put that on me," I spit, anger coursing through my veins. "Your parents might have needed you before, but I will not be the thing that holds you back."

"I'm sorry. That wasn't fair. I'm gonna go."

He brushes past me, storming back through the bedroom and down the stairs, not daring to look back in my direction. I hear the roar of his engine from the balcony, then the chugging of diesel as he drives off into the night.

And then I'm alone, my only company regret, and the gut-wrenching ache that guilt brings.

Chapter 27

OLIVIA

The whole town knows about my mother, and they've made up their small minds about me too. It came as no surprise to me when Sean dumped me. His connection to me would no longer help his chances of getting into Milton, and would no doubt ruin his reputation as well. My father's status is tarnished, so he doesn't need him anymore either.

What I really didn't bargain on though, was finding Sean's tongue thrust down Katerina's throat in the hallway of D block, Katerina's back hard up against her locker while Sean's left hand explored her thigh underneath her pleated skirt.

Fuck both of them. They deserve each other.

I take a seat in the corner of The Espresso Room, aware that I've never set foot in this café alone. I never went anywhere alone.

What has become of my life?

How did I get here?

I can't pinpoint the exact moment everything began to spiral. Was it when my mother was admitted to Rykers? Or was I already on this path long before?

Frustration and anger forge a path for sadness and despair. I don't want this life. I don't want to be here. I want a mother who isn't sick. I need a father that's around enough to notice that I'm drowning.

"Olivia!" The barista calls out, holding up my skinny latte.

When I stand up, I'm met with fifty pairs of eyes. Every single person in the room becomes fixated on me, their stares unnerving. The café falls silent, the only sound coming from my footsteps along the hardwood floor.

A trail of whispers follows me to the register, words and phrases that find my ears in random order.

"Elle Huxton's daughter…"

"….that's her…"

"She's an alcoholic…"

"….lied about…"

"…tried to kill herself…"

Oh, I'm suicidal now? That's news to my ears. It shouldn't shock me, considering these people have no shame in concocting bullshit theories about whoever's in their line of fire at any particular time.

Fuck them. Fuck all of these people.

I lift the cardboard cup to my lips, the hot liquid burning on its way down. I pause, my eyes preoccupied on the cup.

"Is something wrong?" the girl at the counter asks.

"Yeah," I answer. "I guess you forgot the shot of whiskey."

I turn to the wastebin in the corner and toss the cup at it. I miss and the light brown liquid splatters onto the stark white wall behind it in trails. Someone gasps from behind me.

Fuck this. I need a real drink.

Chapter 28

LIV

The Haven is quiet the next day. Carla had taken it as the perfect opportunity to have Kristen and I train a new waitress up on the register. Her name is Gwen and she's Sammy's replacement.

So far, Kristen has done most of the talking, and I've fumbled my way through the morning with a persistent frown on my face. I sensed that Kristen knew my depressive state had something to do with EJ, but she hasn't had an opening to ask me about it.

I'd barely slept last night. My head was a mashup of all the hurtful words EJ and I had thrown at each other. I truly feel sick to the stomach about it.

I zone out again for the millionth time today, when Kristen bangs on the counter with a spoon to get my attention. My head shoots up in her direction. "Liv! It's time for your morning tea break."

I glance at the clock. "What do you mean? It's only nine thirty." I don't usually take my break until ten.

Kristen nods to the far window where EJ leans his shoulder up against the glass, watching us. He waves a hand, gesturing for me to come outside. My breath hitches at the sight of him, and in my hurry to get to him, I don't even bother to take off my apron. In an instant, I'm standing in front of him.

"I'm sorry," we both blurt at the same time.

I breathe a sigh of relief, knowing he feels the same way as I do. My pulse races and there's a fluttering in my gut. A grin surfaces on EJ's face as he combs his fingers through his hair.

"I'm sorry for bringing up Bruxfield. It was wrong of me and really insensitive and I'm a jerk…"

"No." EJ cuts me off. "I'm the jerk. I shouldn't have questioned the plans you have with your dad. I feel like an idiot about how I acted. I didn't mean to hurt you, Liv."

"It's okay. You were only telling the truth." I'd be lying if I said the things he said to me weren't hurtful, but they were things I needed to hear.

"Well, maybe when I said you were smart and beautiful and talented…"

"Shut up," I cut him off, teasingly, throwing my arms around his neck and bringing my lips to his.

He reciprocates, pulling me in tight, his mouth lingering over mine. I wince at the thought of never being kissed by EJ again. Our lips part, but he keeps me close, holding me against him.

"I never want to let you go." His tone is playful, but his expression serious. I can feel his chest rising and falling, his racing heart beating against mine.

"Then don't," I whisper.

"I wish I didn't have to, but my shift starts soon. I've gotta work a double. I owe this guy for covering for me so I could see this really hot girl last night."

"I hope she was worth it."

"She's always worth it. I totally blew it though." EJ's face fills with genuine remorse. It hurts me to see him at war with himself.

"No, you didn't." I take his face in my hands and kiss him again. Then I rest my forehead on his chest. "I'm gonna have to get back in there before Carla cracks it. Can I see you later?"

"I'll be working late, but I can call you."

"Okay," I answer. "I'd like that. Don't forget."

"Never," he replies, releasing me from his embrace.

I instantly miss his arms around me, but reluctantly return to my place behind the counter at the Haven.

"Thank God you sorted whatever the hell that was out!" Kristen comes from behind me with a refill of Greek salad. "I've never seen anyone so depressed."

"Sorry," I cringe.

"I meant EJ. He was watching you like a little lost puppy through that glass."

I roll my eyes and slap her arm playfully, almost causing her to drop the salad tongs. "Stop!"

"I'm just kidding," she laughs. "But are you guys okay?"

"Yeah. We're good." At least I think we are. There's still the unresolved issue of having EJ meet my dad, but I have a plan for that in place. I'll get through the benefit and then I'll arrange for them to meet soon. "Where's Gwen?"

"Just on break. I don't think we've scared her off yet," she jokes. As if Kristen could scare anyone away. She's the friendliest, most accommodating co-worker in the world.

It isn't long before a rush of customers scramble in for lunch, making the rest of the working hours fly by in a blur. When the bustling of people and the clattering of plates finally dies down, it's almost time to close up.

"You better get going before the storm hits," Carla suggests. "You don't want to get caught out half way up the mountain."

"Are you sure? I still have another half hour left," I say, squinting at my watch.

"Yes. I think it would be best. This storm is supposed to be a big one. There's a severe weather warning."

"Okay. Thanks Carla." She may have been agitated with me these last few days, but her kindness and compassion never fail to shine through. I'm blessed to have a boss that cares about my well-being.

A chilly gust of wind hits me when I step out onto the sidewalk and I hear the rumbling of thunder in the distance. I think of EJ, busy at work behind the bar. Happiness surges through me at the thought that he'll be calling me soon.

Large, fat raindrops fall ahead of me on the pavement and I quicken my pace, eager to make it to the car before the downpour soaks me thoroughly. I round the corner, but in my haste, I collide with someone coming from the intersecting street. His tall frame jolts me, sending my bag to the ground.

"Ouch," I say, reaching for the throbbing pain in my shoulder.

"Stupid bitch. Watch where you're going." His tone sends shivers down my spine, the familiarity puzzling.

I scramble to gather the contents of my bag together, then rise up to stand tall against his hostility. Cayden glares down on me with hatred in his eyes.

"What's your problem?" I ask him. "It was an accident."

I'm trying to sound brave, even though he intimidates me more than anyone I've ever known. I can sympathise with what he's been through in the past, but it doesn't give him the right to walk all over me.

"You're my problem," he spits. The scent of alcohol lingers on his breath.

"Whatever," I mutter, readjusting my bag strap over my shoulder.

"You think you're so smart, don't you? You think you've got everyone fooled." He fights against the wind to keep the dark strands of hair out of his eyes.

"What?" It's getting increasingly difficult to hide my fear.

"I remembered where I know you from." He's smiling now, but it's more of a grimace, mean and ugly.

"I don't know what you're talking about," I state, honestly.

"Yes, you do," he scowls. "Stay the fuck away from EJ. You're no good for him."

With that, he shoves past me, knocking my shoulder forcefully again with his own. I can't deny that his words have left me rattled. Where is it he thinks he knows me from? It's impossible. I'd never set foot in Cliff Haven until a few months ago. And he's obviously inebriated. This has to be a case of mistaken identity.

I've never seen him before.

Right?

Chapter 29

OLIVIA

The tiles are cold beneath me. I see the white porcelain of the freestanding bath tub in the corner. My cheek is pressed to the fluffy, white bath mat.

The room slopes, swimming to and fro, like a ship on a stormy sea. I don't know how long I've been lying here. I don't know how much time has passed since the aching turned to euphoria turned to disorientation, but somehow I've found myself unwilling to move. Unwilling or unable, I'm not sure.

How did I get here?

Why am I here?

The answers don't come. I roll onto my back. My right arm flings violently onto the ceramic tiles.

It doesn't hurt.

Why doesn't it hurt?

My fingertips touch on something, and the ping of glass echoes throughout the bathroom. I reach for the bottle, grasping it with weak hands, and draw it to my mouth.

Only a single, tiny drop of moisture falls onto my bottom lip and I lick the bitter liquid away.

I'm tired. So tired. But when I close my eyes, the darkness churns and bile rises in my throat. My head was a freight train earlier, loaded with fear, doubt, anger. Now it's empty.

Numb.

A voice, muffled, as though underwater, gets louder with every breath I take. The words are indecipherable. What is it saying?

"Olivia, what did you do?"

"Nothing."

"Olivia! Did you take anything?"

"No."

"Did you drink this whole bottle?"

My head lulls in an attempt to nod. My eyes roll, allowing only glimpses of the person that hovers over me.

Tessa?

"I'm here, Olivia. I'm going to help you."

Don't.

"It's all going to be okay."

No. It's not.

Nothing will ever be okay again.

Chapter 30

LIV

When morning arrives, no sunshine pries its way through the slats of my shutters, filling the room with its golden glow. Instead, there's an eery gloom occupying the space, and the pitter patter of heavy rain dancing on the rooftop. The storms were set to last through till this evening and I have no intention of leaving my bed in a hurry, having not been rostered on at the café.

Cayden's words had kept me awake last night. I know it's stupid to let a drunken asshole get to me like this. He clearly has no idea what he's talking about. But still something about the whole situation seems off.

EJ never called me last night. And he never answered the text messages I sent to him asking if he was alright. Our relationship is new, but I can't help feeling as though this is totally out of character for him, especially after our conversation outside the café yesterday. I don't want to seem like a stage five clinger, but it's driving me insane not knowing if something has happened to him. Storms always seem to bring out the anxiety in me. I send him one more message, promising myself that if he doesn't reply, it will be my last.

Me: *EJ, I'm worried about you. At least let me know you're okay.*

Half an hour goes by. Then an hour. Then two.

I'm sinking with every minute that goes by. Then there's a knock at the door. My heart skips in my chest at the possibility it could be him, but a quick glance at our security camera shows Tessa's small frame. She isn't meant to work today, although I welcome the distraction.

Throwing open the front door, I fling my arms around her neck. "Tessa! I've missed you so much." Besides our brief encounter the other night, I've barely seen much of Tessa since I started working.

"Aww. Liv, I've missed you too," she replies. "That's why I'm here."

"What about Mila? Doesn't she have dance lessons this afternoon?" I ask. Tessa is a busy woman and I hate to think she's giving up time with her family to check up on me.

"She does, but she's with her dad. I don't see you as often now that you're working so I thought I'd stop by."

"You are such an angel," I say. She truly is the greatest human I've ever known. "Come on in. I was just watching TV."

"Ha! Of course, you were! It's your favourite thing to do on rainy days."

I don't mention that I'm hardly paying attention to the screen. That instead, my mind is occupied, wondering what the hell could have possibly happened, for the guy I've begun to tear down my walls for to go radio silent on me. Or that I've turned into some kind of psycho stalker girlfriend type that plays out so many scenarios in her head, probably none of which are close to the actual truth.

"Your dad's at work, I assume?" she questions.

"Yeah. I kind of slept late, but he left a note. He has a big surgery, but hopes to be home before dinner tonight."

"That's good. That will be nice."

"Yeah," I answer. "As long as he doesn't try to cook again."

Tessa lets out a hearty laugh, then her tone softens. "He's trying. He really does mean well."

"Yeah, I know."

"But in case he fixes you something totally inedible tonight, why don't I fill you up on some chilli cheese fries for lunch. We need some comfort food in weather like this!" Tessa puts her handbag down on the counter and heads straight over to preheat the oven.

"You don't have to do that Tessa." Another pang of guilt resonates with me at the thought of her own family missing her today.

"Nonsense!" she exclaims. "It will be fun! We need a girl's day! Go on and choose a movie and I'll get these fries in the oven."

Tessa ushers me over to the living room. We have a huge home theatre room set up like a cinema with surround sound and leather reclining arm chairs, but Tessa knows me well enough to know that I'm more comfortable on the sofa, curled up with a blanket and whatever delicious comfort food she'll feed me.

She spoils me. It hurts to think that she does more for me than my own mother ever did. But it's true. One day, when Mum was having one of her manic episodes, she'd arrived home, probably from the arms of another man. She'd neglected to pick me up from school on the wettest day we'd had all year when my car had been put in for a service. I'd walked all the way home in the downpour. She'd barged through the front door, only minutes behind me, disregarding my rain-soaked hair and the droplets of water that fell from the hem of my skirt into a puddle on the marble below. I waited for her to notice, to apologise. Instead, she told me to make a start on dinner. And that she needed to have a shower because she was freezing. Despite those awful days, I still long to have her back here with me. I would give anything.

The scent of melted cheese and crispy bacon travels to my nostrils. "Just a few more minutes!" Tessa calls. "Have you picked a movie yet?"

"Almost," I lie.

I steal a glance at my phone on the arm of the sofa. Still no reply from EJ. What is his deal? I shake the thought aside and begin flicking through channels. I log into Netflix, hoping to have better luck choosing something.

I'm not sure how long I absentmindedly scroll through the menu before Tessa rounds the corner into the living room, carrying two plates of the most delectable carbohydrate meals, laden with three different kinds of cheese. She sets one in my lap and then takes her position on the sofa next to me.

"This looks amazing, Tessa. You've outdone yourself again," I stab at the cheesy fries with my fork and revel in their taste. I realise now that I'm starving, having skipped breakfast.

"What's going on, Liv?" Tessa asks, concern crossing her features.

"Huh?" I manage to say through a mouthful of crunchy potato.

Tessa nods toward the screen. "That 70's show?"

I hadn't even realised I'd put it on, but sure enough there was Eric Foreman and the gang hanging out in the basement,

Kitty's piercing laughter cutting through the air. Tessa knows me too well. She knows I watch this show when I need cheering up.

I sigh. "It's EJ."

"The boy from the bar? What's he done?" she asks, taking a bite of her fries.

"Yeah. The boy from the bar," I confirm.

"Why do you seem so sad? What happened? Did you talk to him about your past?"

"Not exactly." I don't want to go into all the gory details of our fight, so I fill Tessa in briefly. "I wanted to tell him, but I ended up going into self-sabotage mode and we had an argument. But then we made up, and he was supposed to call me last night but he didn't. He's not even answering any of my messages."

"Well, it sounds like you sorted everything out if you made up."

"I thought so."

"As for EJ ghosting you, there could be a million reasons why he hasn't replied. Maybe he lost his phone."

I smirk at Tessa's use of the word 'ghosting'. "I don't know. Maybe."

As if on cue, my phone screen lights up on the sofa arm beside me. He's finally texted back.

EJ: *I'm sorry. Phone trouble. I'm okay. Got really busy last night.*

His words are blunt and to the point, but void of feeling. At least it's a partial explanation. At least he's okay. It's highly possible that the bar was packed out last night and he couldn't get away to call or text. That doesn't, however, explain why it has taken until almost two in the afternoon to text me today when he isn't working. Or why his temperament has gone from scorching hot to ice cold.

269

Chapter 31

OLIVIA

"She's fine. She had a bad day. That's all." My mother's whispers are louder than she intends them to be, I'm sure.

"She isn't fine, Elle. She is on a very dangerous path."

I crouch on the staircase as Tessa comes into view in the lobby, torn between whether to keep listening to this conversation or run back to my room and bury my head under the blankets.

"Tessa, she's a teenager. Teenagers do dramatic, stupid things. She broke up with her boyfriend, but she's strong-willed. She'll get through this," my mother says.

"She drank so much she had to have her stomach pumped! She's lucky I found her when I did!"

I shudder. Although I don't remember much about the ambulance ride or being admitted, the burning in my windpipe remains a constant reminder of the tubes that had been force fed down my oesophagus, clawing their way to the pit of my gut.

When I'd awoken the next morning in my hospital bed, with the crunchy, white sheets beneath my limp body, and the worst headache of my life, Tessa had been the one to hold my hand and tell me everything was going to be okay. My parents had been there too, she'd told me, but I guess life goes on. Dad had to go to work. Mum had to be wherever it was that she went these days.

"I really think you should talk to her. She needs her mother right now. She needs guidance," Tessa continues.

I watch as my mother fusses over her Gucci belt in the wall length mirror, still unseen from the top of the stairs. She pulls out her lipstick, painting her pout a deep crimson, then tosses it back into her bag.

"Alright, alright. I'll have a chat with her when I get back, okay?" she mutters, as she reaches for the front door handle. "But I'm sure this isn't the crisis situation you're imagining, Tessa."

Only when the door has firmly clicked shut behind her, does Tessa turn around. A sigh escapes her lips and her hand goes to her forehead. She's visibly stressed and a twinge of shame squeezes my chest knowing I'm the reason for it. Having a conscience is emotionally draining.

She does a double take when she catches a glimpse of my hunched over frame on the staircase.

"Olivia, how long have you been sitting there?"

"Long enough," I respond, my voice still hoarse from the tubes.

"I'm sorry. You know your mother loves you, right?" Tessa begins to climb the stairs, stopping halfway up.

"She has a funny way of showing it," I reply.

"She has a lot on her plate right now, what with adjusting to this new medication and all. None of that changes how she feels about you though."

I give a small nod in Tessa's direction, but I don't say anything.

"Have you given any more thought to doing those therapy sessions at Ryker's?" Tessa asks.

Ever since I drank myself into oblivion, Tessa has been trying to get me to go to therapy. My father has arranged for one of the top psychologists from Rykers to treat me with some one-on-one sessions. She's the same doctor that diagnosed Mum. I can deny needing treatment all I want, but the real reason I don't want to go is because I'm terrified she will find something wrong with me. I'm afraid she'll tell me I'm exactly like my mother.

"No," I say quietly, with a small shake of my head.

"Alright. You know my thoughts on it, but I won't keep pressuring you. I have to go now, but I want you to call me if you need anything. Anything at all. Okay?"

Tessa had said this exact thing to me every time she'd gone home from her shift for the past three days since my return from the hospital, and while it's excruciatingly repetitive, it helps to know that she cares. It seems she's the only one who does. Yet, I still haven't found it in me to thank her for saving my life the other night.

I nod again and a sympathetic frown fills her features. "It will be okay, Liv. I know it doesn't seem like it right now, but the clouds will part. You will see the sun again."

Her kind words instil in me something I don't recognise at first.

Hope.

I fling myself forward onto the landing and throw my arms around her. "Thank you, Tessa," my words come out whispered, a silent tear running downward to my chin.

Tessa's hug is warm and I didn't know how much I needed it until now.

"Try and have a chat with your mum when she gets back, okay?" she says.

I nod again, although I don't hold out much hope for a heart to heart with my mother. Tessa smiles as she descends the stairs, and gives a wave before exiting through the front door, leaving me with nothing but the whirlwind of thoughts that sweep through my mind.

My mother's downplay of recent events no longer phases me. My concern no longer lies with the way in which I'd handled my life imploding.

I know the facts. I drank way too much. I didn't mean to. I just wanted it all to go away. The rumours. The pain. The image of Katerina, her fingers sliding under Sean's belt that has played on repeat in my head. I know I went too far, but now I know my limits. It won't happen again.

What does concern me are the answers to the burning questions that no one is asking. Like, how did I have an almost full bottle of alcohol in my possession, when my father had rid the house of it during my mother's stay at Ryker's?

Only two people know the answer. Only two people could know, that when I went to my mother's closet to return a pair of Louboutin's that I'd borrowed without asking, that the top of a vodka bottle peeking out from a knee-high boot might grab my attention.

But the questions that plague me most are the ones surrounding my mother's condition.

Why is it taking so long for her to adjust to her medication?

Why is her mental state vastly different to when she'd first returned home from Ryker's?

Why is her current behaviour seeming more and more like her old behaviour, the way she was before she was even prescribed medication?

Is there anyone besides me that suspects she isn't taking her medication at all?

Chapter 32

LIV

EJ is avoiding me. That's the conclusion I drew from the facts I'd learned at the Haven on Friday morning, but what I can't figure out is why. When I'd asked Kristen if she'd seen or heard from EJ yesterday, her answer had been vague, but weird.

"Yeah I saw him across the street sometime in the morning. Cayden was with him. It kinda looked like they were arguing," she'd said.

"Arguing? Why would they be arguing?" I'd questioned.

"Who knows with those two? Their personalities clash all the time. They've kinda always fought like brothers." Kristen had answered matter-of-factly, then shrugged it off like it was no big deal. "They'll sort it out. They always do."

Maybe it's true that they butt heads on occasion, but my takeaway from all of this is that EJ had time to fight with Cayden yesterday, yet couldn't seem to find ten seconds to send me a quick text. A sick feeling boils in my stomach remembering my altercation with Cayden the other day. He'd told me to stay away from EJ. But why?

I push the negativity aside. I have other things to focus on today. Among the fact that a mass of customers has just stormed the café, my dad's charity gala is tonight. I hadn't really thought too much about it, but now that the day is upon us, anxiety is setting in. The last one of these functions I'd attended had been well over a year ago and, much to my father's dismay, I'd hidden out in the corner of the balcony from view. Mostly because I couldn't stand to hear the whispers. It seemed everybody in Hampton Ridge had an opinion about me and my parents. I never understood how my father never let it get to him.

When I arrive home that afternoon, Tessa is out the front polishing the frosted glass window panes in the front door. "Your father is in the shower. The limo is coming at 5pm."

I wince. "Thanks, Tessa."

"Hey," she says, placing a gentle hand on my shoulder. "Maybe it won't be that bad."

I shoot her a cynical look, which she counters with a sympathetic one. She knows of my reluctance to go, but understands my need to attend in support of my dad.

"What's this event for anyway?" Tessa asks.

"I think it's to raise money to support medical care for the homeless. Dad mentioned something about opening up another clinic outside the city somewhere." The old Olivia wouldn't have had a clue about which cause the benefits she attended were for.

Maybe I have changed after all.

"That's definitely something worth supporting. Good luck tonight." Tessa picks up the bucket of cleaning products and heads into the washroom.

"Thanks," I mutter, then I make my way upstairs for a shower.

Allowing the hot water to melt away the day, I attempt to let go of my worries about EJ, temporarily at least, while I envision the night ahead. I focus my energy into helping the cause. Like Tessa had said, it definitely is a worthy one.

I suddenly wish I could do more in support of it than just show up to a fancy ballroom and eat canapes off a silver tray. Of course, there would be the silent auction, and I could make a donation, but there has to be more that I can offer. An idea begins to form in my head.

I shut off the water and wrap a towel around myself. Throwing open the doors of my ridiculously huge closet, I survey the rack of designer gowns and the stacks of designer shoes that line the top shelves. Some have been worn once. Most had been gifted to me, or collected from my mum's visits to fashion week shows and have never been worn before at all.

How is it possible that I own tens of thousands of dollars' worth of designer couture hanging in a closet, untouched, while there are people in the world struggling to visit a doctor when sick, or refusing to accept referrals to specialists because they simply can't afford the care? How is it possible that there are homeless people at all?

A sense of revulsion emerges from within me as I sift through the dresses, their contrasting fabrics swaying together in unison. Tom Ford, Valentino, Armani, Gucci, Chanel. I could choose to wear any one of these gowns tonight, but I have a better idea in mind.

I scoop armfuls of dresses together and hoist them off the rack, throwing them down in a pile in the middle of the dressing room. These gowns are not me anymore, and I refuse to wear a single one of them.

Instead, I reach for the one dress that represents me best. The simple black sundress Kristen had spotted in the window of the boutique store down from the Haven hangs in the far corner of the wardrobe. We'd ducked into the shop one day after closing and I'd bought it. It's the only dress in this closet that I purchased with my own hard-earned money, and for that reason, it means the most to me.

I stare down at the pile on the floor, an entanglement of satin, silk, leather, sequins, and lace in different hues. Then I hurry down the stairs, my right hand gripping the railing as I jump the last couple of steps, and burst through to the kitchen. I rummage in the cupboard under the sink until I find a wad of extra-large heavy duty garbage bags, then on returning to my closet I begin scooping the gowns into it. It takes four large garbage bags to contain them, and an extra one for the shoes.

I shuffle to the edge of the staircase, wrestling a bag in each hand, then launch each one over the banister. I glance over the edge, watching as they fall to the lobby below.

"Aargh!" Tessa shrieks. The fourth bag must have only just missed her.

"Oops! Sorry, Tessa!" I call.

"Olivia, what is going on? What is in these bags?" My dad's voice echoes through the lobby and carries up the stairs.

"It's for the homeless!" I shout down to him.

He shoots a suspicious look at Tessa, who then shrugs back at him. He loosens one of the garbage bag ties and peers inside.

"I'm not sure the homeless have much use for designer formalwear."

"Well, sell them off in the auction or something and donate the money to them. I don't need them," I say, stubbornly.

He smiles up at me, then with a resigned look, he turns to Tessa. "Tessa, can you please arrange an urgent courier to have these bags taken to the Cape Edison ballroom?"

"Of course, Mr. Petersen," Tessa replies politely, before scurrying off into the kitchen.

"Olivia, you better finish getting ready. The car will be here in ten." My father follows after Tessa, fidgeting with his neck tie.

Back in my room, I check myself in the reflection of the floor length mirror. I comb my hands through my straight dark-brown hair and apply some mascara and tinted lip gloss.

The girl that stares back at me is different, but for just a second, I see her. I see the other version. I see her face, concealed by too much makeup, her bright platinum hair pinned uncomfortably. She wears a shiny ballgown and spins in her highest heels.

People love her.

They want to be her.

She thinks she's happy and confident, but she is naive. She isn't me, but she's within me. She'll always be there, haunting, but it's time to leave her behind. I blink away her image, vowing to learn from the lessons she taught me.

"Olivia! The car's here." I hear my father call.

"Okay. I'll be right there!" I say, as I pull on a pair of flat sandals and rush downstairs.

"Is that what you are wearing?" Dad asks.

"Um, yes," I reply nervously, wondering if he's going to march me back upstairs and have me change.

Instead, he smiles. "You look different. I like it."

"Thanks." I accept his compliment and then reach up to adjust his crooked tie.

"Come on, the limo is waiting."

"Why do we have to go in a limo?" I ask him as we pass Tessa at the front door. "I could just drive us."

"The foundation takes care of us, Olivia."

My father's response is ironic. I thought we were supposed to be taking care of the foundation.

Dad's regular chauffer, Elliot, awaits us at the limo door. I steal a glance back at Tessa as I climb inside. She waves and gives me a thumbs up. I smile timidly and return the gesture.

Once seated, my father takes a cracker from the grazing plate that has been arranged for us. I usually didn't eat in the limo, but my stomach is rumbling from having not eaten much throughout the day, so I pick up a cracker and top it with a slice of brie.

The gala is being held inside the ballroom of the Cape Edison Clubhouse; a country club situated right on the beaches of the cape on the northern outskirts of Milton. I prefer the airy seaside location to the claustrophobic city. It would offer a much better view when I needed to escape outside from the whispers and taunts.

My dad uses the forty-minute car ride to fill me in on the specifics of the purpose of tonight's gala. He explains the importance of supporting the medical needs of the homeless, and how they're hoping to raise enough money to open up another free clinic outside the city, based on the success of the clinic that has been up and running in the inner city for the past year.

It arms me with a new appreciation for my father and his work. I'm proud of him for all of his accomplishments and impressed by his ability to help so many people. It dawns on me how selfish I've been to criticize him for never being home. While it's true that his absence hasn't helped our family situation, his passion for his work has been what has helped so many. And I know that he is a good and honest man, a trait that a lot of other money-hungry jerks in powerful positions lack.

The limousine comes to a standstill at the doors of the clubhouse, and we are ushered into the ballroom by Susannah, one of my father's personal assistants. Crystal tableware and vases of peonies adorn the room, and elaborate glass pendant lights hang suspended above every table. The floor to ceiling windows boast a 180-degree view of the ocean, the sun disappearing halfway beyond the horizon in a violet and auburn sky.

A throng of Hampton Ridge housewives crowd an oyster tower in the corner, no doubt gossiping about whichever one of their posse hasn't arrived yet. Their husbands, the pompous men in designer suits, prattle on about God only knows what meaningless bullshit as they sip from champagne flutes. As if any of them cared to ponder what it would be like to be homeless. Hypocrites.

I catch sight of Bryce Lundgren and my breath hitches in my throat. I'd forgotten all about the fact that Sean would most likely be here, and my father had neglected to mention anything about it either. Bryce wanders over in our direction.

"Olivia, nice to see you," he says, gruffly, eyeing me up and down. *Oh please, spare me the pleasantries.* "If you wouldn't mind, I'd like to discuss a few things with your father."

Dad nods once at Bryce, then to me he says, "This will just take a minute."

This is the part where I'm left standing awkwardly on my own. My nerves get the better of me, the single cracker and slice of cheese churning in my gut. I used to have Katerina to entertain me at these events. We would steal champagne and guzzle it like water, our parents none the wiser. They were too wrapped up in themselves to pay any mind.

"Hey, you came." Sean's voice resonates over my shoulder.

"I'm just here to support my dad, Sean." I surprise myself with how firmly and confidently I speak to him.

"Fair enough," Sean says. "Look, I want to apologise for ambushing you at the café that day. It was wrong of me to come looking for you. Your dad mentioned that you worked there and I don't know… I guess I was curious."

"About what?"

"Your dad said you had changed. I guess I just wanted to see what he meant. And when I saw you, well, I couldn't help myself. What can I say? I like your new look. You're hot." Sean rubs the back of his neck and turns his eyes toward the ground. Is Sean Lundgren actually nervous around me?

I raise my eyebrows at his admission. I'm not sure which shocks me more; the fact that he stated so blatantly that he thinks I'm hot, or the part where my dad had told him I'd changed.

"My dad said I'd changed?" I can't help wondering exactly what he means by that.

"Yeah. And once we started talking that day, I realised he was right."

"Oh." My tone is one of disappointment.

"I meant in a good way. You've changed in a good way," Sean blurts, as though needing to rectify his comment.

"Okay," I say, sceptically.

"I mean that. You called me on all my bullshit that day. I don't blame you. I deserved it. Your dad told me he was worried about you taking on that job in the café in a different town, but I knew as soon as you opened your mouth that you were taking charge of your own life. I knew you were going to be okay."

These words right here are probably the nicest ones Sean has ever spoken to me.

'Thanks, Sean. That actually means a lot."

"It's the truth."

"Have you heard anything from Katerina lately?" I'm slowly discovering a new found respect for Sean, but I'm not going to let him off the hook that easily.

"No, I told you. That ended before it begun." Sean looks away guiltily. "But I did hear that she was in Europe somewhere, trying to start her own fashion label. I'm not sure how that's working out for her though."

I roll my eyes in response. Knowing Katerina and the lengths she'll go to in order to get her way, I figure her fashion dream probably isn't too far from realisation. I wonder if she'll be able to sleep at night when it does, and if there'll be anyone left to keep her warm.

"For what it's worth," Sean reaches for my hand and holds it firmly. "I really am sorry. For everything."

I nod. "Me too. For everything."

Sean smiles, then letting go of my hand, he drapes his arms around me. His embrace feels more genuine than ever before, and I find a certain comfort in his arms knowing that we've forgiven each other, and ourselves, for the mistakes we made in the past.

But it also makes me long for EJ. I miss him holding me.

"Ahem. We've gotten your mother's attention." I clear my throat loudly as Carol Lundgren swaggers toward us, no doubt having a major freak out that her son is about to make the biggest mistake of his life by getting involved with me again.

"Olivia, darling!" she exclaims, her voice friendly, her expression evil bitch mode. God, she's so fake.

"Hello, Mrs. Lundgren," I say, unfurling myself from Sean's grasp.

I could be polite to the woman, but I will never forgive her for the hurtful things she said about my mum after her death, or what she'd said about me for that matter.

"How are you? How are your studies treating you?"

"I'm not studying, Mrs. Lundgren. I'm working as a waitress." I say, partly because it's the truth, but mostly to get a rise out of her.

"A waitress!" She doesn't even try to keep the disgust from her tone. "Oh well, I suppose someone has to take care of the rest of us educated folk. Have you heard how well Sean's been doing in medical school?"

I nod, my mouth clamped together in a straight line. Sean is then summoned away by another guy in a suit, leaving me cornered by his awful mother.

"Did Sean tell you? His younger brother has been accepted into business school, too!" Carol has no shame. Her bragging is incessant.

"Oh, he didn't!" I reply in my best superficial tone. "How lovely for him! He always was quite boring so I suppose that suits him to a tee." I flash a fake smile her way, then strut toward the oyster tower, leaving Carol Lundgren confused.

She's just as dumb as she is fake.

It's times like these that I can relate to Tolstoy. I mean, the man abandoned a life of wealth to live among the poor. The guy was definitely on to something.

I search the room for my father, only to find him standing a few feet away from where I'd been talking to Carol. Some old guy with a bald head and a monobrow is deep in conversation with him, but his eyes are on mine. I catch a glimpse of something in them. Is it sympathy? Or annoyance? Did he hear my sarcastic remarks? My mind shifts back to my conversation with Sean, when he'd told me my dad had said I'd changed. I'd been right all along. He was disappointed in me.

A few moments later, my father takes to the stage to deliver a speech about tonight's valuable cause. He outlines the foundation's plans to support the medical needs of the homeless, introducing some other important people involved with the gala. He also explains the rules of the silent auction, of which the items have been set up along the back wall. My dresses are exhibited elegantly on mannequins, and I wonder how they'd managed to get them displayed so exquisitely with such short notice.

After my father descends from the stage, I step out onto the balcony for a much-needed deep breath. I draw my phone from my clutch purse. My heart skips a beat when I see a text from EJ.

Ever since he'd gone silent the other night, our texts have been short and strangely impersonal. I'd began to fear he wanted nothing to do with me anymore, that maybe he'd reconsidered his apology for our fight, but this text seems a little more promising.

EJ: *I hope you're having a good night. Miss you x*
Me: *I miss you too. I made a mistake not letting you tag along.*

I suddenly wish so badly that he was here. I wonder what he would think of these people. EJ is so polite and kind, he'd probably just take it all in his stride. I was stupid to think he would judge me for coming here to support my dad. I think back to what he'd said at the stream, when he'd told me that he knows who I am now, and that the past version doesn't matter.

The weight of a hand on my shoulder startles me and I spin around quickly.

"Dad!" I gasp. "You scared me."

"Sorry," he says sympathetically. "Trying to escape already?"

"No… I…" I hesitate, failing to concoct an excuse in my head. He knows me too well.

"It must be hard. Seeing Sean and his parents after all this time," he states.

"Actually, it was okay. Sean and I worked everything out. A kind of truce, I guess."

"And Carol?" he asks, a stern look on his face.

"You heard that, huh?" I hang my head in shame. I'd come here to be there for him. The last thing I wanted to do was upset him.

"Why don't you get out of here? The limo is downstairs. It will take you wherever you want to go."

"Seriously?" I'm dumbfounded. He's been trying for months to get me to attend one of these benefits, and now suddenly I'm off the hook.

"Yes. Go. I'm sorry for dragging you along." His expression is unreadable. "The truth is you really don't belong here."

My heart sinks. "You're angry with me. I'm a disappointment."

"No, Olivia. I'm not disappointed in you. I'm proud of you."

"What?" Now I'm confused.

"It means a lot to me that you wanted to come along and support me, but I can see how uncomfortable you are. I'm sorry for putting you in this position. You're better than these people, Olivia. I want more for you."

"Sean said you told him that I'd changed."

"Yeah," he admits. "I did say that. You have changed. You're living again. I know life hasn't been easy these past few years, but watching you go out there and forge your own path, I couldn't be prouder. I know you're still trying to find your place. Take my advice. Don't choose money over what you're really passionate about."

All this time, I thought he wanted me to have a prestigious career, or to follow in his footsteps. It never occurred to me that he could be proud of me for just being me.

"Thanks, Dad." A surge of tears stings the back of my eyes, but at least this time, they're happy tears.

"You know, enrolments are still open for that music school."

"Dad," I warn him. "Don't push it."

He smiles. "Go on, get out of here. Go find that boyfriend of yours."

"You know about EJ?" I ask, bewildered, then at the same time, we both say, "Tessa."

I reach out and hug him tightly. "Thankyou."

I rush back through the crowded room and burst into the lobby. I can't leave this clubhouse fast enough. The limo is waiting out front, as promised. I throw open the back door, almost scaring Elliot to death.

"Elliot, can you take me home?"

"Sure thing, Miss Petersen," he responds, slightly breathless and still clutching at his heart in shock. "Your father is alright with this arrangement?"

"Yeah," I reply. "It was his idea."

"The night is still young. Are you sure you want to go home?" he asks, as he pulls out onto a busy city street in the direction of Hampton Ridge.

I run the calculations in my head. It's only 8:15pm. EJ's band will be on in fifteen minutes. I could possibly make the end of their set. I need to see him. It's time to tell him the truth.

"Elliot, do you think you could drive me into Cliff Haven?"

"Sure," he nods.

"Thanks."

We hit heavy traffic on the way out of Milton and I start to worry that I'll miss the gig entirely. Would EJ even want me to turn up unannounced like this? I have to assume that from his last message he isn't angry at me anymore, and that this whole avoiding me scenario has been a figment of my imagination. I become so impatient in the back of the limo, I have to sit on my own hands. Every minute is like an hour. After what seems like an eternity, we're finally winding our way down the mountain.

"Alright, Miss Petersen," Elliot calls to me from the front. "We're approaching Cliff Haven. Where do you want me to take you?"

"There's a bar in the main street called Steve's Tavern."

"I know the one," he replies, as we drive down the esplanade.

Elliot pulls over outside the tavern as Kristen and Sammi are coming out the door. Henley leans against the exterior wall, Cayden beside him with a cigarette pursed between his lips.

Even with the long tendrils of hair that fall on his face, there's no mistaking the cold black stare he aims in my direction when I open the back door of the limo. I don't have time for him right now. I have to find EJ.

"Kristen!" I shout.

Kristen and Sammi do a double take when they see me in the limousine, their mouths hanging open in amazement. "Liv? What are you doing? Where have you been?"

"Have you guys seen EJ?"

"Yeah, he left straight after the set. Said he wasn't in the mood to party. I thought you had a family thing." Kristen's face is a picture of genuine confusion.

"Yeah, I did. Did he say where he was going?" I know Kristen and Sammi deserve clarification on this whole situation too, but EJ is my priority right now.

"I think he just went home." Kristen shrugs.

"Okay, thanks." I crawl back inside the limo, leaving the two of them standing on the sidewalk, gobsmacked.

"You owe me an explanation, Liv!" Kristen hollers. "And a ride in one of these things!"

"You know it!" I call back to her as I shut the door, laughing at the expression of awe on both of their faces.

I explain the directions to EJ's house to Elliot, and within minutes, the limo is parked on the curb out front. EJ watches the car from the porch, slumped in a double swinging chair, cradling his apple red fender. The house is in darkness, his silhouette only visible for the single streetlight and the full moon above that bathes the night in soft blue light.

I thank Elliot for the ride, and give him a wave as he drives off. EJ remains silent as I tiptoe up the stone path, my hands nervously clutching at my purse. As I climb the stairs, the wind chimes sway softly overhead in the light breeze. EJ plucks a few guitar strings, but other than that, he makes no attempt to move. It only serves to heighten my anxiety.

"Hi." I speak softly, but somehow my voice still seems too loud in the quiet of the night.

"Hey," he replies, his eyes glistening under the moonlight.

"We need to talk."

"About why you just pulled up in a fucking limo?" Despite his words, his voice remains calm. I don't blame him for being defensive. I'd told him I'd had a family thing to go to and then I'd rocked up in a stretch limousine. What must he be thinking?

"About a lot of things." I honestly don't know where to start.

He slides across on the chair swing, allowing me room to sit, his eyes never leaving mine. I perch on the edge of it, leaning forward slightly with my elbows resting on my knees.

"My dad's rich," I divulge, splaying my palms out in front of me as I offer the information. I turn to gauge his reaction.

"Yeah, I caught that," he says. Relief floods me to see a small smile on his face.

"He's probably richer than you thought," I say, slowly.

"Yeah, I'm getting that too," he smiles again, picking at the guitar strings to create a slow melody. I recognise it as the song he sang in the bar; the one that he said had been inspired by me.

"The thing tonight was for my father's work. You were right. I didn't want you to come." EJ stiffens, his nostrils flaring defensively. "Not because I'm embarrassed of you, but because I'm embarrassed of them, of me. I've always been expected to act a certain way. To dress a certain way."

A sigh escapes him, but he lets me continue.

"I don't like the person I have to be when I go to those things. The person I pretend to be. But tonight, I didn't pretend. I was just me." Something tells me I have him to thank for that. "I don't expect you to understand it. I just need you to know because I care about you. I would never want you to feel like you weren't good enough because you are." I wave a hand back and forth between us. "This. Us. It's everything to me."

EJ sets down his guitar, leaning its neck against the porch railing, and positions his arm around my shoulders. He catches a loan tear with his thumb as it rolls down my cheek.

"Liv…"

"No, there's more," I cut him off, knowing that if I don't keep going, I'll never get the words out. "My parents aren't divorced."

"It's okay, Liv. You don't have to explain."

"I do," I let out a sob and he pulls me in closer. I pause to exhale, preparing myself for what I need to say next. "My mum died."

"Liv, I'm so sorry." His own voice cracks with the words and he envelopes me with his other arm, kissing my forehead tenderly.

I can't bring myself to look at him as I continue. "She was the one who taught me how to play the piano."

More tears move down my face, then his lips are on mine and all the hurt is washed away, at least for now. I pull away from him. He needs to hear the whole story. I need him to know. "My parents…"

"Shh, it's okay," he says softly, his hands cupping my face. "You don't need to say anything else right now."

There's anguish in his eyes, like it's too much for him to bear to hear whatever I'm about to say. As though watching my heart break might break his own.

So, I say nothing else.

And he keeps kissing me underneath the blue glow of the full moon on the front porch swing, and for this moment, I can pretend that everything is how it should be.

If only we could live in a moment forever.

Chapter 33

OLIVIA

It figures. I finally give into Tessa's pleas to see the psychiatrist at Ryker's, only to get there and find that there's been an emergency and she's had to cancel on me.

I curse the traffic on the way back to Hampton Ridge from Milton. City driving has always put me on edge. Now that I've ventured out for the day, I want nothing more than to curl back up in bed, with the covers swamping out the daylight. I've already decided I'm not going back to school, at least for the foreseeable future.

I don't expect anyone to be home. My father has back-to-back surgeries to perform and my mother gave Tessa the day off.

Mum is barely ever at home these days. God only knows where she's been flitting off to. Whenever I ask, she rambles on about random social gatherings and charity organisations. One day she even mentioned that she had book club, yet I haven't seen her pick up a book in years.

My hopes of arriving home to an empty house are dashed when I pull into the driveway and see an unfamiliar vehicle parked out the front.

I push open the heavy, glass panelled front door and enter through the lobby. The stereo volume is so high, I can hear it echoing from the courtyard before I've even entered the house.

In the past, when the music was turned up this loud, it usually meant that my mum would be wasted, and if I dared questioned why she was drunk at 4pm, I'd be bombarded with excuses about how depressing it is to be the trophy wife of Milton's top cardiology surgeon, how she deserves to have some fun. That was before my mother went to rehab though. I immediately fear she's relapsed, if she hasn't already before today.

And who the hell is here with her?

There's a loud crash from upstairs and I hear her cry out.

Assuming the worst, I race to the top of the stairs, stopping in the hall outside my parents' bedroom.

"Mum?" I call.

There's no answer. I creep slowly toward the double French doors, reaching out cautiously for the handles. I push the left door open slightly. I don't know what I'm expecting to find, but nothing could have prepared me for what I see.

Through the crack, a shirtless man leans, suspended above mum's body which is draped seductively over my parent's marital bed. Although I can't see the man's face, I know instantly that he's not my father. My mother is wearing a red satin slip, which leaves little to the imagination.

I heave, my lungs heavy like bricks. The man, spins around, hearing me gasp. His eyes glare back at me, his expression one of total shock. I've seen this face so many times before. I stumble backward, my bag dropping to the floor, its contents bouncing on the cream plush pile carpet.

"Olivia." I hear my mother say under her breath. "Dammit."

I don't know why I bother, but I scramble to pick up the contents of my bag. I guess shock does funny things. I hurry myself, throwing the last item into the bag, a perfume my mother let me borrow last week. A random thought enters my head and I wonder if she bought it to impress him.

I rush into my room and throw my bag down on the bed, slamming the door shut behind me. I pace the length of the room, balling up my fists in anger. I squeeze my temples, shaking my head with my eyes closed, as though I can shake the images of what I've just witnessed from my mind. I can't. I can see them even with my eyes open.

I'm anger and sadness, confusion, and hate. If that's even an emotion. I hate them for doing this. They're the ones committing adultery, and yet I'm the one feeling as though I've done something wrong by discovering them.

I stiffen at the sound of footsteps in the hall. I hear their goodbyes to each other. I want nothing to do with the man, but knowing he is sneaking off like such a coward conjures up an intense fury within me. He doesn't even have the guts to face me.

I've eaten dinner at his house and swam in his swimming pool. He'd driven me home in his Saab when I'd been stranded in the rain. I've always seen him as a family man and a respected businessman, but now I see him for what he truly is. A coward and a fake, who now holds the power to alter my entire existence.

What will my dad do when he finds out that my mum has betrayed him again? And with someone he knows this time?

There's no way their marriage can survive this. I don't know if I can even survive this. It's as if my whole world has been slowly crumbling over time only to come crashing down completely in this moment.

I need to confront her, although it's the last thing I want to do. I need to know how she could do this to Dad. To me. It had taken everything within me to forgive her for last time. I couldn't do it again.

Is all of this happening because she stopped taking her medication? And if that's the case, if all it would take for her to be normal and healthy is for her to just take a little pill each day, then why the hell did she decide it wasn't worth it? Why did she give up on us? Why did she give up on herself?

I storm the hallway, briefly pausing when my fingertips meet the cold metal of her bedroom door handle. I should manage this situation with tact. I know that, but I'm furious. I want her to know how much I hate her for what she's done. Mothers are supposed to be nurturing, to be relied on, but she has been a shitty mother lately, and she's failed as a wife.

When I shove open the door and burst into the room, I find her sitting at the dresser in the master bathroom. She's thrown a dress over her satin slip, and her face is marked with black smudges, the result of tear drenched mascara.

I wonder if she's crying because she's remorseful of the damage she's caused, or simply because she has been found out.

She holds her most expensive crystal, scotch glass in her bony, shaking hand. It's almost empty, confirming my fears of a relapse. She attempts to place it down on the dresser as her eyes meet mine in the mirror. She misses and it tumbles down onto the white, marble bathroom tiles, shattering into countless pieces.

I glare at her reflection. I don't see the woman that raised me. I don't see the kind, caring, supportive woman from my childhood. This version of her is broken and lost. There are a thousand insults I want to scream at her, but when I open my mouth to let them out, the words fade away. My anger dissipates, replaced by pity.

"Olivia," she gasps. The desperation is evident in her eyes.

I prepare myself for the list of excuses that I'm sure will follow. That she's lonely. That she's depressed. That dad works too much. But then she surprises me with one that I'd never seen coming.

"I love him, Olivia."

My anger returns. The words burn like lava as they reach my ears, my head hot with rage. My mother has been unusually absent lately, but I never expected she would be standing here before me, confessing her love for another man. For a man that isn't my father.

"What? What are you talking about? How can you say that?" I plead with her, wishing that this is all a wicked nightmare that I'll eventually wake up from.

"He says he loves me too. I know he means it, Olivia!" She desperately clings to the hope that she can justify her pathetic actions. "Graham is a good man."

She hurls herself out of the dresser chair, almost toppling it backwards in her drunken stupor.

"A good man?" I argue. "Mum, he's married! And so are you. I can't believe this…" my voice trails off. It sounds so ridiculous, I almost want to laugh.

A good man? My father is a good man.

And of all the men she could have chosen to have a sordid affair with, why did it have to be Graham Van Sant? As if Katerina needed another excuse to hate me.

"How long has this been going on?" I ask her.

"It doesn't matter." She waves her hand at me as though she can brush me aside, which only infuriates me further.

She reaches upward to open the bathroom cabinet. I slam it shut before it even opens half way.

"How long!" I demand. She jumps a little, either at the sound of the cupboard slamming or the volume of my voice, I can't tell.

"About six months," she whispers, her voice shaky. She can't even look at me.

I hold my hands up to my face, my cheeks wet with tears. She has been deceiving us for six whole months. She was seeing Graham long before her stay at Ryker's. All those charity benefits she'd supposedly attended. All the times she'd given Tessa a day off. All the times her stories didn't add up, and I had put it down to the fact that maybe she'd just had one too many drinks that day.

"You disgust me." I turn and storm out of the room, but before I reach my own bedroom door she is behind me, clawing urgently at my arm.

"Please, Olivia! Don't walk away from me!" she begs.

"Oh, but it's okay for you to walk away from me? To walk away from this family?" I whirl back around, holding a cold, bitter stare, our faces only inches apart.

There's despair in her eyes as she pleads with me to understand. But how can I, knowing that our lives are about to be turned upside down? I can't stop the words as they tumble out of my mouth. I want her far away from me.

"I don't want to see you. I can't even look at you. Just get out." My voice is bitter, my tone harsh.

"Livvie." Her eyes brim with fresh tears. Hearing her use her pet name for me only fuels my anger.

"I said get out!" I scream the words into her face, my temper reaching its peak.

There's pain in her expression. The kind of hurt that comes from realising you've disappointed the one person in your life that should matter most to you, and I know then that she's only just now comprehending the magnitude of what she's done.

I'm trembling. I've never spoken this way to anybody before, least of all my own mother. This woman brought me into this world, and now she's tearing it down right before my eyes. Her betrayal is unforgiveable. Tears continue to stream down her red, blotchy cheeks. She wipes them away with the back of her hand.

"I love you, Livvie," she whispers.

Something resurfaces from within her, a flame that flickers ever so slightly. I see fragments of who she used to be, as though that version of her still burns somewhere inside of this ghost she's become.

I know her words to be true, that she does love me, despite this web of lies she's spun. I almost want to reach out and touch her, but then she's gone, scampering down the stairs. I retreat back into my room.

I'm remorseful of the things I said, which frustrates me, because she brought this all on herself. If anyone should be crippled with guilt right now, it's her. It's not like we haven't fought before, but it's different this time. This is bigger than anything we've ever faced.

The truth descends on me like gravity, the reality suffocating. I run to the double French doors and burst through them. The sea crashes wildly below. I fall to my knees, the sadness suddenly paralysing.

I've lost my mother. We can't go back. She will never be the same again, forever damaged, like her broken crystal glass lying in pieces on the bathroom floor.

There is no way to fix her.

Chapter 34

LIV

I wake early to the doorbell ringing incessantly. I practically suffocate myself with a pillow trying to ignore it, but nothing I do can drown it out. I throw the covers back, glancing at the clock.

Who the hell rings a door bell at 6am on a Saturday morning? Grunting, I drag myself out of bed and down the stairs, my eyes barely open, and heave open the front door, ready to give whoever it is a piece of my mind.

But the words stall in my throat when I come face to face with EJ.

"EJ? What's wrong? Why are you here so early?" My voice comes out groggily.

EJ had driven me home after our conversation on the porch swing at his house last night. He wouldn't have arrived back at his place until well after midnight. He's the last person I expect to show up at my door this early.

I rub my eyes and blink until he comes into focus. He appears dishevelled, his hair a little more messy than usual, a couple of days of facial hair growth present that I somehow never noticed last night. But more than that, he looks exhausted, with visible bags underlining his eyes, which appear greyer today than green.

"I need to show you something," he states.

"Now? EJ, are you okay? You look like you haven't slept."

He steps backward as I reach out to him.

"It's really important. I need you to come with me. Please."

From the serious expression he wears, I can tell this isn't going to be another fishing trip to a mysterious stream in the middle of the woods. Whatever he wants to show me is something he's been losing sleep over.

"Okay," I answer. "Come inside while I get dressed."

"It's okay. I'll wait out here," he says, as he shoves his hands into his jacket pockets and starts toward his ute.

His distant demeanour is beginning to scare me, but I do as he asks and get dressed, then join him in the car. It's so early that even the sun is still asleep, the orange glow only just beginning to peak up from under the ocean.

Still weary, I close my eyes to rest them while EJ drives in eery silence. A few minutes pass, then his hand covers mine, clutching it firmly.

"We're almost there," he says, his husky voice coming out not much more than a whisper.

"EJ, what's wrong? Where are we going? I'm worried about you," I plead with him.

His eyes stay focused on the road ahead, but I can still see the glassiness in them. Is he holding back tears?

The car winds around a tight bend and his hand begins to tremble in mine. I watch him, becoming more concerned with every passing minute.

I scan the scenery outside. We had been following the coastline earlier, but it's evident to me now, that we are somewhere at the bottom of the ridge, on a section of road that is unfamiliar to me.

EJ removes his hand from mine so he can steer with both hands around the next bend.

That's when the unfamiliar surroundings become somewhat recognisable to me. I've never actually stopped here, but I've driven through it, seen the area in photographs. He brakes slowly and pulls the car over on a straight stretch of road.

I start to panic, unable to breath. My body quivers involuntarily as my heart pounds against my rib cage. Why the hell would he bring me here?

"EJ, what are you doing?" I hear my words as if someone else is saying them. "I can't be here. I can't."

All the colour has left his face when he turns to me. "I'm sorry," he whispers, as a single tear tracks down his cheek.

My face scrunches in confusion. What does he mean he's sorry? I open my mouth to ask him, but no words come out. I want him to take me home. Take me back away from this place. But he's exiting the vehicle now.

Cold air brushes my cheek as the passenger side door opens. I notice him standing there, see his hands held out to me. "It's okay. We can do this together."

I barely hear his words over the pounding of my own heartbeat. My body is frozen in fear, my stomach twisted in knots, the nausea rising in my throat. The same question plays on repeat in my head.

Why is he doing this?

Reluctantly, I allow him to take my hands and pry me from the car, my body like a dead weight bearing down on him.

We step up onto the curb of the footpath that traces the edge of the river.

This doesn't make sense.

This can't be real.

Chapter 35

OLIVIA

I have no more tears left. I've cried myself dry, having wallowed in this pity party for one for I don't know how long. I've never been one to feel sorry for myself, but I'm so alone. I have no one.

Katerina had always been my person in times of crisis. In another life, I'd call her and she would come to my aid, usually with chocolate or vodka, or both. How times have changed.

There will come a time where I need to pull myself together, and maybe that time has to be now. My mother will surely be back soon from wherever she's escaped to, and I need to be ready to deal with that. I wonder if she's with him. She can't have gone far on foot. Maybe she called to have him pick her up.

I stagger to my feet, using the balcony railing for support. I walk back through my bedroom in a daze. I've only taken a few steps out into the hall when I see my mother's phone, face down on the cream carpet. I guess that answers my question about whether she called him. I don't pick it up.

Instead I descend the stairs, slumping on the bottom step, my head resting on the wall.

I wrestle with denial. Maybe Mum will have sobered up when she returns. Maybe she'll take back what she said about Graham and we can go back to how things used to be. Maybe after she apologises I could tell her what she wants to hear. I could tell her that I love her too, that she'll always be my mother. And that I'll always be here for her.

My stare remains on the front door. I sit there for what seems like an eternity, until the light coming in through the glass panels fades to a dull blue glow. I wonder which one of my parents will enter first. At this point, I can't decide which alternative would be worse. If it's my mother, we could end up in a full-blown argument again, but if it's my dad, what the hell am I supposed to say to him?

My eyelids are heavy, the emotionally draining events having taking a physical toll. I close my eyes for an immeasurable amount of time when a click disturbs me. The front door handle turns and it opens. My father enters, bringing with him a gust of crisp Autumn air.

"Oh, Olivia!" Dad says in surprise. No doubt he isn't expecting me to be lounging on the staircase. He leans on the doorway as he removes his shoes. "Where did your mother go?"

His question strikes me as odd. How does he know she has gone anywhere? "I don't know," I answer, truthfully. "Why?"

"Her Audi is gone," he replies casually.

"What? She took the car?" I jolt upright.

Mum was not in a fit state to drive when she left. Why had I just assumed she'd gone on foot?

In my state of distress, I hadn't heard her pick up the keys. I never even heard the car engine.

Where is she? Why has she been gone for so long?

I push past Dad and burst out onto the front porch, as though hearing him say the car is missing isn't enough. I need to see for myself. Sure enough, it's not there. She didn't even bother to close the garage door.

A pit forms in my stomach. Fear surges through my veins, turning my blood ice cold. My mother had driven under the influence of alcohol.

"Olivia." My dad's voice startles me. "What's wrong? You're as white as a ghost."

I can't find words to answer him. I knew my mother had driven after a couple of drinks on more than one occasion, but never as wasted as she was when she left this afternoon.

My Dad watches me, anticipating my response. I tell myself I'm overreacting.

Maybe I misjudged her.

Maybe the half-drunk scotch in her broken crystal glass had been her only drink today.

I could easily have mistaken her panic-ridden guilt for intoxication. Maybe, apart from the fact that my parent's marriage is over, everything else is just fine.

The possibilities whirr through my mind, until they're silenced by an unnerving sound that will forever haunt me.

My panic is mirrored in my dad's eyes as we listen to the high-pitched wail of distant sirens, echoing through the valley below.

Chapter 36

LIV

"EJ, take me home," I beg.

EJ's eyes are trained on the river below. I don't think he even hears my pleas to leave this place. The place I told myself I would never see. A place I drive the long way home just to avoid. I move closer to him to get his attention, to force him back from wherever he's gone.

He crouches down, slowly running his fingers along the guardrail. "My parents have been here more times than I can count, but I've never been able to bring myself to come."

I feel my forehead crumple in confusion. Then I notice the section of guardrail he touches. There's a part that looks different to the rest, as if it has not too long ago been replaced.

He sucks in a deep breath, and then continues. "My sister was amazing. I wish you could have met her. She was beautiful, talented." He looks out at the river, the early morning sun reflecting off the still water. "In so many ways she was a lot like you. I guess that's why I snapped at you that day. I'd hate to see you waste your potential when she never had the chance."

I stare blankly into space, taking in all of his words. They register gradually, washing over me like a tidal wave in slow motion. Then I ask him again, the question that I'm starting to believe I already know the answer to.

"EJ," I whisper, as I collapse down beside him, my hands still shaking uncontrollably as I grasp the smooth metal railing for support, cold beneath my fingertips. "Why did you bring me here?"

He doesn't answer me. He doesn't have to. Now that I'm on the ground with him, I can see what he's seeing.

There's a makeshift shrine at the base of the railing post on his right. A small teddy bear, an assortment of flowers, and resting in the midst of them, a photo frame that displays a picture of a beautiful young woman about the age that I am now.

I've seen her before. Not in person, but on the front page of the local newspaper, alongside my mother's photograph. The headline above it had read "Alcohol fuelled crash kills two."

I remember her name. Madelyn Jensen.

EJ picks up the photo frame, stroking the picture with his thumb. "I miss you, Mads," he chokes.

"No," I stammer, rising to my feet, and stumbling backwards. "No. I don't understand. None of this makes sense. You said your last name was James."

"My middle name is James," EJ says, still looking at the photograph.

"You said that she… that she drowned." I'm momentarily aware that I must sound deranged.

I'd assumed his sister's death had been a simple tragedy. That she had drowned in a lake or on the beach. That maybe she'd been out with friends, or at a party, and a horrible accident had occurred. Now that it's all coming together in my mind, I feel sick. EJ turns to me, his eyes full of despair. "I'm so sorry, Liv. I wanted to tell you, but I didn't know how."

I squeeze my eyes shut, wishing I could erase this moment from my life. I want to unsee this place, the shrine, the sorrow in EJ's expression.

"You knew." Tears flow from my eyes now. I couldn't hold them back if I tried.

He nods, swallowing hard, tears falling from his own eyes now.

"Why are you so calm? Aren't you angry?" I can't imagine how I would feel if the roles had been reversed. He must hate me.

"I was. I was angry at her. For a long time, I had so much hatred for this person that took my sister's life. She took her away from us, and tore our whole family apart. And I was angry that she died with her. Because she never has to live with what she's done."

No. I do. I have to live with it.

Because she'd left me all alone that night when her life ended, and I'd been angry at her too. Frustrated to the point I would write myself off every night in an attempt to numb the pain. But all I was doing was trying to avoid the truth. That it was my own fault.

All of it.

The police report determined that my mother's blood alcohol level was three times the legal limit. Her Audi R8 convertible had slammed through the guard rail and into the river, taking with it an innocent bystander, a college girl, who'd been walking along the footpath with her boyfriend.

The impact had sent the girl plunging into the depths below. Her boyfriend's attempts to rescue her from the dark water had been unsuccessful.

Cayden.

"Did you know this whole time?"

"No." He shakes his head. "I swear I only found out the other night."

The night he went silent on me. The night he'd failed to call when he said he would. The same night Cayden threatened me to stay away from EJ. Because he knew who I was.

"Cayden told you."

"He said he remembered you."

I can't breathe. It's as though a thousand knives are stabbing me in the chest. It will never cease to amaze me how emotional agony can cause such physical pain. I stagger backward, my foot clipping the edge of the gutter. I gasp as I fall backwards only to be caught by EJ's strong arms. I savour his touch, then remember I don't deserve it. I push away from him.

"No," I sob.

He looks back at me, hurt, and confused. It's killing me, knowing that I did this to him.

"Liv, come here. Everything's going to be okay."

"No, it's not," I weep. "It's all my fault. I'm sorry."

"What? Don't say that." He watches me helplessly, his hands falling to his sides. "What are you talking about?"

Memories of the worst night of my life come flooding back in a blur. I'm unsteady on my feet. He rushes toward me again, always ready to catch me if I fall. Lightheaded, the ground shifts beneath me and his hands are on my waist.

Sweet, dependable EJ. So steady and loyal.

I'm about to ruin him.

"My mother was having an affair," I begin, my voice quivering. "I found her in my parent's bedroom. With *him*. I couldn't believe that she could do that to my dad. I confronted her about it and we got into an argument."

I pause and lower my gaze to the ground. I can feel EJ's eyes burning through me, but I can't bring myself to look at him.

"I screamed at her. I told her to get out. I knew she'd been drinking. And I told her to leave. I let her leave." I bring my eyes up to meet his. "It's all because of me."

I watch as understanding passes over EJ's face. I can't see what he sees, but I imagine, that for a second, he sees *her*. The other version. That he understands what she was capable of and why I've been trying so hard to run from her. Not a day has gone by since the accident, that I haven't wondered how the situation could have played out if I'd done things differently that night.

I wasn't there with him the night his life had been shattered and his family torn apart, but the look of anguish on his face right now tells me that he's reliving it all over again. What little light had been left in his eyes this morning has now diminished, leaving a dark, muddy grey, vacant stare.

I never wanted to be the reason that light went out.

And now I am.

"I'm sorry," I say, my voice a mere whisper. "I can't do this. I can't be here."

I turn my back on him, not knowing where I'm going to go. It would take me hours to climb the ridge back up to my house, but anything was better than having to see EJ's pain, knowing that I'm the one who caused it.

How many times since we met had he thought about coming to this very spot, to mourn for his sister, not knowing that it was also the place my mother's life had ended?

All this time I'd been worried about introducing EJ to my father when they'd already met. After the accident, my dad had met the family of the innocent girl whose life was cut short. I'd wanted to join him, but he'd thought it best for me not to get involved, considering my fragile state. I realise now that when EJ had mentioned he'd once met someone from Hampton Ridge, he was referring to my dad.

I trail the path that winds along the coastline, the waves crashing violently on the dark grey rocks below, forming deep blue ripples marred with streaks of white foam. I reach the second bend before I hear EJ's footsteps on the gravel road behind me, feel his palm gently slide into mine. I shrug him off and quicken my pace, despite my increasing fatigue.

"I told you. I can't do this, EJ!"

"Liv, please!" he pleads from behind me.

"Just go home," I sob. I kick myself for not telling the truth earlier. Maybe we could have avoided all of this if I'd ended things before our relationship had begun.

"Liv! Don't do this!" he cries. "Just stop!"

And then his arms are encasing me, holding firm at my waist. I fight against his grip, but he's much stronger than me. He turns me around to face him.

"Look at me, Liv!" he insists. "I'm not leaving you!"

Despite his demands, I can't bring myself to look him in the eye, instead burying my head in his chest.

"My mum killed your sister, EJ. You lost your sister."

313

"Yeah," he agrees sadly, blowing out a breath. "And you lost your mum."

His words stop me in my tracks. It's the first time anyone, other than Tessa and my father, has acknowledged the fact that I've suffered a loss too. The rest of the town had labelled Elle Huxton an alcoholic, a murderer, but first and foremost, she was my mother. And she was gone.

I look at him then and when our eyes meet, I see only compassion and sympathy within his. He's still here. Even after everything. He found out about this days ago, and sure, he'd avoided me for a short time while he obviously struggled to process the information. Last night, on the porch swing I'd tried to tell him the truth and he'd known all along. And still, he'd comforted me when I cried. He'd wiped away my tears and kissed me so tenderly.

I surrender to his embrace, collapsing into his arms. The cry that leaves me, agonising and raw, is evidence of all the emotion I've pent up inside for too long. I can't bear the weight of it any more. EJ clings to me tightly, his solid arms enveloping me with warmth and love. The kind of love I don't believe I deserve. I cry even harder, burying my face in his chest.

"It's okay." His voice cracks with the effort of the words, his hand stroking the back of my head. He continues to let me cry, for how long I can't be sure. "Come on. Let's get out of here. I'll take you home."

I nod as he helps me dry my tears with the sleeve of his sweatshirt, then leads me back to the car. We drive in silence, neither of us really knowing what else to say. EJ reassures me that it will be okay, but everything is far from okay. This situation is beyond messed up, and I can't see how we'll survive it.

What will happen when he wakes up tomorrow and realises this isn't just some twisted nightmare, and every time he looks at me he sees his sister's face and what was taken away from him?

Every day I fight a battle with my conscience, knowing that if I'd handled things differently that night, I could have prevented a tragedy. Will seeing EJ be a constant reminder of that now?

"I'm sorry, Liv." EJ blows out a shaky breath as he turns off the ignition. We're already back at my house. "I shouldn't have dumped all of this on you. I didn't know how else to tell you."

"I can't believe this is happening."

"We'll get through it, Liv. We have each other."

"How can you say that? How can you stand to be near me after everything I've done? I told her to leave."

The last words I ever said to my mother replay in my head. I hadn't heard the scraping sound of the keys being dragged across the stone bench. I never stopped to think she might take the car. I just wanted her away from me.

"Liv, listen to me." He turns his whole body toward me and takes my hand in his. "There is no way you could have known what would happen. If you'd tried to stop her, do you really think she would have listened?"

"I don't know," I say. "We will never know."

"I don't blame you for what happened. I told you there was nothing about your past that could change the way I feel about you. I still believe that."

"Is that why you've spent the last few days avoiding me?" It's a low blow, but I need to make him see that he's better off without me. I need him to hate me. It's what I deserve.

"That's fair. I'll admit it freaked me out at first. I didn't know what to think." He closes his eyes and pinches the bridge of his nose. "I didn't even know if you knew who I was."

A bitter laugh escapes me. "I didn't."

"Look, I've had three days to process this. Maybe you'll feel different in a couple of days too."

"I doubt it, EJ."

"So what? You just want to walk away from us? Come on, Liv. There's a reason we met. There has to be."

"Maybe there is. But maybe it's not the reason you want to believe."

"Don't say that." He looks straight ahead, his jaw ticking with anger.

I blink more tears away as I reach for the car door handle. "I'm sorry."

"Please Liv, just think about this!" EJ pleads, reaching across the car to thumb the tears on my wet cheeks. He swallows hard. "I love you."

A physical ache rips through my chest as my heart is obliterated into thousands of tiny shards. I can't say those words back to him, no matter how badly I want to. I can't throw myself into his arms and tell him I need him more than he will ever know. The irony of the situation isn't lost on me. How many people can say they've broken their own heart?

His bloodshot eyes plead with mine not to give up on us, but I can't see past my own guilt and the damage I've inflicted on so many lives.

I jerk my hand free of his and exit the car, slamming the door shut and leaving him alone in the silence of his own suffering.

I dare a glance back once I reach the front door. The ignition is on, but through the mud splattered windscreen I can make out EJ's form, his shoulders slumped, his head buried in the steering wheel.

My worst fears have come true.

I've ruined him.

Chapter 37

LIV

I want a drink.

Vodka, bourbon, scotch. I don't care. Anything that will numb this heart-wrenching pain would suffice. I'd happily welcome whatever could silence the screaming in my head, but we don't keep booze in the house and there's no way I'm leaving this bed. I roll over throwing the covers over my head. The darkness will have to do.

Six days have passed since my world came undone. Six days since I discovered my newly reinvented life is just as shitty as the one I tried to leave behind.

My dad is getting worried about me. He's even taken leave from work. I hate that he's put his life on hold for me, yet I'm grateful for it. Tessa has been around every day, but I refuse to let her see me. I don't deserve whatever kind and beautiful things she will surely say to me.

My phone is blowing up regularly with calls from Carla and texts from Kristen, none of which I have the courage to answer. I heard my dad answer one of Carla's calls yesterday when he thought I was sleeping. I overheard him tell her that

I need to take a leave of absence and her calls have since ceased.

"Olivia," Dad says softly from the doorway of my bedroom. "You really should come and eat something."

Food is another thing I've refused the past few days. That and sunlight and basic hygiene.

"I'm not hungry," I answer, my voice muffled by the sheets.

"It's not doing you any good being in bed, Olivia. I'm worried you're going to make yourself sick." My father's feet pad softly on the carpet, edging in my direction.

The mattress dips as his weight bears down on it next to me, then he pulls the covers off my head. I understand his concerns. The poor man is probably terrified that I'll relapse and end up right back in Ryker's the way I had after my mother's death, but that had been a long twelve months and, despite wishing there was an easier way to numb this pain, I intend on keeping as far away from there as possible.

"I can't believe this is happening. I finally found this one person that I wanted to let in. I thought he was my person."

He nods solemnly. "Maybe you should talk to him."

I shake my head profusely. "I told him we couldn't be together anymore. It's too hard."

"Nothing worth having is ever easy. I don't know Emmett. I only met him after the accident that one time, but I do know something. He brought a light into your life. After you started seeing him, it was like you were this brand-new person. It was the happiest I'd ever seen you."

"Yeah," I sigh.

EJ made me want to be better. But right now, I'm all the versions of myself that I never wanted to be.

"You can't stay up here forever though, okay? Maybe you should give that friend of yours a call. The one from the café."

"Kristen."

I can't begin to fathom how Kristen would be feeling about my deception, or if she even knows the truth yet, but I assume she has spoken to EJ. She probably hates me. Madelyn was like family to her. Either way, she's been a good friend to me and I owe her an explanation.

"I have to go grab a few things from the office. Just promise me you won't be in bed when I get back, okay?"

"I'll try."

"Okay," Dad pats me on the shoulder awkwardly. I can't imagine it's easy for him to navigate this situation either.

After he leaves, I lay flat on my back staring up at the ceiling, willing myself to get my act together. I wonder what EJ is doing. I picture him strumming his guitar, his pick wedged between his front teeth as he frowns in concentration. He hasn't attempted to contact me since the day I left him shattered.

Fresh tears fill my eyes remembering the hurt and anguish on his face as I'd walked away from him. Maybe he was right to think that we'd come into each other's lives for a reason. Perhaps he's here to help me heal, and I, to allow him to let go.

I inhale a long breath, then clamber from my bed. I know my dad is right. I'm not going to find the answers in the confinements of my room, and after all we've been through, if anyone knows what is best for me, I trust that it's him.

I take a long shower, allowing the scalding hot water to run over my skin, willing myself to feel something other than searing guilt. I dress in a pair of grey sweat pants and a loose, cropped black t-shirt, then drift down the staircase and into the lobby.

I stare at the haze of black and white before me. My fingertips trace the lengths of the keys, my mind having no memory of how I came to be sitting here in front of the piano, with the stool bearing the weight of my tired body. A pang of hunger hits my stomach, but I need to feed my soul before I replenish my food stores. EJ's words echo in my head.

Find whatever it is that's holding you back from playing.

Use it.

It will only hurt for a little while.

Then it will heal you.

So, I play. I play until my fingers are sore, my body is spent and the tears stream down my face. Although it helps immensely, I have a feeling I'd have to play for a lifetime to recover from the emotional damage I've suffered this past week.

My phone rings and as I pull it out of my pocket, Kristen's beautiful smile fills the screen. I've ignored her for long enough. She deserves better. I swipe the answer key and hold the phone to my ear.

"Kristen," I choke.

"Liv?" Her voice is frantic. "Liv, what's going on? You've had me so worried."

"Have you talked to EJ?" My words come out cracked, barely a whisper.

"No. Nobody has seen him. It's like you both just dropped off the face of the planet!" she cries. "Please tell me what's happened. Did you guys have another fight?"

"It's bad, Kristen." Another tear falls from the corner of my eye, tracking its way down to my chin. "It's really bad this time."

"Are you at home? I'm coming to see you. What's your address?"

I absentmindedly splutter out my home address, then Kristen hangs up on the call.

Chapter 38

LIV

By the time Kristen arrives at my house, night is beginning to fall. Dad still isn't home, but called to tell me he'd been summoned into help with a surgical procedure. He was relieved to hear that I'd left my room and that Kristen was on her way.

When Kristen arrives, her face is panic-stricken and I instantly feel guilty for making my friend worry. "What happened, Liv? You're Dad told Carla you need to take leave. Neither you, nor EJ have been answering my calls. I was starting to think you guys were mad at me for some reason."

My face crumples with emotion. "I could never be mad at you. You've been such a great friend to me."

"Oh, sweetie! Don't cry!" she gushes, as she rushes forward to hug me. I don't deserve her comfort.

"I'm sorry, Kristen. I'm a horrible person and I've been a really shitty friend to you."

"What are you talking about?" Kristen's face drops, her bright smile falling into a frown of suspicion.

I wipe my eyes with my palms and sink down onto the lounge, its blue velvet fabric wrinkling under my weight.

"My name isn't Liv Peters," I blurt. "It's Olivia Petersen."

"Olivia Petersen," Kristen echoes, squinting in thought. "Why do I feel like I know that name?"

"My father is Victor Petersen," I say, bluntly.

I watch as understanding passes slowly over Kristen's face and her hand goes to her mouth.

"My mother was…"

"Elle Huxton." Her voice is barely audible as she utters my mother's name. Her eyes seem to look everywhere except at me before she finally falls down onto the lounge beside me. "Oh god, Liv. EJ knows, doesn't he?" It's more of a statement than a question.

I nod. "Apparently Cayden remembered my face from somewhere. I still don't know where. I don't remember ever meeting him."

I can see Kristen's brain ticking, her mind racing desperately to fill in the blanks I haven't yet revealed. So, I tell her everything.

I tell her about the accident and how I blame myself, about EJ taking me to the river and how I'd broken his heart. She listens intently to my explanation and when I'm done, she is silent for a long while. It's impossible to tell what she's thinking as her own eyes brim with tears.

"I remember seeing pictures of you in magazines and on the news. You looked so different. After the accident, the newspapers mentioned your parents and there were photographs of your dad, but there was nothing about you."

"My dad paid the media a lot of money to leave me alone. Besides, I wasn't around much for a while after the accident. I was abusing alcohol and I was sent to Rykers Institution."

324

I don't need to mention how I'd drastically changed my look, cutting my platinum blonde locks into a choppy bob, and dying them back to my natural dark shade.

"I knew my dad was going to meet with Madelyn's family, but he wouldn't involve me in it. I didn't even know she had a brother, or that she lived in Cliff Haven." I pause again. "Do you hate me?"

She looks up at me sympathetically. "No." She takes a seat beside me on the lounge and pats my knee with her hand. "I'm sorry you had to go through all of that, Liv,"

I'm not worthy of her compassion.

"EJ is hurting and it's all my fault. You warned me he'd been through enough heartache, and now he's reliving the worst night of his life all over again."

"So are you, though. You didn't know who he was. None of this is your fault. Not the accident, and not this."

"You're not angry at me?" I ask her.

Her eyes find mine, and within their warm chocolate brown I only see understanding. There isn't a trace of hatred or hostility. "EJ doesn't blame you for any of it. Why would I? You're being too hard on yourself. I mean, EJ still wants to be with you."

I squeeze my eyes shut. "I can't. Too much has happened. He deserves more than this."

Kristen throws me a sympathetic look and wraps her arm around my shoulder. "Maybe you both need time."

"Do you think he's okay?" I can't shake my concern after Kristen mentioning she hasn't seen or heard from him.

"He will be. He probably needs space, that's all."

I nod. "Do you think you could do me a massive favour?"

"Anything."

"Could you go check on him for me?" EJ could probably use a friend right now.

"Of course. I'll swing past his place on my way home tonight. But first, I need to make sure you're okay. When was the last time you ate? You look wrecked."

"Yesterday, I guess," I answer, remembering the chicken caesar salad my dad had left on my nightstand. I'd only picked at it. Nausea had washed over me as it hit my stomach, but now my hunger pangs are increasing with the thought of food.

"I'm going to order us some pizza, okay? Do you have any take-out menus around here?"

"In the kitchen. Bottom drawer on the left." I wave a hand in the direction of the kitchen.

"Okay, I'll be right back. Pepperoni and meat lovers okay with you?" she asks.

"Sure," I respond.

In all honesty, I'm not sure that pizza is the best thing for my stomach right now, but Kristen means well and I have no energy left to refuse her.

After about five minutes, she skips back into the lobby from the kitchen, her phone still in her hand.

"Good news is I've placed the order. Bad news is delivery will be up to an hour and a half." She slumps back down next to me on the lounge, a look of annoyance on her face.

"You don't have to stay. If you want to get going, I understand."

I'm relieved to have Kristen here, but I don't want her to feel as though she has to babysit me or anything. Plus, I'm anxious to have her report back to me after checking on EJ. My worry for him is growing by the second.

"Don't be silly. I'm not going anywhere until your dad gets back. I'm not leaving you alone." She smiles and then her forehead wrinkles at the sound of shouting coming from outside at the back of the house.

"Stop!" An urgent voice shouts, sounding far away, but uniquely familiar.

"Is that…" Kristen leans forward on the edge of the sofa, straining to listen.

I know that voice anywhere. "EJ," I whisper.

We both spring to our feet, somehow acutely aware that there is nothing normal about this situation. As we run through the kitchen to the back of the house, the sound of EJ's voice gets louder. Closer. Another voice yells in response to him. He isn't alone.

"Cayden! Don't do this!" EJ yells.

I hurl the sliding door across and lunge out into the alfresco, conscious of Kristen's footsteps behind me. I struggle to comprehend as I watch this scene play out.

Cayden's lanky form lingers in the darkness, his silhouette defined by the aqua glow of the pool lights, a flaming red ember emanating from the lit cigarette pursed between his lips.

He carries something in his right hand, a square-shaped container held by a handle. My heart jolts as he tosses it aside, casting it out of the shadows and into the beam emanating from the kitchen pendant lights. A jerrycan hits the cool, marble tiles with a hollow clatter. The distinct scent of petrol travels into my nostrils. Kristen's hand reaches for mine.

"This isn't right, Cayden!" EJ pleads. "This isn't you!"

"This is what they deserve. Don't you see that?" Cayden bellows back, plucking the cigarette from his mouth. "Mads is gone. They ruined our lives and look how they live! Like spoilt, privileged fucks in a fucking mansion." He swings his arms around, waving them upwards at the house.

"Come on, man. You're not this guy. You don't want to hurt anyone."

"I want the pain to stop."

"This isn't the way," EJ begs.

"Cayden," my voice comes out shakier than anticipated. "I'm sorry for everything. I'm sorry you lost Madelyn. If I could change things I would."

Cayden laughs bitterly. "Wow. Thanks princess, but it's too little too late."

Princess. The word strikes a chord with me. Not because it's insulting, but because I've heard it before.

"The Salt Factory." I think out loud. "You used to work as a bouncer."

"Ding ding ding! Right answer!" Cayden mocks me in a sarcastic tone. "You might have guessed that earlier if you weren't such a superficial bitch."

"Cayden, that's enough," snaps EJ.

Cayden momentarily shifts his attention to EJ, then turning back to me he says, "You always used to walk into that club like you owned the place. So high and mighty with your stupid, little friend. And then I saw you that night at the Twisted Ivy. Oh, how far you'd fallen. Drunk out of your mind, hanging all over that douchebag bartender. You were probably so wasted you don't remember me helping you into your ride home."

My mouth falls open in shock. Cayden had been there the night of Katerina's party too. "That was you? I do remember. You were so kind to me that night. You took care of me."

I'm suddenly aware that there had been another version of Cayden before this one. He used to be the kind of guy that would go out of his way to help a young girl that had found herself in a dark place. Now he is in that dark place. He's merely the collateral damage of a disastrous accident that I still blame myself for. I step forward and Cayden's eyes find mine in the dark.

His glare falters. That guy is still in there. Lurking somewhere in the depths, beneath all of this hostility, is a guy that desperately wants to recover from heart-wrenching pain, but simply got lost somewhere inside of it. He looks at me almost like he wants to say something other than what comes out of his mouth next.

"Your family ruined my life. And now I'm going to ruin yours."

My eyes fall to the cigarette, still lit, hanging by his side. In one swift move, this whole place would go up in flames. Would it really matter?

"You want to burn my house down, Cayden?" I cry. "You want to destroy everything I own? Go ahead. I've already lost everything that matters to me."

EJ's eyes catch mine and he takes a large stride toward me, positioning himself protectively in front of Kristen and I. "Come on, Cayden. You're not really mad at Liv. It's not her fault. She wasn't even there. You're angry at yourself."

"Fuck you," Cayden spits. There's anger in his glare, but there's also something else.

Torment.

"There was nothing you could have done." EJ's tone is softer now. Sympathetic.

"Stop!" Cayden screams, dramatically placing his hands over his ears, as though it physically hurts to listen to EJ's words, the cigarette still pinched between two fingers.

"You have to stop blaming yourself. You did everything you could." Kristen says, taking a step forward.

"It should have been me," Cayden croaks. "We were having an argument. A stupid fight about something so trivial. I don't even remember." Cayden's feet are planted firmly in place on my lawn, but his mind has gone somewhere else entirely. "She stormed off up ahead. I was yelling. And then this car came out of nowhere and just… She was there. And then she wasn't."

Witnessing Cayden's recount of losing Madelyn breaks me in a new way, serving as an unnecessary reminder that my life was not the only one that was turned upside down that night. Just as my grief is connected to EJ's, it is bound to Cayden and his heartbreak too.

"I know, man. But there's a reason you're still here." EJ takes a step in Cayden's direction and Cayden begins to cry. "This isn't what Mads would have wanted. If you do this, there's no coming back from it."

Cayden nods, his expression one of defeat. The fight has left him, but he flinches suddenly when EJ advances on him. The movement causes the cigarette to fall. Regret washes over Cayden as the heavy realisation of what he's done bears down on him.

"No!" he cries, falling to his knees.

A blur of orange and blue races from the lawn to the alfresco, separating the three of us from Kristen. I spin around in time to see her take several steps back, disappearing into the house behind a wall of flames.

"Kristen!" I scream, as I watch the building become engulfed in fire around her. Instinctively, I move in the direction of the house only to feel EJ's strong arms grabbing me from behind. My fingers fight to pry his from my waist.

"Liv, stop. Listen to me. We need to get to the front of the house before the other side catches." EJ points to the far-right side of the house and I instantly understand what he means.

If we wait too much longer, we'll be trapped at the back on the cliff's edge with nowhere to go. We have to get to the road, and hope that Kristen is already out the front waiting for us.

I nod, then speed towards the right. I steal a glance back over my shoulder. EJ is helping Cayden to his feet and then they're both right behind me.

When we reach the front, Kristen is nowhere to be seen, and a quick glance at the front of the house sets off a new fear within me. An orange glow burns behind the glass panes of the front door, and more smoke billows out from underneath it. Kristen is likely trapped with no way out.

"Shit." EJ's panicked voice comes from beside me. Then he calmly turns to me. "Liv, go to the road and call for help." He slaps his phone into my shaking palm. "Do you understand me?"

I nod as if in a trance, the scent of smoke infiltrating my nostrils, and helplessly watch as he removes a large rock from the garden and uses all of his power to propel it through the front window.

"EJ!" I shriek. His eyes snap to mine, which I'm positive are now filled with intense fear. "I can't lose you."

"You won't," he says above the crackle of the flames, and then he disappears into the furnace that was once my home.

I race to the road, where a few onlookers have congregated, leaving Cayden where he is, kneeling on the lawn. I fumble with EJ's phone, my shaking fingers seemingly unable to make a simple phone call. Sirens wail in the distance

331

as a set of older, wrinkled fingers grasp mine. I look up to see an elderly woman. Her kind face softens as she speaks to me.

"Emergency services are on their way. I called them."

"Thank you." My voice trembles with both gratitude and fear. I can't believe this is happening.

"Liv!" The sound of Kristen's voice snaps my attention away from the woman.

She stumbles in my direction as I run to meet her in the middle of the yard. I throw my arms around her, but the weight of my hug is too much and we both fall to our knees. Kristen is in a state of panic, fighting hard to fill her lungs with air. I lay her down on her side, the tiny blades of evergreen grass pricking at her soot-stained skin.

The sirens draw nearer, resonating through the night. I comb strands of hair away from her face.

"Help is coming, Kristen. You're going to be okay." If anything happens to her, I won't be able to live with myself.

I look up as a loud crack whips through the night air. Fear grips me. The kind that stops your heart right in its tracks and tightens its chokehold around your throat. Sparks roar skyward as a large section of the roof caves. The mansion is now fully consumed by fire.

Kristen whimpers beside me; her eyes still closed.

"Kristen. Where is EJ?"

"Behind me," she murmurs. "He was right behind me."

If that had been the case, then why isn't he here? Where is he? My mind wrestles away the negativity that threatens to arise, but I know that EJ wouldn't want to be anywhere else right now than right here next to me.

The urgent blare of sirens is directly behind me now, as their blurry red and blue glow saturates our otherwise quiet street. My thoughts plunge into darkness, into the space where I'd lost my mother. I pray that this time they aren't coming for somebody else I love.

There are voices all around me. Hands pulling me upwards. Arms lift Kristen onto a stretcher. An oxygen mask is strapped over her nose and mouth as she coughs violently. Fire fighters leap in all directions, working to dampen the flames. Minutes pass before I'm able to get my legs to move. I stagger forward toward the inferno.

"EJ!" I scream with all the air in my lungs. "EJ! Where are you?"

Muscular arms hold me firmly. "You can't go in there, Miss. It's too late now."

"No! You don't understand!" I cry. 'Someone is in there!"

What did he mean it's too late now? EJ is in there. Why are they not trying to save him?

"It's okay." The fireman tries to reassure me. "Everything is okay."

I look at him in confusion, tears stinging my burning eyes. I shake my head in bewilderment. I'm aware that I've become full blown hysterical, but they need to know there is someone inside. "But he's in there!"

"We got him," the fire fighter says, stroking my hair. He is trying to calm me down, but to no avail. I will not calm down until I've seen him with my own eyes.

"What? Where is he?" I cry.

"He's right over there," he says, pointing to the ambulance on the other side of the street. "He's suffered some burns, but he's going to be alright."

"Burns?" I echo.

God, why is this happening? EJ is the best thing to ever happen to me. He deserves so much more than this. None of it is fair to him.

Sure enough, EJ's form fills the back of the ambulance. He sits upright on a stretcher, holding an oxygen mask up to his blackened face, while a young woman wraps a thick dressing around his forearm. My heart hammers at the sight of him as more tears flood my cheeks. He seems so helpless sitting there, and it's all my fault. I edge closer to the ambulance, not wanting to disturb the paramedic from fixing my broken hero.

Seeing me, he removes the face mask. "Liv, I'm so sorry."

A short, bitter laugh escapes me. It's so like EJ to say sorry when he has nothing to apologise for. We both know that this whole mess has everything to do with me, and nothing to do with him.

"Are you okay?"

"I will be." The left corner of his mouth lifts. The light dancing behind his eyes is all I need as proof that he's telling the truth.

The paramedic finishes fastening the bandage and steps out of the vehicle. "I'll give you two a minute here. Don't go anywhere though. The police are going to need your statements."

I climb inside the ambulance, positioning myself on the stretcher opposite him. We're so close that our knees touch, a sense of longing permeating the cramped space.

"You scared me to death," I whisper. "I didn't see you come out."

"I'm sorry," he says, again. "The paramedic kind of intercepted me on my way to you."

I sigh, eyeing his bandaged arm. "Does it hurt?"

He shrugs. "Nah. It's not bad." He's lying for my benefit.

"This is all my fault," I begin.

"No, Liv. This is all Cayden's fault."

334

I shake my head defiantly. "Cayden is broken. And that's on me."

EJ reaches for my hand, gripping it firmer than I expected. "No." His eyes penetrate mine. "Cayden may have been dealt a shitty hand. We all were, but how we react is on us. This is on him. None of this is your fault. Do you hear me?" Even after everything, he still wants to believe in me, in my innocence. I sigh again, then nod. He takes both of my hands in his now, bringing them up to his face. "I don't know what I would have done if I hadn't made it here in time."

"Hey," I whisper, pulling my hands away so that I can see his face. When I see how distraught he is, I wish I hadn't. It never occurred to me that EJ was wrestling with the what ifs of this situation. "You did though. You made it."

He lowers his gaze away from mine. "I'm sorry I didn't believe you when you told me Cayden was dangerous."

"Don't be. You always try to find the best in people. It's what you do. It's one of the things I love most about you." I lean forward, brushing a few strands of hair away from his face. His eyes meet mine again, and in them I can see his heartbreak and everything I've done to him. "Thank you for saving me."

They are only five simple words, but they carry with them so much weight. He's saved me in more ways than I can imagine, long before he'd shown up to rescue me from the fire.

He glances away, like it's too hard to look at me. He fumbles with the blanket that lies in a ball beside him, then swiftly pulls an object from it, offering it to me. "I almost forgot."

I bite my bottom lip, inhaling sharply. EJ had salvaged my music book from the fire. This was the reason he didn't follow Kristen out of the flames. He'd risked his life to go upstairs in a burning house. I'm mad at him for putting himself in danger merely for one of my possessions, but at the same time, I'm ever grateful.

I turn the book over in my hands, then thumb through its pages. I trace over the handwritten message inside the cover, where my mother's hands had once skimmed over its smooth, white pages. "I can't believe you saved it."

"I'd do anything for you, Liv. You know that," he says softly, his eyes falling to my lips.

I nod, reaching upward to his cheek. I thumb away a smudge of soot. His hand covers mine and he closes his eyes, savouring my touch. My hands shift down his t-shirt, fisting clumps of it to pull him near. I cover his mouth with mine, slowly and cautiously, because somehow I know this will be the last time.

His hands come up to my hair and my whole being physically aches for more of him. He smells of smoke and he tastes like ash, but I don't care. I breathe him in, pull him closer, kiss him deeper.

Because this is the last time. Because down to the depth of my soul, I know it's true. This man would do anything for me. And I can't keep letting him save me.

When his lips leave mine, he holds me close, his forehead resting on mine. "I'm sorry, EJ. For everything, for not being honest about who I am."

He pulls back, shaking his head, then tucks a loose strand of hair behind my ear. "I've always known who you are, where it counts. Maybe I didn't know your real name or who you were related to, but I know you."

I exhale, then nod. He's said these same words to me before, but it's only now that I'm actually starting to believe them.

"You need to let go, Liv. You're fixated on this past version of you that doesn't exist anymore. I mean, sure. She exists somewhere deep inside of you. You wouldn't be you without going through all of those experiences, but there are going to be so many other versions of you in the future. Maybe you'll become a mum one day, or a grandmother. You might have seven different careers and each one of them is going to shape you into something else. Everything you do in your life, everything that happens to you, is going to have an impact." He keeps my hands firmly in his and lets out an unsteady breath. "I love this version of you and every other version to come, and I want you in my life, but until you can see that, this isn't going to work."

I bite down on my lip in an effort to keep the tears at bay. "I know. And I can't let you be my saving grace."

He smiles sadly. "And you can't be mine."

"Emmett," a woman's voice captures our attention away from each other momentarily. "Officer Greenberg would like to speak with you first, if that's okay?" The paramedic gestures to a tall policeman standing up on the driveway, before turning on her heel in his direction.

"That's my cue," EJ says, combing both hands through his hair and then crawling out of the ambulance. He turns, taking my hand to help me down onto the road. He takes a step toward the officer when I throw an arm around his waist, attempting to draw him back to me.

"I love you, EJ."

Recognition fills his eyes, and then his arms are around me, encasing me in love and light and all that EJ is made of.

He presses his lips into my hair. "I love you, too, Liv. I hope you find what you're looking for."

Then the air goes cold around me as he lets me go, and my awareness of what is happening sets in. I stare in awe at the house, flames still roaring through the top story windows like dragon's breath in some twisted fairy tale. The noise around me washes away as the shock winds its way through my veins, creeping in like an unwelcome intruder.

I'm only mildly aware that I've fallen down onto the driveway, the cobblestones leaving indents upon the skin of my hands. I am numb. I don't feel my dad's hands on my shoulders, don't feel him pull me into his chest as he drops down beside me, his fingers stroking my smoke scented hair.

Watching coils of smoke billow from the windows of this house I'd grown up in, as everything I own goes up in flames, a deep emptiness opens up within me. There's a void in my life now that I don't know whether I'll ever be able to fill.

My bloodshot eyes sting like hell, but it doesn't stop more tears from falling. I'm not crying for all the things I've now lost to the fire, but for the one thing I lost all on my own. I could get by without my clothes, my TV, my piano. I can even accept the fact that the photo albums my mother had made when I was young are now gone forever.

But how the hell will I ever live without him?

Chapter 39

LIV

EJ left town the day after the fire. He never said where he was going or for how long, but Kristen told me he'd gone by to see her, his car packed with nothing but a backpack and his acoustic guitar.

I'm happy for him, and glad that he's finally doing something for himself for once. And yeah, his absence has left a hole in me that I know no one else can ever fill. It's a little weird that whatever we had was cut off so abruptly, but I know that ultimately, he's never really left me. I carry pieces of him with me. The way that I see it, I have two choices. I can lie down and continue to wallow in self-pity, or I can pick myself up and strive to be the woman that he's believed I've been all along.

My dad and I decided not to rebuild our life up on the cliff, instead choosing to leave it behind in the ruins. We've had some happy memories up there, but also some not so happy ones and in the end, neither of us can say we're the same people anymore.

So for this past month, we've been living in one of my dad's townhouses in the heart of Milton, the only belongings I own barely filling a tiny suitcase purchased from Kmart.

And that's okay. It's liberating. We're starting anew.

Dad is looking to purchase a property overlooking the water in Little Bay. It seems like the perfect location, on the outskirts of Cliff Haven, but also not too far for him to get to the city when called upon. And he always has the townhouse to fall back on if he needs to spend extended periods of time in Milton.

Overall, Dad seems really ready to embrace a quieter life. He's already taken the necessary measures to step back from his work. He mentioned buying a fishing boat last week, and it didn't even seem like he was joking. Whether he cares to admit it or not, recent events have affected him. It's evident in his actions; in the way he speaks to me, and his new found attentiveness toward me. It's killing him to think that he almost lost me.

Despite Cayden being responsible for destroying our house and putting all of our lives at risk, my father didn't wish to punish him. Cayden had owned up immediately, surrendering himself to police as they'd arrived on the scene. He could just as easily be rotting in a cell right now, but Dad had other plans for him. He agreed to drop any charges made against him on the condition that he commit himself to Rykers Institution for treatment.

I don't hate Cayden. What kind of person would I be if I did? I'm thankful that he's getting the help that he needs, and I pray that he will find himself again, the way that I'm slowly finding myself. That kind, young man that helped me on one of my darkest days is still in there. I have to believe that.

For the first time in a long time, I'm learning to be at peace with who I am. My life isn't mapped out and I really don't know what the future has in store, but I'm okay with that too.

I've begun to let go of my past versions. Every day I discover more and more pieces of that girl that EJ saw, and every day the line between who I used to be and who I am now, becomes a little more distinct. I realise what EJ had said to me is true. There will be many different versions of me in this life, but when I look back on all of them, I want to be able to say they were good ones.

With everything slowly falling into place, I'm feeling more content, but there is still a heaviness in my heart that only one thing will fix. I need to see Maggie and Steve. I've been avoiding the confrontation for weeks now, but I owe them an explanation. Madelyn Jensen had been their daughter and their son had saved my life.

"Hey Dad," I say, peeking my head around the wall of my dad's makeshift office. "Do you mind if I take your car? I'm gonna go for a drive into Cliff Haven." My car was incinerated in the fire and I'm yet to buy a replacement.

My father looks up from the piles of paperwork laid out on the desk in front of him. "Sure. I'm just finishing up here and then I've got a few calls to make to the real estate."

"Okay," I respond. "I'll be back in a few hours."

It takes a little over an hour to get to Cliff Haven, due to the lunch time traffic. I park my Dad's Tesla in a vacant spot out the front of the Haven. Kristen spots me through the café window as soon as I set foot on the pavement.

"Liv!" She playfully struts out the café door, her apron still wrapped tightly around her waist. "Ooh, nice wheels, rich girl!"

I laugh at her mock comment as she throws her arms around me in a warm-hearted hug. "How have you been? I miss you."

"Yeah, I'm doing okay. Same old really. Your dad find a house yet?"

I've only seen Kristen a handful of times since the fire. Once in the hospital the day after, and a couple of times when she'd visited the townhouse, but we text every day.

"Nope. He was about to call the real estate when I left, so that might be promising. How's Carla?"

"Strung out." Kristen's laugh rings out through the street. "Your replacement is having a tough time getting orders right. You know she'd take you back in a heartbeat, right?"

"I know." I smile.

I'd resigned from my job at the Haven on account of the fact that it's too difficult to commute while living in Milton. I will always have fond memories of the café, and I will always cherish the friendships I've made there, but I'm determined to find my place in the world. I sense that I'm so close to finding what it is that I'm meant to be doing in this life.

"I actually came down here to see Steve," I say.

"Oh, you mean you didn't come all this way just to see me?" Kristen pouts, light-heartedly.

I roll my eyes at her sarcasm. "You know I always love seeing you. Come over to the townhouse later if you're free."

"Maybe tomorrow afternoon. I have a test to study for tonight. Anyway, I better get back to Carla before she has a breakdown. I'll text you." Kristen gives me another quick hug and then launches herself back through the café doors.

The tavern is quiet when I push past the heavy, wooden door. Only two guys are seated at the bar, dressed in workwear and steel capped boots. A few tables are occupied on the far side of the room. The scent of tap beer soaks me in nostalgia, transporting me back to nights spent watching EJ. The room feels hollow without his presence to fill it.

Henley gives me a nod when he notices me, which I reciprocate with a wave. He continues on his way to a far table, his arms laden with plates of food. Steve unpacks bottles of bourbon from a large, cardboard box, shelving them with his good arm into the cabinet above the bar. I approach him, nervously.

"Hello stranger," he says. I can't decipher his tone.

"Hi, Steve. How are you? How's Maggie?" I ask in a rush.

Steve turns to face me. He looks exhausted. "We're okay, Liv. How are you?"

I shrug. "I'm alive, and I owe that to your son." Damn it. I thought I could do this without crying, but my emotions are getting the better of me. "I wanted to tell you how sorry I am. About Madelyn. About everything."

Steve sighs, then turns and I start to think he's walking away from me entirely, but then he rounds the corner to meet me in front of the bar. "You have nothing to be sorry for. EJ told us you feel responsible for the accident. But you're not."

I nod. "I'm starting to see that."

"Good," Steve says, rubbing the back of his neck. "Maggie and I have spent so many hours wishing things were different, pondering the what ifs. It was a tragedy, but it happened. And when something bad happens it's easy for everyone involved to try to find a way to blame themselves. I blamed myself for letting her go to a party that night. If I'd have just said no, she might still be here."

I understand his point. "It's like the butterfly effect."

"Something like that. Please don't blame yourself. It's not what Mads would have wanted." Steve came to rest his hand on my shoulder. "You know, your father came to see us after the accident. He seemed like a really decent man. I see a lot of him in you."

My eyes fill hearing these words. No one has ever made such a connection between me and my father, and it's only been over the last few months that I've come to realise that it's not so bad to be like him. My heart swells with his compliment. "Thank you."

"Liv, if you ever need anything you just let me know, okay?"

My smile is weak as I nod. "Thanks Steve. Say hi to Maggie for me?"

"Of course."

I scan the small stage, remembering the night EJ had played solo. My eyes drift over the old piano. I hesitate for a moment. "Uh, Steve? There is actually one favour I could ask of you."

"What's that?" he asks.

All of a sudden, I realise how rude it is to ask Steve for anything. What was I thinking? "Actually, it's fine. Don't worry." I shake the idea from my head and turn to leave.

"Liv, I said anything you need. I'm here for you."

"Well," I whirl back around. "It's just… my piano burned up in the fire and I was wondering, if it's not too much trouble…" Even as the words leave my mouth, I know I'm asking too much.

"You want to use the piano here." Steve finishes my sentence.

"Just until I get my own. Only when the bar isn't open of course. It's okay if you don't want…" I know I'm rambling, but I can't help it. Ever since I'd played the night of the fire, I'd been craving the release it had brought me.

344

"Sure you can. You can come by tomorrow morning if you like. I'll be here doing some paper work."

"Really?" I'd half expected him to say no. "Thank you so much, Steve."

"Not a problem. EJ said you were good on that thing. If you're up to playing for an audience that can be arranged too. I'm gonna need some new live entertainment now that EJ won't be around."

His words pummel me like an avalanche. The realisation that EJ is gone indefinitely is crushing. We'd ended things and I'd come to terms with that, but hearing Steve talk about his absence is evidence of the finality of it all.

I force a smile. "I think, maybe that would be a little too ambitious for me. Take care."

"I'll see you tomorrow, then?" Steve asks.

"Yeah, for sure."

I desperately want to ask him. I want to know how EJ is doing. Where is he? How does he spend his time? But it's not my place to know. He isn't my person anymore.

I step toward the door when Steve's voice resonates from the bar. "Liv?"

"Yeah," I say, spinning around to meet his gaze.

"He's okay. He's great, actually." A small smile tugs at Steve's mouth.

Relief surges through me. That's all I need. To know that he is okay is enough. "I'm glad."

"You got that app on your phone? Spotter.. something." He squints in thought, scratching at his forehead. "Spotify?"

"Uh, yeah?" My forehead creases in response to this random question.

"You'll be able to look him up on there sometime soon."

"On Spotify?"

"Yeah. He's been playing some bars and clubs around the place. Got noticed by some bigshot executive record producer one night."

My heart fills with pride and happiness. "That's amazing! I'm so happy for him."

"Yeah. I thought you might be. We're really proud of him."

"Me too," I say.

And I mean it. EJ's happiness means the world to me, and it makes all the difference knowing he's out there living his dream.

I cross the street to the Tesla, tossing my bag across the passenger seat with a little too much enthusiasm, and dive into the driver's seat. I'm flying high on EJ's success, so when the tears come, I know they're happy ones. This is good. EJ deserves all the good things in this world.

I reach into my bag for a tissue, my eyes falling to the passenger seat, where the scarce contents of my handbag lay strewn. My music book lies open, my mother's inscription visible inside the front cover.

Follow your dreams. They know the way.

Is life really all that simple? Maybe it can be. It's all about perspective, isn't it? The rest of my life is being shaped right now, through the choices I make, by the people I surround myself with and the person I decide I want to be.

My gaze is suddenly drawn to the vacant building next to the Haven. The "For Lease" sign still balances on the window sill, but there is another sign above it that I'd never noticed before. There's an apartment above the vacant space.

An idea begins to take shape in my mind. I see the life that I could have, envision a possible future. I reach for my phone, typing the number as it appears in bold.

"Hello, Cliff Haven Realty, how can I help you?" A bubbly voice greets me on the other end of the line.

"Hi, I'd like to enquire about the vacant space next to the Haven Café."

8 MONTHS LATER

"What do you think?" My dad asks, his hands splayed, gesturing to his new prized possession.

I stare in awe at the small fishing boat, bobbing on the surface, anchored in place to the jetty. "I think it's great!" I exclaim. "Can you even drive it?"

"Not quite yet." He smiles, hanging his arm around my shoulder. "I'm working on it."

I laugh as we stroll side by side along the jetty, in the direction of my dad's beach house. Tessa waves at us from the back deck when we reach the lawn. "I'm about to head off, Mr. Petersen. Did you need anything else before I go?"

The worst part about downsizing is that we see less of Tessa. She only works for Dad one day a week now, spending a few hours cleaning and sometimes cooking a meal or two for him, but she always calls me and we try to arrange to catch up as regularly as our lives allow us. She's always been a special part of my life and I intend to keep her in it.

"No, Tessa! You go and enjoy the rest of your day. You've done plenty." My father is so much more relaxed these days. Beach life suits him.

"Bye, Tessa," I say, as I throw my arms around her neck. "I'm coming to visit you next week, okay? Don't forget."

"Oh, I could never forget!" Tessa says. "I'll have a slice of your favourite cake waiting."

"Ooh, ricotta cheesecake? I can't wait!" I bid Tessa farewell, and then my father and I retreat back into the house.

"I really love this house," I tell Dad after Tessa leaves.

Although the beach house is still ultra-modern, it has a humble and homely vibe that our mansion in Hampton Ridge lacked. Even Dad had welcomed its much smaller size.

"Well, you know there's a room for you here anytime you need it."

"I know." Guilt gnaws at me at the thought of my dad living here all alone, but I needed to branch out on my own.

"You want to go out and get some lunch. The café down the street makes a mean Greek salad."

My dad's comment makes me smile. "Oh, really? You're starting to sound like a proper local, Dad. Thanks, but I have to get back to the studio. Kristen said she was gonna stop by after her class and the painter should be coming by in an hour or so."

"No worries," he replies. "I'll stop by as soon as I can and take a look at that leaky kitchen sink of yours."

"Okay, thank you."

I love my new apartment, leaky taps and all. To my advantage, Dad has transformed into Mr. Fix-It since having more time on his hands. Now that he is both living and working in the same place, he no longer has to waste time commuting into Milton every day. He's still a member of the board, but his main priority is getting a new hospital just outside of Cliff Haven up and running. As proud as I am to be venturing out on my own, I'm even more proud of my dad for his accomplishments and the life changes he's making.

When I arrive at the studio, the painter is already waiting outside. "Hey, Olivia!"

"Hi, Bob. I'm sorry. I wasn't expecting you for another half an hour." I fumble with the keys, trying several before I find the right one.

"No problem at all. My last job finished earlier than planned, so I headed right over. I just need to put a second coat on those walls and then I'll be out of your hair."

"Okay. Thanks. Actually, I was wondering if you would mind putting my window decals on. They arrived yesterday and I'm worried I'll mess it up if I try doing it myself."

"Sure." Bob follows me inside the shop, resting his ladder up against the front wall. He makes another trip to his van, bringing back with him a can of paint and other supplies.

I put my bag down on the counter next to the tubular box that arrived yesterday. I'd been too nervous to open it. I still am, which is why I opt to hand it to the painter and have him do the honours.

"Do you just want it in the centre of the window?" Bob asks.

"Sounds perfect," I reply.

I chew my fingernails nervously as I watch him peel back the backing paper and line the decal up on the glass. Within minutes, it's done.

"What do you think?" Bob gestures to his handywork, while I stride out the front to view it properly.

The reality hasn't fully set in yet. That this little shop is my very own music studio, created one hundred percent by me.

There's still a lot of work to be done. Only half of the stock has arrived. I'm still waiting on another shipment of keyboards and guitars, and I'm yet to find a drum tutor. But sure enough, there on the window, are the words "The Music Box," scripted in a font that I painstakingly chose over all the rest, along with the phone number, email, and website details for my little business.

"It's perfect," I state, as Bob follows me out to inspect his work. He gives a nod of satisfaction, then returns inside to continue his painting, causing the entry bell to ding on his way in.

"Wow." I feel Kristen's arm wrap around my shoulder as she joins me in appreciating my new sign. "Your mum would be so proud of you, you know?"

"Thanks," I say, resting my head on her shoulder. "That means a lot. Argh, you're gonna make me cry!"

"Olivia Petersen?" a man's voice startles us both, and I turn to see a guy struggling with several heavy boxes.

"Yes. That's me," I say, opening the door wide for the man. I no longer shudder at the pronunciation of my full name. I'm finally comfortable in my own skin. "Do you think you could leave them on the counter over there?"

The man does as I instruct and Kristen and I follow him inside. I sign for the packages and then he leaves.

"What's in the boxes?" Kristen asks.

"Should be the merchandise I ordered. Wristbands, t-shirts, pens, keyrings. That kind of thing." I pry open a smaller box with a set of boxcutters. "Not to mention, my new business cards."

"Wow." Kristen stands, her hands on her hips, "That's impressive Miss Petersen."

"It scares the hell out of me," I say in reply.

351

In just a few short weeks, the renovations will be complete, the rest of the stock will arrive and the Music Box will be open to the public, offering both music supplies and tuition.

If there's one thing I'm certain of in this life, it's that music is something I was born to gift others. I can't wait to meet my students, to see that light go on when they hit the perfect chord or find the right melody.

On top of that, I was accepted into the Milton Conservatorium of Music, which I plan to attend part time when the next semester starts. I all of a sudden have a lot on my plate, but in the absolute best way.

"You're gonna do great, Liv. This is going to be epic. I promise." Kristen has been my rock throughout this entire process. I'm hyperaware of how lucky I am to have her in my life. "Hey, I'm really thirsty. Do you mind if I grab a drink while I'm here?"

"Sure," I answer.

Kristen follows me out the back and up the narrow flight of stairs that leads to my apartment.

"So there's kind of a big reason I wanted to see you today. I have news." She throws her handbag down on the tiny wooden dining table and collapses dramatically onto the sofa.

"Oh my god, Kristen. If this is about you setting me up on another one of your blind dates from hell, I am so not interested. The last guy was so boring, I nearly chewed off my own hand!" She takes a deep breath, her nostrils flaring. For a second I worry I've offended her. "Sorry, I know you're just trying to help. I didn't mean…"

"No, that's not it," she replies. "It's just… wait, he was really that bad?"

I give her a hopeless look, to which she waves her hands at. "Never mind." She pauses, as though searching for her next words. "He's coming home."

My heart thumps against my ribcage. "Who?" I ask, though I already know the answer.

"EJ. Who else?" She looks at me as though I'm the dumbest person on Earth. "He's coming home to see his mum for her birthday."

"Oh, it's Maggie's birthday?" I say matter-of-factly, turning to reach into the top cabinet. I pull out a glass. "I should get her a gift."

"Oh, it's Maggie's birthday?" she repeats my words with sarcasm. "That's what you're taking away from this? I mean, the guy you've been pining for this whole time is finally going to be in the vicinity and you're concern is buying his mother a present?"

I fill my glass with water from the leaky tap and take a sip, trying my best to seem casual. Of course, he was going to come home eventually. This is his home town. I'd be lying if I said I hadn't thought about his return at least once a day. I wonder if Kristen can see my glass shaking with the tremor of my hand.

"Well, I wouldn't say I've been pining."

Kristen sighs. "C'mon, Liv. We both know you've memorised the lyrics to every one of his songs. You listen to them every day! And don't think I haven't noticed you have a brand-new Instagram account just so you can follow him."

"I created that account for my business!" I retaliate.

Kristen gives me a suspicious look.

"I want to support him." I sigh, placing the glass down on the table a little too abruptly. "So much time has passed, though. We're really just strangers to each other at this point."

353

This is a lie. I know EJ inside out. "When is he supposed to get back?"

"Tomorrow night, I think. You want to hang out tonight? I can help you keep your mind off it all."

"I can't," I answer.

"Oh, are you playing tonight?" she questions.

"Shit, I am actually." I'd forgotten I was meant to be playing at Steve's tavern tonight.

I've been playing covers there for the last few months. Borrowing Steve's piano had led to me filling in as the bar entertainment for one night, which subsequently turned into me playing every second Friday. At first I'd agreed to do it to gain confidence to apply to MCM, but performing live was such a surreal experience, addicting and therapeutic.

"Well, I might go see what Henley's up to before he starts his shift." Kristen stands, reaching across the table for her bag, then glances back at me. That's when I become aware that I'm wearing my anxiety on my face. "Hey, don't stress about this, okay? And call me if you need anything."

I nod. Don't stress. That's easier said than done.

She never did get that glass of water.

***

At exactly eight o'clock, I burst through the doors of the tavern. I've been mentally psyching myself up since Kristen's visit, trying to push EJ out of my head. I have roughly twenty-four hours. Twenty-four stress free hours, and yet EJ's visit is weighing heavily on my mind.

354

What will I say when I see him? I've been in denial this entire time, telling myself that we could leave what we had in the past. But the truth is, I've never stopped thinking about him, and if his return brought the news that he has someone new in his life, my heart will crack in half.

I pass Henley pouring drinks behind the bar on my way into the storeroom. As I shove my satchel bag under Steve's desk, a memory burns in the back of my brain. I can almost feel the pressure of the bar against my back, EJ's mouth hot on mine as he pins me against it.

Get a grip, Liv.

I've been in this room, in this bar, so many times since he left, but suddenly, tonight is the night my mind chooses to start wandering down memory lane. I will my pulse to calm the fuck down and grab my music book, with the sheet music I'd printed shoved inside it untidily.

Steve had invested in a shiny new baby grand piano when I accepted his invitation to play on Friday nights, which made me feel as though he'd invested in me. Like he believed in me. That, or he knew he could just find some other pianist to do the job if I failed. So far, he is happy and the crowd is happy, and I'm happy too.

My first time playing for a crowd on this stage had been scary as hell, and for some reason tonight is no exception. I'd gotten used to the judgmental stares, and even become a pro at drowning out old Tommy's drunken, sexist comments, but there's no doubt that EJ's impending arrival has me on edge.

Just like the first time, my heart pounds steadily in my chest and my lungs feel as though they are made of concrete. Before my first performance, Steve had given me the greatest pep talk I'd ever heard. He'd told me that I would do great, and that I was my own worst critic, which had made me smile because it reminded me of EJ.

Then he'd told me to picture everyone in their underwear and enthusiastically jumped up on stage to introduce me. He'd wolf whistled to the crowd, then tapped on the microphone and said, "A special friend of mine is here to perform for us tonight. It's her first time so let's make her feel welcome!"

And right now, just like that first time, my hands tremble as I wipe my sweaty palms on my jeans. My pulse races as I battle to steady my breath. It's quiet in here. Too quiet for a bar, with everyone's attention focused squarely on me.

I've done this many times, I tell myself. Tonight is no different. I smile nervously at the crowd, running my hands along the smooth leather of the bench, and praying inwardly that I can forget EJ long enough to finish my set.

"How's everyone doing tonight?" I ask the audience.

A few people respond to my question with low cheers. I crack my neck, take a deep breath, and then begin to play. I make it halfway through the first song before I stuff it up. My concentration is lacking in a major way tonight.

"Sorry, let me try something else," I mutter, to no one in particular.

I nervously comb loose strands of hair behind my ears, daring a glance toward the bar. Kristen is perched on a stool at the bar in front of where Henley stands. They're both watching me intently and its obvious in their expressions they can sense I'm not myself.

"You okay?" Henley mouths to me.

I give him a nod.

I try another song. I make it to the end, but my voice falls flat. My heart isn't in it. I rummage through my sheet music, contemplating which song to play next, when my eyes fall on the handwritten notes and lyrics inside the cover.

It's the only song to grace the pages of my music book, and I've never attempted to play it for a crowd, but if I can't get EJ out of my head, then maybe channelling my energy into a song written about him might help.

I balance the book on the music stand. I survey the audience, which all of a sudden seems so much bigger.

Kristen holds her hands up in the air as if to say, "What's going on?" Sammi is now seated next to her, twirling a straw around in her drink.

"Sorry, guys. It seems I'm not having the best night tonight."

"Speak up, darling! We can't hear you!" Old Tommy shouts from the audience.

I cringe and adjust the microphone, wishing the stage would just cave in and swallow me whole. I inhale another sharp breath. I can do this. I have nothing to lose. What does it matter if the audience doesn't like the song? The only person whose opinion I care about isn't here. He won't be here for another twenty-four hours.

"I want to share a song that I wrote for someone that means a lot to me." I say into the mic. I pause, surveying the crowd again, but all I can see at this point is a blur of faces. "For someone that taught me that it's okay to make mistakes, to stumble and fall. And that some of the greatest things we do in this life will be the ones that scare us the most. This song is for the one person who saw the best in me when I couldn't see it myself. Wherever he is, I hope he's happy."

My fingers locate their place on the keys and the introduction rushes out of me, with no hesitation this time. My voice wavers, but after the first line my confidence builds.

357

I'm going to give my all here. If I don't, then what the hell is the point?

You're the anchor
The lighthouse
I'm the driftwood in your sea
I know you're always here beside me.

You're my refuge
My safe haven
My gravity
I carry pieces of you within me.

We can never change what's written
You said it's time to start livin'
You showed me how to be better
But I'm better with you.

When I reach the chorus, my emotions overwhelm me, and the reality of what I'm doing hits me like a ton of bricks. This song, written for the man I loved, still love, pours out of me like rain in a drought. Every pent up feeling I've held in for so long comes rushing out, and the unfairness of it all makes my bones ache with longing.

And I'm happy that you're happy
And we tell ourselves we're fine
But the pieces left of your heart
Match the missing parts of mine.

And I know we're doing what's right
And our souls have been set free
But freedom feels so heavy
When you're not here with me

You breathed colour
Into this black and white space
But I could never let you
Be my saving grace.

You're the place I call home
And I just wanna go home.

The final chord echoes throughout the bar. The eery silence that briefly follows gives way to an eruption of cheers.

A tear falls from my eye, splashing onto middle C. I'm still fixated on the questions I'd reflected on during the song writing process.

Could it really be possible, that after everything that has happened in our lives up until this moment, that EJ and I were just supposed to go our separate ways?

Suddenly, even the space surrounding me on the stage isn't enough. I stand up so abruptly, the piano bench topples backward behind me with a loud thunk on the wooden floor. I swipe at more tears that cloud my vision as I escape through the back exit of the claustrophobic tavern.

I hurry to the beach, knowing that the ocean will be the only thing that can help soothe the ache inside my chest. The summer air warms me and I welcome it, letting it fill my lungs as I collapse down onto the wooden paint-chipped park bench.

I'm suddenly aware of how dramatic I'm being, which only serves to deepen my reaction. I pull my knees into my chest and bury my face in them, listening to the waves as they crash on the shore.

"Are you okay?" A husky voice comes from beside me, sucking all the breath out of my lungs.

A sexy, husky voice.

I slowly raise my head, turning it towards the man now sitting beside me on the park bench.

"Yes," I stutter, then shake my head. "No. I don't know."

I don't know what I expected him to be like now. Whether months on the road would have changed him, whether he would be more 'rockstar' than before.

But he is just EJ.

My EJ.

With the same grey-green eyes that dance with flecks of light. His mouth pulls up on one side forming that crooked grin I know and love.

"What are you doing here, EJ?" I ask, still trying to get air into my lungs.

"It's my mum's birthday tomorrow." His casual response throws me.

I sigh. "I know. But I mean, here. Right now."

EJ tilts his head to the side, still grinning. "I heard that Steve's Tavern had new live entertainment."

"You were there?"

He nods. "In the back."

"You saw that?" My eyebrows lift in surprise, and then the humiliation sets in. EJ had heard my song. What must he be thinking? I don't know whether to laugh or cry, so I just bury my head into my knees again.

"It was fucking incredible." The park bench shifts beneath me as EJ's weight transfers closer. I feel his fingers stroke my hair. His touch sends electricity and heat through me, the same way it always had. "I missed you. That's why I'm here. I haven't stopped loving you, Liv. I never stopped missing you. Not for one single day."

These words are all I've wanted to hear for so long, but knowing he would be leaving only makes them painful. I look up into his sea-green eyes. "I can't say goodbye to you again, EJ."

"You don't have to. I'm not going anywhere."

"What? What about your music?" I love every word that's coming out of his mouth, but I could never watch him sacrifice what he was put on this planet to do.

"I can record anywhere. And I don't want to make music unless I can do it right here where you are." EJ's fingers graze the back of my neck and then his other hand comes up to cup my cheek. "I'm home, Liv."

His bottom lip softly grazes mine, lingering, his unsteady breath increasing in its pace to match the rhythm of my heart. I press my mouth to his, the kiss slow and light at first, then building into something deeper. His skin is hot under my touch as my hands reach up to his neck.

This is all I've thought about for so long and I know now, without a doubt, that he is everything. We are everything. We are the one good thing to come out of all the tragic moments of our pasts and I don't want to let us go.

With the passing of time I've come to realise that maybe EJ was right all along. Maybe what happened on that fateful night was a senseless tragedy that never should have happened, but maybe there is a reason we met.

I know I'll never take him for granted. He is both my safe haven and the adventure my soul craves. Sometimes home isn't a place. Sometimes home has a heartbeat.

And I'm finally home.

I pull away from him briefly so I can see that light dancing in his eyes again. I've missed that. And I know that there will be days where that light goes out, but I'll be here by his side.

We can take on the world together.

Follow me for more info and updates...

📷 eveblakelywrites

🐦 eveblakelybooks

♪ authoreveblakely

www.eveblakely.com

QUEEN B INX

Printed in Great Britain
by Amazon

21448111R10212